To Rule Britannia

THE CLIFFSIDE CHAPEL SERIES

To Rule Britannia

Alison Longstaff Moore

A Moore Publishing
Kitchener, Ontario

TO RULE BRITANNIA

Published by AMoore Publishing
116 Queen St. North. Kitchener, Ontario, Canada N2H 6T7

© Copyright 2025 Alison Longstaff Moore

Cover artwork by Drayton Mapp
Cover design and internal layouts by Donna Heldon
First printing 2025

PUBLISHER'S NOTE:
This is a work of fiction. All of the main characters, their families, and friends are entirely fictional. Occasionally, a real live human being will walk onto the pages and interact with the characters, but in each of those incidences it will be with the full consent of the live individual, and with full thanks recorded in the acknowledgments. Cliffside New Christian Community and the town of Ben Kirk exist nowhere but in the author's mind.
Their inspiration is drawn from existing Swedenborgian communities in the Kitchener, Ontario, and Bryn Athyn, Pennsylvania areas, with certain homes and an actual building of worship used as settings for this novel. Past that point, the similarities rapidly drop away.

Canadian Cataloguing in Publication Data
Longstaff, Alison, 1961–
To rule britannia

(Cliffside Chapel series)
Includes bibliographical references
ISBN 978-0-9687329-2-2

1. General fiction. I. Title. II. Series.

Fonts used in print edition, EB Garamond and Beau Rivage, are from Google Fonts.

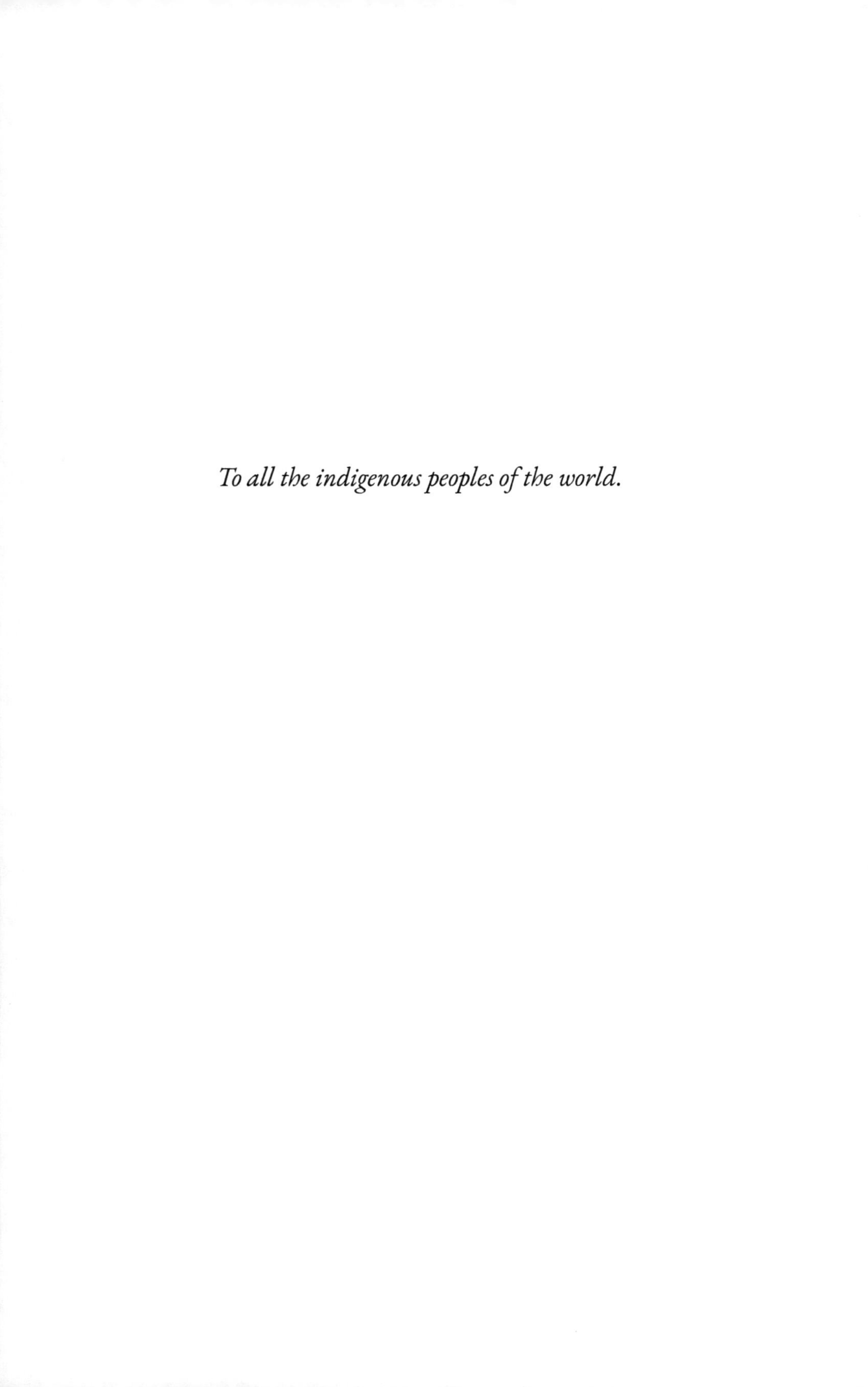

To all the indigenous peoples of the world.

ACKNOWLEDGEMENTS

Over twenty years

Calvin Sault: Back in 2004-2006, as I was struggling to build a backstory for the hero in this second novel, I met an indigenous gentleman named Calvin Sault, from the Six Nations of the Grand River. He was willing to meet with me, answer my many questions, and tell me stories of healing. He gave me the indigenous name "Waubunanung" which means "morning star". I am grateful for his wisdom and guidance to this day.

Paula Naill: In the 2000s Paula Naill, who hails from the Grey-Bruce region of southern Ontario, invited me to various places and events for research into indigenous customs and beliefs. Paula and I attended the annual Pow Wow at Cape Croker Park, Neyaashiinigmiing, Ontario, run by the Chippewas of Nawash Unceded First Nation. Though it was many years ago, the conversations and impression have been lasting and unforgettable.

Michael Vincent David: "That Swedenborgian out in Hawaii" (Chapter 4) said many smart and funny things in his lifetime. He passed on from this earth on October second, 2022 and is missed every day by his siblings, wife, daughter, stepchildren, and friends. He was a trusted and valued connection going back to college. I'm sure he is doing great things where he is now.

Kenneth Carman Veitch: Is a historian in Bracebridge, Ontario. He has written many books on the history of the town and has been a big help in my Bracebridge research.

Real live humans gracing this novel: Bet Giddings – wonderful accompanist and human; **Lauren Anderson** – wonderful human being and excellent relative. These friends supported this work on Patreon and earned the right to be featured in this novel.

And so many more.

PREFACE

Reflections on the journey, twenty-five years after "Heaven Sent"

It has been a quarter-century since I first released "Heaven Sent" into the world—a stretch of time that feels both impossibly long and startlingly short. Looking back, I am struck by the way grief and struggle have changed me through the years. When I began this journey, I was deeply embedded in my childhood denomination, held fast by the ties of intentional Christian community. My wusband and I were raising our children with ritual, firm beliefs, and the conviction that we were building something beautiful and enduring.

I remember the dreams that kindled "Heaven Sent." I wanted to write Christian fiction that offered romance, intimacy, and longing, yet never transgressed the sexual mores I cherished at the time. It was important for me to show believers living ordinary lives—playful, complicated, imperfect—without being preachy nor implying all readers should be Christians.

In short, I set out to write Christian fiction that anyone could read. My intention was to tell a good story, full stop. My characters happen to be a particular flavour of Christianity, but their struggles and joys echo those of Muslims, Jews, Hindus, Buddhists, Atheists, Agnostics, and all other human beings. We are, all of us, stumbling along, reaching for meaning, belonging, and what some call grace.

But as I reached the words "the end" on the manuscript of "Heaven Sent," my own world began to unravel. That very day, my wusband lost his job—a loss that became insurmountable in the aftermath of 9/11. Opportunities vanished, our community was shaken, and financial realities pressed hard upon us. Despite the chaos, I managed to shepherd the book to publication in December, clinging to the exhilaration of seeing my words in print and the thrill of sharing my story on television and in bookstores. For a brief span, I rode a crest of accomplishment.

My wusband was ineligible for unemployment insurance for reasons unknown to our community, and by February, the stark truth came: we would lose the house. The sense of displacement was profound; with each loss—a home, a beloved pastor, a cherished community, even our country as we moved to the States for two years—the writer in me grew quiet. Years of writer's block followed, haunted by grief, uncertainty, and spiritual dislocation.

In time, I was shattered by the experience of spiritual abandonment by my childhood denomination, yet I would learn I was not alone . Many souls have walked the path of losing their church home. Many also grapple with wounds of exclusion or betrayal at the hands of their faith communities.

Necessity led me into unexpected fields. I became a professional organizer, which has its own "pastoral" quality. Eventually I returned to school, driven by a calling ministry despite my inner prejudice set by the men-only clergy policies of my former denomination. Still, I pressed on, determined to use my gifts where I could.

Over the years, I earned two Master's degrees, gained Canadian citizenship, achieved ordination, and, eventually, navigated a divorce. I have moved eleven times, six of those across international borders. Each milestone demanded courage and invited transformation. I learned to support myself, balancing the work of ministry and organizing, meeting new faces and building new communities. I re-married—a dear college friend—and together we survived the pandemic in New York City. We now live together in Canada and all is going well.

Through all these upheavals, the writing remained frozen. It wasn't until I made a commitment—a new chapter every other week for my readers—that the creative ice began to thaw. The promise of accountability, the gentle encouragement of a waiting audience, helped me rediscover my voice. Words began to flow again with increasing confidence. By the spring of 2025, the manuscript for this second novel was finished. Looking at it now, I am reminded of the resilience of hope and the mysterious ways that stories demand to be told.

I offer this new novel as a testament to endurance, change, and the fierce grace that threads through every chapter of life. These pages are the fruit of years marked by loss and renewal, by questions that deepened rather than diminished my faith. I no longer belong to the denomination of my childhood, but I remain a seeker: looking for the Divine in unexpected places, listening for wisdom in the stories of others, believing that love—however imperfectly lived—still matters most.

To those who have walked alongside me: thank you. To those who have found resonance in my writing or in my journey, I am grateful for your companionship and curiosity. My hope is that this story, like "Heaven Sent," invites you to see the sacred in the ordinary, to honour the complexity of faith, and to extend compassion to yourself and to others, regardless of creed or circumstance.

Twenty-five years ago, I dreamed of writing fiction that would open doors rather than close them, that would welcome the reader—whoever they might be— into a space of possibility and growth. I am still dreaming. And I am still writing.

Here it is—my offering, my story, my hope—twenty-five years in the making. May it speak to you, wherever you are on your journey.

AUTHOR'S NOTE

Anachronism

My first novel, "Heaven Sent" was set in 1998-1999. This second novel follows immediately after but was written primarily between 2022-2025. Because of this giant jump in writing time, my characters started using the technology set in the years of *writing*, which is nothing like what it would have been in 1999. Anachronism (from ana meaning "against" and chronos meaning "time") is what one calls mismatched technologies from their historical setting. The story had to remain set in 1999, or none of the relevance of Britt's WW II history would make sense. Given the rush to complete chapters on a schedule, I wrote what I knew, rather than take the time to research what technologies were used in 1999.

Call me lazy. Call me pragmatic. If I was a paid writer and not doing this in snippets of spare time, I could have taken the time to research and rewrite the portions that are so anachronistic.

Please just run with it. The year is 1999. The characters are using 2025 technology.

Thank you, dear readers.

One

February 13

Britannia Suzanne Smith, "Tanny" to her friends and family, stood on the chancel of her home-town chapel, air-bouquet in her hands. She took a breath and gazed up the aisle.

There at the back of the church, glowing with happiness, stood Susie, Tanny's best friend. Of course Susan was radiant. Susan Rennie was about to walk down the aisle on the arm of the most incredible man God had ever created.

Finding herself a maid of honour for the third time in her almost twenty-eight years, Tanny Smith suspected that she would never, ever get to be the bride. She reminded herself that she was not jealous.

What a wild week it had been. What a crazy month. In fact, nothing had been quite the same since the new assistant pastor had arrived on the church's doorstep in late November. Fresh from the airport, he had poked his head in to watch the choir practice. He had looked like a modern-day Jesus leaning there on the door frame with that dark hair and beard.

Then he'd said something in his unusual South African accent, and Tanny had been smitten heart and soul—soon to be joined by virtually every other female in the congregation.

But the Reverend Jonathan Haley, from his very arrival, had only had eyes for Tanny's cousin, Susan.

This was Susan's second walk down the marriage aisle. Widowed at age twenty-four, and with twin girls in tow, Susie had been scooped up by a second terrific man before her twenty ninth birthday.

Not that Susie even tried to attract men. She was just quiet and sweet, and an absolute man-magnet. Susan had the dark-chocolate eyes that ran in the Bender family. Tanny hadn't been so lucky. Hers were an undecided hazely-greeny-muddy colour. And her ears stuck out a little.

Tanny sighed.

So here she was, helping Susan prepare for a rushed Valentine's Day wedding.

Sue's shy face glowed as she progressed down the aisle on Jonathan Haley's arm.

Good heavens, but those two will have gorgeous children, Tanny mused.

The tall South African looked down at his bride. Tanny had to blink and look away.

Will anyone ever look at me that way?

Across the chancel from Tanny, grey-eyed, sandy-haired Conrad Knapp also watched the approaching couple. Conrad and Jonathan had become fast friends in the two months since the South African's arrival.

Just then, Conrad's eye caught hers and he smiled. Tanny remembered then the brief revelatory exchange they had had as they stood, arm in arm, the best man and maid of honour, waiting to practice their walk up the aisle.

Tanny grinned. Conrad was one of the kindest, most empathetic men Tanny had ever known. She liked him an awful lot. But Conrad Knapp, registered nurse, son of "Heinrich the Horrible", was ... well ... gay. Nobody ever talked about it, but everybody knew.

Jon had brushed past them to jog up to the chancel. The two had watched the South African as he'd held a friendly exchange with their pastor.

Upon a sigh from Tanny, Conrad remarked, "So. You too?" He hadn't looked at her.

She'd been puzzled. Was he teasing her for being yet another susceptible female? *Or* ... it had occurred to her: *Does Conrad have a crush on Jon too?* Tanny had looked at the sandy-haired nurse. His gaze had flickered slightly, and he'd looked away.

So, it's true?

Tanny had felt what?—camaraderie, empathy, sympathy? *If he's saying what I think he is saying....* Was Conrad confiding in her?

And I thought I *was lonely.*

From that moment, Tanny had felt an almost maternal protectiveness toward Conrad. Neither of them might ever get married, but at least they could be good friends to each other.

Tanny crossed her eyes at Conrad now, communicating humour over their situation.

Conrad's eyes crinkled.

So, she and Conrad were in the same boat. How weird was that?

Well, if there was one thing of which Tanny was certain, she knew that she herself wasn't gay. Not even close! She'd spent most of her girlhood going from crush to crush. Her adolescent diaries seemed to hop from one unsuspecting youth's glorious attributes to another. Good heavens, she'd found "The One" so many times, she concluded that she'd never recognize the real "One" by now, even if she tripped over him.

Meanwhile, the current object of Tanny's infatuation was walking down the aisle on the arm of her best friend.

Another sigh.

Does the name "Britannia" curse the bearer to spinsterhood? Tanny thought about her great-aunt, Britannia Bender. Britt had never married. But unlike some women, Britt had never fretted about being "unwanted goods." On the contrary; apparently it was all the men around Britt that had been the unwanted goods. What had she said? "I will never marry until I find a man that I can't live without. And so far, there isn't a man alive that I can't live without."

Tanny understood Britt more and more over the years. Oh yes, she got crushes! But a few weeks into any relationship, she found herself bored. Was there *no* man who was deeper than beer and hockey? Was there any guy who would rather be with her, having a great conversation, than watching the Super Bowl? Was there any guy that cared about *her,* instead of how many dates it would take to get inside her pants?

Just then, Andrea and Alyssa, Sue's twin girls, stepped sedately up onto the chancel. One dark, one fair, the seven-year-old twins took their places by Tanny and Conrad. They turned to watch their mommy come down the aisle with Jon. Andrea was the one next to Tanny—mouthy, independent, chin-to-the-world Andrea, with the brown, brown eyes just like her mother's. Neither of the twins had inherited the Bender sticking-out ears

The other twin—blond, crinkly-haired Alyssa—would probably be the "approved of" one of the two. Tanny's mom had always entreated Tanny to "be more lady-like." Her dad teased her regularly about being strong-willed and opinionated, saying it was the "American" blood in her coming out. They implied that she should shut up and be meek and accepting if she wanted to get married. But blast it all! What about just being herself? And why did her whole identity have to pivot around getting married? That was her parents' issue, not hers. Tanny insisted on the right to express her opinions. If Tanny had something to say, she said it, especially if something stupid was going on and nobody was saying anything about it! And honestly! If a man couldn't love her for who she was, strong opinions and all, she wasn't interested. Seriously, if getting married required squelching all her own ideas so as not to make a man uncomfortable, she didn't want to get married. That wouldn't be a marriage anyway, unless marriage was defined as "between one man and one woman-who-is-hiding-and-lying."

Tanny came back to the present, resolving *again* to stop fretting about her single status. She *knew* life wasn't only about men, finding love, and getting married. It's just that sometimes she felt her loneliness keenly—especially within this congregation that seemed to value marriage and children almost to the exclusion of anything else.

She counted her blessings: 1) a job even though there was a recession, 2) great friends, 3) a home....

Sue and Jon approached the chancel steps, their dear faces a mixture of solemnity and joy. Sue's hand was tucked around Jon's elbow, and he hugged it to him in a sweetly possessive gesture.

The thought was there before Tanny knew it. *Will there ever be someone who loves me like that?*

Sue arrived, glowing, at Tanny's side, slightly teary, radiant. Tanny abruptly hugged Susan, then solemnly accepted the bride's air-bouquet.

These two people mean the world to me. No matter what happens, Lord, thank You for finally bringing them together. I'll do anything to help them be happy. I'll be a spinster all my born days without a peep of complaint if that is what it takes. I promise.

Tanny bounced slightly on her toes and grinned at the pastor. If ever there were two souls that deserved peace and happiness, these two did. Jonathan Haley and Susan Rennie had been through hell lately. It had seemed as if the very universe sought to drive them apart. Tanny herself wouldn't have believed their story if she hadn't lived through it.

But here they were, marrying quickly, before any new disaster struck.

The pastor smiled broadly at the couple, his grey eyes twinkling. He began to review the service.

Tanny mused about the "quickie" service. The couple's plan was inspirational. They had not wanted to wait another minute. There was no time for invitations or a big reception; and certainly not time enough for Jon's South African family to come from overseas. So, the couple was marrying legally *now*, in a simple dawn ceremony. There was to be a small breakfast reception, and they'd head off on their honeymoon. However, in June, when there would have been time enough to send out invitations and find dresses and hire a photographer; and for all the South African connections to book flights, they would have their "Wedding Celebration." That is when they would have all the trappings—the special music, the photos, the cake, the dancing—all the bells and whistles usually associated with the marriage ceremony.

Tanny looked at the little crew on the chancel. It was just as well that Jon and Sue were putting off the grand celebration for a few months. This was a pretty battle-scarred looking group for wedding photos. Though blond Alyssa was injury-free, Andrea still sported the marks of her terrible sledding accident. Sue had only just gotten the stitches removed from her bruised face, and Jon's right hand was heavily splinted.

The sledding accident wasn't what had caused the adults' wounds. Tanny grimaced. Tanny's charming brother-in-law, an "upstanding" member of the church board, had ... he had—Tanny's mind could barely touch it—one week ago Terry MacGregor had entered Sue's home in a drunken temper and tried to rape her. In the struggle to overpower Sue, Terry had split Susie's lip, bruised her face and broken the pinkie on her left hand. Jon had arrived only just in time, and in the process of expressing his objections, had broken his hand on Terry's face. Terry's face had fared much the worse for the encounter. It was about time somebody had pounded her rotten brother-in-law into a bloody pulp, Tanny thought with guilty satisfaction.

The maid of honour snorted softly. How fitting a metaphor that this couple's wedding photos could have looked like war images. Cliffside, as a congregation, had a lot to learn about "Christian" behaviour!

Well, Sue's splinted pinkie wasn't enough to stop Jon from sliding a wedding band onto Sue's ring finger.

The Pastor was speaking about the ring exchange. Tanny went through the motions of giving an imaginary ring to Sue.

Tomorrow, when Tanny walked down the aisle, she would have the real wedding ring around her thumb. Jon's wedding ring.

What would happen if I just refused to give it up? I'll just pop it on my own finger....

She smiled to herself. *"Thou shalt not covet. Thou shalt not covet."* Then, looking at the dear and handsome face, Tanny sighed again. *Lord, why did you only make one of him?*

Tanny pouted just a little. *There's nobody else like him. There can't be. He's one in a million, and he's taken, and that's all there is to it. Deal with it, Tanny.*

Pastor Stephen was suggesting, "When you slide the ring on Susan's finger, Jon, take your time."

I am not jealous.

"Do it in stages as you say your vows. Push it a little way, then stop, then push it a little farther, then stop again. It will help you pay attention to the significance of your commitment to each other. Really pay attention to what you are doing. There's no rush."

Tanny shivered.

Jon was practicing now. "In giving this ring, I wed you...."

Jon's face was a mix of emotions, wonder, joy, happiness, solemnity.... Sue's cheeks were pink.

Tanny blinked hard. *And this is just the rehearsal!*

Now Susan was taking her turn. Jon's glance was tender as he watched his bride. Tanny saw him swallow, visibly.

They so deserve each other. They so deserve this.

Stephen said, "Now you join your left hands like so, and I place mine over them and pronounce you man and wife." His voice was solemn, his face wreathed in smiles.

Lord, let me be the best friend I can be! I'm sorry for the jealousy. Please take it away. I promise to try harder! Just let me be a wonderful aunt to their kids and friend to their marriage. Tanny determined in that moment to enjoy her life as it was—to stop longing for pastures greener than the one she was in.

"Will there be a veil?" Stephen asked. The couple nodded and Stephen said, "Then this is when you would lift the veil and kiss her, Jon."

Maybe acceptance of what is, is the key. Maybe Britt's happiness came from accepting her situation and making the most of it. Maybe that's what I need to work on. After all, how can I ever be happy if I'm constantly wishing for something other than what I have?

Lord, Tanny prayed, *give me a wonderful man just like Jon and I'll never ever wish for greener pastures again....*

"Tanny?"

Tanny jumped. Stephen had had to say her name twice to get her attention. He said, "I understand that it's your job to smooth the veil at the back and tug out any kinks."

Tanny nodded. Yes, she knew. She'd done this several times before. *I am a veil-smoother, not a veil-wearer. Got it.*

Tanny pretended to smooth Sue's imaginary veil as Jon gave his bride a tender kiss. Tanny gave Stephen a thumbs-up.

"Okay. This is where we would kneel for the prayer. So, let's all kneel down." Tanny juggled her two imaginary bouquets and tugged at the skirt she wore to practice in. She tipped Andrea on how to adjust her skirt so that her heels wouldn't catch in her hem when she stood up again.

Stephen, kneeling at his prayer bench said, "Now I would lead us in prayer. When I rise again, Jon and Sue—you stay kneeling. Everybody else can rise."

Tanny murmured to Andrea, "So you want to watch that your heels don't catch in your hem and try not to step on the front of your skirt either, as you rise." Andrea rolled her eyes.

Stephen had risen and was standing over the kneeling couple. "I invite the congregation to rise if they haven't", said Stephen, "and then I say a blessing on the couple." Stephen laid his hands on their bowed heads and murmured, "Lord, bless these two darling idiots." He was grinning.

"Now you rise, Jon and Sue." Everyone waited as the couple struggled to their feet.

"This is where I bless the congregation, acknowledge the open Word, and send you off in peace. And ..." he checked his notes, "that's it. The music starts and off you go."

Tim Galloway, the congregation's electronics guy was up in the church loft, leaning on the railing. "Time for the recessional?" He disappeared from view, and soon a gentle, jazz-style acoustic piece started over the church speakers. Tanny wracked her brain to identify the familiar piece. Jon and Sue had turned to face the pews, but were just standing there, gazing into each other's eyes. The music was ... Oh yeah, Kenny G! A song with lyrics. Susan had told Tanny about having to dance with Jon as this song had played when things between Sue and Jon were in a hopeless deadlock. The singer described wonder at finding love when all hope was lost. Tanny shook her head. Things had worked out miraculously for these two, just like they had for the singer. The hopeless romantics. Tanny took charge, indicating to Andrea and Alyssa to head off down the aisle. The sisters stepped off the chancel and skipped toward their grandma who waited at the back. Jon and Sue stayed a moment longer, just gazing at each other. Then, at a look from Jon, they broke their gaze and began their grinning stroll to the back. Jon murmured something to Susan that widened their smiles.

Tanny sighed.

She gave Conrad a "well, it's our turn", look and they stepped together. Tanny couldn't quite read Conrad's expression. It wasn't particularly happy. The music crooned in tango with a saxophone, the words describing despair about finding love, and God providing someone at the last minute. She squeezed his arm, and they headed down the aisle.

The rehearsal dinner was a simple buffet of take-out Chinese food at Kate's house. Stephen's wife, Liz, had joined the small group and they all had settled around the fireplace in the comfy furniture. Jon had described his scramble to get a wedding license in just a week, with much animation, nearly spilling his chicken almond ding in Sue's lap in the process. The group was roaring with laughter as he finished.

Tanny just sat in amazement, marveling at his eye-stopping beauty, lively wit, and adorable accent. *Does a man come more perfect?* she wondered. *Lucky, lucky Susan!*

Inevitably, the conversation turned to Cliffside congregation's ongoing struggle to maintain a hold on its property and buildings.

When Britannia Bender had died, her last will and testament revealed that she was the sole owner of the land on which Cliffside Chapel and School stood. Instead of willing the land to the congregation freely, she bequeathed it conditionally. Over the next several years, Cliffside's members would be required to solve several puzzles and complete a series of tasks. Only if these were accomplished would the congregation inherit their land. If not, the whole property would be sold, and Cliffside congregation would be left with no school and no place in which to worship. They would receive only $150,000.00 in compensation for the loss of their buildings.

"It was so close. So close!" Liz commiserated. Tanny had been describing last weekend's near miss in completing the first task.

"Heinrich can be a very giving man—on *his* terms. He's very dutiful about managing the ushers' schedule and is passionate about keeping this place running efficiently," Stephen said.

"Well, we nearly didn't have a place to run, efficiently or otherwise, thanks to him", Tanny snorted. "Honestly, it's a miracle that we still have our buildings."

"Who knew that a little Canadian coffee could accomplish so much?" Jon added, eyes twinkling.

It was a little incident with coffee that had swung the power struggle out of Heinrich's control.

"What would we do without our coffee?" Stephen murmured.

There was a general chuckle.

"So, you're off to Cedar Haven for the honeymoon?" Liz asked Sue.

Sue nodded, her hand to her mouth to show she was finishing a mouthful.

Tanny had wanted to join the team of women who had gone to help ready the old Bender homestead for the honeymooners. But her work schedule and her unreliable car had prevented her. It would have been great to see the old place again. It would have been neat to meet the old caretaker that Britt had appointed to watch over the place.

That old caretaker, as well as Tanny, Susan, and Uncle Jake were the four "stewards" appointed to look after Cedar Haven. She wasn't even sure what a steward was, but she was excited to be one.

Sue said, "Mmm. Yes. We liked that idea. Just us, and the peace, and the snow."

Liz smiled. "That'll be nice. Is it a big place?"

Sue said, "It's a big old house and barn on a bunch of land. I love it. Maybe we can have a mini retreat there someday, just the ministers and their wives, and then you can see it."

Ouch, Tanny thought. She had watched Sue bonding increasingly with Liz over the week. They would both be minister's wives now—a unique role in life that seemed to carry a sort of special club membership. Now Liz and Sue belonged together. Tanny felt as if she was again on the outside of a candy store looking in. *Heck,* Tanny thought. *I can't even figure out how to join the* marriage *club, let alone the* minister's wife *club. All I know is that I'm losing Susie again. I'm losing Susie again and I don't know what to do about it.*

She rose to take her plate to the kitchen. She wasn't hungry anymore. *Except maybe for those brownies....* She grabbed an especially moist looking one and turned to watch the happy group from across the room. Then her lips closed on the sweet-dark confection, and she closed her eyes. *I'll just marry this brownie,* she decided.

Two

Tanny sat, picking at the remains of her eggs. The wedding was done; the lovely, celebratory breakfast was over, and the happy couple were now on their way to old Britannia's farm. There had been no rice-throwing, no streamered and tin-canned bridal car, just prolonged, jubilant hugs, and good wishes. Sue's mom was settling the bill with the restaurant while Pastor Stephen chatted with Sue's twins. Conrad was at Tanny's right, occupied with removing mushroom bits from his omelet remnants, using the tine of a fork.

Tanny said, "I guess that's it."

"Yup," was Conrad's response.

"They're on their way."

"Yup."

They sat in mutual preoccupation.

Stephen said, "There comes Kate. I need to get going. Tanny?"

She looked up. "Hmm?"

"Three o'clock?"

"Yeah, great. Thanks."

He gave her a nod as he tugged on his gloves. "Good. See you later, then. Bye, Conrad." The tall pastor gave him a friendly pat as he pushed his way past their chairs.

Kate had returned. "Shall we get going?"

"Su-re," Conrad drawled, pushing his chair out slowly.

Tanny threw her napkin onto her plate. She stood and gathered her coat off the back of her chair. She looked at the twins. "Who wants to ride with Aunt Tanny?" she asked.

"I do!" Conrad piped in unison with the girls.

Andrea laughed and hit Conrad with her mitten. "She's not *your* aunt, silly!"

"She's not your aunt!" echoed Alyssa.

Conrad made a face of confusion, "Aw. Why not? Why can't she be my aunt?"

"Because she's not!" Alyssa laughed delightedly.

"Because she's your same age!" insisted Andrea. "And you're not.... She's not.... One of you would have to be married to somebody," she finished with finality. "-like Uncle Paul."

"So, if I married your Uncle Paul...." Conrad said slowly, trying to figure it out, "Then... Tanny could be my aunt and I could ride in her car?" he finished cheerfully.

"No! No! No!" the girls giggled.

"*Do* you need a ride?" Tanny asked him.

"No." He shook his head, grinning.

"You can't marry Uncle Paul! He's a *man!*" laughed Andrea.

"He's already married!" chimed in Alyssa.

Conrad shoved his hands in his pockets and sighed melodramatically. "'Aye, there's the rub.' I guess I'll never figure it out."

"You could marry Tanny," suggested Alyssa.

"Girls, we really need to go," insisted Kate.

Conrad looped his hand though the suggested bride's arm. "Would *that* make you my aunt?" he queried of Tanny.

"Con-rad," choked Tanny, pushing his arm away.

"No! No!" giggled the twins.

"I need them to come with me, Tanny," inserted Sue's mom. She reached out a hand to guide the girls to the door.

"Of course, Aunt Kate." Tanny moved to help usher the girls along. When they complained, she lifted her chin. "Nope! Nobody gets to ride with Aunt Tanny today. Tanny wants to ride all by herself. You get to go with your Nana."

Eventually the bright-eyed young ladies had exited the restaurant with their good-natured grandmother.

Tanny watched them go. Were those girls really going to turn eight in a few months? She pushed at a lock of hair. Golly, that made her feel old.

Conrad walked with her to the parking lot. As she pulled out her keys he said, "Tanny, would you like to go out for coffee some time?"

Tanny looked up in surprise. "Well, sure! Um, did you want to talk about..." she shrugged, "...anything in particular?"

Conrad was tucking his scarf tighter about his neck. "Just ... life," he grinned. "Common complaints, you know." He dropped his hands. "Well, great. Can I call you later you about a time?"

"Sure. Yeah. That works." Tanny watched the slight man head off toward his car. *I wonder what that's about.*

She inserted her keys and began the wiggling, jiggling, jumping routine that was involved in unlocking her old beast. "Come on, Herman. Open up!" The lock finally shifted with that satisfying *chunk* that meant success. Tanny climbed in and soon had the engine warming. She waved at Conrad as he passed behind her in his little Mazda. Then, huddled in the chilly interior with nothing to do but wait, she brooded. *I wonder what he wants.* She smiled. Conrad was always good company.

Her thoughts turned to her three o'clock appointment with the pastor. She felt some misgivings about consulting him. What could she say? What could *he* say? But she needed to do something about her turmoil. With a grinding feeling in her stomach, she recalled a decidedly unhelpful conversation with her mother.

It was when she and her mom were folding some wash that Tanny's mom had asked her if something was wrong. Tanny hadn't felt very close to her mom for a long time, but ever willing to improve that, Tanny had responded with simple honesty. "Mom, I'm just feeling ... jealous, I guess. Susan— Susan gets everything. Here she is, on her second marriage, with kids, and a house, and an *awesome* new husband, and I don't even have... I haven't even had a ... a really decent boyfriend. I mean, I don't *begrudge* her. I wouldn't want to take anything away from her, I just.... I just don't get why life is so uneven—why it's *so* unfair. Sue's life seems charmed."

Emily picked up a towel and shook it out. "Having your husband killed in a car accident isn't exactly 'charmed.'"

Tanny's stomach twisted. "That's not what I meant. Because you see ... Well, look how it turned out: Duncan— I saw stuff you didn't, mom. He wasn't a great husband. He was a control-freak. Sue's far better off—"

"Britannia Suzanne Smith. Don't say unkind things," Emily frowned.

Tanny ground her teeth. *Mom can't even come close to understanding what I'm trying to say. Why do I keep trying?*

Emily deftly folded a tea-towel on her lap. Her voice became conciliatory. "I still think, if you'd gone down to the church college in Ben Kirk like we'd wanted—"

Tanny made a face, "'—I'd have found and married a nice "church" boy by now.' Yeah. Thanks for that, Mom. Not to mention that you and Dad would have had to remortgage the house to afford the tuition."

"A price we would have gladly paid."

"But that's not the point. Susie found somebody *here*—twice. It isn't about *here* or *there*. It isn't even about finding a 'nice Swedenborgian boy.'"

Tanny's hands stilled, and she looked at her mom. "I just start to wonder if I'm somehow too... 'messed up' to find someone. Or maybe the 'right one' lives in Tanzania, and that's why we haven't met. Or for some reason I'm just not able to fall in love." *Well, except with Sue's fiancé.* She tossed a sock back in the basket and reached for a washcloth. "I certainly get crushes easily. But nobody ... Nobody holds my interest very long. The few remotely serious relationships I've had never went anywhere. And most of the men that actually interest me aren't interested *in* me, or they're not available. Maybe I'm broken. Maybe I should just give up."

Her mom was supposed to say, "Of course not, sweetheart." And give her hope and confidence and reassurance. Instead, Emily said, "Who knows? Lots of people don't find true love. Besides, I suspect that 'true love' is a fairytale." She set the folded towel down and reached for another. "Sue and Jon are going to have all the same struggles every married couple has, no matter how 'in love' they look now."

"I can't imagine them disagreeing about anything. They're simply perfect for each other. For some reason, they're more deserving than I am, or something. People like me might not ever find what they have, but *some* people do. I have to believe that. *I have to.*" Tanny felt the sting of tears in her eyes.

Emily shrugged. "Maybe you're right. But my experience is that marriage is just something you get through—like life. It provides a service to the world. It gives kids a starting place and a stable environment. It holds the world together and makes us all feel more secure. 'True love' is just a romantic ideal. I don't even know if I've ever experienced it."

Tanny's hands dropped. She gazed at her mother.

Emily kept folding with energy.

Tanny took a deep breath. "Mom. I never knew you thought that way. That's so sad."

"Is it? I guess I'm just so used to 'what is' that I long ago let go of 'what should have been.' I spent a lot of years being mad. My early forties were the worst...."

"But.... Did you have true love with *Jenny's* dad?"

Well, of course I thought I did! But that relationship was so ... melodramatic in its way. We never experienced normal marriage, really. I always knew I could lose him. So, we never fought much; there wasn't time, really. His remission was so short-lived. Our love wasn't ever tested by passing time." She sighed, reflecting. "Then there was Gilbert—so persistent, so adoring, so sweet with Jenny—it seemed the only choice, really, to marry him."

"So, you didn't love Dad when you married him?"

"Of course I loved him. But what I felt for him and feel for him isn't anything like what I imagined true love would be when I was your age—hang on, I was married with two children by your age...." She thought a moment. "So, when I was a *teenager*," she corrected herself. Then she brightened, "But the religion teaches us to marry in our religion, so I did. God's Providence looks over it all. I followed God's commands, and it will be okay. I just have to work harder and trust harder, and it will all make sense in the end."

Tanny blinked. She had seen genuine tenderness and friendship between her mom and dad through the years. Her mom could be a bit prickly and critical, but Gilbert always took it with humour.

Tanny said, "So, you are saying that marrying in the religion is the answer, and feeling love comes later? You are saying that the most important thing is marrying in the religion, more than feeling love?"

Emily looked frustrated. "The ministers go on and on about how wonderful marriage is—and it makes me wonder if they are just charmed, or perhaps not truthful. I was raised to expect that getting married in the religion would fix everything." There was a pause. Then she said with some force, "Well marrying in the religion doesn't fix everything. Some people don't get a 'happily ever after' like I was taught, and it's not fair!"

Tanny just stared at her mom. Emily was clearly struggling to hide tears. Tanny asked, "Are you saying that because of Jenny?" Jenny, Tanny's older half-sister, was married to the slime-ball that had tried to rape Susan. Now Terrence was going to jail, and Jenny was alone with a toddler and no job.

"What?" Emily looked confused. "No. I'm sure she'll find someone better. She's young yet. Terrence wasn't really in the church anyway, was he? We need to find her a good church boy, not an outsider, like Terrence was."

"Wait, so you think it was Terry's status in the church that—"

"No.... I just don't want you to be set up for disappointment. People start out 'in love' but over the long haul, marriage is just hard work, and not always very fun."

Tanny laughed in amazement. "Now *there's* an endorsement nobody can resist. Mom, why would anybody ever get married then?"

"Well, for security, I guess. For the comfort of knowing that somebody is there for you, even if they're flawed. And because we're supposed to. It's God's plan." She set aside some single socks and reached for some briefs. "But being single doesn't mean you can't live a full and useful life; look at your aunt Britt."

After a pause, Emily patted Tanny's arm, "I think you simply haven't found the right man yet. Just look at Mr. Haley. Thirty-one years old before he found Sue. Surely, he must have had a hard time waiting."

He's also gorgeous and incredibly funny and smart and kind and talented. It wasn't for lack of willing partners—of that I'm sure, Tanny mused.

Emily suggested, "Maybe Jon would counsel you about waiting."

Tanny stifled a laugh.

"But you know, I still think you should go for courses in Ben Kirk. There are always several available *Swedenborgian* men down there." Emily's hands rested on a neatly creased T-shirt. Maybe one of the professors...."

"Mom!" Tanny had exclaimed, and grabbing her laundry, marched off to her apartment. She shut the door with more force than necessary, growling.

"Maybe Jon would counsel me?" Oh, that wouldn't be mortifying at all. Not embarrassing in the least. Though he certainly would know about "waiting." Tanny laughed as she thought, *my mom is NUTS if she thinks he's still a virgin. Heck, she thinks I still am. That's what she means by "waiting," as if SEX is the thing that is hard to wait for, not a decent, healthy, deeply compatible LOVE. Jon would definitely understand waiting to find that. But as he's off on his honeymoon, it's not like he has time to counsel an insecure, neurotic maid-of-honour.*

Tanny had decided to talk to Stephen, and the meeting time was nearly upon her. She hoped Jon and Susie's drive north was smooth and without much traffic. At least the weather was behaving.

Three

February 14, noon

The dark blue van sped north. There wasn't a sound in the car save for the muffled engine noise and whir of the tires on the road. Jon drove with one hand on the wheel, leaving his right hand free to hold hands with Susan.

It was a comfortable silence, pregnant, yet peaceful. The usually busy 400 highway was blissfully clear of traffic. It was an early Sunday morning in February. No surprise there.

Sue stirred and asked, "Want me to put on some music?"

"Sure," said the new husband.

There was a pause, then Susan said, smiling, "You'll have to let go of my hand."

"Already so demanding," Jon sighed, and released the item in question.

"What're you in the mood for?" asked his bride.

"Anything. Anything you like."

Sue made a little noise of frustration. "All right," she pouted. "I choose heavy metal." She lifted a CD out of its box and slid it into the player. Something gently acoustic with piano and guitar wafted out of the speakers.

"Plastic, recycled milk carton music," Jon exclaimed, grinning. "I like it." It was an inside joke.

"If you're not going to vote, you don't get to complain," Sue returned. They clasped hands again, interlacing fingers.

After a moment Jon asked, "Did you sleep last night?"

"Not much. You?"

"Not a wink."

After another comfortable silence Jon asked, "So what did you think about, all those hours awake?"

Sue looked at Jon's hand, interlaced with hers. She loved his hands—long-fingered and graceful, beautifully proportioned, and strong.

"I was feeling excited and so good about us. I was also ... wondering ... um, what it will be like to share your bed."

Jon jerked the wheel over and back in pretend shock. He said, "And there I was, wondering if I had packed enough warm socks, and if my alarm would go off in time."

"Liar," she grinned. Sue surveyed her new husband's face as he concentrated on the road. A gentle seriousness came into his eyes.

"I am as eager as a horny teenager and extraordinarily nervous," he admitted. He glanced at her with an eyebrow lifted. His thumb rubbed gently where their hands were clasped. The road whirred under their wheels.

"No, seriously," he continued. "I know it is completely unorthodox, but there's something quite sensible to the modern way young people are doing things, where couples have already incorporated their sexual relationship into their general functioning *before* the honeymoon. They don't have to wait through the ceremony and reception and everything with 'what will the sex be like?' hovering in the background." He gave a snort. "I rather envy that. It keeps the focus on the powerful commitment rather than on 'now we get to have sex.'"

He continued, "I mean, I get it: Before the advent of reliable birth control, couples really couldn't sleep together before marriage without risking pregnancy. These protections go back beyond Biblical times. Impregnating and abandoning a woman back then was to create two outcasts, an unmarried mother, and a bastard—an "orphan and a widow." But these days women are educated, independent, have access to birth control, and can often support themselves. There's a lot more informed consent happening now."

After digesting this Sue asked. "So ... are you sorry we waited?"

He squeezed her hand. "Not at all. For us, I can't imagine any other timeline. We've only known each other, what ... about ten weeks? And after 'saving myself' for thirty-one years, I might as well finish what I started. But the nerves I am feeling now are making me ... think again about how morality has changed since our grandparents' day."

After a comfortable silence, Susan added, "I am glad we waited too."

The snow-covered fields scrolled by in the sunshine.

Jon suggested, "So tell me more about this Cedar Haven."

"My great, great grandfather settled on the land way back when the first white people were moving into the area. Somehow, he and his wife survived and raised three kids. Their son inherited the land from them—that was Britt's father. He built the Cedar Haven that stands there today. Then Britt inherited it.

"Is it made of cedar?"

"Well, no. They say there once was a log cabin on the site, but that burnt down before Britt was born. It was Britt's dad—my great grandfather—who built the big house that stands there now, out of *brick*. Yes, 'Cedar Haven' is a big, *brick* farmhouse. Don't laugh! They called it that because there are so many cedars on their land, and because cedars are such a sweet-smelling, resilient tree. But it's definitely not built out of cedar."

Sue continued, "But the name suits it. I have always loved the big kitchen and the cozy, stone fireplace."

"I'm looking forward to meeting this Cedar Haven."

Winter views rolled by the windows. Acoustic guitar danced in the air.

Then Jon said, "I'm also really looking forward to sharing your bed."

There was an old sedan parked outside the house when Jon and Sue rolled up. Cedar Haven's front door opened as the newlyweds climbed out the car. It was Susan's aunt and uncle, Jacob and Eileen Bender who lived in nearby Bracebridge.

"You made good time," greeted the balding man with warm brown eyes. "Welcome! Can I help with the luggage?" He had boots on and was pulling on his heavy coat.

"Uncle Jacob. Aunt Eileen," Sue exclaimed. She waved at the woman with the messy topknot who emerged from behind her husband.

"Such congratulations!" Eileen greeted. "I'm so happy for you."

Susan's uncle clapped Jon on the shoulder. "Congratulations, young man. May you two be very happy."

Jon appreciated the clear eyes and firm grip of his new uncle-in-law. "Thank you. I think we will. So good to see you again."

Jacob smacked his gloved palms together and said, "How can I help with the luggage?" He eyed a small cooler on the front seat.

Meanwhile, Eileen was ushering Susan toward the house. "The men can get the luggage," she was saying. "But you, Susan, take a deep breath. Close your eyes. Britt did some renovating."

Under Emily's guidance Sue stepped into the house and stopped.

"Open your eyes," said Eileen.

Sue opened her eyes to an almost unrecognizably beautiful space. She walked forward slowly. "Whaaaaaat?" Her eyes flitted from the completely renovated kitchen to a grand view of the water. "That's so .... I can see the.... But where's the

.... WHA-A-AT?!" She stopped near the familiar stone fireplace, now part of one great room. Sue gazed at the view of the trees and water, the grand dining table, the open kitchen with its big, central island. "This is amazing! I had no idea this view was even here." Where once had been wallpapered solid walls, with pictures and a few curtained windows, there was a now wall of glass with a large, wide deck beyond it.

"Cedar Haven has entered the twenty-first century," said Eileen. "Britt really wanted the old place to be made welcoming and usable by today's tastes, and this is the result."

Sue called, "Jon, you have to see this!"

Jon looked up and said, "Ni-i-i-ice!" as he wrestled two cases in the front door. He then continued wrestling the cases up the stairs.

"Not too shabby, eh?" said Jacob, burdened with a cooler and several bags. He dumped them on the kitchen island. "I don't know where you want these."

Sue said, "I'd heard something about renovations, but had no idea...." She was walking slowly around the space, moving freely from the former living room to the former dining room, then gazing straight into the generous kitchen where there had once been a solid wall. It was now one unified space. "This is GORGEOUS!"

"Britt never talked about what it cost, but it must have been a fortune." Eileen dropped her voice. "Jacob was NOT happy with her. It was his childhood home too and he didn't want it touched. I mean, I had my doubts too. But it has come out really beautifully. I have to give Britt credit. Even Jacob has come around to liking it now."

Jon came downstairs and moved over to slip his arm around Sue's waist. "What did I miss?"

Jacob was setting a few more bundles on the kitchen floor. "I think that's all of it," he panted.

Eileen became brisk. "Okay! Here are the keys. The heating controls are there by the basement door. There is more wood for the fire in the basement; I think Jeff left you more than enough. I wrote out some instructions which are there, on the kitchen island. If you have any other questions, we are a phone call away." She paused. "Jeff is away for the week, so you have the place all to yourself."

Susan, puzzled, said, "Jeff? You are talking about the caretaker, Mr. VanGalen?"

"Of course," said Eileen. She then gave Susan and Jon each a big squeeze before heading toward the door. "Ready, Jacob dear?"

Uncle Jacob shook Jon's hand again and gave Sue a quick hug. "Enjoy yourselves, now," he said. And with a firm click of the front door behind them, the kindly couple were gone.

"Hmmmm. What shall we do first?" asked Jon, his arms encircling his bride.

"Make sure everything is really out of the car and put away the food," grinned the practical mother of two. Then we can think about ... er... other ... things..."

Jon had started kissing her under her ear, moving down her neck.

"Jo-on," she sighed, chuckling. "Not yet." She placed her hand between his lips and her skin. "We really ought to—."

But Jon had closed his lips around her fingertips and was sucking on them, the heat of his mouth and soft lips contrasting with the bristly moustache. Sue felt that increasingly familiar rush through her core. She longed to let go of common sense; just for a minute. She tried feebly to pull her fingers away from his kiss. Sensations rose from where his mouth was tasting down her neck toward her collarbone. Her head tipped back to allow more access, and her eyes closed. She whimpered in frustrated amusement when his arms started tugging off her coat.

He murmured, "Please, sweetness. Please. I've waited so long." His lips came back to her jawline; his kisses crept closer and closer to her lips until he murmured right at the corner of her mouth, "Please, Susan." His voice was low and husky. "No more waiting." His bearded mouth closed over hers.

Sue made a noise of surrender and desire. The house keys hit the floor.

Off came winter coats, sweaters, jeans. Jon glanced around out the windows. "Do we have to worry about prying neighbors?" he asked as he helped her out of her blouse. He rumbled approval at the sight of her.

Sue laughed. "Are you kidding? There is no one for miles."

Jon slipped his fingers under her bra straps, and reverently, slowly, slid them off her shoulders.

After many delicious moments they were on the floor, the cool air on their excited skin. Jon stopped, poised over Sue. He looked Sue deep in her eyes and murmured, "I've waited so long for this, I feel like I ought to say a prayer."

Sue's cry of impatience brought him hard into her, again and again and again.

Susan cried, "Yes! Yes! Oh ... God. Ohhhhh, GOD! OH. MY. GO-O-O-O-OD!" And with a squeal of pleasure Susan shuddered, clinging to Jon, her face pressed into his moving, sweaty shoulder. Jon followed with noises of rhythmic, guttural astonishment. Finally, he collapsed over Susan, both of them laughing. Then they wept with the enormity of their experience. They rested, locked together, stunned, and spent.

Jon eventually lifted his head so as to look down into Susan's face. He tenderly brushed the hair out of her eyes.

She said with a half-grin, "I'm sorry I said, 'Oh my God.'"

Jon looked at her with absolute delight. "That is your first thought? Seriously?" A low, delighted chuckle moved through his body. "You are apologizing because you called God's name during your orgasm?" His deep and rhythmic laughter moved his body wonderfully against her own. "Sweetness, if there was ever a time you could call out God's name with complete reverence, this would have been it." Jon pressed tender kisses into her hair as she giggled. "I do so adore you, Susan."

Four

February 14, afternoon

Embarrassment pushed forward as Tanny approached the office door. At her knock she heard a cheerful, "Come in!"

Pastor Stephen Shantz stepped around his desk to greet her when she opened the door. "Hello Tanny." He offered a warm handshake and indicated a stuffed chair. "Have a seat. Get comfortable." He shut the door and settled into a chair facing her.

Tanny removed her coat and sat. She was about to speak when Stephen said, "How about we start with prayer? I find that always sets a good tone for whatever follows." Tanny nodded and bowed her head.

Steve said, "Heavenly Father, we come before you today with questions on our hearts. We know you answer every prayer, just not always in our timing or in the way we might expect. We ask today that you open our minds and hearts to your leading and wise guidance. We trust that you will show us which way to turn our attention and our feet, to become the people you would have us become, fully alive and a blessing to all we meet. Amen."

Tanny reflected that Steven had a gift for prayer, as she said, "Amen." Then, "Fully alive and a blessing, huh?" she asked. "Not, 'Thy will be done?'"

The sandy haired pastor cocked his head, grinning. "In what way is 'fully alive and a blessing' *not* God's will for us?"

Tanny mused on that one. "Hmmm, good point. It just doesn't sound humble enough or something." She laughed at herself. "I guess I somehow expect God's will to be a burden, not a joy. Maybe I should rethink that."

Steven raised his brows, the smile still in his voice, "'My yoke is easy, and my burden is light,'" he quoted. "We religious folks tend to take ourselves way too seriously." He paused and looked at her with gentleness, "Now, tell me what is up for you...."

After her convoluted attempt to lay out her struggle, Steve summed things up for Tanny.

"This is what I hear you saying: you are longing for that thing that I believe everyone longs for: true love with one perfect soul mate. You see it happening for people around you, and wonder if there is something wrong with you, or something different you could do to make it happen for you in your life. On top of that you then judge yourself for wanting such a thing, because it means you are somehow weak. Is that about it?"

Tanny was stunned. She had not realized that she was judging herself on top of everything else until she heard Steven's analysis. "Yes.... Yeah. Pretty much. I think you nailed it."

Stephen settled back into his chair. "There are two answers *at least* that I can think of for you, but I'm not sure either will satisfy." He looked rueful. "The first is quite simple, and the second fairly complicated."

"Okay...." Tanny waited.

Steve steepled his fingers and looked at Tanny, "The first is this: I believe it is God's will for every single one of us to find and live with one true love. And I absolutely believe that you will find and have your special someone at the perfect time for you. I also am sure you are doing nothing wrong. The one and only thing you can do is live your life and trust God's providence. That's the simple answer."

A big sigh breathed out of Tanny, as if she had been holding onto something and finally released it.

Stephen paused a beat and said, "Now here is the complicated answer: Every single one of us is on our own spiritual journey. That journey is a solitary one. We are born alone, and we will die alone to all intents and purposes. When it comes to our deepest pain, we face it alone. Our whole spiritual quest is a lot like many of the hero stories in popular fiction—*The Lord of the Rings* in my day, and *Harry Potter* today. The hero has terrific friends who are there on the journey too, who ease the loneliness and provide laughter and companionship, and who watch their backs and occasionally rescue them. But when it really comes down to it, the hero must face his—or *her*—" Stephen added with a nod at Tanny, "—demons alone. Just you and the monster—you and the battle—with only God as your ally."

"So, it is a paradox," Steve continued. "We are always alone, *and* we are made to live in community, and especially with one special someone—that's *my* belief, anyway. And as paradoxical as *that* sounds, there is one more hitch: Unless and until we make our spiritual journey and do our spiritual work, *any* relationships we are in will be dragged down and messed up by our own unconscious baggage. It's not just a matter of *finding* the right person, it is also a matter of *becoming* the right person. Like every archetypal fairy tale, the lovers will be torn apart by the villain's darkness until the hero battles and defeats that darkness. That hero is in-side each of us, male or female. We each, in a way, live out our own inner arche-typal fairy tale, with all the characters living inside us. And until our own inner wholeness is restored, by doing that spiritual work—by facing and overcoming our inner demons—it won't matter what relationships we are in *outside* of us—"

Steve stopped abruptly, struck by a thought. Tanny watched the light play across his face as ideas danced through his mind. He looked at Tanny, coming to a conclusion. "In fact, Tanny, I think the church's obsessive emphasis on *getting* married is a big mistake. What does that Swedenborgian out in Hawaii say? 'Stand-ing in a garage doesn't make you a car.'" Steve chuckled and shifted his weight in his chair. "His point is that *being married* doesn't mean one is in a great relation-ship any more than being inside a gym means you are an athlete. You have to do the work. The inside character needs to come first. Any shelter around a car can be called a garage, but any item which happens to be in a garage is not a 'car' simply because it is in the garage." Stephen looked befuddled. "Am I making sense? I'm not nearly as eloquent as he is, but maybe you get my point?"

Tanny nodded, enjoying the subject, though unsure where Steve was headed with it all.

"Okay, so my point," Steve continued, "is that you can go ahead and work on becoming a better and better 'car,' whether or not you are in a 'garage,' and the 'garage' will appear in its right time. Do you see? And even if the garage were to appear right now in front of you, you might at this point only be a scooter or skate-board...." He trailed off with a look of bemusement and sympathy. "If you have any idea of what I'm trying to say."

Tanny made a face of exaggerated concentration. "So...you are saying that finding my soul mate is kind of like 'the garage', and the 'car' would be what I bring to the relationship as to my personal character and maturity—which by the way, you are calling a 'scooter'! Thank you so very much!" She made a noisy rasp-berry in Steven's direction. He shouted in laughter. She folded her arms in front of herself and pressed her lips together, trying to smother a smile. "So what you are *really* saying is that I'm a spiritual kindergartener, and there's no point in even *looking* for someone to love as all I bring to the game is a roller skate?"

The kindly pastor played along, nodding in enthusiastic agreement. "Yes! That is *exactly* what I was saying. *That* was my pastoral message of comfort and hope to your bright and attractive and talented self."

Behind her own laughter, Tanny captured *bright, attractive, and talented* and stored them up in a secret nest to pull out and muse upon at a later time. She sighed. "So, just keep on living my life and doing my best and trust in God...."

"...And build your own wonderful self—becoming more and more the angel that God is already making you. Then, when the magical 'he' appears, the fit will be that much more perfect, straightforward, and delightful, because you will both have already been transforming and growing into the angel God intends you to be."

Tanny sighed. "So, the folks who are already married aren't necessarily way ahead of me on the road? Sometimes I feel like I'm standing at the starting line without shoes or feet or a horse!"

"Or a car?" Steve laughed. Then a mild wistfulness crossed his face, and he became quiet. He sat back in his chair and steepled his fingers again. "The thing is, so many marriages that you see out there aren't the happily-ever-after that we would like to think. We are all so busy, so ill-equipped, and so mired in our own baggage, it is amazing that any marriages work out at all. A fifty percent divorce rate doesn't seem so unreasonable to me anymore, having worked in the field as long as I have and having seen what I've seen." He shook his head. "Honestly, there are some couples who really *ought* to get divorced—they seem to be such bad news for each other." He half-laughed. "I sometimes think ongoing therapy should be a *requirement* of married couples. Kind of like we have regular safety inspections for cars, and they have to pass inspection to be driven." He made a noise of bemusement. "*And* ... we are back to the car metaphor again." He sighed.

Tanny found herself wondering if Steve's own marriage was doing okay after hearing such honest admissions, but when she pictured the kind pastor and his warm-hearted wife, she simply couldn't imagine them having problems. "I don't know," she said. "I guess I didn't really expect that you would have some magic formula for me so I could find Mr. Right. I'm just tired of feeling left out of the game and need some kind of hope or guidance or comfort.... I look at Sue and Jon, and most of the other women my age, and even my sister Jenny, and they all have homes and kids. It is like a club I can't join. I'm on the outside looking in through the glass, and it's all warm inside and everyone is laughing...and I'm outside on the street in the cold, alone." She felt tears sting her eyes again and felt annoyed at herself. "I haven't been in a rush to get married, but lately I'm wondering if maybe I *should* be! My big career hasn't materialized, thanks to the economy. My job's not all that soul-filling, and as more and more friends get married and have kids, I find I'm scrambling to figure out how to be happy being single, or how to join the marriage club."

Steve had looked down and away when Tanny had choked up. Whether it had been coincidental or gracefully intentional, Tanny was relieved. She realized that if the pastor had shown her sympathy just then, she would probably have fallen into sobs of frustration.

Steve sighed and said, "One of my biggest challenges in this pastorate, Tanny, has been how to help this congregation remain a comfortable home for single adults. So many churches become marriage- and child-centric. Singles often feel like fifth wheels, even though no one intends that. We have parenting classes and marriage classes, but not a lot that is for individuals, regardless of marital or parental status." He sighed. "And no matter how many ways I try to push for it, it all seems to keep re-setting to marriage and family social events."

Tanny chimed in, "To which singles are invited, but are expected to think it is just great and fun to only talk about kids, school, and marriage. I always feel a little odd when I go. Everyone is nice, but I just don't have that much to say about babies who won't sleep or husbands who don't take out the garbage. I feel like I'm seen as someone *who is not yet married,* not someone of worth in my own right. It's just no fun."

"I have heard this before and no doubt I'll hear it again," Steve said with some apparent frustration. "It takes a long time for a culture to change, and for a dominant culture to make room for alternative ways of living. Christianity has been so very marriage-centric for so long—our entire Western culture has thought in terms of heterosexual couples for so very long—that there is a lot of inertia to overcome in shaking up the status quo." Steve's brow took on a look of concern and his eyes assessed Tanny. He said at last, "I want you to understand me when I say this: I want nothing more than for you to find a happy home to worship in, *right here at Cliffside Chapel.* But if you feel increasingly on the outside here, I encourage you to be open to exploring other spiritual communities. You need and deserve belonging, and if Cliffside's congregation can't be more inclusive of singles, we will continue to lose them. You are one of the last of our young singles who still come, have you noticed? The congregational groupthink needs to change radically if the not-married are going to feel just as much a part of things as the families. I totally want this to change, but there's only so much I can do as a pastor, especially as *I'm* married and raising six kids myself."

Tanny hadn't realized that Stephen had been conscious of the singles' plight and felt grateful for his sympathy.

Steve continued, "It was looking like Jon Haley was going to be reviving the adult singles when he arrived, but that didn't last long. Oh well!" Tanny's disappointment resurfaced at the mention of Jon's name. *If he had stayed single, even for a little while,* she mused, *a group with him at the helm would have been awesome.*

It was resolved that Tanny would consider Steve's words, pray about it all, and revisit the issue with him in a few weeks. As he stood at the office door bidding her goodbye, Steve said, "In no way am I wanting you to leave our Cliffside congregation, Tanny. But more than anything, I want you to be in a good spiritual home where you feel like you belong. If you find a congregation that has a happening young adults' group, go there!" He paused, considering. He then said, "Maybe I shouldn't advertise for another church, but Conrad Knapp has been going to the Unitarian Congregation across town, for example, and been quite happy there. You might ask him what he thinks about it. Anyway, I look forward to hearing how things go, Tanny.' He paused. "See you in a few weeks?"

"Absolutely," she smiled and gave her pastor a hug.

Tanny let herself out of the church into the chilly afternoon air. She felt both soothed and somehow even lonelier than before. *Conrad Knapp again*, she reflected. We can get together and drool over Jon and commiserate over our broken hearts. She kicked a chunk of snow, stubbing her toes inside her boot. She swore before she could stop herself. *Life is often like that*, she thought. *Sparkly and fluffy looking on the outside, but cold hard ice in the middle.* Tanny trudged back to her lonely basement apartment feeling once again thoroughly out of sorts.

Five

As Tanny walked home, her cell phone chirped. It was a text from her friend Shelley, an excessively talented photographer and friend from university. "You up for coffee and a visit?" it said.

Tanny texted back, "Sure! When, where?"

"Uptown? Organic Cup?"

Tanny reflected that she had forty-five minutes to get herself up to the high-end coffee chain near Waterloo Town Square. "It's a date", she texted back.

She let herself into her parent's front door rather than going down and around into her apartment.

"Hi, Mom!" she called. "I'm back!" The dogs crowded around her feet as usual. Tanny tried not to trip on them as she wrestled her boots off.

Emily poked her head around the head of the stairs. "I'm up here, Tanny. How was your meeting?"

Tanny climbed the long, straight wooden stairs, experiencing a nostalgic flashback of giggling blanket-wrapped sledding excursions down them with Jenny. She found her mom in the sewing room, folding some fabric. "Oh, hey, that's beautiful", she remarked, fingering the white-on-white textured brocade.

"I saw it on sale in a fabric store a few years ago and just had to grab it. I have no idea what to use it for", said Emily a bit wistfully.

"Maybe a tablecloth?" Tanny suggested, then, "Hey wow, you bought a ton of it! Why did you get so much?"

Tanny's mother tossed her head a little and said, "Well, if you must know, I thought it would make a wonderful wedding dress for you. Since I made Jenny's, well, I thought it made sense to get this for you while it was on discount. But now I feel silly because you may never use it".

The brocade was exquisite, but not necessarily what Tanny might want. She got that too-familiar grinding sensation in her gut. Now she felt obliged to use it if she ever got engaged. Tanny wasn't even dating anyone, yet should the day ever come that she was a bride, her fabric was pre-ordained. She wondered if her mom wanted to pick the pattern of the dress too. *Heck, how about mom pick the groom and maybe even just walk down the aisle herself? I will just wait in the car.*

She realized the silence was stretching awkwardly, and quipped, "I think I'll elope. It's cheaper. Besides, now that Terry is out of the picture, maybe Jenny will find someone decent to marry, and *she* can use it". She straightened and turned to leave. "Anyway, I wanted you to know I'm heading out for coffee with a friend".

"They are just separated, dear", her mother commented. "Maybe they can still work things out".

Tanny's eyes widened. She had had this discussion with her mom already several times. Tanny knew that any comment she might make at that moment would plunge them back into the same ugly go-round. Emily refused to believe that Terry had tried to rape Susan and clung to the hope that her eldest daughter's marriage could be salvaged. Her mom insisted on it beyond all rational explanation. It disgusted Tanny.

"And pigs might fly", Tanny called brightly over her shoulder, and she scurried back down the stairs grabbing her boots on the way toward the basement. Once in her apartment she locked the door and glared at it. What planet was her mom born on?

Charm trotted over and licked her hand. Tanny crouched down and ruffled the thick fur, brooding. "We need to get out of here", she said into the panting face. "I am twenty-eight and still living at home". As if responding to Charm's objection she said, "Yes, I am paying rent to my parents for this apartment, but who am I kidding? I *haven't* left home yet. It's just semantics". She stood and gave the soft fur another few good scrubbing pats. "Nope. I have failed to launch. I am just a Velveteen Rabbit".

Tanny sighed. Her cool job was temporary, and the school debts still had to be paid. She had been trying to save for a trip to Scotland. But every time she made any progress; some unexpected expense would come up and eat away all her hard-won savings. She had lost any sense of purpose in trying to save money anymore. Plus, her faithful old car Herman was about to die, and Charm, her sweet golden retriever, was showing increasing signs of her age. The vet bills were only becoming more frequent and more expensive.

"Blast". She grabbed her car keys. Coffee with Shelley would cheer her up. "See you in a bit, my sweet", she said, crouching down to croon in Charm's face. Charm licked her nose. She seemed a bit listless. "Do you want a walk when I get back?" Tanny asked. The mention of a walk usually got Charm excited. Instead,

Charm weakly thumped her tail. "What is it, girl?" Tanny crouched down to rub behind the retriever's ears. "Look. I'll be right back. I'll leave the door to upstairs open in case you want to join Rory and Elmer or have them come visit". These were her parents' dogs, a collie-mix, and a beagle. Tanny then left by her own door.

Just after locking the door, she turned and promptly fell on the ubiquitous icy patch that lived just outside her entrance. *Right. The reason I like to come and go through my parents' door in the winter.* "Shit!" she cried. "Shit! Shit! Shit! SHIT!" Her pants were all wet where she had landed on her right hip. Her hand was scraped. Now she had to go change before she could start the thirty-minute drive from the south-western suburb of Kitchener into Waterloo's downtown.

She scrambled back inside, removing boots and coat, grabbed the first clean thing she could find—grey sweats—transferred everything from her pockets, climbed back into her coat and boots, and exited *carefully,* climbing the icy steps up the grade to where Herman waited. Her hip hurt where she had landed on it, her back ached too, and she felt generally discombobulated.

"If my life was going well, would I be 'bobulated'?" she wondered out loud as she traversed the yard toward her car. "Or maybe '*com*bobulated'?" as she strapped herself into the seat.

"I'll take anything", she concluded as she headed toward Waterloo.

Six

February 14, late afternoon

Tanny pushed open the glass doors of the beloved high-end coffee chain in "Uptown" Waterloo. She scanned the heads in the crowded shop until she spotted the abundant blond tresses of her tall friend. Tanny wound her way through the crowd and joined Shelley in the line-up.

"You didn't need to dress up for the occasion," was Shelley's wry comment on Tanny's grey sweatpants.

Tanny looked down. "Yeah, I know. Well, I fell on the ice, and this was what I could find—" She stopped. "I've got my pants on backwards. How did I not notice this?" Tanny plucked at the fabric, trying to adjust how it lay. "I hate how this feels—all baggy in the front and binding up my butt." She looked at Shelley. "How bad does it look?" Tanny twisted around trying to see. "Does it show? How obvious is it?" She looked at Shelley again for help.

Shelley just watched her with that delighted, wide-eyed smile that said, "I can't believe you."

Tanny asked, "Tell me how bad it is."

Shelley blinked, "You want me to look at your butt." The line moved forward.

"Yeah. How bad does it look? Do I have a wedgie? Do I lose my place in line and go fix it right now, or not worry about it?" She made a face and pulled at the fabric again and wiggled her bottom around, trying to shift it to something more comfortable.

Shelley just said with a smile, "You are awesome."

Tanny opted to order her drink and then go make the switcheroo.

On coming back into the room, she found Shelley had grabbed them a table. She tapped her paper cup to Shelley's and took a sip of her latte. Her noise of pleasure was followed by a small groan of discouragement. "I'm going to have to put a stop to this expensive latte habit. Old Herman needs another $800 of work, and I can hardly make my payments on my school loan as it is."

Shelley pursed her generous lips and looked thoughtful. "I don't know if our friendship will survive that. I'm just not a fast-food-coffee kind of girl."

"Ha! I'll trick you into treating me, or I will sip my tepid tap water while making puppy-dog eyes at you until you relent-"

"Which would be tricking me into treating you."

"Um, yeah."

"Same thing," they said in unison.

"So, we've got a plan," said Tanny in contentment.

Shelley shook her head at Tanny, with a "what am I going to do with you" look in her eyes. There was a companionable silence.

Then Shelley said, "Well, I have a proposal for you. Sometimes I need an assistant on my wedding shoots. It wouldn't be regular, but if you are up for tagging around after me for a day carrying my equipment once wedding season starts, I'm always looking for someone."

"Okay," Tanny thought for a while. "Sure. That sounds like fun." Tanny removed the lid from her drink. "I am free most Saturday's anyway, and I always need more income." She licked the foamy sweet residue on the underside of the lid.

"Awesome," said Shelley. "I will put you on my list."

"I will be your caddy."

"Well, it's mostly my camera bags."

"I will be your bag lady," Tanny amended.

"My bag lady," Shelley responded. She shook her head, grinning. "Awesome."

Tanny pressed her lid back into place and took another sip.

The two friends spent the next hour in happy chatter. When she spent time with Shelley, Tanny often marveled that she had found someone even more talkative than herself. Shelley was older, had traveled much more, and Tanny thoroughly enjoyed their wide-ranging and intelligent exchanges.

With an abrupt lift of her arms Shelley said, "OMYGOSH! I have found the most amazing energy worker."

Tanny choked slightly at the unexpected announcement. She was used to Shelley's "Ooh! SHINEY" way of narrating her latest passionate interest, but it still had made her jump. She gurgled, "So, what does she do?"

"Remember that I was having trouble with my right shoulder and arm from all the computer-work I do? Well, she's fixed it." She sat back with finality, looking at Tanny with wonder. "She fixed it. Just like that." She made a tossing motion with her arms.

"Tell me more."

"She's got this wild space which she has had Feng Shue-ed—it's fricking awesome—and these three dogs, one of which has a Level One Reiki certificate. I kid you not. Anyway, my car mechanic went from unable to walk due to back pain, to back on the job in a day thanks to her, when no one else had been able to help him, so when I heard that, I had to give her a try."

Tanny loved Shelley's animated, run-on delivery and the way she used her hands with dramatic emphasis.

"So ... what does she *do*?" Tanny repeated.

"It's called 'craniosacral,' and she hardly does anything. You lie on your back on this treatment bed-thing, and she might hold your head or your feet, or put her hands on your back and move them very slightly. And you go into this kind of trance. And the next thing you know you are sighing, and things are feeling better. She said I was carrying too much responsibility and had a lot of anger to release." Shelley's wide eyes regarded Tanny with a dead-pan expression. "I know. Right? It was so freaky."

Tanny felt her bruised hip and the way her low back had started aching since her fall and wondered if she should try this "energy-worker."

Shelley continued, "The funny thing is, my car mechanic? He's the straightest guy you could ever meet—NOT at all flakey. So, the fact that *he* recommended her makes it extra funny." She sipped her latte and continued, "He said," and she imitated his voice and speaking style, "'I don't know what it is that she does, and I don't *want* to know. All I know is yesterday I couldn't walk and now I am back on the job.'"

Tanny said, "So, I would look up 'energy worker' if I wanted to find her?"

"Oh! No. Here." Shelley pulled out her phone and started thumb-typing on it. "I'll just text you her contact information. Her name is Adina Kinsey, and her place is near St. Mary's Hospital. It's easy to find. It looks like no other place on the block—all plants and fountains and Buddhas and wind chimes, even in the snow—well, not the plants part."

"Is she expensive?"

"That depends," Shelley was still tapping on her phone. She said, "Send," with finality. He eyes lifted to Tanny's. "There. You should get it any second. Do you have coverage for physiotherapy?"

"I'm pretty sure I do." Tanny's phone dinged.

"Then you are covered."

"Cool," smiled Tanny.

"How does a dog get a Reiki certificate?" she wondered as Herman chugged through the gathering evening.

Just as she pulled into the driveway at her parents' her phone dinged. It was a text from Conrad saying, "Hey Tanny, can we grab a coffee tomorrow?

"Sure," She texted back. "When?"

"Before work or first thing after?"

"Before," replied Tanny.

"Seven-thirty a.m. Tim Hortons on Bleams? "

"I'll be there," agreed Tanny.

She sat in her quiet car wondering what he wanted to talk about.

As she closed her car door, Tanny remembered to use her parents' front door to avoid the ice by her own. Once in, she kicked off her boots, noticing the quiet. Tanny remembered that her folks were out at a gathering with their cronies. Her parent's beagle and collie-mix bumped up against her in greeting, but there was no sign of Charm.

"Hey, you two," Tanny murmured as she gave them each a welcoming scrub, "Where's Charm?"

Tanny jogged down the dark wood-paneled stairway and entered her unit. It was completely quiet. Charm was laid out on her bed in the dim light. Tanny rushed over to stroke the sweet, golden head, noticing the half-closed eyes.

"Charm, honey? What is it?" Charm gave no response. Tanny immediately grabbed one of her largest towels and wrapped Charm in it, gathering Charm's legs close to her body. She wanted Charm to feel secure. Then Tanny hefted her beloved retriever back up the narrow stairs. Laying the unresponsive golden on her parent's couch she scribbled,

Taking Charm to the vet.
I don't know when I'll be back.
Pray for her!
T

Charm was so quiet. Tanny had found a thready pulse but trembled as she pulled on her boots. She carried her companion of almost ten years out the door and laid her gently on Herman's back seat.

"There you go, my girl," she murmured. "Nice and comfy. We're going to get you some help. Hang in there." A sob caught in Tanny's throat. "Please, please don't die." Then, with one, final caress of the soft head, Tanny buckled herself into her old car and roared off to the emergency veterinarian clinic.

Seven

February 15, morning

Tanny jolted awake to her alarm as the night's memories flooded back to her. The technicians at the clinic had gotten to work quickly on Charm, giving her an injection and hooking her up to a fluid drip. Charm had seemed to rally a little. She even thumped her tail once when Tanny spoke to her. The staff wanted to keep Charm overnight for observation; the Dr. would see her first thing and possibly order tests. They promised to call Tanny as soon as they had any information.

Tanny resisted the urge to call the vet immediately to ask for news. Instead, she called work and asked for a personal day. It was granted.

So promptly at seven thirty Tanny eased Herman into a parking spot at Tim Hortons. She could see Conrad through the window at a table. It looked like he was sitting with someone already. Tanny pulled off her scarf and gloves as she entered the familiar-smelling coffee chain. Conrad stood up, smiling, and reaching a hand. The young man he was with also stood.

"Tanny! Thank you for coming. How are you?" Conrad grabbed her in a big hug. She had forgotten how warm and bracing his hugs could be.

"Gosh, your hugs are so amazing," Tanny gasped.

"Tanny, I want you to meet my friend, Gary." Conrad indicated a wiry man about their age in an opened peacoat, and newsboy cap. His smile was warm in his boyish face.

Intrigued, Tanny said, "Hello there. It's nice to meet you, 'Conrad's friend, Gary'."

Gary offered a fist-bump. "I hope a fist-bump is okay. Some of the kids I work with are immune compromised."

Tanny held her two hands up in happy surrender, "No complaint here. You work with kids? That's really great." She had so many more questions. She settled her things on a chair. "I'm just going to get myself a coffee and I'll be back."

"No. Please let me get this," said Gary still standing. "How do you take it?"

"Are you sure, Gary?" At his insistence Tanny gave him her order. She settled back in her chair, adjusting her purse. "He seems nice," she said to Conrad. "A friend from school?"

Conrad scratched the back of his neck. "Not exactly...."

"Work?" At Conrad's continued hesitation she said, "Never mind. It doesn't matter. How have you been?"

Gary returned with the three coffees and an apple cruller. Tanny murmured her thanks. She appreciated the well-tailored vest and pants that showed under his peacoat. He set his tweed cap on the table revealing some mouse-brown hair thinning on top.

Conrad said with fondness, "Gary loves Tim's apple crullers. He always gets one."

Gary just grinned and popped open his coffee.

So, they know each other's habits?

"How long have you two known each other? Tanny asked. "I have so many questions."

Conrad raised an eyebrow, looking at Gary, who just gazed back at Conrad with a "go ahead" kind of expression.

"Tanny," Conrad hesitated. "I wanted you to meet Gary because I thought, um, I thought you might be a safe person to tell. You see, Gary and I are a couple." His eyes showed hope, happiness, but also hesitation.

Before she knew what she was doing, Tanny had jumped her chair towards Conrad in excitement. "That's amazing!" She cried, a little too loud for a coffee shop. "That's so cool!" she added in a stage whisper, her eyes twinkling. She squeezed his sleeve.

Conrad's eyes filled with wonder. "What? Just like that? Even with the church's teachings?"

A whirl of thoughts went through Tanny's mind. She had already known Conrad was gay. She'd only recently been questioning the church's teachings about same-sex relationships because of his painful loneliness. She simply couldn't understand how the existence of same-sex couples could "hurt" heterosexual marriages. *As if Jenny's marriage was over because of letting same-sex couples marry. Duh. As if I can't find love because Conrad did.* And seeing Conrad happy, with someone who loved him, only made her joyful. Something let go in her heart and she shifted fully into acceptance of same-sex relationships. All she felt was joy for Conrad. Maybe she was supposed to feel disapproval and disgust, but she didn't at all. She had known Conrad a long time. He was kind and funny and, well, a good friend. She only felt happiness for the couple; and fierce protectiveness as well.

Conrad was saying, "As you know, I don't have a lot of people in my life that I can trust to accept this about me. I thought you might be someone who would."

"Of course! Oh my gosh! This is great news!" Tanny threw her arms around Conrad and then paused in midair, wondering if Gary was a hugger. He was.

"I'm so glad you decided to tell me." She looked them each in the eyes. "I'm here for you. I support you. I think this is great."

Conrad grinned broadly. Gary's expression was warm and relieved.

Tanny sat back and chewed her lip, "This *does* throw off my plans for making one of those 'if we're still single in X-number of years we'll marry each other' pacts with you though, Conrad." She cocked an eyebrow and waggled a finger between the two of them. "Do you think this will last?"

"Look," said Conrad pretending seriousness, "if this doesn't work out, I'm there for you. We can say, 'by the time we're sixty and neither of us are married'; how does that sound?"

Gary, meanwhile, though enjoying their banter, had a look on his face that said he didn't think Conrad would be available any time soon.

Conrad said, "The only other person in the church who officially knows is Jon. He assures me I'm not a mistake or a 'sin.'"

Tanny said, "And if Jon says it, it must be true." After a moment Tanny asked, "What happens now? Are you going to tell your parents some time? Have you told Gary's parents? The church will never recognize or approve of you two."

Gary said, "My family have welcomed Conrad with open arms. They already love him. I think they already see him as a member of our family. We have my family's support no matter what Conrad's parents say. And my church welcomes us as a couple."

"That's great news! Except, maybe for you, Conrad." Tanny looked at him, thinking about his extremely conservative parents. She felt a twinge. Then she said, "Wait, how long have you two known each other?"

Conrad's eyes twinkled. "We've been dating on and off since early January. That's when I first attended Gary's church. I can't go often, or my parents start asking questions. But from the moment our eyes met—"

"—The moment our eyes met," murmured Gary, grinning.

"We both felt it."

"That's so romantic!" said Tanny. "So, you just randomly met at a church? What church?"

Gary said, "I attend the U.U. church here in Kitchener. One day, this gorgeous stranger walked in looking a bit lost."

Tanny remembered that Stephen had said some of the young adults had been going to other churches in the city. He had even suggested the U.U. church to her.

"Does Stephen know? I mean, not that he has a right to know."

"Funny you should say that," said Conrad. "He does know I attend another church. It was actually him that pointed me at the U.U. church as a place my soul might be more comfortable."

"No kidding!" said Tanny. "He's cooler than I thought."

"But he doesn't know about this," Conrad lifted his and Gary's clasped hands. So don't you tell him. I'm waiting for the right time."

"Of course, " said Tanny and she drew a zipper across her lips.

They chatted for a while, easily comfortable and laughing a lot. Gary's sneaky sense of humour helped him jump into the conversations seamlessly. Soon it felt like Tanny had known him forever. He also showed such a thoughtfulness and tenderness toward Conrad that her heart filled with joy.

They were laughing at one of Gary's stories from teaching when Tanny's phone buzzed in her pocket. "Ooh. I have to get this. My dog...." Fear for Charm rushed back to the front of her mind. "Hello, this is Tanny."

Conrad flicked a piece of shredded napkin at Gary while they waited. Gary flicked it back, and the game was on.

Tanny was feeling the room recede as the technician was telling her about Charm having brain cancer. Charm had had two seizures overnight. They said that Charm was lucky that she had been so asymptomatic up until now because the cancer was well advanced. They were saying there were some treatments they could do, but as the voice faded into terminologies of radiation and chemotherapy, Tanny only heard that Charm would never be her sweet self again. Her loving golden girl was facing more seizures, changes in personality, and loss of balance, among other things.

Tanny started shaking, "Okay, so how long does she have? What should I do? What do I do now?" Tears crowded the corners of her eyes.

The game had ended at Tanny's first noises of sadness. Conrad had shifted his chair so he could set a hand on Tanny's shoulder. Gary did the same putting a hand behind her heart.

Tanny listened some more and then gave a shaky, "Thank you. I'm on my way," and hung up.

She looked at her companions and after a beat said, "I have to go. Charm—" she choked. "My dog is dying."

Conrad cried, "Charm? Sweet old Charm? Noooooo!" He shook his head in dismay, his eyes never leaving her face. Then recognizing that Tanny was going into shock, Conrad took charge. "We're going to stay with you. We are here for you." Gary murmured his assent.

"Um... um..." Tanny was fishing for her keys. "Dumfry Animal Hospital, out on New Dundee Road."

Conrad took her keys from her. "I will drive you there in Herman. Gary can bring my car," and handing his own keys to Gary he ushered Tanny out to Herman. "It's going to be okay. We are going to get you through this." And gently he settled Tanny into the passenger seat of Herman (after moving some packages and books and napkins into the back seat.)

Eight

February 15, late morning to evening

*C*onrad and Gary entered the veterinary hospital right behind Tanny and followed her to the room where Charm was resting. Charm recognized Tanny and licked a little at Tanny's hand when Tanny cuddled her face and spoke to her. The motherly technician explained that Charm had experienced another seizure and some vomiting.

It was increasingly clear that Tanny's choices were between attempting treatment (likely to extend Charm's life only a few months), taking her home to die slowly, or euthanasia.

If she wanted, they could put Charm to sleep right there and dispose of the body for Tanny.

"Um, couldn't I take her home and bury her there?" Tanny asked, her eyes never leaving the retriever's sweet face.

"Unfortunately, no. There are laws against that now, unless you live on a big farm."

Tanny thought of her parent's half-acre lot and all the family pets resting there already. "Oh, we have lots of land," she said. "I'm sure we are covered under the farm exception." She didn't even question the fudged truth. Charm was coming home just like their other family pets.

She looked at Conrad and Gary in despair. "I can't choose. Tell me what to choose."

The technician left quietly so they could make decisions.

"They said they could buy her at most six months with treatment," Tanny said ruffling Charm's fur gently around her ears. "But she wouldn't be well. She'd have a lousy quality of life. And the treatment might cause her more suffering than no treatment at all."

Tanny spread her hands to Conrad and the tidy, kindly Gary. "I knew she would die someday, but please, not today!" Tanny dashed away tears. "If I *don't* put her to sleep, Charm's life is going to be pretty terrible from now on. *I* want her treated because *I* want her around more." She looked at Conrad. "But I shouldn't prolong her suffering just because..." her eyes refilled with tears, "...just b-because I'd m-miss her so much!"

As Tanny covered her face and started weeping, Conrad put both his arms around her. Gary added a supporting hand behind her heart. Tanny wept and wept, her forehead resting on Conrad's sweater, her hands covering her face. Eventually the wave of grief passed, and she quieted. The men's support was deeply comforting. She sniffled loudly and muttered, "Can I please have a tissue?" hiding her face.

"Right here," said Gary, and he waved a box down low, where she could see it.

Tanny grabbed several and started mopping up. "Thank you, you guys. That really helped." As she finished cleaning her face she narrowed her eyes at Gary, "Wait, you had that box of tissue in your hand? You had it ready? What kind of man are you?" Tanny had a look of astonishment on her teary face.

Gary grinned and shrugged.

"Men never think about providing tissues!" Tanny continued. She poked Gary experimentally in the arm. "What manner of creature is this?" she asked Conrad, sounding like Igor from a B-movie.

After the chuckles died down, Tanny again faced reality. Her face crumpled again.

Conrad said, "Tanny, what does your gut say? What does your heart tell you?"

Tanny gave a small nod. "I know what my gut is telling me, and I don't like it." After a pause she said, "I need to put Charm down before she suffers any more. She's had a great life ... well, right up until yesterday. It would be selfish for me to try to keep her around." Tanny took a shaky breath. "I need to ask them to put her out of her misery—" another wave of quiet weeping choked her. Again, Conrad held her, and this time Gary had his arm around her shoulders, his head resting against Conrad's.

Not too much time later, they were all sitting by Charm as the anesthesia began to do its work. Charm's eyes were closed, her retriever face looking, as retrievers do, as if she was smiling. "Goodbye, sweetheart," Tanny whispered through her tears, "Sleep well, sweet girl." Tanny's breath was coming in shuddering inhales as tears streamed down her cheeks. Gary was ready with tissues; Conrad supporting her.

The retriever's body became increasingly limp; her breathing slowed and slowed. "No..." whimpered Tanny through her tears. "No.... Please.... I'm going to miss you so much." Eventually it was clear that Charm was gone. "Nooooooo!"

Tanny wept. She bent over the still form resting her head in the fur. Full paroxysms of her grief swept through her. Next Tanny cradled Charm's head and rocked and rocked and wept some more, while Gary and Conrad stayed near and ready.

The men availed themselves of the tissues as well.

Eventually Tanny whispered, "Goodbye, my sweet, sweet, Charm." She slowly lifted her head and looked at the men. It was clear that it was time to take Charm's body home.

Charm was wrapped in the towels that Tanny had brought her in. Conrad laid the dog on Tanny's back seat. Conrad looked into Tanny's face. "Let us help you bury her, okay? We've got the time today. We'd like to do this with you." Tanny nodded and so, after a big hug, Gary settled himself back in Conrad's car, ready to follow back to Tanny's place.

Conrad was giving Tanny another hug as Tanny requested to ride in the back with Charm's body. As they stepped apart, another car pulled into the parking lot. In the driver's window they saw the gaping face of Margaret Inquist.

"Oops. Now we are dating," Tanny said. "We are practically engaged."

Conrad's eyes twinkled. "I don't know about you, but it works for me to let the gossips think that. It explains why I'm so happy."

"Con-rad," Tanny replied, "You are trouble," but her eyes were twinkling.

Margaret was carrying a cat-box. Her eyebrows were up in her hairline as she approached them.

Conrad gave Tanny a light kiss on the cheek and said, "Let's get going, sweetheart."

As Tanny turned to climb into Herman she greeted Margaret with a polite, "Hi, Miss Inquist," and settled herself in the back seat. She took Charm's head into her lap and stroked it. *Why do I get silly when I am most upset?* She enjoyed the distraction, but the roller-coaster drop of coming back to reality was not fun at all.

Tanny let the tears fall on the drive home; she wept as they passed fields in which Charm had run and would no more. She half-laughed when they passed that muddy pond that Charm loved to romp in. Oh! She always smelled so terrible when she came out. She remembered introducing her to baths as a puppy, and saw Charm settle down through the years to love them. Silent tears dripped on the golden head.

Tanny's mom, Emily, was bringing the recycling bins back from the end of the driveway in a housecoat, scarf, and boots as the two cars turned in. She waved and then looked surprised to see Conrad emerge from the front seat as Tanny clambered out of the back.

When she saw Tanny's tear-streaked face she dropped the bins and hurried over to hug her daughter. "What's wr—" she began to say, and then she saw Charm's still body in the back seat. "Oh no! Is she...? She looks—"

Tanny confirmed what her mom already could see. She rubbed her mom's back as Emily began to moan and weep. Her mom truly loved animals and loved all the dogs equally.

When Gary joined them Tanny said, "Mom. This is Gary, a friend of Conrad's. These two stayed with me at the vet and have come to help me bury Charm."

Emily pushed back her scarf and adjusted to Gary's fist-bump when she offered her hand. She hugged Conrad saying, "How sweet of you two. That's so very nice."

Together with them she helped Tanny pick the right spot, being sure not to dig where another pet rested. She showed them where the shovels were and said, "If you hit roots, just chop through them. We have so many trees, it's the only answer." Then she said, "I must go take care of things inside. If you need a break, do come inside for tea or cookies or something after all your hard work." With a smile of sympathy, Emily returned to the house.

With a look of "it's now or never" Tanny pressed her shovel into the partially frozen earth, grateful for the thaw of the last week. She jumped on it to drive it deep. Gary followed suit. Meanwhile, Conrad ran over to Isaiah Bender's to ask the loan of a third shovel. When he returned, he panted, "Isaiah wasn't there, so I just borrowed it. I'll put it back and let him know when we're done." Then he struck his blade into the ground, as well.

It was hard work. In no time Tanny's blade hit a root. Tanny ran back to the tool shed for various hacking tools to help them through it. They also had to deal with partially frozen soil. They debated pouring boiling water on the harder spots to see if that would help.

"I'm not waiting to bury her," Tanny panted. "I KNOW we can do this," and she growled as the shovel went in again.

"We are blessed to have had this thaw," Gary observed. "Even a week ago this would have been too hard."

Slowly and surely the hole deepened and widened. Tanny's gasps of exertion sometimes felt closer to sobs, but she just kept going. The physical labor felt cathartic, and the warm, strong presence of the men uplifted and heartened her. Conrad's wiry, strong frame flung his dirt wherever he could. Gary was more methodical, piling his dirt in one area, and puling the bits of root away to pile in another place.

After a hard ninety minutes, they chose to take a break. They tramped toward the house, leaving their muddy footwear by the door. Emily was waiting with a pot of tea, water, and lemonade. She also had set out a tray of cookies.

"I don't know if lemonade is what you want in February," she said. "I can make hot chocolate if you prefer."

The men murmured their appreciation and gratitude. Tanny, having washed her hands, went to her mom and rested her head on Emily's shoulder. She gave a shuddering sigh. Emily patted her back and held her.

Conrad helped himself to tea and dropped on the bench to rest. Gary poured himself water and took a cookie. He took a chair at the table.

Emily said, "The Lord knows we've had to do this often enough. It's the downside of having pets." Her tone was matter of fact. "We know how deep to dig, how to keep other animals from digging them up, and even to put cat litter in the grave. Thank goodness we still have a supply since Stinky died."

"Stinky," Tanny giggled. "That was one goofy cat."

"We let Eric name him," Emily chuckled. "We never should have."

"I remember Stinky," Conrad added, "He was the one with six toes on one of his paws?"

"That was Stinky," Tanny affirmed. She finally stepped away from her mother and took a cookie. She plopped down on the bench near Conrad. "Oh, Mom, I should warn you. Conrad and I are engaged." Tanny started giggling; then she couldn't seem to stop. In her fatigue the whole thing seemed funnier and funnier.

Emily's expression switched quickly from surprise to confusion, to suspicion.

Conrad stepped in to help. "Margaret Inquist was arriving with one of her cats as we were leaving. She saw me comforting Tanny, and as her eyebrows approached her hairline, I knew we were doomed."

Tanny waved her hands weakly and shook her head, giggling too much to speak.

"So, you're not engaged," Emily confirmed.

"Not as yet," Conrad agreed, "Though we've discussed it."

Tanny slid lower on the bench still convulsing, alternately shaking, or nodding her head depending on what was being said.

Conrad continued straight faced. "But Tanny was right to warn you. Soon half the town will be expecting us to set a date." This started fresh gales from Tanny by now nearly under the table.

"S-set a date..." she squeaked.

"You will be the first to know, if that should happen," Conrad assured Mrs. Smith in all seriousness. Meanwhile he was trying to heft Tanny back up onto the bench in vain.

Tanny completed the journey to the floor, finding even this funny. "Nooo.... Oh, nooo...

Gary remained silent, but his eyes showed his delight in the mischief.

Emily sighed and left them to their amusement.

Eventually Tanny settled down, astonished at how similar laughing could be to crying. "I'll take giggling any day," she told them. They found Emily and thanked her for the refreshments and then headed back out to finish the grave. It took another hour, but in the end, they were satisfied it was the depth they needed.

Before burying Charm, Tanny wanted to present Charm's body to the other dogs. She wanted the other dogs to know what had happened. She laid Charm in her blanket on the kitchen floor and let Elmer and Rory check her over. They sniffed and whuffled over their still companion's body, and then, as if in acceptance, they trotted off. Tanny murmured "Bye, Charm," as if speaking for the dogs. She wished her own process could be so easy.

They carried Charm out to her grave, and, using a blanket, lowered her down in.

Emily joined them. She brought a lit candle and held it in the gathering gloom.

"I want to say, you were a great dog, Charm. You kept me company and were so loyal. I hope you had a good life." There was a pause. Tanny's face crumpled. "And I'm really going to miss you." She leaned sideways against her mom's shoulder.

Emily said, "You certainly were a great dog, dear Charm. Thank you for being Tanny's good and loyal friend all these years."

Conrad cleared his throat. "Charm, I have known you since Tanny got you. Rest well. You will be missed by many of us."

After a pause, Gary added quietly. "Everything they all said. Thank you for being a great dog."

The wind creaked a bit in the pines. The temperature was dropping, and the winter sun was setting.

"Okay then," sniffed Tanny bravely, tucking away her tissues. "Let's do this." She grabbed a shovel and ladled the first shower of dirt on the still, wrapped body. Gary and Conrad followed suit as Emily stood watch. It was a quicker task to refill the grave and mound the dirt than it had been to remove it.

After another moment of silent reverie Emily blew out her candle. "Gilbert is going to be home soon and it's getting quite cold. I'm going in. Thank you again, boys. It was nice to meet you, Gary."

"It was nice to meet you too, Mrs. Smith. Thank you for the refreshments," he responded.

Conrad added, "We were glad to help. Do say hello to Mr. Smith for us please." And Emily made her way back inside.

Gary turned his gaze on Tanny. "We don't have to leave if you'd like more company. We could order in some pizza or something, our treat, and just hang out with you." He hesitated. "Unless you are ready to be alone now?"

Tanny felt like she had two guardian angels. She did not want to be alone yet. "I'd love that," she agreed, and hugged them both.

They went into Tanny's basement apartment by the separate entrance. Upon entering, Tanny immediately felt the loss of Charm's presence and was glad the men were joining her. She saw Charm's big empty bed and dragged it off to a storage cupboard to get it out of sight. She emptied the food and water dishes and put them in the dishwasher, making small noises of distress. Gary, having hung up his coat and enjoyed a quick tour, phoned for pizza to be delivered. Conrad had run the shovel back to Isaiah's, returning to say Isaiah sent his condolences. Tanny found some beers in the fridge. The pizza arrived, smelling heavenly. Together they picked a movie. Tanny grabbed a slice of pizza and sandwiched herself between her two guardian angels on her small couch.

In the morning, she awoke to find herself in the same place, tucked in snuggly with a fuzzy blanket and the dishes washed.

Nine

February 16, all day

Tanny phoned work to take another personal day. She shuffled upstairs into her mom and dad's kitchen, still wrapped in the fuzzy blanket. Emily was there starting a lasagna.

"Good morning, honey," Emily greeted from where she was mixing eggs and ricotta cheese. "Did you take a day off? How are you doing? There's coffee if you want some."

Tanny did want coffee. She got herself a mugful and sat carefully at the table. "Yeah, I took another day off. I'm just feeling a bit lost. Not having Charm is going to take some getting used to."

"Of course," Emily agreed. A silence stretched out while Emily stirred a ground beef mixture in a skillet.

Eventually Emily said, "You know, I was thinking .... Jenny needs to get out of that house and be with family, now especially. She needs help with Will."

Tanny grunted agreement.

"Well, I was thinking, if you moved back upstairs, into your old room, Jenny could move into the apartment with Will." Emily seemed unaware of the cinderblock she had just dropped in Tanny's stomach. "She would have her own place still but be right here if she needed help with Will. It would be so much easier for me to look after him for her. And she'd be back with family."

Tanny lost interest in her coffee. She hunched deeper in the fuzzy blanket.

Emily continued, "I was discussing it with Jenny. I was thinking she could move in for March first, or thereabouts?"

Tanny had been attempting to escape all thoughts and feelings. Instead, she was faced with a whole new onslaught. She could see the logic in her mom's thinking, but she felt erased at the same time. It *would* be good for Jenny to move back with Will, and the apartment made a lot of sense. But what was she? Chopped liver? Why hadn't her mom consulted *her*? Why couldn't Jenny and Will move into the spare upstairs bedrooms and leave Tanny in her home of four years?

Then Tanny reflected that her rent would go way down, which would help with her many bills. On the other hand, her mom's interference and expectations for help with the housework would ramp up. Could she stand that? There was a reason Tanny had been desperate to get her own place four years ago. Besides, didn't Jenny need to save money too? Tanny felt a sickening sense of injustice, while her mom's words inspired guilt for not wanting to agree.

Standing up and gathering her blanket around her Tanny mumbled, "Mom, I can't think about this right now." She descended carefully back to her haven, wondering for how much longer it would be her home.

Tanny turned on music to keep her company. She'd been listening lately to an artist named Karla Bonoff—someone a cousin had put her onto. There was something about KB's chord progressions and lyrics that lifted her spirits. The four albums she rotated through were all so familiar, she could sing along to most of them. She dressed and brushed her hair and started a load of wash. "Fool in love with a fool that never cared..."

She decided she wanted to go visit Jenny and maybe do some cleaning or cooking for her. She texted if that might work for Jenny and got a simple, "sure," back.

"Stay, on the way of the heart .... You know that we'll find love," she sang as she exited her house and began to walk the half kilometre to Jenny's. She cut through Susan's, (and now Jon's) yard, remembering that they were still on their honeymoon. This brought her out to the loop road that included Jenny's home. *Golly,* she thought, *Poor Jenny!* She felt a pang of guilt for how infrequently she visited her sister and hurried her steps through the sunny, cold air. She knocked and then let herself in, as had been her custom whenever Terry wasn't home.

Shutting the door, she called out, "Hey Jenny, I'm here!" She pulled off her mitts and kicked off her boots simultaneously.

There came a faint, "Hey Tanny, I'm in here," from the kitchen. Tanny moved into the sunny kitchen where she could see Jenny, still in her pajamas, over by the coffee maker. She crossed to her sister and hugged her, noticing how tired she looked. Will was in front of the fridge playing with magnetic letters. As usual he didn't seem to notice the newcomer but kept holding his left ear and sucking his pacifier.

Tanny crouched down beside him and set a hand on his back. "Hey Will, how's it going?" After the customary silence Tanny said, "Are you playing with your letters?" She indicated the one in his hand, "What's this one, Will? Which letter is this?"

"Dubboo," Will slurped around his pacifier.

"That's right, Will! You are amazing, you know." She kissed his red head and stood up.

"You 'mazing," he said, never taking his eyes off the fridge.

Tanny stared at Jenny. Jenny's eyes registered humour.

"He's kind of like a parrot," she said of her son. "He imitates all sorts of things, really well, but he doesn't use his words to communicate. I can't even get him to make eye-contact anymore. Is this normal? Nobody else's toddlers are like this."

Tanny looked at William speculatively, "Well, I don't know. He is unusual. But you've heard the stories about Uncle Brains; he was a weird sort of kid. It just turned out he was brilliant. Maybe it's just the Bender brilliance?"

Worry creased Jenny's tired brow. "I have a feeling it's something more than that. I've got him scheduled for an assessment in April. Maybe they'll be able to tell me what's wrong with him."

"Or tell you he's just fine, and too smart for words."

"Mart for words," stated the toddler.

"Hmmm. Maybe not 'for words'; he's got the words all right..." mused Tanny.

There was a pause. Then Jenny said, "Want some coffee? It's butter pecan flavoured."

"Ooh!" jumped Tanny. "Absolutely. You've always got such yummy coffee, sis." She helped herself and joined her older, half-sister at the table.

Jenny was shorter than Tanny by a head. She had the rich brown eyes and dark hair that cousin Susan and so many of the Benders had. Jenny had inherited the short-waisted genes that also ran in the family and the metabolism that tended toward extra weight. Jenny had put on a bunch of weight since Will's birth. Tanny thought Jenny was beautiful, weight or not, exhaustion or not. She also felt protective of Jenny for some reason, going way back, though Jenny was the older of them.

Jenny's father had died of leukemia when Jenny was only three months old. Tanny remembered hearing vague stories of Emily having some sort of breakdown, and family having to step in to care for both her and the baby for many months. Tanny guessed that was why Jenny had always seemed like a favorite, yet her mom also treated Jenny as if she was breakable. Tanny, on the other hand, had been treated quite the opposite. She felt like she had been sent out in the yard to raise herself—and like she was expected to be the strong one for all three of the women. Tanny *was* the strong one AND chopped liver, apparently.

Tanny was about to ask Jenny how she was doing when she looked at Jenny. Her sister was staring strangely at her wedding ring. "What's up?" she asked instead.

There was a pause as Jenny tilted her head, gazing at her fat, golden ring. She said, "I can see my reflection in my wedding band." She frowned and lifted her chin as she stared. "But that angle makes my neck look fat, so if I stretch my neck ... No. It's weird. Well, look!" Jenny thrust her hand at Tanny. "Look at your face in there."

Tanny did so, not sure where this was going.

"Now, make some faces. Waggle your eyebrows, twist your mouth like you do." She waited. "Can you see any change? Does it even look like you?" Jenny pulled her hand back to stare at her own reflection again. "It doesn't even look like me. It's just a face. It could be anybody. I'm trying to make an expression that even looks like me. You know, so I can see myself. So that it is *my* face."

Tanny shifted uncomfortably. Will said, "Face."

"But it's just a stranger. An expressionless stranger."

Tanny sipped her coffee, wondering what to say.

"Really. Is that me?" Jenny asked sounding irritated. She blinked. Suddenly Jenny grabbed her ring as if to pull it off. "Why am I even still wearing this?!" she cried. She struggled with sudden determination. "Ow. It won't come. Get some lotion, will you? I've gained so much weight..."

Tanny leapt up to grab some hand lotion and bring it over.

"Ow. OW! Thank you." Jenny tried lathering on some lotion. "Damn. I can't get it."

Drawn to the drama, Will had brought a fistful of letters over.

"No. Damn it! No. It's not coming," complained Jenny. "I'll have to cut it off or lose some weight."

"Dammit!" said Will, with big eyes.

Jenny, who had started to weep in despair, laughed instead at the one phrase Will had decided to repeat. "Of course that's what you repeat you funny boy," Jenny complained, her laughter turning back into tears.

"Dammit indeed!" she asserted, looking right at Will. She looked at Tanny who had moved to her side. "He should have a father, Tanny! A GOOD father. He shouldn't be learning swears from a fat, depressed..."

"Shush." Tanny murmured holding her sister. "A BEAUTIFUL, kind, loving, exhausted mother," Tanny completed with emphasis.

"It wasn't supposed to go this way!" wept Jenny. "Will is so sweet! How could such a sweet kid come from ... from ...."

"I know. I know," reassured Tanny.

"Tanny, sometimes I wish so hard that this had never happened. That we could go back to... to... how it was before. But ... it was no fairytale." Her tears were quieting. "I thought I loved him. How is it that somehow, I still love him? Terry could be so sweet, and yet he could be so horrid. Both at once. No one thinks that is how marriage will be."

Tanny's heart was breaking for her sister. She had seen Terry's duplicity and skeezy energy long before. But she had also kept her mouth shut just in case Jenny was actually happy.

"I'm so scared for Will," Jenny continued. "What if, what if I'm raising a monster? What if he's doomed to turn out like his father? What if it's my fault Terry tried to, tried to..."

"You can stop that right there!" Tanny said, taking Jenny's face in her hands to look into her eyes. "Jenny, there is no way this is your fault. This is not your fault!" Tanny wished she could push her own certainty of this right into Jenny's mind. She hated to see her sister blaming herself for her creepy husband's choices.

Tanny took a deep breath, and a certain clarity came to her mind. "I think we need to get you out of here. Did mom talk to you about moving back home? Would you like to move back home?"

Jenny nodded, looking lost. "She did. But she didn't explain what you were going to do for an apartment. I can't expect you to leave because of me. And besides, I don't think I have the energy to even think about moving. I can barely get through my days with Will and no Terry. I don't even know what I'm supposed to do now."

Tanny was struck with certainty that Jenny needed to get away from the marital home and back near support. Her own problems seemed insignificant. "Look, I've got the rest of the day. Let's start with some cleaning and organizing— whatever you feel up to or whatever is most bothering you."

"The laundry!" Jenny said, without hesitation.

"And we will see what you most want to do. Maybe you'd rather stay here?" Tanny asked, a little hopefully.

"Absolutely not!" said Jenny with such vehemence that Tanny wondered just how unpleasant Terry had been around the house with Jenny.

"Well, it's absolutely clear then. You've got me for today, so let's see how much we can get done to start preparing."

In the late afternoon, the two sisters decided they had done enough. Several boxes had been started, and the laundry was completely caught up. Tanny had handled the unpleasant task of looking after Terry's ignored washing, so as to pack it off and get it out of sight. Jenny was flushed with their effort, looking more alive than Tanny had seen her in years.

Jenny stood with Tanny in the entryway as Tanny laced up her boots. "Thank you, more than I can say, Tanny. You have been a lifesaver."

"Well, maybe a life-preserver," Tanny mused, standing up, her boots laced. "Something to hold you up a bit while you live a nightmare."

Jenny tossed her curls and looked thoughtful. "I think I am finally waking up from the nightmare. I think my new life has begun today. You are showing me the way forward."

"I'm just being a sister," Tanny said. "What else are sisters for?"

They shared a final embrace. "Well, you're the best," said Jenny. She slowly closed the door as Tanny headed back to her parents' home.

There was a real bite to the wind walking home, and Tanny zipped her coat tighter and repositioned her scarf to protect her cheeks. She felt alive and good and heroic. She also felt baffled by her sudden shift in loyalties. Five hours earlier she was feeling resentful and abandoned. Now she felt like a linebacker pushing through walls of defenses to rescue her sister. Her own place of residence seemed somehow unimportant, in the light of things. Was that quite healthy? She shrugged. Whereas she had felt lost and victimized, now she felt powerful and strong and capable. She liked feeling competent and capable, drat it all! She felt sure something would turn up in the way of housing for her just now. She wondered how long that feeling would last.

A fragment of a Karla Bonoff song wafted through her mind, and she started humming, "Isn't it always love that takes the tears away... and you wouldn't have it any other way."

Once home, the reality of Tanny's decision to surrender her apartment hit hard. She stared at the cozy space. She scrambled to imagine what sort of accommodations she could find on her budget. She shuddered. So, her apartment only had two windows, all in the main room, but still, it was safe and clean and snug. She plopped down on the small sofa that was still coated in Charm's hair. *Maybe it will be nice to have a fresh start where there are not so many reminders of Charm.*

She gazed on the tiny corner kitchen which still managed a dishwasher. *I hope my new place has a dishwasher. I hate doing the dishes by hand.* A big sigh moved through her. *Hey, maybe I could move into Jenny's house while we figure out what to do with it?* That prospect lifted her spirits. Then she reflected that it would still mean she'd have to move again probably within a year.

Within a year. Tanny shivered. She remembered Britt's last dying words to her, "There is a great and tender love for you, just around the corner." Britt's fierce eyes had twinkled. "It will come within the year. But you will fight it." She had paused for more oxygen. "Just don't fight too hard, my darling."

"It will come within the year." That message had at first thrilled Tanny, and she had started looking at all the eligible men in her life with new eyes. But after three months, she had given up. The thought just exhausted her. What did that prophecy even mean? What was she supposed to do with that promise? Tanny shook her head. Didn't Britt know it would be terribly disappointing for Tanny when it didn't come true?

Tanny dropped her head back, closing her eyes, and running her fingers into her hair. Oh, how it would make her life so much easier if someone could scoop her up and look after her. With a loving relationship would come a home, or at least someone to search with. With a loving relationship would come someone to talk to, someone to hold and be held by, someone to figure things out with, *someone who would have her back.*

Tanny heaved another great sigh and sat up. Well, she was powerless to make that prophecy happen, and meanwhile, she had to soldier on with the life that she had.

Tanny got herself a quick dinner and shower and went to bed.

Ten

Tanny tossed her gear on the counter, her keys and gloves followed, then her scarf.

"Rats. RATS. RATS!" she cried and stamped her foot. She was freshly back from a job that was no more. She was unemployed. And there was no Charm to come sniffing, showing concern.

Tanny had enjoyed her job. She had gotten her degree in animal psychology. She was paid to focus on the lab animals' comfort and well-being, while performing experiments that measured their behaviour. It was fascinating and fun. Unfortunately, Tanny had developed an allergy to the lab rats. It was one of the dreaded hazards of being an animal technician. Tanny had seen it happen to others before her. Over time, the body builds up a sensitivity to the animals' dander, and the outcome makes it nearly impossible to work.

At first, the symptoms hadn't been too distracting. They had manifested as abrupt bouts of sneezing requiring Tanny to flee outside and gulp large amounts of fresh air to clear her passages. It was rather funny, actually. But now, even wearing a mask didn't prevent or delay the onset of the sneezing, and the bouts had become so violent and so frequent, that she was basically unable to perform much work in the lab at all.

She was looking into having to wear a gas mask full time to continue, when Professor Clark insisted she stop work. "There's only two months of funding left, Tanny. It's not worth it. It has become ridiculous. We can finish and close the project without you. You get yourself a better job with more stability and no allergens. We'll be okay. Let's call this your last day, so you might as well go home now before the next bout comes on."

So Tanny was standing in her kitchen at ten am, out of a job.

"RATS!" The double meaning was not lost on her.

On top of Herman's repairs, her school debt payments were continuing to come due, and now there were vet bills. It was more than clear that she should give up her apartment now, whether she wanted to or not. Yes, she could get the school debt payments paused while she was unemployed, and could file for employment insurance, which would give her some financial ease for a bit. But truthfully, she had to get right back out there to find another job. She dreaded the process. She was a job-search virgin when it came to writing resumes and interviewing. The job she had just lost had come to her through a university co-op program.

"Many bad words!" she added.

She turned on her Karla Bonoff playlist and a gentle song wafted into the air, "The whole world's blue... and nothin' ever goes right..."

"That's a little too on the nose," she complained. She switched to a different playlist.

Tanny plunked down on her hairy couch and wondered about packing. She should let her mom and Jenny know. She would need to get boxes. No, maybe she should figure out where she was going before she started packing; moving upstairs was an entirely different animal than moving into a new apartment ... which wouldn't be happening so long as she was unemployed. If she just moved upstairs, she'd need laundry hampers and garbage bags more than cardboard boxes. And she could do it over the—she counted on her fingers—the next eleven days left until March first (though she wasn't sure Jenny would be ready by then). She considered again moving into Jenny's house temporarily. This seemed increasingly ideal.

"We could share a truck, taking a load of my stuff over there, and then a load of her stuff over here, then another load of my stuff over there, until it was all swapped," she said aloud in the room. She smiled with the clever idea.

Tanny had an impulse to take Charm for a walk and was smacked with the realization that her retriever was dead, as if it was new information. How long until these Charm-connected reflexes would stop triggering, like an alarm clock that could not be reset? Each new reminder ached.

Tanny climbed the stairs to see if her mom was home. She found Emily watching old episodes of "Due South" on the family television. She was also knitting.

Tanny plunked down on the big family sofa and watched Paul Gross lick a rock.

Then she plunged right in. "I just lost my job, mom. Just now. My allergies have become unmanageable, and the grant is nearly used up as it is, so they let me go."

"That's terrible!" Emily responded, though she didn't stop knitting or watching the show.

"So, I need to talk to you," stated Tanny.

Emily's needles continued clicking. "You can always talk to me, honey."

Tanny's temper flared. "So, can we turn this off? Can you look at me?"

Consternation covered Emily's face and the knitting hesitated, "Oh, but, this episode ... uh ..." Emily sighed and put her needles down. She grabbed the remote and jabbed it at the TV. She turned in her chair and looked at Tanny. "Of course. Of course. You've just lost your job. I'm sorry." Emily shook her head in sympathy. "Would you like a hug?"

"Um, not now. I need to talk."

"Okay, honey." Emily folded her hands and gazed at her daughter.

Tanny was a bit confused by Emily's "listening" performance. Maybe her mom's therapist was making headway? Nevertheless, Tanny said what she came to say.

"I agree to surrender my apartment for Jenny. As I have no job, I will have time to help Jenny in packing and preparing, and we can probably do the switcheroo in one day with a truck and a bit of help. I can be ready for March first, and maybe we can get Jenny ready by then too. Maybe you could babysit Will while we get it done? Then we get Jenny somewhere snug and safe and near family, and I have somewhere to be until I work something better out."

Emily beamed. "Both of my daughters under my roof again."

"Well, no," corrected Tanny. "I was thinking I could live in Jenny's house to help fix it up to sell...." As she watched Emily's frown and dawning objection she added, "You know, and for security. Somebody should be looking after it. It should look lived-in."

"You'd move in there?" Emily asked. Then her brow cleared, "That's actually a good idea. Though I hope you remember you can hang out here any time. This is your home too."

Is it? Tanny thought. *Or do you just want free help with Will and Jenny and the house?* She instantly felt guilty for the negative thoughts, though she was pretty sure she was correct in her assessment. She heaved a big sigh. "Of course, Mom," she said with warmth, choosing to respond to the sentiment rather than her lived experience.

"Well honey," said Emily, reaching for her knitting and then stopping herself. She folded her hands again and gazed at Tanny, "as always, I am impressed with your ingenuity and resourcefulness. I hope it won't be too hard leaving your home of, well, almost 28 years. I mean, your birthday is coming up soon now. Do you still want a party here?"

My mom is so weird, Tanny thought. *Is she trying to get me to stay by imply-ing I won't get birthday parties anymore?* But she said, "If you want to throw me a party, mom, I won't object. Thank you." She cleared her throat, "But I'm going on thirty. Heck, Liam is 23. We are all adults. You are not obliged to throw any of us birthday parties anymore." Tanny suddenly wondered if her mom was struggling with a kind of empty nest syndrome. Did she know who she was without children and grandchildren to manage? Tanny softened a bit towards her mom.

"So, anyway, I'm going to go see what Jenny thinks about all this. It's still just a plan." She stood and kissed her mom on her cheek. "Thanks for listening, mom. It really helped." She wasn't sure that last bit was entirely true, but she was trying her best to hide her annoyance.

Tanny switched on the TV again. "Sorry for interrupting your show." Then she scampered back down into the apartment to prepare for Jenny's.

As she walked, she texted Jenny. "You awake? Can I come over?" Though it was nearly eleven, she had become hesitant to disturb Jenny since Will was born, so much so that it had become a habit to text or simply walk over rather than call.

"Sure," was Jenny's response. Jenny was rarely effusive. It seemed Tanny got all the emotional expressiveness for the two of them.

Tanny tapped and let herself in. As she was kicking off her boots Jenny came to meet her holding out her wedding ring. "I got it off!" she exclaimed with satis-faction. "It took cold water and soap and ffff---uhhh---" Jenny's eyes searched for a more appropriate word, "---fierce determination, but I did it."

She threw the ring down in disgust and it pinged dramatically before it bounced and rolled.

Tanny said with a straight face, "You could get some decent money for that...."

"Whatever. I'm free! I am no longer married to that man." Jenny was more animated than Tanny had seen her in a long time.

Tanny bit back her, "It doesn't quite work that way," and instead let her sister enjoy the symbolism. She said in agreement, "You are FREE! That is so good, sis."

"Fee," they heard from the kitchen.

"I've made coffee; want some?" Jenny asked, heading back into the kitchen.

Tanny followed her, bending to retrieve the ring and set it somewhere safe. They settled at the table again, and Tanny laid out her plans.

Soon the sisters were hard at work dismantling, packing, and creating piles ready to be hauled to a thrift store. It was clear they would need to get boxes, but a lot of clothes and linens could be used to pack breakables, and any other soft items could go in garbage bags.

"Just be sure to mark them or label them, so they don't get taken out for garbage!" Tanny declared, tying a bright ribbon around the neck of one bag.

Jenny said, with rosy cheeked Will on her hip, "There's that new family moving in just up the road from me. I wonder if we could get boxes from them?"

"Right! What a great idea! I've been meaning to go say 'hi' to them," Tanny responded.

Tanny bundled up and trudged up the road several properties to the Chalet-style house that sat back from the road behind a wall of bare forsythia.

The front door looked like it was never used, so she knocked on the door off the car port. Eventually the door was pulled open by a middle-aged woman in a winter-themed tracksuit. The two women stared at each other.

"Barb!" Tanny exclaimed simultaneously with the woman's "Hi, Tanny!"

Tanny's second cousin welcomed Tanny into the crowded half-flight and led her up into a sunny kitchen. The whole place smelled of the cedar paneling that covered the stairwell walls.

"Wait," Tanny said. "I had heard a family from Ben Kirk was moving up here. Somehow, I didn't put together that it was you guys. However are you? It's been ages." She exchanged a hug with her comfortably plump, long known second cousin. Barbara was taller than Tanny, with thick, curling brown hair, and a playful smile. She was Tanny's cousin through the Smith side, not the Bender, but had grown up in Kitchener. She was several years older than Tanny, had gone down to school in Ben Kirk, married an American while down there, and been living there ever since.

"I have been so homesick for Canada." Barb explained. "So when Fred lost his job, and Ian needed special medical care, and my business was doing so well, I convinced Fred to sell our house down there—we got a small fortune for it! — and look for something up here. I sold my business too, so we have a tidy sum to get started here. I have jumped through hoops to get our kids registered as Canadians born abroad. Once we get landed immigrant status for Fred, he can look for work. And I can set up my business here." She gasped as if she had said it all in one breath.

"You've said that to a lot of people, haven't you?" Tanny said, smiling.

"I sure have," Barb replied, turning to her coffee maker. "It's my new elevator speech. Want some coffee?" She pulled out a big can of Tim Hortons.

Tanny put a hand on her arm. "I've got a mugful waiting at Jenny's, about two houses that way. I wanted to check with 'the new family' if we could have your spare boxes?"

Barb paused and looked at Tanny in surprise. "Well of course! Jenny is moving?'

Tanny realized she would be there a long time if she started to explain. It was funny how some news got everywhere, and other news didn't—like the fact that *Barb* was moving back to Cliffside. "I would LOVE to explain, but we are moving Jenny in kind of a hurry and doing it ourselves. Otherwise, I would totally be here, helping you."

Barb waved her hands and shook her head. "I completely understand. I'm a professional organizer, and I would come help you if I wasn't facing this..." Barb indicated the half-empty and still sealed boxes around the kitchen and in the next rooms.

A red-headed boy of about seven wandered into the kitchen, strumming a ukulele.

"Hey, Ian," said Barb, putting her hand on his shoulder. The boy kept strumming and humming. Barb explained, "The girls are already up in the school. But Ian is here with me while we look for a placement. He's on the spectrum." She bent her head to look more directly at Ian. "Ian, this is Tanny. She's our cousin. Can you say 'hi?'"

Ian's eyes flicked up to Tanny's and away as his head bobbed gently to his tune. "Hi," he said.

"Hi Ian, nice to meet you." Tanny was struck by how stressful Barb's life must be. She wasn't sure what to say.

"Anyway, help yourself to all the boxes you want. They're in here." Barb showed a thick stack of flattened boxes tucked behind a chair in the living room.

Tanny hugged her cousin tightly and said, "Thanks so much. I'm thrilled you're back." She grabbed several sizes. "Coffee, soon, okay?"

"You bet," assured Barb, and she let Tanny back out into the chill air.

As Tanny walked back to her sister's her mind whirled. What amazing luck that "the family" had not only had ready boxes, but that it was Barb Fraser ... uh... what was her married name? MILLWOOD. That's right. Her husband's name was Ventnor Millwood (also Tanny's cousin). But everyone called him Fred. And their boy, Ian. There was a lot about Ian that reminded Tanny of Will, and it wasn't just the red hair. And Barb was a professional organizer? That was a thing? Tanny wondered if she could become one of those too. It sounded like fun. She looked forward to many more visits with Barb.

Eleven

February 18

Tanny was gliding along in the dawn light. The dark waters of Lake Muskoka lay remarkably still as the prow of her canoe sliced through. The only sounds were the slight plop and dribble of her paddle, and the call of a loon. She and Aunt Britt were heading off to ... to .... Tanny couldn't quite remember where they were going. But it was somewhere exciting.

Tanny twisted slightly to smile back at Britt, and Britt's words instructed her, "Keep your eyes on the prize, darling. This is your journey. This is about you."

Tanny turned back to the prow, only to discover Britt sitting in front of her, with Tanny in the rear of the canoe. She shifted her paddle hand and drove the paddle in deep, knowing which direction was needed.

"That's it. We're getting close now. You are getting closer," encouraged Britt, who looked young and healthy.

Then Tanny realized that they were headed back toward Cedar Haven. She saw the mouth of the river, and knew the dock was just up ahead on the left. She paddled harder, and suddenly Britt was on the shore, beckoning her in. There was a man with her, but Tanny couldn't make out his face. A wind was rising, coming from the shoreline.

"Come find someone who adores you, Tanny! He's here! Come soon!" Britt was beckoning with both hands, even as the indistinct gentleman tugged Britt's elbow.

Paddling with all her might, Tanny called, "I'm coming Aunt Britt! Wait for me!" She dug deep, pulling in long, strong strokes. The rising wind was in her face, raising wavelets against her progress. The closer she drew to Cedar Haven's dock, the stronger the wind was in her face. A strange mist was rising on the shoreline, swirling around the figures' legs, and Britt was moving backward into it, smiling and beckoning.

With a desperate plunge of the paddle, Tanny pulled herself upright in bed. Still the smell and feel of the Muskoka dawn air seemed to linger around her as she sat in her tiny, windowless bedroom, panting. She felt like an hourglass that had just been tipped upside down—like she was needing to reorient to a new vertical.

It had been a dream. It had been an intensely real-feeling dream, involving all her senses. She still felt an urgency to get back to it—to get back to the canoe and reach the dock and find Aunt Britt in the mist. She HAD to find Aunt Britt....

But Aunt Britt was dead. There was no way this was anything besides a dream because Britt had been so young. She looked like the Britt in the pictures from World War Two France, not the frail woman Tanny had visited on her death bed.

Tanny was staring unfocused across the room as she tried to hold on to as many of the images and feelings of the dream as she could. There were clues there, she knew it. She reached over to scratch Charm and was vaulted more completely into her waking reality. No Charm. *Right.* And she had ten days to get moved out of her apartment. The final wisps of the dream melted into irrelevance. She had work to do.

But as Tanny moved through her breakfast and dressing, the *feeling* of urgency and promise remained. She felt very close to Britt, as if she had truly just spent time with her. Tanny carried her dishes over to the dishwasher, thinking again about Britt's deathbed prophecy: "Don't settle for just anybody. There is someone who adores you. You will find him within the next year." So, combining the prophecy with this dream, was Britt telling her she would find her true love if she visited Cedar Haven?

Tanny moved to go brush her teeth. As she did, she resolved to go to Cedar Haven as soon as possible—maybe even today? Except ... Tanny deflated. Jon and Sue were there on their honeymoon. The place wouldn't be available until sometime after the weekend.

Okay, that gave her time to help Jenny a lot and THEN go see what was awaiting her at Cedar Haven. But she *could* call Aunt Eileen to set it up. It would probably be good to get the number of the fourth caretaker too, the old man that Tanny suspected might have been Britt's secret love—so she could contact him directly in future. Apparently, this fourth caretaker lived at Cedar Haven, but had vacated it for the honeymooners. He lived on site while the church and caretakers worked to figure out what would happen to the property in the future.

But old Mr. VanGalen wouldn't have to vacate it again for her. It was a big place, and she wasn't going to ... she was going to .... *Why was she going? Because Britt told her to go in her dreams?*

She would need to think of a plausible reason. Regardless, she didn't need to render him homeless just because she wanted to stay there a bit.

Meanwhile, she had planned to spend the intervening days cleaning and packing for herself and with Jenny. She tried not to worry about money. Not yet. Surely, she could stay rent-free in Jenny's empty house for a bit?

She grabbed some coffee from her parents' kitchen—her mom always made some for Tanny—and was heading toward the car when Emily entered the kitchen and stopped her.

"Sweetheart! I'm glad I caught you. I've found you a job."

"You what?"

"Yes, I was talking to my cousin Doris who has just moved into the Ben Kirk Estates, and she says that a rich woman is looking for live-in help there. I think you should jump at it!

"Wait, what?"

"You could get a ride down with Stephen when he goes to the ministers' meetings. And you'd be right there in Ben Kirk, where there are so many eligible church boys—I mean, *men*. I'd be okay if you married a Ben Kirk man, so long as you are happy."

"Whoa, mom. How did we get to marriage?"

"Well, these things happen," continued Emily. "I want to help, and I want you to be happy. Doesn't it seem like God's Providence is looking out for you? This job has your name all over it."

Tanny abandoned her coffee. "Mom, I can't think about this right now. Thank you, but I need to get to Jenny's. We'll talk about this later, okay?" And she scurried out of the kitchen to grab her coat and boots. "Love you!" she called as she slammed the front door.

The job had *Emily's* providence written all over it. Yes, her mom wanted her to "be happy" but only if it matched with what would make her mom happy. Tanny had no interest in moving to Ben Kirk to work for some rich octogenarian.

But the morning organizing with Jenny didn't go as planned. Will was having one of his fussy days, pulling at his ears, crying, and clinging to his mom. While Jenny could tell Tanny what needed packing, she wasn't able to help much physically, occupied as she was with soothing Will. Then towards noon Tanny tried to lift a heavy box up onto a dresser by herself, confident in her ability, only to feel a sudden spasming pain in her back. She got the box up but couldn't do anything else for Jenny but apologize. She then hobbled home to lie down. She was thoroughly discouraged.

As she eased herself into her bed, Tanny's phone dinged with a message from Shelley, her coffee-loving photographer friend. "Hey Tanny, my usual helper abandoned me for this Saturday's gig. Wanna be my bag lady?"

Yes, if I can walk and move comfortably by then, thought Tanny. She texted as much to Shelley who instantly suggested her healer friend, Adina Kinsey. "She's amazing. She'll have you back to your healthy self in no time! Let me give you my appointment for this afternoon. I'm doing great this week. I'll arrange it."

Tanny, fearful of the cost for alternative health care texted, "No. You don't need to. I'll manage." But it was too late, Shelley had already set it up before she looked at Tanny's response. In fact, she planned to come drive Tanny to the appointment by two-thirty p.m. Tanny sighed and shook her head at her friend's abundant enthusiasm and eagerness to help. She reasoned that the money she earned from Shelley (if the treatment worked) on Saturday might cover the expense and accepted her fate. If she was honest, she was grateful to have a friend come roaring to her aid, even if it meant she spent money she otherwise wouldn't have.

No sooner had Tanny lain back wondering what to do about lunch when Jenny texted to say she had arranged a doctor's appointment for Will the next day, so tomorrow could be a day for Tanny to stay home and rest.

Then her phone dinged again. It was the pastor's wife, Liz Shantz. "Hi Tanny! I heard you were out of work and might welcome some extra income, and I really need help with housecleaning. Do you have time tomorrow?" Tanny reflected that she now would, if this Adina Kinsey was all she was reported to be. She said she'd love to, but was a bit under the weather, could she get back to her in the morning? "Sure! Feel better," responded Liz.

Tanny lay there a bit longer, hoping more job offers would come in. But her phone remained silent. She reflected that life was looking up again, so long as the healer did her thing. She closed her eyes and rested. Eventually the pain killers had done enough work that Tanny was able to get up again and get herself some lunch.

Promptly at 2:30, Shelley was waiting for Tanny in the driveway in her little Cooper Mini. Tanny was fascinated by this car, not knowing anyone else who owned one. She eased herself into the tiny but comfortable machine and off they set towards central Kitchener. Adina Kinsey's practice was in an eclectic old brick home near Saint Mary's hospital. The entire yard was landscaped with plants and winding brick paths, windchimes and fountains, with mystical creatures peeking out from plants and hanging on the wooden fence. They followed the twisting path to the front door and entered the home's front room. It had once been a hall with a room on each side but had been opened up to be a large living room/waiting room. A grumpy black dog growled from the top of the second-floor steps, while two spaniels greeted them with wagging tails.

"This is Ginger," said Shelley, scratching behind the ears of the butterscotch and white spaniel. "She has a Reiki certificate." Shelley's face was straight, but her eyes twinkled merrily. She pointed at the black dog who gave a low rumble in response. "That one is a negativity vacuum," she continued. "Adina takes him regularly to a dog psychic who cleans out all the negative energy. He's nice for a few weeks, then gets increasingly unpleasant, until she takes him for another clean-out." Again, the straight face but twinkly eyes.

"What about this one?" asked Tanny, giving the brown and white spaniel some nice rubs behind the ears.

"Oh," responded Shelley. "That's just a dog." Her blue eyes danced, and she couldn't quite keep the chuckle out of her voice.

"I see," said Tanny, wondering what new wonders were ahead of her. They found a smoothly sanded wooden bench and settled themselves. Shelley started describing her experiences with Adina as Tanny looked around at all the amazing, brightly-coloured platters, tribal textiles, and unusual paintings that decorated the space. She could hear some murmured conversation and occasional laughter coming from behind a set of glazed French doors.

There was an odd black metal contraption in one corner, taller than most humans. Shelley saw Tanny's gaze and explained, "Not a torture machine. That is an anti-gravity device for stretching out your back."

"Suuuuuuuure it is," grinned Tanny.

After several minutes, the French doors swung open and a tall woman in peasant style clothes ushered a grateful and relaxed looking older woman out into the main room. In the treatment room Tanny saw a table with a mattress on it. Ginger trotted over and lay down under the table.

When Adina was done seeing her prior client out, she turned her broad, merry face toward Shelley. "Hello Shelley! So, you brought me someone new?"

Tanny accepted a warm handshake and looked into the smiling brown eyes of the taller woman as Shelley introduced them. Tanny liked the woman immediately. As Adina walked with her toward the treatment room, Tanny described her situation.

"Low back, eh? Been having financial troubles, have you?" asked Adina.

Tanny stopped in her tracks. "How did you know that?" she asked.

Ms. Kinsey gave a low chuckle. "Low back is always money worries. It's a lack of feeling supported." She said this with such a matter-of-fact tone that Tanny was less inclined to doubt her, even though it seemed a bit "woo-woo." Tanny often reflected on how open she was to accepting spiritual realities, despite her scientific training. (Sometimes the two halves of her way of understanding reality—science-based vs. mystical openness—were barely on speaking terms with each other.)

She didn't have to undress. She simply lay on her back on the twin mattress. The dog, Ginger, leapt up to join her and settled down with her paws on Tanny's hip joints. Then Adina lifted the table with hydraulics, murmuring "Good girl," to the ginger spaniel.

Tanny found it hard to describe what happened over the next fifty minutes. The weight and warmth of the dog's paws felt amazing. Adina held Tanny's feet for a while, pulling on them gently and stretching her legs a bit. Tanny told her about losing her job and then her apartment. She talked about losing Charm while tears rolled down and pooled in her ears.

Finishing with Tanny's legs, Adina placed her hands between Tanny and the mattress, under Tanny's hips, moving them almost imperceptibly slowly. Tanny talked about her mom finding her a job in Pennsylvania, and how thoroughly uninterested Tanny was in it.

Ms. Kinsey said quietly, "I think the universe is taking you there for a reason. I see you going there. It will help you accomplish something."

"No! Don't say that. I don't want to hear that," Tanny complained. But it was as if something inside her recognized that it was true. It made no sense. She didn't have to go if she didn't want to. But her consciousness was already shifting to include the possibility.

Tanny heaved a deep sigh, as Adina murmured a low, satisfied, "There ...." Ms. Kinsey then moved her hands behind Tanny's heart, continuing her gentle, barely perceptible movements.

As the treatment progressed, Tanny found herself becoming very still and quiet, with regular deep sighs springing from her involuntarily. Often as Tanny sighed, Ms. Kinsey would say that low, "There...." as though something had been accomplished. She moved her hands to support Tanny's shoulders.

Eventually Adina's warm hands were holding Tanny's head, moving it slowly and slightly in various ways. Tanny stayed in a deeply relaxed place, finding her usual chattiness silenced by whatever was happening to her. She never fell asleep, but she did feel like she was returning from somewhere far away when Ms. Kinsey indicated that it was time to sit up slowly and carefully.

Once Tanny was sitting up with her feet over the bedside, Ms. Kinsey invited her to stand and then checked Tanny's stance and balance. "Good," she said. "How do you feel?"

Tanny realized she had almost no pain in her back.

"I want you to take it easy and drink lots of water," Adina advised her. "There will be some residual achiness from those overworked muscles, but otherwise you should be good to go now."

Ms. Kinsey popped open the French doors and lead Tanny out to an excited Shelley.

"Amazing, right?" Shelley grinned.

"Ummm, yes. 'Amazing' about covers it," agreed Tanny, with wonder.

"I'm not charging you for this," said Ms. Kinsey, looking squarely into Tanny's eyes. Then she added, "I sense that you are seeking your soulmate. He will reveal himself soon, but not until you've done some more healing. Don't try to find him. He will find you when the time is right." She chuckled. "And when he does, boy ... fireworks!" She looked at Shelley as if to share in delight at Tanny's future. They both grinned broadly at Tanny.

Tanny received their looks of delight. Her mystical side was intrigued, enchanted, and grateful. Her scientific side grumbled, "I'll be in the car," and evaporated.

Twelve

*T*anny awoke the next morning feeling like she had slept several days. She moved with caution, then with increasing confidence, finishing with a grateful back-arching stretch. She lay a moment marveling at how painless she felt. She rose carefully, not quite believing she was completely healed. But by the end of breakfast, dishes, and an abrupt bout of weeping when her reflex to feed Charm banged into reality, she was still moving easily and painlessly.

Today she would be going up to Liz and Steve Shantz's to help with some housecleaning. With six kids—was it a rule that ministers had to breed more than the average congregant? —the pastor and his wife certainly needed the help.

Tanny texted Shelley that she would love to be her "bag lady" on Saturday and what time should she be ready? She then opted to walk the quarter kilometre to the Shantz's. It was heavily overcast, and a rain/snow mix was predicted.

The manse was situated facing the church, not the road—one of the many idiosyncrasies of Cliffside. The garage faced the road, and one had to walk up the left side of the garage to find the entrance to the generous side-split home.

An untidy collection of strollers and shovels and stacked firewood sat off to the side under the same overhang that protected the front door. Liz opened the front door almost immediately upon Tanny's knock, looking like Rosie the Riveter with a toddler on her hip.

"Hey! Come in!" and Liz stepped aside with a welcoming gesture. They got Tanny's gear stowed, and the two women moved stocking-footed up the half-flight into the bright living room. To the left was a large picture window framing a view of the church across a small field. Straight ahead was a sizable fieldstone fireplace. A dining area nestled in the corner to the right of the fireplace, with a cozy kitchen directly to Tanny's right through a small doorway.

Liz asked after Tanny's back prompting an abbreviated but glowing review of Ms. Adkins' skill. Liz took down the name and number of the healer, murmuring something about Stephen's stress level.

"But," Tanny asked, pushing up her sleeves, "I'm here to help you. Where would you like me to start?"

"Let's see," said Liz, bouncing the impish girl on her hip. "Tomorrow is Stephen's and my seventeenth wedding anniversary. We plan to have a small gathering tomorrow night to celebrate. So, I want to focus on this living room, the kitchen, the entry, and the bathrooms."

"Okay," nodded Tanny.

"I'd love it if you would do a counter and cabinet scrub-down in the kitchen. I'll do the floor tomorrow. I'll take Grace with me and tackle the bathrooms. How would a James Taylor, Carole King mix do for cleaning music?" Tanny agreed and the two women got to work. Tanny, who had fought chores tooth and nail as a child had discovered a love of cleaning in her late teens. She found great satisfaction in turning something that looked dingy or neglected into its shiny best, even if it was old and worn kitchen cupboards. Tanny sang along as she worked.

Eventually, as the noon hour approached, Liz returned from the nether regions having finished with the bathrooms. Tanny was finishing up polishing the stove.

Liz puffed at her bangs and settled Grace into her booster seat at the table. "Steve and the kids will be arriving home for lunch in about twenty minutes. How are you holding up?" Tanny assured Liz she felt fine and could clean for several more hours if needed. Liz set Tanny to polishing and dusting in the living and dining rooms, suggesting that they have lunch after the kids had returned to school. Grace happily munched on an apple while Liz set out lunch for everyone. In no time at all, Liz and Steve's four middle children marched in with their dad. Steve greeted Tanny, thanking her for helping.

The middle four were all in the church school. Tanny greeted the pastor and four children but kept cleaning, listening to the stories and squabbles. It became clear that their second youngest, Ben, would be staying home now as he only had half-days. No wonder Liz had wanted to start early!

Tanny was finishing polishing the upright grand as three kids gathered their things and trooped back to school, after only a half-hour for lunch. Tanny remembered that crazy scramble to get home, eat, and get back from her childhood. She didn't miss it. At least these kids had the shortest walk of all. Stephen was staying home a bit longer too, to enjoy time in the relative quiet and see his wife.

Liz called to Tanny, "Now that the hordes are gone, come sit, eat, have some coffee." Tanny did so gratefully while Ben asked what hordes were.

Stephen said, "Hordes are lots of noisy, busy people."

Ben looked thoughtful and said, "So I'm not a horde?"

Stephen and Liz shared a look of humor.

Liz said, "One person can't be a horde. So, no."

Stephen added, "But if you are with a bunch of noisy, busy people, then you are part of a horde. In this case, the horde left you behind."

Ben thought some more and said, "So, after church is a horde. Everyone is so noisy and busy, when all we want is just to go home and play."

Steve surrendered. "You are right, you know. Maybe every large group of—" and he stopped himself, knowing that his silly off-hand comments often came back to him as "facts" from his kids' mouths. He substituted, "Actually, no, not all groups of noisy, busy people are hordes. So it's a confusement!" and he ruffled his son's hair. He stood up, signaling that the conversation was over. He moved to fill his coffee mug and stood, leaning against the counter.

"I want a dorde," complained Grace, who was done with her mix of fruit and hot-dog pieces. Liz moved to wipe her youngest off and lift her clear of her booster.

"We'll see if we can find you one," murmured the busy mom. Tanny noticed that Liz had managed to finish most of her sandwich before she was launched back into motherly responsibilities.

"Let me get this," said Steve. He reached for Grace announcing, "Benjamin, it is quiet time now. You know the drill. Gather the books and stuffies you want, quick-quick. I will read Grace her naptime story, and you can listen, or you lie on your bed and do quiet things until the timer goes." Carrying Grace, he ushered Ben along towards the bedrooms.

Liz plunked herself down with a groan at the table again.

"Finish your sandwich," Tanny suggested with a sympathetic grin.

"Just a short moment of rest," Liz sighed.

Tanny rose and started clearing the kids' dishes. Liz flapped a hand. "Don't bother. I can do that. Just sit with me." So Tanny sat.

"It's just a small gathering, but it means a lot to me," Liz explained. "Jon and Sue will be coming. The twins will hang out with my kids in the basement play-room. One of Ally's friends will be helping her babysit them all." Liz was referring to their oldest child. A thought crossed Liz's face, "*You* come! Of course you are invited. I am inviting you to join us if you like. It is from four to six p.m. Hors d'oeuvres and some wine and some lovely people. Do come!"

Tanny was delighted.

After a little more rest, Liz and Tanny got back to work. Liz set Tanny to vacuuming the living room, while she finished the dishes and wiped the table.

Then she joined Tanny with a long fluffy stick designed to bring down cobwebs.

"I HATE spiders," Liz was grumbling as Stephen came down from settling the kids. Tanny was appreciating how badly the living room needed a good vacuuming as she uncovered loads of cobwebs in the corners, behind drapes, and even between chair legs. She moved slowly and methodically so as not to miss any.

Liz shrieked and jumped back from where she had been dusting the ceiling. She had thrown her dusting stick away from her and was doing a sort of jumping dance, shaking her arms and hopping. "One dropped at me! Oooooh!" She made rapid brushing motions off her arms and body, as if to swipe away the nasty creature. Stephen was laughing.

Liz grabbed the vacuum away from Tanny and used the long tube attachment to hunt the offending spider. She flipped back a drape and shrieked again. "There he is. DIE SUCKER!" And stabbing the vacuum hose at the creature, she disappeared him with satisfaction.

Stephen said to Tanny, "Liz's dark side comes out when she's vacuuming." He then teased his wife, "You're murdering them."

Liz, holding the vacuum tube like a weapon said, "No. I'm evicting uninvited guests." With an "Aha!" she stabbed at another, followed by an, "Ewww. Gross!" as she found several balls of eggs and had to scrub the tube end against the curtain to try to remove the sticky things.

"Tanny," she said, "Please get a bucket of warm soapy water and follow me around the room. I want you to get the remaining gunk that the vacuum can't get once I'm done."

"And technically, I'm not murdering them," she continued with Stephen, her eyes hunting. "We don't know for sure that they die. They're just sucked into a black hole and then cast into outer darkness."

Stephen added, "Where there will be weeping and gnashing of teeth."

Liz grinned and asked, "Do spiders have teeth?"

"Where there will be weeping and gnashing of weird, ugly suckers," amended Stephen. He kissed his wife and thanked her for all her hard work. "I'll tidy up the entry porch a bit, and then I have to get back to the school." He took several steps and said, "I'll be sure to release any spiders I find into our welcoming home." Liz dropped the vacuum and went after him.

"Don't you dare!" She was swatting at him as he dodged and twisted, laughing. Liz was laughing too, and eventually they ended up in a tussle which became a kiss.

Tanny turned her back, polishing fiercely, touched by their open affection.

When Liz returned, the Rosie scarf was falling off her messed hair, and she was smiling with delight. She said, "They work him too hard. We tracked his hours a few months ago; he was working as many as eighty hours a week. Jon was supposed to ease that burden. Then there was all that drama about Jon, and now he's on his honeymoon. It's like Stephen can't get a break. Not that it's Jon's fault. I have been insisting Steve work no more than ten hours a day, forcing him to stop, no matter what still isn't done yet. But he's a bit of a perfectionist, and he doesn't want to anger the board by starting to draw boundaries after all this time. Congregations see a pastor like children see parents—always on call and having no personal needs." The two women vacuumed and scrubbed. "I shouldn't be telling you this; you are a member of the congregation. I'm sorry. Please forget what I said."

Tanny wanted to say she wasn't really a member, except she was. It was the first time it struck Tanny how isolated Liz was as a minister's wife. Who could Liz confide in without it being a breach of trust? Tanny said, "Well it makes complete sense to me that we want to keep Steve in good health! I had no idea he worked so many hours."

Liz grunted. Tanny guessed she was choking on a "See?!" that she couldn't say. Liz's jaw was clamped shut. Tanny dropped her cloth and grabbed Liz in a hug. Liz struggled and then burst into tears. Tanny held on firmly saying, "I had no idea. I am grateful to know, because now I will stop taking him and you for granted."

Liz struggled again, "But—"

"I understand that you said this in confidence, by accident. I won't say a word. I know nothing. Just let it out, and we'll pretend this didn't happen."

Liz laughed through her tears. "Thank God I've found a group of ministers' wives in the city to meet up with. We can gripe and complain freely with each other. It does help! But I've realized how some other denominations have much clearer and more thorough contracts. Some ministers get the occasional Sunday off! They get a whole month off in the summer AND a month for study! It's all built into the philosophy of how the denomination takes care of the pastor, with a whole system for finding supply preachers and student preachers to cover the Sundays. And they don't even have a school to run as well!"

Tanny absorbed the level of frustration burdening the pastor's wife. She felt protective and wanted to champion her cause. This bright, cheerful, insanely competent, everything-rolls-off-her woman was stressed and lonely. "I can't even imagine how hard it must be," she offered. "I wish I could help."

Liz looked into her eyes. "Thank you, Tanny. You ARE helping by cleaning with me. But please don't say anything about this to anyone. This is our battle, and we need to fight it ourselves. This cannot become part of the gossip. Steve's job could be on the line."

Tanny wanted to reassure Liz that the board was made up of reasonable people, but after the craziness they'd just been through with Britt's will, she wasn't so sure. "I understand," she said.

They pushed on until the living areas were fresh and bug-free. Tanny chatted about her upcoming job helping her photographer friend. Liz speculated that they needed some painting done at the church, and would Tanny be interested?

By three in the afternoon, Tanny was heading home feeling content, with a tidy little packet of cash in her hand. If only she didn't have eighteen ways to spend it already.

Thirteen

Tanny's morning and most of the afternoon were spent tagging along after her hilarious and quirky photographer friend. She learned a surprising amount about professional wedding photography. Most of the church weddings Tanny had attended used someone from the congregation for the photographs, which Tanny had thought were lovely.

But this venture started with photographing the ladies sitting around in satin robes waiting for their turns with hair or makeup, drinking Prosecco and eating tiny quiches. Shelley stood in odd places and turned the camera for unusual angles. She photographed the shoes, the satin robes, the makeup application, the hairstyling. Some shots were posed but many were candid. Tanny instantly liked the wedding party, and they welcomed her as the photographer's "bag lady" with laughter.

Next, Shelley drove to where the gentlemen were preparing, and did much the same thing, with Tanny handing over whatever camera or lens Shelley requested. Tanny even helped with the odd boutonniere when the young men looked lost. She enjoyed the obvious good feelings among the men.

Finally, it was time for the two groups to meet. Shelly had funny and creative ideas for the photos that would never have occurred to Tanny. When Shelley suggested the party reach behind and pinch each other's bums during the group shots, Tanny laughed out loud. It worked to make the smiles and laughter genuine and fresh, avoiding the frozen, self-conscious expressions that could creep in.

Eventually, the shoot done, Shelley dropped Tanny off at home with a wonderful wad of bills, a much larger payment than Tanny had expected. Tanny also understood why her photographer friend charged so very much for what she did. She worked hard, she was funny and lively, and she still had hours and hours of selecting, editing, and compiling to do for the couple.

The party at Steve and Liz's started at five. Tanny was excited to see Susan and Jon again and happy to be included in this pastoral social group. She dressed up in a stylish wool pantsuit, gave up in frustration on her hair, and set out through the still, gathering darkness. She appreciated that the sunset was later and later each day.

Stephen welcomed her in with a hug, accepting gratefully the bottle of wine she handed him. Tanny shed her boots and coat, listening to the happy chatter coming from the living room. Stephen had taken the wine up to show Liz. Tanny padded up the half-flight behind him, noticing immediately the radiant newly-weds, as well as several staff members and their spouses. It was all couples, as usual. Tanny realized that the only single teacher, the one who taught the third and fourth grades, hadn't come.

Liz greeted Tanny with thanks for the wine and showed her a selection of beverages as well as yummy hors d'oeuvres. Tanny selected a spring roll and something with bacon wrapped around it and moved over to welcome Sue home.

Sue's face lit up when she saw Tanny, and her hug was warm and long. Tanny noticed that Sue's nose and chin were a bit chapped. Tanny asked, "How was your honeymoon? How are you?"

Susan slipped her arm around Jon's waist and said, "Wonderful. It was . . .wonderful." They were radiant. Tanny realized that the chapped nose and chin were probably from kissing her bearded husband a great deal, and felt a shiver of ... what? Envy? She gave herself a shake to clear those thoughts.

"Good to see you, Tanny," said the new husband, and gave her a one-armed embrace.

"What did you think of Cedar Haven?" Tanny had to ask.

Jon said, "It was kief—I mean, gorgeous. Apparently, Britt did a lot of up-grades in her final years. Have you seen it?"

"It's all open concept on the main floor now," Susan added. "It's remarkable."

"Ja," continued Jon. "I look forward to what you all decide to do with it from here." He was referring, of course to the fact of Susan and Tanny recently being made stewards along with Uncle Jacob and the old caretaker, Mr. VanGalen. Jacob wanted to call a meeting about it, but the weather and a certain wedding had forestalled this first meeting. It didn't seem it was urgent, but Tanny really was eager to move forward on it. Which reminded her that she wanted to call Uncle Jacob to set up a visit.

Liz came over at that moment to join them.

Is it just me, or does Susie look relieved to see Liz?

Sue said, "Um, I need to talk to you.... Do you have a minute?"

"Well sure," Liz responded with concern. They went off, arm in arm.

Tanny felt the room recede a bit. She was hit by a wave of disappointment. *Wait! What about me? Don't leave me out. You can still include me...."*

She looked to Jon, who was already engaged with Stephen and the Mac-Arthurs discussing something to do with the kindergarten. She listened a bit to the funny story that Nancy was telling about one of the kindergarteners. But there was no point of entry into the conversation. She looked around for another group to join. The room seemed to be broken up into discussions all about marriage and children.

Liz and Susan were down in the entryway, talking closely and quietly.

Tanny sighed and pushed herself over to join Daniel and Lisa Nesbitt to ask about their cottage adventures. (They owned a cottage a few kilometres from Cedar Haven, and the last Tanny had heard, a family of skunks had set up residence in the crawl space.) But the Nesbitts were discussing the upcoming play with the teacher of the seventh and eighth graders. They were so engaged; it felt a bit random for Tanny to suddenly ask about their cottage.

Finally, Susan seemed to be finishing up with Liz. Tanny took a few steps toward Sue when Stephen called everyone to quiet. He beckoned Liz to his side and proposed a toast to his beautiful wife of seventeen years. He also proposed a toast to the institution of marriage. "Liz is the biggest blessing of my life. I don't know who I'd be without her. So, let's raise our glasses to marriage, to wives, and to Liz in particular!"

"Hear, hear!" the room cried.

"Hear, hear," said Tanny, raising her plate of hors d'oeuvres, as she hadn't chosen a beverage yet. As glasses were being clinked, she went to the kitchen to grab a glass of wine, only to discover the clinking was over by the time she returned. She belatedly clinked her glass against one that somebody had already set down on a table.

Tanny looked at Susan, already back in conversation beside Jonathan. Tanny just wanted to talk together with Susan alone. She had really missed her! She realized she didn't really belong in this group, and she was tired. Tanny set down the wine, untouched, quickly downed the bacon thing—amazing! —and then went to make excuses, citing a long day.

On the way home through the darkness, she fought back tears. No one had meant to ignore her. No one had actively snubbed her. But somehow, she had lost interest in approaching any of the guests to find topics that interested them both.

No one had done that for her, though they might have if she'd stayed. But she was too discouraged and sad. She knew she had been invited as an afterthought, but she hadn't minded. Now she understood. She didn't fit in ... because she wasn't married. The sadness just grew as she hurried through the darkness.

Once home, she let herself in the front door instead of going down the icy steps. Emily perked up at the sight of her and began talking to her, but Tanny put her hand up, shaking her head, and ran to the stairs down to her apartment. She slammed her apartment door and was soon face down on her furry couch, sobbing.

It's so unfair!! I feel so helpless! There's nothing I can do to join the marriage club! I don't know who I am in this church if I'm not married! Where is my group?

There came a gentle knock on the door. Emily pushed the door open a bit, quietly calling Tanny's name. "Oh, sweetie!" she cried when she saw her daughter's misery. Emily sat on the edge of the sofa and started rubbing Tanny's back. "I'm sorry. I'm so sorry. Whatever it is, I'm here."

After a bit more of Tanny's weeping Emily asked, "Do you want to tell me?"

"Oh, mom, why is it so easy for everyone else to find love and so hard for me? I don't fit in with the marrieds in the church and it hu-urts ... so ... mu-uch!"

Emily made a sympathetic noise and continued gently smoothing Tanny's hair and rubbing her back. She found some tissues and reached them around where Tanny could see them.

Eventually Tanny sat up, grabbing for more tissues. "Mo-om, I want somebody to love me the way Jon loves Susie. I want someone who *gets* me. Will I ever have that? Ever?"

"I'm sure you will, sweetheart. You are too smart and funny and lovable not to find someone."

Tanny leaned into Emily's arm and rested her head on her shoulder. "I hope so. Most of my friends have moved or married. I feel so ... lonely."

Tanny was slumped, tissue box in hand. "Everything has been taken from me, mom. I've got no job, no apartment—Charm's gone. I don't know who I am anymore." Another sob choked her. "And I've lost Susie a-gain!" Fresh tears found her leaning into her mother's comforting shoulder.

"You haven't lost Susie, honey. She's a bit preoccupied right now. She's got a lot of adjustments to make. Don't give up on her."

Tanny realized that her mother was right. She resolved to ask Susan for a visit, or at least a chance to help. She gave her mom a big hug and thanked her. Sometimes her mother really came through for her. She was a bit of a Jekyll and Hyde. Tanny never knew which mom she would get, but she was very grateful right now. She got herself to bed early and slept long and deep.

Elizabeth Doering Shantz lay tangled in the sheets, her hand on her husband's chest. The morning light lay in thin strips across the bedding. Liz grinned. "So, who would have thought I'd have such a high sex drive?"

"We do have six children, honey."

Liz chuckled and nestled her head into his shoulder. "Yeah but, all ministers have lots of kids. It's like ... it's part of the job description. And yet, ministers and their wives were the last people I imagined would have sexual feelings when I was younger. Because sex was such a taboo topic."

"So how did you think ministers got so many kids?"

"Oh, you know, 'Immaculate conception,' or 'Lie down and think of England.'"

"Hmmm. I'm so glad that's not how we do it."

Laughter bubbled out of Liz. "Me too."

There was a companionable silence as the two of them rested and reflected.

"Still, I have worried," Liz continued. "You know I have struggled with ... having a high sex drive. It makes me, somehow, 'not a good woman.'"

"When we were engaged, you worried that I would think you were ... what was it?"

"Oh yeah...."

"'A wanton yuck,'" they said in unison.

Liz started giggling. "But I am. I *am* a wanton yuck!"

"I LIKE my wanton yuck," Stephen growled.

More bubbling laughter curled out of Liz, followed by noises of pleasure as Steve backed up his declaration with some masterly kisses.

When they had settled back into the pillows Liz asked, "Do you remember, after Benjamin was born, when I lost all interest in sex? It was so odd."

"I do remember," Stephen murmured with some emphasis.

"I could remember that I used to like sex. I knew that I had liked it a lot. But for some reason—I had no idea why—the very thought of lovemaking left me cold."

"I remember."

"It was so strange. I just wanted to nurse my baby and be a mommy and cook and clean."

Stephen continued, "And be left alone."

Liz said, "Yeah," and then lightly, "Sorry about that."

Steve responded, "You couldn't help it. It was hormonal. And we survived."

"I had absolutely no choice. It was like I had become a different person. It was so weird."

There was a silence and then Liz said, "I tell you, Stephen, it gave me a lot more understanding and sympathy for women who have a lower sex drive. I could much better understand what it's like for them—with the husband always wanting sexual attention while they are mostly not interested."

"And it did help me better appreciate the frustrated husbands who came to me for counsel," mused Stephen.

Liz snorted. "So, it was a gift from God."

"Yay," said Stephen without enthusiasm. "Another gift from God."

"May such gifts be few and far between," agreed Liz.

"Amen!" said Steve with a lot of enthusiasm.

Up on her elbow, grinning, Liz said. "I got bettah."

"Indeed, you did," chuckled Steve, with satisfaction. "You are no longer a newt. But now, you wonderfully sexy woman, I have to get a shower and go preach."

"Maybe comb your hair too," grinned Liz.

By Sunday afternoon, after a sermon about the joy God has in store for us, Tanny had left a voice mail for Uncle Jacob, telling him she would be coming up to Cedar Haven the next day.

Fourteen

February 22

$\mathscr{T}$anny's little car chugged along the packed snow of the road. The wheels slipped and grabbed valiantly, and Tanny wished again that she could have afforded snow tires. After three hours of driving, it was warm in the car; but the squeak and creak of the snow under the wheels advertised the extreme cold outside. She was almost to the driveway into Cedar Haven. Just a few minutes more.

Up ahead at a bend in the road, a sheen indicated an icy patch. Tanny steered toward the middle of the road, leaving herself plenty of room to slip and yet still be on the road. She didn't like the way the road angled down a bit toward the ditch just there at the bend. As she approached, she could even see skid-marks where some unfortunate had slid off into the gully. Tanny wondered …maybe if she gunned it now, her momentum would zip her right across the ice and back onto solid snow again….

"No, no, NO!" was all Tanny had time to bellow as Herman careened crazily around and slid backwards into the ditch with a CRUNCH.

"Fork!" Tanny smacked the steering wheel in frustration. She set the gear to low and tried to drive up and out, but her wheels just spun in spasms, which simply settled her more deeply into the icy ditch.

"Damn, damn, damn!" Tanny smacked the wheel with each word. Then she wilted and rested her forehead on the top of the steering wheel with a long, frustrated groan. The silence settled around her. She sighed. She was tired and frustrated and mad at herself.

"Okay, fine," she announced to her car, "Be that way." She shut off the engine, pocketed her key, and unbuckled herself. Then she went to open the door. It wouldn't budge. "Hermannnn!" Tanny howled on a rising note of frustration, "Don't DO this to me!" She heaved and heaved against the door, slamming her shoulder repeatedly into it. Nothing.

She sat there in silence. "Duh." She rolled down her window. Once she had scrambled out through the window, Tanny surveyed her crazily angled steed. She saw that her door was wedged shut by snow. Herman looked like he'd be staying in the ditch for quite a while. He'd need a tow truck for sure. Tanny sighed. The cold was already biting at her cheeks and forehead. Tanny considered. She was only about a half mile from Cedar Haven. She would walk, get herself a fortifying cup of tea, and then come back with a sled for her stuff.

She closed the window the best she could, tucked her scarf more closely around her face, and scrambled up out of the ditch. A field stretched behind Herman, frozen and hard under the icy sky. The pinewoods that ran onto Britt's property loomed dark and dense on the other side of the road. Tanny started walking. Up ahead, the afternoon sun showed as a vague milky whiteness in the winter haze. The sky was an unnerving greyish-yellow, and Tanny moved faster. The invasive wind held enough bite to assure Tanny of the extreme cold. She pressed her mitted hand against her stinging forehead and trudged on. The cold began to grab at her legs through her jeans. She had forgotten how useless jeans were in cold weather. She could hear her mom's warnings, "Do you have enough warm clothes? Do you have your emergency kit? Do you have a full tank?" Why had she ignored her? But Tanny was so near her destination. Surely, she could walk the last bit to the house, cold or no.

Soon the cold that had taken over her legs had begun seeping upward under her coat. It had crept up her sleeves as if she had no coat at all. And it was Canada cold! She tugged her sleeves down and hunched her face lower in her collar and wrapped her arms tight around her body. She kicked herself for her naïve assumption that she wouldn't need her long underwear or balaclava, "because the car was so warm." She had the proper gear with her! But it was all packed in her suitcase in the back of Herman. She had set off for the house thinking it would be faster than trying to dig it out and put it on. She was already regretting that choice.

The cold air attacking her face forced her shielding hands up to cover her cheeks and forehead. Breathing made her nose hurt. She pressed a mitten over it, then decided to pull her scarf up over her nose and mouth. The warm breath helped her nose to thaw, but now her neck was exposed. The wind stung everywhere it touched.

Tanny tucked her chin down closer to her chest, and with mitts pressed against her cheeks and forehead, she trudged on. Her legs were getting clumsy as her muscles succumbed to the cold. *Just keep going.*

Tanny reached the familiar driveway to Cedar Haven and turned onto it with relief. It was icy on the slight slope down into the woods and after a few careful steps, she fell, landing hard on her left hip and elbow. She scrambled to her feet, heart hammering, hands shaking. Now her hip and elbow throbbed.

She took two stumbling steps, then leaped back as a bellowing snowmobile fish-tailed across her path. The driver shouted and swung his exhaust-belching beast around to face her. A large, wolf-like dog appeared, barking furiously just out of reach.

The shock gave Tanny a much-needed surge of anger. Her discomfort disappeared behind outrage that anyone would snowmobile on her aunt's land. The driver shouted something, and the dog retreated to his master's side. Switching his machine to a lower roar he bellowed, "This is private property. You are trespassing." His tone was authoritative, his eyes hidden behind snow goggles. When Tanny didn't move or reply he continued, "You'll want to go back home immediately. A storm is coming. You don't want to be out in it."

Tanny took in the muscular build, unshaven jaw, and the tattoo showing above his left glove. She shouted, "My car is just back there," and waved toward the road. He sat watching her, so she turned and started to march back up the driveway, seething. There was silence behind her for several steps. Her back prickled from the man's watching eyes. Finally, she heard his engine rev and, to her relief, growl off into the woods.

She took a few more steps, then turned. No sign of the snowmobile. She could hear its roar far off in the wooded valley. No sign of the dog either.

Who was that guy? He chased me off my own property! The surging anger fueled her tired muscles, and she stomped onward toward the house in fury. Some territorial white guy, she decided. He took advantage of Britt's un-patrolled acres for his own joyriding, then got thrills ordering other trespassers off the land, the hypocrite. I'll be sure to alert Mr. VanGalen about him when I get up to the house. Tanny pictured old Mr. VanGalen. What would he look like? She gave him a wizened, kindly face, a stooped body, and a sweet smile. What a cutie! He was Britt's secret love. Tanny was sure of it. Why had Britt never told anyone? Why had she kept their love a secret? Tanny persevered, eager to meet the man that had finally won Britt's heart.

The sky had a strange smoky look to it. It wasn't smoke though. It looked almost like ... locusts? Tanny cursed her luck as snowflakes assaulted her on a freshening wind. Storm coming indeed! She turned her back to the onslaught and struggled on sideways, head bent. *Not much farther!*

Tanny realized how lucky she was that the old caretaker kept the driveway plowed. At least the banks offered some protection from the wind. Even so, she could barely see where she was going. The snow was coming fast and hard. The driveway was going to need another good plowing soon if this snow kept up.

Tanny peeked out from behind her shielding mitts just often enough to stay on course. Otherwise, she was locked in a world of stinging, stumbling cold. She couldn't really feel her feet and knew it was not going to be comfy when the boots came off and they began to warm up. *Just keep walking. You're nearly there.*

Tanny jumped. The dog was back, barking and barking, keeping pace with her, just out of reach. After her heart settled back in her chest, Tanny yelled at him to go home. When that didn't work, she gave up and ignored him, utterly intent on getting to the front sidewalk, the front porch, the front door. The caretaker must be home. He lived here. She couldn't even let herself consider what she would do if the house was locked, and no one answered her knock. The dog continued prancing around her, barking and barking. She wished he'd shut up, but she lacked the strength to chase him off. She just wanted to get into the house and get warm. *I can break in if I must. It's my house too.*

The dog followed her inside. She swatted at him and grabbed for his collar to shoo him outside. "You dumb dog!" she yelled. "Get out of here! Go home!"

A large, tattooed arm appeared over Tanny's head, pushing the door shut. "This *is* his home," said the owner of the arm. "Who are you?"

Tanny was appalled to find herself nose to nose with the scruffy man from the driveway. He was tall, and a snake tattoo writhed up his muscled left arm. He had a shaved head. Tanny's heart took up residence in her throat. *How did he get in here? Has this biker taken over Cedar Haven? Where's the caretaker? Just be calm and assertive...* She lifted her chin. "I don't think so. I'm Tanny Smith," she thumped her breastbone in emphasis, "I own this place, and you can take your dog and just get out now before I call the police." She pointed with emphasis toward the door, hating that her face was so numb that she had actually said, "Caw duh powice."

The man was younger than he had first looked. Now he ran a hand across his hairless head, looking at her like he was seeing a ghost. For a brief second, Tanny wondered if she had stumbled onto the wrong property—certainly the main floor looked entirely different. But no, there was the familiar coat cupboard, and there was that paint splash on the third step to the second floor from when she had been "helping" do some painting upstairs.

A gust of wind roared against the house, making the windows shudder. Snow rasped against the panes like hungry locusts. Tanny shivered, feeling less and less confident. *I am trapped in this storm with this skin head .... with amazing eyes.* They were golden in colour. Not brown, not hazel, not grey, but a remarkable yellow gold. She had seen eyes like that once before.

"M-M-Mr. VanGalen?" she shouted into the house. "Can you hear me? Are you okay?" *Could he even answer?*

Tanny's was trembling with fatigue. "T-tell me what you have done with the c-caretaker. Where is Mr. VanGalen? Have you hurt him?"

The man dropped his arms to his side. "Tanny, it's me, Jeff. Jefferson VanGalen. I'm the caretaker. I'm Jacob and Eileen's foster son."

Tanny's gaze scoured his face for recognition. *Jeff....* Her eyes flew open. "Wait, you're Jeffy? *The* Jeffy we played with that summer when my folks were travelling? You're *that* Jeffy?" She had memories of scooting down cascades in one of the Muskoka rivers and jumping off a cliff into the water on Lake Muskoka, and canoeing ... everywhere. Memories of laughing over card games with Jenny and her brothers along with this kid. Jacob and Eileen had brought him to Cedar Haven when they came to help Britt "babysit" them all. "Jeffy" had been a bit scrawny and non-descript, except for those amazing golden eyes. He had been quiet. And she had forgotten all about him. How long had it been? Over fifteen years at least.

"You're Jeffy?" Tanny asked, again recognition dawning. He was not non-descript now! He was well-muscled and tall and was leaning toward her slightly.

"I go by Jeff now." After a pause he added, "It's good to see you again."

Abruptly Tanny's romantic fairy-tale about Britt's secret love collapsed in dusty rubble. She felt suddenly exhausted now that the threat was over. Another strong gust shuddered around the eaves and lashed the windows. The thought of having to walk back to the car for her suitcase in this weather made her feel too tired to stand.

"Look, can I...?" she tipped her head toward the living room.

Jeff caught her when she staggered. "Let's get you to the couch." He helped her over and settled her on the comfy sofa. "You were not dressed for the weather. Where did you come from?"

She winced as he lowered her down. "My car went into the ditch not far from the driveway."

He grumbled, "That ditch! I keep telling them the road is not graded properly there." Turning his back, he poked and fed the fire until it was roaring again.

Tanny appreciated his muscled back but quickly looked away when his face swung around again.

"Just rest," he said, and handed her another pillow.

Moments later Tanny was snuggled up under Britt's favourite afghan in front of the crackling fire, a mug of chicken soup at her elbow. She rested her head back on the couch, looking up at the great stone fireplace, trying to adjust to the turn of events.

Britt's property manager was this young man. She remembered that the caretaker had "right of residence" or some such but had never expected it would be a problem for her to come stay for a few days. Tanny's folks would be outraged if they knew he was her age. She could hear them now, "trapped in a blizzard all alone!" She knew their instant assumption was, "They will have sex!"

Tanny snorted. Honestly! Her parents were so weird. As if! She barely remembered the man. She sipped the soup and made a face. Ugh. It was the freeze-dried kind with the cardboard noodles. Still ... it was very un-thug-like that he had made it for her. And covered her with the afghan.

So, this was Jeffy, that quiet kid with the golden eyes. Jeff had disappeared down into the basement with his dog "Mack" after seeing that she was settled. She tried to remember what was down there ... not much. The furnace and water heater, the laundry, the single-car garage, and mostly the big Muskoka rock that the foundation rested on. Many Muskoka houses had to accommodate the massive Precambrian shield that lay under so much of Ontario.

The fire crackled. Jeff didn't come back up.

Tanny awoke when the basement door burst open. Jeff was trying to drag something big through it while "Mack" pushed past him. Mack was covered with melting snow, which he proceeded to shake off right in front of Tanny.

"Ahhh!" she complained, shielding herself with the blanket.

"I'll put this stuff up in the right-hand bedroom for you."

He was carrying her bags! He must have gone out in the storm and fetched them for her. She struggled to sit up, noticing his ice-reddened cheeks.

"Thanks...." was all she managed to say. Then, after he had shuffled several steps down the hall and started up the stairs she realized, "Wait! I can do that."

"Sit!" He barked.

Both Mack and Tanny sat. Tanny waited in meek silence as the shuffling ended in a series of muffled thumps overhead. She waited for her host to return, but he never did. Mack yawned and dropped down onto the rag-rug to doze by the fire.

Now Tanny was awake and rested enough to feel uncomfortable. Should she get up? Should she stay seated? She remembered the grumpy command to "Sit!" and knew it had been aimed at her, not the dog. If she went upstairs, would he yell at her again?

She waited for a long moment. The dog gave another loud yawn. Tanny felt awkward. *What is he doing? Is he riffling through my stuff?* She pictured her lacy

　　　　　ALISON LONGSTAFF MOORE

bras and panties and leapt to her feet, bolting for the stairs. She bounded up them, two at a time, coming to a halt at the top. There were her bags, tumbled in a heap in the right-hand bedroom, just like he had said. He was in the left-hand room, sitting on the bed with his face in his hands. He was still in his winter gear.

"Oh," she said, and felt uncomfortable. Then, "sorry..." and feeling like she had intruded on something, she went into her room, pushed her stuff inside and shut the door. The thunk of his door followed.

Tanny sat on the bed, bewildered. She was supposed to be having a heart-to-heart with Britt's true love right now. She was supposed to be sharing the house with a kindly old grandfather.

Why on earth had Britt picked *this guy* as the fourth caretaker? Why was *he* living in the family homestead? He was the only non-relative of the four appointed stewards—well, she guessed being Jacob and Eileen's foster son made him kind of a relative. She wondered what had happened to his parents. She was so grateful he had brought up her bags! The storm beat around the eaves, as she unpacked and wondered what she would tell her parents.

After some unpacking, Tanny heard a knock at her door. A voice announced that he was going back out to get the car out of the ditch before it was buried deeper in snow.

"Oh! Thanks!" Tanny called back, moving to open the door. He was gone down the stairs by the time she flung it open. "Can I help?" she asked. But there was no answer. She heard the basement door slam, then the garage door opening and the truck starting up. She found slippers and padded down to the main floor, stopping to take in just how changed it was. She heard the garage door rumble closed and Tanny ran to the window to watch the pickup with a plow on the front head off down the driveway, plowing as it went.

Tanny walked around the remarkably open-concept main floor. She ended up in the kitchen and turned on the kettle. She unpacked her small cooler which Jeff had set near the fridge and decided to make up some "stew" (a couple cans of Chunky soup plus some extra sauteed vegetables and a chopped-up leftover steak). She looked in the cupboards and discovered she could make biscuits. When the kettle clicked, she poured a pot of tea.

It was quite a while before she heard the rumble of the plow returning. Out the window she saw Herman being towed behind the plow right past the house and up towards the barn. She guessed he was putting Herman in the barn, out of the snow. That was thoughtful.

Eventually she heard the plow returning. It entered the garage followed by the rumble of the garage door closing. She felt a flutter of nerves. She sipped at her tea. The oven dinged on the biscuits just as Jeff came up through the basement door followed by Mack. He had his boots in hand. Again, Tanny felt something in his presence, as if his energy filled the space. She had a hard time not watching him as he shed his coat and ski-pants.

"Something smells amazing," he said, tipping his head toward the kitchen.

"I uh, I threw together a kind of stew and made biscuits to go with it. I made enough for two if you want some. I know it's only late afternoon...."

"Fresh biscuits," he rumbled. Jeff strode into the kitchen and produced some butter as Tanny was tipping them out onto a cooling rack.

"Thank you for getting Herman out of the ditch," Tanny said with all sincerity.

"That's not the first car I've pulled out of that ditch, and it probably won't be the last," the tall man said, biting into a freshly buttered half-biscuit. His noise of pleasure was like a basso profundo purr. "These are great!"

Tanny felt his gaze and she turned to look into those remarkable golden eyes.

"Herman?" he said.

Fifteen

*J*eff lay awake for a long time. Tanny Smith had just shown up, unannounced, and his crush had returned full force. All those years ago, when his foster parents brought him to Cedar Haven when they had agreed to babysit some nieces and nephews, Jeff was completely taken by the warm, friendly girl from Kitchener. He'd always wished he would see her again, but there was never another circumstance that put them in the same place after that. Though she was technically his foster cousin, Jacob and Eileen didn't spend much time with Jacob's side of the family. They had Eileen's family in the area, and Britt.

Being taken in for fostering by the Benders at age nine probably saved his life and had given him the stability he had sorely needed. They stood by him even as his birth parents were in and out of rehab. They had welcomed him back after each time one or both of his parents earned custody only to fall short a few months later. And they had stood by him when, at age fourteen, he had eventually buried his parents—killed by driving drunk.

Britt "adopted" him as a sort of grandson, hiring him to help on the property and supporting him financially when he wanted to be a paramedic. Britt had been the adoptive grandmother of his heart; Jacob and Eileen the parents his own simply couldn't be. When Britt had died so suddenly, Jeff had been in the Netherlands researching his family roots. He had not made it back in time for the funeral in Kitchener. But shortly after he had arrived home, he spoke at the United Church memorial service for her in Bracebridge. Nearly the whole community had turned out for that. How he missed her!

And now her namesake was sleeping just across the hall. Why had no one warned him of Tanny's arrival? It wasn't right. The other "stewards" shouldn't just be able to arrive unannounced. This was his home! He'd have to talk to Jacob.

Before turning in for the night, he had chatted with the still delightful woman over dinner. She had explained that Herman was her car, as if everybody named their cars. When he'd asked "why Herman" she had answered, "because that's his name" as if that wasn't circular reasoning and explained everything. And then she'd dimpled, and he lost the ability to speak.

They had both retired early. Tanny had cleaned up the kitchen and Jeff saw that the fire grate was safely in place and everything secure. He'd let Mack out and waited for him. He felt tremendous relief when Tanny had gone into her room and closed the door.

He called Jacob then, getting voicemail, only to remember that his foster parents were up in Parry Sound, visiting her mother for a few days. Jacob was not a fan of cell phones and still relied on his landline. Jeff left a message on Eileen's cell phone requesting that Jacob call him. Eventually he accessed the bathroom at the top of the stairs, then shut himself in his room.

Jeff saw himself as a confident man. He wasn't uncomfortable with other people; in fact, as a paramedic he dealt with a whole array of humanity, giving them reassurance and comfort during some of their most vulnerable moments. He knew how to display the confidence and competence required to ease the anxiety of struggling patients and families.

So why was he tongue-tied around this woman—his former friend? Was it her lovely curves and feminine mannerisms? Was it her stormy and changeable eyes? Maybe it was just the whole package, the transformed ideal girl and friend into this stubborn, confusing, attractive woman? He sighed. Eventually he slept.

Jeff had awoken early, having dreamt of trying to rescue Tanny from a human-car hybrid named Herman. He had tried all sorts of things to get Herman to release her. It was only when he threw a porcupine at the monster that it had shrunk back into a normal car and Tanny had rushed into his arms. They had made wild, passionate love.

Jeff got himself a chilly shower, shaved, and headed out with Mack to shovel, plow, and get some work done on the small apartment he was building in the barn. The workshop out there was heated and insulated. The apartment was not yet, or he would have moved out there immediately to give Tanny (and himself) more privacy.

But by ten in the morning, he couldn't ignore his hunger or desperation for coffee. He also was missing the plans for the apartment, and he wondered if he had left them in his room. He squared his shoulders, reminded himself of his confidence and capability, and headed back to the house.

When Jeff let himself in the front door he was hit by the smell of coffee and the sound of Tanny singing in the shower. Mack squeezed in beside him, and looked up the stairs, waving his tail.

"This heart's crying just like YESTERDA-AY," came Tanny's voice booming through the floorboards along with music she had playing in the bathroom with her.

Jeff looked up the stair at the closed bathroom door. Surely, he had time to run up and grab the plans and get out before she even knew he was back in the house. "Stay here, Mack," he commanded. He dashed up the stairs and into his room, glad his stockinged feet made no noise. His heart was racing. So, where were the plans? Hadn't he left them there on the desk?

Tanny continued singing at the top of her lungs. She whooped. Jeff heard thumping in the tub from Tanny stomping to the rhythm. "Oh, won't ya tell me?" Jeff grinned despite himself.

Mack whined from the bottom of the stairs. "Stay, Mack!" Jeff's whisper was fierce. He wanted to get his plans, maybe get some coffee, and food, then get out so he didn't have to encounter the woman he had just been making love to in his dreams. He lifted papers on the desk, frantic to find the plans.

The song came to an end. Jeff froze, afraid to make a noise.

Another song started. Tanny was singing again—this time a love song.

She doesn't hear me. She thinks she's alone in the house.

"All my life—blub-flub." Tanny laughed out loud, having put her face under the shower mid-verse. Jeff felt like a sneak and voyeur. *Where are those blasted plans?*

"Ask for a little help from above," Tanny crooned.

Jeff realized he had started looking in ridiculous places. He was on his hands and knees looking under the bed when the water stopped. He heard the sound of a shower curtain being pushed aside.

Now what? Dash for the stairs? Close the bedroom door? If he could just get out to the barn....

He heard the bathroom doorknob squeak. He opted to stay down behind his bed. *I'm hiding behind my bed in my own house.*

He heard her footsteps and the sound of her door shutting. A door that was exactly across the hall.

Jeff gave up on the plans. He decided to make a quick dash for the stairs when—oops! He dropped down so fast, he nearly hit his head when her door opened again. He'd had a quick glimpse of her toweled head. Tanny was singing absentmindedly. She returned to the bathroom, but he did not hear the door shut. He heard a hair dryer start up.

Now what?

Jeff just wanted to get out to the barn. Forget food. Forget coffee. But the bathroom door was open with a direct line of sight down the stairs. Jeff reasoned that if he could get to the wall beside his door, he could flatten himself there until either Tanny went back to her bedroom or shut the bathroom door, *then* he could hot-foot it down the stairs.

He could vault the bed....

Jeff heard, "Where's my...?" and the hair dryer switched off.

He dropped his head again and heard feet padding to her room. But he didn't hear the door shut. There were rustling sounds like clothes being put on as she hummed. Jeff put his head in his hands. *If she finds me here, how on earth do I explain this?*

There is more rustling. *Is she dressing? Had she not been dressed?* The humming continued. *Was that a "zip"?* Her player started a new song with a strong beat.

"There you are!" Tanny cried.

Jeff jumped while simultaneously realizing she had said it across the hall in her room. Her feet started thumping again. The trapped paramedic peeked under his bed to see two bare feet in jeans, dancing down the floor. *She is dressed!* He sighed in relief.

He lifted his head slowly, hoping she wouldn't see him behind the pillows. There was Tanny fully dressed, dancing with a round hairbrush, eyes shut, wet curling tendrils swaying. She froze at a dramatic point in the music and wailed, "When I finally find, FINALLY find MY LOVE!" She then shifted her hips and danced away out of sight into the bathroom.

Jeff considered leaping over the bed but Tanny hopped back into view, clearly lost in her world of music. She jogged back into her room, spun, danced back out, rounding the corner into the bathroom hopping on one foot in time to the beat. Jeff couldn't stop himself from watching. *She is annoyingly cute.* Tanny jogged back into the bathroom.

That's it. Jeff rolled quickly across the bed and came up beside the door. He peeked around the door frame. He could just see Tanny, hair blowing back from the dryer. She had a look of concentration as she did something mysterious with the strange round brush. Jeff realized that if she knew to look, she'd see him. The chorus of the song started again. Tanny whipped the dryer to her mouth as if it was a microphone only to splutter at the blast of hot air. She laughed and switched hands to sing into the brush instead. "When I finally find MY LOVE!"

Jeff pulled his head back. *This is private. I'm not meant to see any of this.*

Then came another refrain, and Tanny switched to add a high sweet line of harmony.

Mack's questioning face appeared in Jeff's doorway.

Mack! Jeff grabbed his shepherd-mix and dragged him out of sight, blood pounding.

"Down!" he whispered, pushing Mack down.

But there was no gasp and yell. The hairdryer was still humming away. *Okay. She didn't see. How do I salvage this?*

Jeff peeked around the door frame. Tanny's stringy mop was becoming a soft, fluffy cloud. There was a pleasant, feminine smell. He had a hard time not watching her. She was mesmerizing. He absently ran a hand over his prickly pate. Then he noticed that Mack was standing out in the hall.

Jeff caught Mack's eye and pointed hard to his side. Mack simply looked confused and didn't move. Jeff peeked around the corner to realize Tanny had disappeared into the far side of the bathroom.

Seized with desperation, Jeff grabbed Mack's collar and dashed down the steps. He grabbed his boots and moved out of sight into the kitchen, hopping while putting them on. He saw his plans sitting on the kitchen counter. He remembered putting them there now.

He contemplated pouring himself some of that coffee.

"Ain't nothin' love can't dooooo," Tanny was singing. But then she stopped. "Hi Mack," she said.

Jeff swore under his breath.

"Mack? What're you doing here?"

The tall paramedic grabbed his plans and sprinted for the back door like the devil was after him. *Didn't he have some meal bars in the workshop? He'd have to get another coffeemaker for out there too.*

Tanny scratched Mack under the ears and crooned to him. "Hellooo gorgeous. Where's your master? Is he back?" She looked down the stairs and called, "Jeff? Are you here?" She would have to get his cell number so she could text him—so they could communicate if he disappeared like he did this morning.

Tanny had woken to find neither sight nor sound of the Jeff from her childhood. His bed had been made. Tanny wanted to find out if Herman could make the trip home soon or if she'd have to take a bus. She finished everything upstairs, even putting on a touch of make-up, and descended to the kitchen. Her hair had come out really well. Tanny assured herself that she had put in a real effort on her appearance only because any self-respecting girl keeps herself looking good. But the niggle in her stomach told her that maybe she wasn't being honest. She was both relieved and disappointed that Jeff wasn't around to share breakfast.

The coffee was still on, so she poured herself the second cup and switched the machine off. She had wondered how long Jeff was going to be out and had made the second cup for him. Oh well! So, she got two cups this morning.

She looked around the large, renovated space and really took it in in the daylight. The snow had stopped, and the sun was out. The brilliant white light filled the space, highlighting every change and detail. *These new windows!* Where there had once been a masonry wall with narrow windows there was now a window wall facing a lovely view. Britt had even put a deck on the other side of the windows with outdoor seating. But now, everything was covered in white, the chairs, the pines, the scrub brush, the hills, even the inlet was blanketed. It must have been cold enough for it to still be frozen over. Tanny's eyes scanned the warm expanse of the interior and stopped on the great stone fireplace. This space had once been chopped into three, the kitchen, the living, and the dining room, with no attention paid to any view. Now the view travelled from the dining room to the living room. From the couches one could enjoy the fireplace and the view. Tanny realized that her bedroom sat above the living room, so she must have the same view from up there if she bothered to look.

Tanny sipped her coffee and moved to the mantel. There were Britt's special pictures. There was an old black and white one which must be of the French family Britt knew during the war. There was young Britt sandwiched between two handsome young Frenchman and a young woman.

There was another black-and white photo of the same young woman with one of the young men, holding a baby. That baby must be Britt's godson—what was his name? Pierre? The next images were a triptych of what must be the godson as he grew: one when he was an early teen, one when he was a young man with a bride, and one again with his wife and two small boys. Sweet! They were a nice-looking family. The godson looked particularly pleasant. It was like she was looking at a friend. Tanny wondered if Britt had written to or heard from her godson much through the years. Perhaps his parents had been writing to her. How else did Britt get these pictures?

Tanny was surprised to find that the next picture was of Jeff when he was a young man. He was in his late teens, but recognizably him. In this picture he was standing with his arm around Britt in front of Cedar Haven. His thick hair was golden-brown; it matched his eyes. And did he have man-dimples? With that hair and that smile he was rather handsome.

Jeff finally came in around three in the afternoon. Mack greeted him at the door, whining. "Oh, now you want to listen to me?" Jeff said to his dog. "Do you need to go out?" Mack wagged his tail. Jeff let him out. He shut the door and slowly removed his boots, then his coat.

Tanny was poking through the cupboards. She greeted him warmly and asked how his day was going.

Good. She has no idea about me hiding in my bedroom. He said, "I'm getting some good work done out in the barn. I came in to get a sandwich," not meeting her eyes.

Tanny closed the cupboard door and said, "The barn? Were you working on Herman?"

Jeff remembered throwing a porcupine at "Herman" followed by hot kisses and was pretty certain his face was giving him away. But he said, "Herman? No. I have a workshop out there."

Tanny said, "Oh. I thought.... So, when you have a minute, would you please look at Herman with me and tell me if I can drive him home?"

Jeff thought, *I want to do a lot more than look at Herman with you, damn it.* But he made himself look her in the eye, calling on his professional demeanor and said, "Of course. How about after I eat something?"

Tanny was taken aback by the dilated pupils he turned on her. She had seen the flaming red neck and cheeks and wondered what was going on in his head. *Was he smoking weed out there? Is he ashamed and lying about it? Is that why he's so red and his pupils are dilated?* She said, "Great. I need to go home in two days, and I need to find another way if he's kaput."

The man formerly known as "Jeffy" grabbed the bread and a jar of peanut butter. His man-dimples were out in full force as he deftly whipped up a sandwich. He turned and leaned on the counter. He said, "I will do my best to insure he is not 'kaput.'"

Tanny felt a flutter as the big man faced her. He was ripped! Would she be safe out in the barn with him?

Meanwhile, Jeff was thinking "kaput?" *Who talks like that?* He was trying not to smile too broadly. He asked, "Why did you come? No one told me you were coming." He took a big bite of his sandwich. He could feel his flush receding and hoped she hadn't noticed.

Tanny leaned on the counter facing him. "I called Uncle Jacob and let him know. Well, I left a voicemail."

Jeff nodded and took another bite. He said around his mouthful, "Jacob doesn't have a cell phone. You never know if he gets his voicemail."

Tanny's voice was smaller. "Oh." There was a silence. "I'm sorry. You see, I just lost my job, and I needed a break, so I thought I'd come up here a few days. But I didn't realize—I thought.... I just thought you were an old geezer so I could just stay here without there being a problem—"

Jeff choked on his sandwich and was laughing and coughing at the same time. "An old geezer! Why did you think that?" Eventually he recovered. He grabbed himself a seltzer from the fridge. "Sorry. Go on. I'm an old geezer." *Because you completely forgot about me from our childhood while I have been unable to forget you.*

"I—" Tanny sounded apologetic, "I didn't realize that Jacob wouldn't clear it with the old, well, with you. I know my folks would have a fit if they knew we were sleeping together—I mean, in the same house." Now it was her turn to be flaming red.

Jeff was struggling not to remember sleeping with her in his dreams. He also grinned at her slip. How he wished it was Freudian! He said, "I'm guessing Jacob and Eileen won't be thrilled to discover it either." He took another bite.

"Maybe I should just leave today? If Herman is capable, that is."

Jeff waved his seltzer in dismissal before taking a sip. "Look, I have no intention of molesting you. It's just not my thing. I'm into full consent." He said this with a smile that showed his understanding of the fearfulness of the older generation. *In his dreams he'd had full consent....*

Tanny flipped her hair and promised, "And I will not lure you with my irresistible femininity. You are safe with me." Her adorable dimples were back.

Too late, was Jeff's thought as he stoically finished his sandwich. He knew she was safe with him, but it was not going to be easy or comfortable. Wiping his hands he said, "I'm ready to go. Are you?"

"Oh! Sure!" she leapt for her coat and boots.

Tanny enjoyed Jeff's presence, though she had trouble reading him. She liked the feeling of walking beside him across the snowy yard towards the barn. Being a steward with him wasn't going to be bad at all, she thought.

He let her into the large upper expanse of the barn where he had stashed Herman.

"Hey, Herman. How are you feeling?" Tanny said walking slowly around the old car. She ran her mitted hand along the grey-blue flanks.

"Why don't you try starting him up?" suggested Jeff.

Tanny looked at Jeff, liking the way the thick toque framed his face. He was actually quite nice looking. She could see the boy beneath the man, like a layered image. She felt a wave of affection as memories returned of their many adventures. "Okay," she said.

She got herself into the front seat and turned the key. Herman started up with a noisy growl. Startled, Tanny turned the key to off.

"It sounds like the muffler has come loose," said Jeff, looking thoughtfully at her wounded steed. "I will see if I can get it reattached, though it can be driven as is. It will just be very noisy."

"Yes please; try to fix it, I mean. When might you fit it in?" Tanny found herself hoping he couldn't fix it today. She was loving being at Cedar Haven and liking getting to know Jeff again.

"I can start right now. I just need to get my tools."

"Oh. Cool. Thank you." Tanny tried to muster more gratitude than she was feeling. After an awkward pause she said, "Uh, I was thinking of throwing together a stir fry with stuff I found in the freezer. Maybe I'll go do that now? Or do you want my help?"

Jeff waved her away. "I can do this on my own. And I will appreciate *any* hot meals you feel inspired to make—that is, if you were intending to share?"

"Of course! It's the least I can do for all your help. Thank you!" Tanny nearly fled back to the house. Why was she feeling flustered? She realized that she felt ashamed of her need for help from this man. She felt like an interruption and a burden.

Meanwhile, Jeff felt a wave of relief that she had gone. He knew how to be alone building or repairing things. But he also realized that once Herman was repaired, this irresistible, adorable woman would be leaving his life again. He sighed. It was probably for the best.

Sixteen

February 23, later

$\mathcal{T}$anny found rice in the cupboard and veggies in the freezer. She also found frozen burger patties which she figured she could chop into chunks in the stir fry. She found some tahini and a bunch of spices and was satisfied. She didn't have onions but there were minced onions among the spices. She would make do. She got the vegetables and meat out to thaw, but decided it was too early to start cooking yet.

She wandered around the main floor. There was a den across the front hall from the kitchen. It had been Britt's office, so Tanny pushed the door open and looked in. This room had not been touched by the renovations. It still had the original windows and custom bookshelves lining the walls. There was the big, roll-top desk, covered in papers. Had anyone looked through them? There was a small bed in the corner, and pictures everywhere. Again, Tanny strolled around looking at the photos.

This room had a lot of the Bender family photos. There was young Britt with her brothers and their parents. That one must have been taken shortly before the original house burned down. They were in front of a two-story log cabin, sitting where Cedar Haven stood today. Both of Britt's brothers had the sticking-out Bender ears, while Britt had escaped them. All three of the children had the rich brown Bender eyes, like their father, though the mother looked Scandinavian. Tanny couldn't remember who her great-great grandmother had been. She had a niggling feeling that she might have been an Inquist, which meant that Tanny was related somehow to the bossy and generally disapproving Margaret Inquist—a never-married, large blond woman who was a significant presence at the church. Margaret *never* kept her thoughts to herself.

Tanny speculated that the occasional blond, blue-eyed Benders came from recessive Inquist genes, if Inquist genes they were. Susan's dad, Noah, had had that Nordic look, as did Cousin Isaiah, and her own brother, Liam. But most of the Benders had brown eyes, and bunches had ears that stuck out a bit.

Tanny pressed her own ears flat against her head. Hers weren't too bad, though she often liked to cover them with her hair. Gorgeous Susan had flat ears, as did her girls. Some people got all the breaks!

Thinking about ears gave Tanny pause. She moved back to look at the pictures on the mantel. Britt's godson had ears like Tanny's. They stuck out a bit too. He had brown eyes that looked so familiar....

Wait. What? Tanny looked carefully at the picture of the godson with his boys. The younger boy had ears that stood out like Will's. They stood out like Maggie's and Ingrid's, Micah's and Ivan's, and so many more of the cousins. *What? Could the baby possibly be Britt's baby?*

Tanny moved back to look at the picture of Britt with the young adults from France. The taller young man was standing close to Britt. The second woman looked so much like the taller man it was almost comical. Was this a picture of two sibling with their sweethearts?

Tanny looked again hard at the baby, the young teen, the young groom and the young father. She felt goose bumps rise along her arms. *That man could absolutely be Britt's son. That would explain the family resemblance in his kids. And in him.*

The fire crackled. Tanny's eyes tracked back and forth between the pictures. Did that tall Frenchman have his arm around Britt in the picture? Or was he simply slightly behind her? *Am I just being my ridiculously imaginative self?* No one had ever implied anything about Britt falling in love in France let alone having a baby. Britt had always been independent! What had she said? "I will only ever marry a man I can't live without. And so far, there isn't a man alive that I can't live without!"

There isn't a man alive.... What if Britt had been in love with this Frenchman, and he had died in the war?

Tanny stomped her foot and shook herself. There she went again, imagining secret loves for Britt, and she'd just seen how well that had turned out. Britt's "secret love" at Cedar Haven had turned out to be Tanny's age. She sighed. She decided to go out and see how Herman was coming along.

Covering a mug of fresh coffee with her mitt, she walked carefully across the yard to the barn. She wondered if maybe she should leave tonight if Herman was ready in time? She felt a bit leaden at the idea. She didn't want to leave.

She pushed open the door to the large, dim space and called out, "Jeff? I brought you some coffee. How's it going?" She couldn't see him anywhere. The space seemed empty besides Herman. Just then she heard a phone ring in the depths of the barn. She ran around the car to go find it, felt weight catch her feet, heard a grunt, and found herself airborne, the coffee flying out ahead of her. She spread her hands to break her fall. She slid on her hands and chest until coming to a stop.

"Owwwwwww." Tanny just lay there, absorbing that she had tripped over Jeff's feet and thrown his coffee all over the floor. At least she hadn't gotten any on herself. The mug had even survived. The wide wooden planks must have been soft enough to cushion its fall. They had also left several splinters in her palms. Tanny heard a scrambling as she pulled herself up to a sitting position to assess the damage. She felt winded and achy. She noticed that both knees felt skinned though her jeans looked okay. Her palms were scraped and bleeding a bit and she had several splinters. She had started sucking on the heel of her right hand when she felt Jeff's presence at her side.

Jeff's heart was racing as he knelt beside Tanny. He was relieved to see that she was sitting up, but the tripod position could mean that she was having trouble breathing. He assessed her quickly. Her color was good; she seemed alert; her breathing was not laboured.

Jeff put a gentle hand on her back and looked into her face. "Hey. Are you okay? Can you tell me your name?"

Tanny laughed. "I'm Margaret fricking Atwood, Jeff. Who do you think I am?"

Jeff chuckled, but took her chin and turned her face slightly, looking into her eyes. He was checking for unusual eye-tracking or changes in her pupils. He released her chin. "Does it hurt anywhere?" He held up a finger and asked her asked to follow it with her eyes as he moved it around. She seemed okay.

"My hands hurt, and my knees, and my pride. But I'm otherwise fine. Except I spilled your coffee."

Jeff sat back on his heels and looked towards the spill. He swiped a hand over his eyes, feeling the concern for her settle until he wanted to laugh.

"You didn't just spill that coffee; you launched it into outer space. Are you sure you are okay?"

"I didn't see you from the doorway. Then I heard the phone, so I ran around Herman to go answer it. The next thing I know, I'm flying across the barn and throwing fresh, hot coffee all over the floor. Seriously. Who has such big feet?"

Jeff watched the wisps of hair dance around her temples as Tanny focused on her palms. He could hear the laugh she struggled to hide. "Let's get you into the house and clean up those hands," he suggested. "Can you walk?" When she struggled to get up without putting weight on her palms, he put an arm around her waist and a hand under her elbow and helped her.

"I can walk," Tanny said shrugging his hands off. Jeff fetched the fallen mug. "Did you finish fixing Herman by any chance?" Tanny asked, holding her hands stiffly; they were probably painful.

"I was partway done attaching the muffler when somebody tripped over my apparently enormous feet," he answered. "So, no; not yet." They walked back to the house, Jeff keeping a hand ready if she slipped on the packed snow.

Once inside, Jeff settled Tanny at the kitchen island under the bright lights, then went to grab the first aid kit. He returned with Dettol, tweezers, cotton pads, gauze, medical tape, and a lot more. He took the seat next to Tanny and asked her consent for him to clean and disinfect her palms.

Tanny meanwhile was still recovering from the shock of her fall. She was also noticing how distracting Jeff's presence was. She had felt every second of his hold on her chin, the strength of his arms as he lifted her, and the intensity with which he looked into her eyes from so close to her. She was struck by his concentration and efficiency. There was nothing sexual about his attention, yet she felt decidedly aware of him as a man.

Tanny watched Jeff's face and profile as he carefully swabbed and examined her hands. His touch was confident yet gentle. It felt remarkably intimate even as he was working so clinically to find and remove splinters. *He has a nicely shaped head.* She saw that his hair was starting to grow out a bit. She noticed the faint golden hue among the stubble and asked without thinking, "Why do you shave your head?" Then she kicked herself inwardly. *That's none of my business!*

He took a firmer grip of her right palm and said, "Hang on. This might hurt a bit." He yanked, pulling a big splinter free. While he set it carefully on some gauze he said, without looking at her, "Every few years I donate my hair for cancer. I just got it done last week. It's easiest to get my head shaved afterwards and start fresh. Take a deep breath—"

Tanny gasped as the next splinter came free. *He cuts his hair for cancer?* The shiver that went through her was more than respect. She was silent a while and then observed, "You seem to have medical training." She winced as another splinter came out.

Jeff swabbed her palm checking for more splinters. "There's one," he said under his breath and shifted his grip. "I work part-time as a paramedic." He yanked the next one free. There was a tidy stack of splinters growing on the gauze. He looked up at her then, from only a few inches away. Her heart began to race as she watched his pupils go from normal to dilated. He set her hand down and stood up, turning his back to her. "Perhaps I went into overdrive when you fell. It's my train-ing." He took a few steps away, still presenting his back and gave a light laugh. "Maybe you'd like to finish up by yourself now? The worst of the splinters are out." He grabbed the unbroken mug and walked it to the sink.

The last thing Tanny wanted was for Jeff to stop working on her. Something intense had just happened between them. When Jeff's pupils had dilated Tanny had felt intensely attracted to him. She felt that she wanted to fall into him—into his eyes, his soul, his whole self without reservation. Now it seemed as if a door to a big, warm space had just closed, leaving her outside in the chill. She barely knew Jeff, but she couldn't deny the powerful draw he had for her. Though she had not been with him even twenty-four hours, she wanted him to come back and hold her hands and bend his head again. She wanted him close to her.

Tanny wanted to know so much more about this tall, golden-eyed paramedic.

Jeff turned sideways to her. He said, "I have a shift starting at seven tomor-row morning. You may not see much of me after that. So, I will try to reattach your muffler before tonight. But if I can't, I can point you to several mechanics in Bracebridge."

Tanny felt him pulling away and ached.

"Thank you for bringing me coffee," he continued. "I'm glad you weren't hurt too badly when you fell."

The phone rang in Britt's office and Jeff left like a jackrabbit to answer it, leaving Tanny alone with her splinters. She picked up the tweezers and got to work.

As Tanny was wrapping gauze around her right palm, Jeff returned to the kitchen. He still wouldn't meet her eyes. He said, "That was Uncle Jacob. He's wondering if you arrived, and how long you thought you would be staying." Jeff rubbed the back of his neck. "He wants you to go stay with them until you leave because, well, you know."

Tanny groaned. She rolled her eyes ceilingward. After thinking things over she said, "I think that if Uncle Jacob wants to invite me over, he can ask me directly, and not through a messenger. Even if he does, I will turn him down, as all my stuff is here and I'm leaving tomorrow anyway." There was a pause as Tanny sat, her face weary. "I wonder how long until mom is calling in an effort to save my virtue."

Jeff felt the pull of Tanny's dilemma and felt a similar frustration. They were both nearly thirty! Even when he had been a teenager, consent had been his pri-mary code. He had never liked the feeling of being policed.

Why did adults of a certain persuasion think that all young people, regardless of taste, orientation, or moral code, would leap into bed the minute they were left alone together? The data wasn't there. Basic psychology wasn't there. It was maddening.

Jeff had never felt like he couldn't control himself around a woman. Women weren't objects, they were thinking, feeling beings. He wouldn't cross anyone's boundaries any more than he wanted someone to cross his. He had never been with a woman intimately unless it was clearly mutual, and the boundaries were understood. His first experience had been when he was seventeen. He and a friend of many years had been speculating about how to negotiate a first time. While they had discussed it, they broached the idea of leaping over that waterfall together, in the safety of their friendship, just to check off that box. So, they had. Neither of them expected it to become anything else, and it hadn't. He felt a tenderness toward her that would never change, but they had gone on with their lives, grateful, but not attached. Every sexual relationship for Jeff since had been thoughtful, consensual, and ended with good will. All three of them.

Besides, Tanny had forgotten all about him. They were starting at the beginning, if they had a relationship at all. Even if they were beginning a relationship, they were both old enough to make their own choices. They didn't need policing. The problem was, in that older generation's way of thinking, they assumed sexual activity was there the minute they suspected it. And the consequences always landed more on the woman than the man. This made him feel extra protective of Tanny.

Jeff stole a look in Tanny's direction. He realized it was a good thing that she was leaving. He desired her like he had never desired a woman before. *Was* she safe with him? He certainly wanted to think so! But he was increasingly aware that the two of them could—might, possibly fall into something spontaneous. Even though it would be consensual, if it was discovered, they would become the objects of gossip in her world. He couldn't let that happen. Unfortunately, the thought that he and Tanny might be overcome by passion did not help the fit of his pants.

"I'm going to see if I can finish the muffler," he muttered, grabbing his coat, glad it was long and bulky. "Coming, Mack?"

Tanny watched Jeff go, emotions swirling. She had realized this time that his eyes had widened from attraction, (not from smoking weed). She was stunned that someone could have that level of attraction for her. She was trying to take in the undisputable evidence, even as she realized that the attraction was completely mutual now. She didn't really know him, but she *felt* like she knew him. She didn't know about his original family, or who his friends were, or his taste in music; but what she did know stunned her. He had loved Aunt Britt; he really loved Cedar Haven. He was a paramedic; and he fricking donated his hair for cancer!

Tanny wanted to follow Jeff out to the barn and ask him so many questions. But Jeff had clearly closed a door. She was wondering if there was a way to draw him into conversation later when her cell phone rang. It was Aunt Eileen.

"Hi Tanny! How are you? Jacob and I wanted to invite you over for a meal and to stay while you're up here. How does that sound?"

Tanny rubbed a gauze-wrapped hand over her face. She then thanked her kindly aunt for the thought and wished it could have worked. She let her know that Jeff was out in the barn trying to fix her broken car (so no way to get over there) and then she was leaving Bracebridge tomorrow. She fended off questions about which bedroom she was enjoying, steering the conversation to the amazing renovations. She then asked about Eileen's mother, which lead into several stories about the Flaherty family. Finally, she asked Eileen if she could speak to Uncle Jacob.

Once Jacob had come to the phone Tanny asked him, "Hey, now that Sue and Jon are back from their honeymoon, can we schedule our first meeting of the stewards of Cedar Haven? I have so many questions about what is expected of us. I want to be part of the decisions. I want to hear about the upgrades and Jeff's duties, and everything. I mean, should I have a key, for example? It seems like a lot is happening, and I want to be up to speed."

Jacob responded, "Well, I didn't want to rush things, but sure; we should definitely schedule a meeting."

Then silence. Tanny realized that Jacob wasn't going to follow up that statement with action, so she suggested, "Perhaps Sue and I could come up in a few weeks so we can all meet here? That would make it easy for everyone. How about the weekends of the twenty-first or the twenty-seventh of March? I'd have to check with both Jeff and Susan, but it would be good to get something on the calendar anyway."

There was a pause while Jacob considered. He said, "I'm sure either would work fine. I have all the paperwork here. I meant to get everyone their copies, but I guess I never got around to it."

"Could you please just email them to us all, Uncle Jacob? Do you have the electronic copies?"

"Ummm, yes. Of course I do. I'm sure Eileen can help me get them to you. We'll try to do that tonight." Tanny heard Eileen's, "What are we doing tonight?" in the background.

"Thanks Uncle Jacob." Tanny had been pacing around the kitchen. She stopped to look out towards the barn. The dusk was gathering. She saw the lights in the barn go out and Jeff exiting the big door. "I need to go now, Uncle Jacob. Thanks for answering my questions. It was good to talk." Tanny received Jacob's farewell and ended the call. Jeff was circling around toward the lower floor of the barn, where the snowmobile was parked.

Disappointed, Tanny turned to the unmade stir-fry and began to put it together, bandaged hands and all.

Seventeen

February 23 to February 24

*I*t was much later when Jeff came into the house, banging his boots on the door frame to knock off extra snow. He had disappeared on his snowmobile for a long while and then started up the truck and plowed the driveway of the extra inch of snow that had fallen that day.

Tanny had covered the finished stir-fry and set it on warm. She had then started gathering her things back into her suitcase, ready for the trip home tomorrow. She was drinking tea and researching on an online genealogy program when Jeff finally came in, Mack frolicking at his side.

Tanny jumped up and grabbed Mack before he tracked snow everywhere even as Jeff's sharp, "Mack!" reminded the big dog to stay in the entry. Tanny grabbed one of the big towels on the floor for the purpose and started toweling the dog's fur and paws.

"I've made a stir-fry if you'd like some. There should be enough for leftovers too," said Tanny. She tried to ignore the close quarters, and the two times they bumped butts as they respectively wrestled with the dog and winter boots.

Jeff grunted his approval, setting his boots on the mat and hanging his coat in the closet. He dragged off his toque and ran a hand over his stubble.

Tanny had danced away into the kitchen as soon as she could. "I found some red wine," she added. "I'm going to have some with dinner. Would you like some too?"

"I'll get a beer," he said. "First I need to feed Mack." The husky-shepherd mix was already by his big metal bowl, whining.

"Let me refill his water," Tanny said, and reached down to grab the water dish in time to bump heads with Mack's master.

"Oh! Sorry!" Tanny said, having splashed slobber-dregs over her wrist. The gauze was slowly soaking it up.

Jeff took the water dish from her and said, "Sit. I got this." He pressed her gently into one of the stools at the counter—the stool where the gauze and scissors were still sitting. Flustered, Tanny removed the soggy gauze and re-wrapped her palm in fresh bandages. They had gotten a bit soiled during cooking anyway.

Once Jeff had set the special mix down for Mack and refilled the water he washed his hands, grabbed a beer, and got two plates. He started serving the stir fry. Tanny tidied the medical supplies aside and got herself a glass of wine.

"It smells great," Jeff said, putting plates down for both of them.

Then they both sat, facing each other across the center island.

Tanny realized that she felt the old habit of blessing the food rise up, but didn't know what Jeff's habits were. Jeff bowed his head, and she watched his lips move. Clearly, he had some habit, probably from Aunt Eileen and Uncle Jacob, but he was keeping it private. She bowed her own head and ran through a blessing in her mind. When she looked up, Jeff's glance moved to his plate, and he began to eat. She sipped her wine.

The silence stretched, their eyes dancing away if they caught each other looking up. Jeff took another scoop of the stir fry.

Finally, Tanny said, "I'm assuming you fixed Herman? If so, I can't thank you enough."

Jeff waved his beer glass and said, "I did. I can't guarantee the muffler will hold, but I bought you a bit of time. Just don't go over any big bumps." He got up to let Mack out for a romp once his dinner was finished.

After another long pause he said, "I will need to be away from the house by six tomorrow morning. Can you leave the house through the garage? That way you can leave it locked."

"Of course," responded Tanny. "Again, sorry for showing up unannounced." She hesitated then asked, "Might we exchange cell numbers or emails so I can contact you directly next time?"

Jeff felt a lurch in his stomach. He would love to have her cell number. He swallowed and said, "That's a good idea." He pulled up his phone. "Tell me your number and I'll send you my contact information." He typed in her number, feeling a swoop of joy. He asked, "So, should I list you as 'Britannia?' Or just 'Tanny?'" He was half teasing.

Tanny made a face and said, "Tanny, please! I loved Aunt Britt, but I don't want to be confused with her." She sat up straight, holding her fingertips to one ear and said, "Afterlife Switchboard; how may I direct your call? Britannia Bender? One moment please," and she mimed plugging lines into an invisible wall. She froze mid pantomime and looked at Jeff. "Why do I think the technology in heaven is way behind the times?" She dropped her arms and dimpled. "Just 'Tanny Smith' is fine."

Jeff was glad to drop his eyes to his phone and type her name in. He kept making mistakes, so distracted was he by her adorable looks and behaviour. Finally, he said, "There. I've sent you my information by text. That should give you my email and phone number."

Tanny was watching her phone. When there was a ding, she opened his information with a look of apparent delight. She added him to her address book. "Great," she said, and sighed, putting her phone down.

"This is good," Jeff said, eyes on his food so as not to look at her.

Tanny told him she would put the leftovers in the fridge for him.

Jeff was aware she was looking at him, and, using a long, slow breath he steeled himself to return her glance.

But she jumped up, going to put the leftovers away as she had said.

"Don't you want to finish first?" Jeff asked, noticing her unfinished dinner and wine. He took a long pull at his beer wishing he would stop feeling so intensely aware and self-conscious.

Tanny stopped and turned, looking surprised. "Oh!" she said. "Of course. Silly me." She considered. "But while I'm up I might as well do this. It has been sitting out a while and it's best to get it in the fridge."

Jeff tried not to stare at her shapely figure as her back was turned. *Why did she have to be so desirable? What if she never reciprocated his feelings?*

Tanny popped the leftovers in the fridge and turned to face him, her eyes both happy and sheepish. She turned pink when their eyes met.

What if she already did reciprocate his feelings?

Jeff realized he had stopped breathing. He imagined his bounding pulse must be visible to the naked eye. He made himself look down at his plate and somehow scooped the last of the meal into his mouth. Tanny had returned slowly to her chair and was sitting tentatively, looking out the window. Jeff downed the last of his beer and stood up, holding his plate.

"Thanks again, Tanny. I have an early start so I'm heading up now." He took his plate to the dishwasher and set it in, dropping the silverware into the holder. He took a deep breath and said, turning, "So I might as well say goodbye now." He held out a hand.

Tanny launched herself at him, throwing her arms around him in a big hug. "It was great to see you again, Jeff," came her voice, muffled against his shoulder. Then she had sprung away and turned to clear her dishes.

Jeff needed a breath to regain his equilibrium. He had been ready for a proprietary handshake to keep things from getting steamy when she had vaulted into his arms. She had smelled feminine—both flowery and tantalizingly earthy. He had just realized she was in his arms when she had sprung as quickly away. Now her pink cheeks were barely visible as she made herself busy with the cleanup on the far side of the kitchen.

Gathering himself, Jeff said, "Safe drive tomorrow." He let Mack back in, dried his paws, and headed up to his room.

In the morning when Tanny awoke, she could feel the emptiness of the house. She sat up with the blankets gathered around her waist and stared out at the scrap of view she could see from her bed. It was grey and overcast. She opened her phone to check the weather. It was meant to be overcast but mild—above freezing anyway. The back roads might be slippery from snowmelt, but the main roads should be clear.

She took herself down to the lovely, empty-feeling kitchen, and started some coffee. Mack wasn't even there. Tanny wondered what Jeff did with Mack when he had a shift.

Tanny wrapped her arms around herself and walked over to the window-wall, looking out at the overcast day. The inlet no longer looked like a snowy plain. It was grey and smooth, probably treacherous ice. Tanny wandered over to the mantel and the mysterious photos. She decided to snap pictures of the images on her phone. So much had happened that weekend that she had not had time to follow up on all her questions about Britt's possible illegitimate son. *Were there Bender cousins in France?*

Tanny got herself some breakfast and poured her coffee into a travel mug for the road. When she went upstairs to finish up and close her bags, she stopped and looked into Jeff's room. This had been the room she and Jenny shared all those years ago. Jeff kept his bed made-up. There weren't clothes draped here and there. If only she could be that tidy! She rested a hand on the door frame, gazing in, not really looking at anything. Remembering moments and feelings.

The next thing Tanny knew she was lying on top of the bedclothes, remembering Aunt Britt, remembering the one time when Jenny had had a nightmare, and Britt had climbed in with them for the rest of the night. A bunch of fond memories assailed her, and her heart ached. Tanny flopped on her side and was immediately aware of the smell of the bedclothes. It was subtle, but recognizably

Jeff's. Tanny's pulse responded, and she got up, feeling like she was trespassing. She crossed the hall for her bags.

Tanny stopped once more in Jeff's doorway before she hefted her bags down the stairs. "Goodbye," she said. Then she headed down to go out through the basement.

Tanny's drive was uneventful. Her muffler even managed to hold on for the entire trip. She pulled into her parents' driveway, feeling a sinking sensation. Her life was unsettled and uncertain. The answers she had been looking for at Cedar Haven had just produced more questions—confusing questions, "what the heck am I doing with my life" questions.

Tanny considered that she had about five days until she and Jenny would be making the switch. Was she ready? The long list of things she had to do overwhelmed her.

"Just do the next thing," she told herself. The next thing was to unload the car and get unpacked. What she wanted to do was run over to Susan's to talk about Jeff. Maybe she could do that after she had unpacked? It was early afternoon.

Tanny's mom pushed open the front door and waved. She called something. Tanny exited her car. "Hey mom, I'm back."

Emily wanted to know how her drive was and about the other caretaker, whom she heard was a young man. "Eileen said you were staying in the house with him. Just the two of you. How... how did that go?"

It's like clockwork, Tanny thought. *So predictable.* She thought of several sarcastic things she could say but finally said, "Jeff has a great big shepherd-mix named Mack. He was gorgeous."

"Jeff?" Emily asked.

"Jeff VanGalen. Do you remember that Jacob and Eileen have a foster son? His name is Jeff. It turns out Jenny and Liam and Eric and I all met him that time you and dad vacationed in Prince Edward Island."

"I had forgotten they had a foster son," Emily said.

You and me both, thought Tanny.

"What is he like? Did he behave himself?" asked Tanny's mother.

Tanny hefted her bags into the front entrance of the house. She thought of several more sarcastic responses to her mom as she kicked off her boots. *He barked like a dog and licked crumbs off the floor....* She said, "He was a perfect gentleman. He takes good care of the place and even put Herman's muffler back on so I could drive home." Tanny carried her coat towards the top of the basement stairs and came back for her bags. "How were things here?"

Emily gave news about Eric's hockey exploits, Liam's new girlfriend ("she's not from a church family") and Will's on-and-off health problems. Had Tanny had lunch? Yes, from Tim Hortons. Emily announced that Jenny had made progress with the move while Tanny had been away. Tanny wasn't sure what to think of that last.

Finally, Tanny got her things down the stairs and shut the apartment door. She turned to see no couch. The living room furniture that was still there had been pushed onto the kitchen tile. Clearly the rug had been steam cleaned, and a fan was running to help dry it out.

Couldn't they have at least asked? Tanny thought. She hefted her bags over the damp rug as carefully as she could, then moved back towards her bedroom. At least her bed was still there. Her bathroom fan was running, she supposed to help vent the moisture out. She'd have to check in with Jennie to find out what had happened to her couch. She was too annoyed with her mom to talk to her just now.

Eventually Tanny had unpacked and was happy to discover that the living room rug was drier than she had feared. She could put the couch back tomorrow if she still had a couch. She checked in with Jenny to discover that her couch was over at Jenny's, taking up room.

"Mom's idea was to get your rug cleaned and then move my sofa over there. I convinced her not to throw yours out. Instead, it is jammed into my living room, with my sofa and chairs."

"That must be really crowded," Tanny commiserated.

"It really is. But Will is loving it. As long as he can watch his weather network or Raffi videos, he's happy. But just picture how fun it is to change DVDs for him when your couch is up against the tv cabinet."

"I'm sorry, Jenny."

"Hey. Don't worry about it. Fingers crossed, only five more days in this house! Barbara Millwood has been over helping me, and she's amazing. I feel very ready to move."

Tanny felt a squeezing in her heart. Jenny getting a home meant Tanny losing one. On her brave days, it felt like a brilliant idea to trade places. Today she just felt displaced and uneasy.

The world was moving on whether Tanny was ready or not. She needed a job! She needed a new car and her own place and financial stability! Tanny pushed her anxieties into a closet and gave them a valium lollipop.

Staring at the half-filled boxes around her place, Tanny called Susan. Jon answered the phone. He said Susan was sleeping, but could he help in any way?

Tanny sighed. No, she just wanted to talk to Sue. Jon reassured Tanny that Susan would get the message as soon as she was awake.

Tanny settled down to watch programs on her phone in her bed, as there was no couch to sit on. Darned if she was going to perch on a dining room chair to watch TV!

Before she did, she sent a text. "I'm home safe and sound. The muffler stayed on the whole way. Thanks."

She noticed Jeff was responding immediately. "That's great news. Thanks for letting me know." He added a thumbs up emoji.

Tanny wanted to say more but wasn't sure what to say. Finally, she typed, "Say hi to Mack."

There were the wiggling dots of an incoming message, then, "He says hi by slobbering on your hands and sitting on your feet. We both miss you."

Tanny sat frozen. *He said he misses me.* She typed, "I miss you both too." She wondered about asking about his shift, but hesitated, finally opting to leave it there.

Instead of watching shows on her phone, she curled up and relived memories and images of Jeff and Mack and Cedar Haven.

Eighteen

Thursday, February 25

Tanny awoke early, to rediscover the furniture crowded on the kitchen tile. She checked the rug and discovered it dry. She moved back what she could onto the rug, so that making breakfast was easier. Instant oatmeal and coffee. She needed to get fresh berries again.

As she sipped her coffee, Tanny felt a niggling of anxiety. What was she going to do? She guessed that she had to face moving more of Jenny's furniture over, and more of her own to fill Jenny's house. She realized she'd be using Jenny's couch until the final big switch. Well, that was a perk! Jenny's couch was very comfortable.

It was another dark, overcast day. Life near the Great Lakes in winter did include a lot of grey days. Down here in Kitchener there wasn't the snow cover that had brightened the world in Bracebridge. Snow made the world feel bright, especially under these overcast skies. But today it was just gloomy. Tanny hoped there would be more snow to freshen and lighten the outdoors again soon.

Tanny reached for her journal. She hadn't written in it for months, and she knew it always did her good. It helped focus her thoughts, clarify her yearnings, and help her set directions, especially when she felt overwhelmed. What she really wanted to do was text Jeff; but she didn't feel justified. So, she found a pen and got writing.

At around eight thirty, her phone buzzed. It was Susan.

"Hi, Tanny! I heard you called. I just got the twins off to school and had a moment of quiet over breakfast. Now I'm finally dressed. Want to come over for coffee—assuming you want a visit and catch-up?"

"Yes please!" said Tanny. "We are way overdue. Can I come right now?"

"Of course. It will be so good to see you. It feels like ages. Come right now."

Tanny rung off and ran upstairs with her coat to grab her boots. As she was reaching to put one on, her mother came down the stairs.

"Sweetheart!" began Emily. "I'm glad I caught you. I've accepted the job for you."

"You what?"

"Yes. Fifi Dunkirk-Jones is indeed looking for live-in help in Ben Kirk. She wants someone more mature than a student and doesn't want someone from outside the religion. It's like it is made for you! I'm sure she will pay well, in American dollars too. I accepted the job for you. I think you should confirm it immediately."

"You can still get a ride down with Stephen and Jon when they go to the ministers' meetings."

"Mom! I can't believe you accepted it for me. I will have to cancel it. Right now, I have somewhere to be." Tanny hurriedly shoved on her boots and exited the house.

She let out a noisy, frustrated sigh once she was far enough from the house. Everything was coming at her too fast. She wished her mother would stop interfering! First her living room, and now this job that Tanny would have to beg off. Tanny quickened her steps across the white pine needle strewn back yard and onto the winter-browned grass of the Renn—no, Haley's back yard. Soon she was knocking on Susan's side door and entering the mud room to Susan's warm, welcoming hug.

"Ohhh my gosh," grunted Susan, giving an extra final squeeze. "So much has happened since we last visited!"

Tanny had squeezed back and agreed whole heartedly. This was Susan, not the distracted, otherwise engaged woman of the past few weeks. "I have so much to ask you, and so much to tell you."

Susan said, "What happened to your hands?"

Tanny looked down at her scabbed palms. She no longer used the gauze, but they looked pretty sore. "Oh, I tripped in the barn up there. I got a bunch of splinters, but we got them all out. They're not too bad. I'm a quick healer." *And my stomach is flipping at the memory of Jeff cleaning them for me.*

"My gosh, Tanny. First Charm died, and then you lost your job. And I heard something about Jenny getting your apartment. And you hurt yourself. What is going on? Are you okay? Where are you going to live?"

They had moved into the kitchen where Susan flicked on a waiting coffee maker and indicated a chair at the kitchen table. Tanny enjoyed the wide, gentle view that stretched beyond the kitchen's large picture window. As the coffee burbled, Tanny described the plan to move into Jenny's house while they prepared it to sell; then she didn't know where she'd go. She mentioned the job in Ben Kirk that her mother was pushing on her.

Susan sat up straighter and said, "We've been thinking about finishing the basement apartment here. You could totally move in here if you needed to—that is if we finish it in time."

Tanny's heart jumped at the idea. To live in their house, but in her own apartment. It would be ideal. She would see Susan (and Jon, and the girls) much more regularly, rather than her mother!

"I love that idea!" she said to Susan. Susan was rising, and the coffee had come ready. She took out two mugs then paused, looking pale.

Susan said, "Help yourself. I ... think I will have tea instead." Susan moved to put the kettle on and select a tea bag.

Tanny poured her coffee and helped herself to cream. She stood, staring at the overcast skyline.

Susan turned a wan face to Tanny as she waited by the kettle. She sighed and said, "Tanny, it's too soon to know for sure, but I think I might be pregnant."

Tanny startled, just managing not to spill her coffee, which she quickly set down. "No. What? Really? That's excellent!" She grabbed Susan around the shoulders. Susan drooped a little in the hug.

Tanny slowly let go, realizing Susan's lack of enthusiasm. She said, "You're ... not happy about this?"

Susan shrugged. "I mean, I haven't even missed my period yet, but my appetite is off, my boobs ache, and my guts feel ... heavy? I feel ... that full, crampy feeling. And I'm suddenly so tired! I haven't actually mentioned it to Jon yet. I need to wait at least until I miss my period and get a positive test result to tell him. So, this goes no further. But it is SO SOON. We hadn't planned this at all. We were going to wait and jell as a family and then add more children." Susan paused. "I'm too exhausted to be happy." Even Susan's hair looked tired.

Tanny looked puzzled. "So, you hadn't planned this. What happened? The condom broke?"

Sue's gaze went into the middle distance. Her cheeks flooded rosily.

Tanny, realizing said, "You ... didn't.... Oh, Susie! You got carried away, is that it? You didn't have time for a condom?"

Sue, laughing and full of misery, covered her face with her hands. She was unable to hide a smile. "Oh Tanny. It was... I never knew it could be like that."

Tanny was thinking about it. "Oh my. Oh ... my...." She sighed. "You lucky girl."

Sue pushed her cousin with both fists, her face both happy and scared. She added, "I was going to go back to school for my voice. So, this is probably God's way of saying, 'Look honey. Your voice is not that good.'"

"Don't be an ass, Sue. Your voice is too that good. And God doesn't work that way. Besides! You're going to have a baby, Sue. A baby! Well, maybe. Maybe a baby. Jon's baby. Yours and Jon's! Good grief, the world's going to need sunglasses to look at him, he's going to be that beautiful!—or her!' she added.

"It's easy for you to be excited," complained Susan. "You're not facing months of vomiting and fatigue and swollen ankles." Susan paused. "Do you realize that this time last year, I didn't even know Jon existed? And now I'm carrying his child?"

"I know!" Tanny said with emphasis, grinning.

Sue made a noise of exasperation. "It's too fast. It's too soon. We were going to wait."

Tanny sobered. "You're genuinely afraid."

Sue nodded, tears welling.

Tanny took the young bride into her arms, crooning, "I'm sorry. I'm so sorry. Here you are, panicking, and I'm just laughing. I'll shut up now. Please tell me."

Sue, crying softly murmured, "It's just.... It's just that ... I'm scared. Tanny, what if it's twins?"

Tanny's eyes widened.

Sue gestured, "Jon is a twin, and my only birth was twins. I love the girls, but I don't know if I could go through infant twins again."

Tanny said, "Wow. Cool! I mean.... Um, I'm sorry! But that's such a cool idea from where I'm standing." The more Haley offspring, the better.... "Look. I'll help you every way I can. I'm out of a job now, so I'll be your nanny. I'll do everything for you but breastfeed. You just might have to feed me sometimes, since I'm out of an income.... But this could work! I'll shop for you and cook for you and just snatch the occasional bite for myself, so I don't starve...."

Sue was laughing, wiping her eyes. "You idiot," she muttered.

Tanny breathed, "Wow, pregnant. So, when are you due?"

Sue said, "Um, mid-November if I'm pregnant. But Tanny, don't you see? If I AM pregnant, I could have Jon's child before I even met him!"

There was a silence, and then both women burst into laughter.

"You know what I mean...." Sue giggled.

Tanny gasped, "Another Virgin Birth!"

"...before a year," Sue explained.

"This is going to be one special kid!"

"...before I'd even *known him* a year...."

"—or two special kids!"

"Jon. Before I'd known Jon a year...."

Tanny was on a roll. "It'll be a boy and a girl!"

Sue complained, "Tanny, don't you see?"

Tanny clapped her hands. "God will be saying, 'Okay, get this—'"

"…It's too soon!"

"'—I'm not just a man. I'm both. Male and female!'"

Sue was laughing, complaining, "It wasn't meant to go this way…. We were going to wait."

Tanny continued, "God and Goddess! Two in one!"

"Tanny, you're awful!" Sue was laughing so hard she had to wipe tears from her eyes.

"Do you suppose Mary had morning sickness?" Tanny concluded, looking at Sue with wonder.

"You are so bad! That's got to be sacrilegious."

"You're going to be all green and swollen for your official wedding pictures in June though, you know?" Tanny added, shaking her head. Then she paused. "I'm sorry. I'm sorry. I'm not much of a friend. I just can't seem to take this seriously."

Sue gasped, wiping her eyes. "You do make me laugh…."

Sue's kettle boiled and she poured her fragrant tea. The two of them moved to the large sectional in the living room, and Susan lit the fire in the fireplace. The conversation shifted to Cedar Haven.

"Did you meet the other steward, Jeff VanGalen, when you were up there?" Tanny asked.

"No, we never did," said Susan. "Aunt Eileen said he was away on some training for his work. Did you know he is their foster son?"

"I just recently found out," replied Tanny. "Right after you and Jon got back, I went up there for a break and met him."

"Did you?" Susan sat up. "What's he like?"

Tanny gathered her thoughts as she sipped at her coffee. "He's got a big dog named Mack. He's a paramedic. He… builds and repairs things."

"Well, but how old is he? Is he nice? Is he going to be easy to work with as a steward?" Sue asked.

Gazing out at the view of the half-acre back yard bordered by the large pines marking Tanny's parents' place, Tanny announced, "That reminds me, Uncle Jacob wants to schedule our first stewards' meeting for later in March. We need to get started working as a team."

Susan took her seat next to Tanny. "Tanny, what aren't you telling me? You are dodging my questions."

Tanny felt her neck warm and a grin she couldn't hide spread to her eyes.

"Tell me right now!" demanded Susan.

"Weeeeelllllll," Tanny drawled. "It turns out I have met him before, when I was about twelve—we were both about twelve. He remembered me from back then." Tanny went on to describe staying at Cedar Haven with her siblings and their adventures with "Jeffy." "For me, I was meeting someone I really didn't know, though small mannerisms and things came back as we talked." She grew thoughtful. Then she straightened up with a breath and said, "So he's a paramedic and donates his hair for cancer patients and is smart and respectful and .... pretty cool." After a beat Tanny added, "And he's really good with his hands—I mean, building and repairing things." She grinned at Susan, remembering his firm and gentle touch, cleaning up her splinters.

"You're blushing, Tanny. What happened?" Susan's eyes were alight with curiosity. "Tell me more about him. What does he look like?"

Tanny tipped her head to the side leaning back into the cushions. "He's, uh...well, at first, I didn't think he was very nice-looking—just kind of ordinary. His head is shaved, which instantly turned me off. I assumed ... well, that he'd be a macho, toxic-masculinity guy, with his snowmobile and big dog and ... um, shaved head...." Tanny trailed off sheepishly. "I guess I profiled him and judged him when we first met, which isn't very cool." But then she went on, "But he's chivalrous and thoughtful. I think he might be a great human, though we ... kind of ... avoided each other a bit." Tanny searched Susan's eyes. "I think .... No. I KNOW I started to find him very attractive. There is something about his presence—his energy field or something—that just made my heart race when he was near."

"Really?" Susan was all attention, "Is he tall? Short? Has green skin and an extra arm?"

Tanny laughed. "Yup. All of the above. Both tall and short." She sighed. "He's tall—maybe six foot two? He has a big presence, though he's not "big" like a football player. He is very fit. His eyes are sort-of golden in color. I didn't know that eyes came in gold. I think his hair is browny-blond when he doesn't shave it. His face is ... okay looking, but then he talks and smiles, and he's ... well, gorgeous."

Susan was looking intently at Tanny. She asked, "soooo, is this maybe another lightning crush—gone two weeks after it hits?"

Tanny sighed. "You know me so well. I do love falling in love. This could just be another wave of romantic wishful thinking." Her brow wrinkled. "But somehow I think this is different." Tanny remembered her prophetic dream in which Britt told her to "come find someone who adores you." She put her hand up to her cheek as she remembered those moments of great intimacy, when Jeff's pupils had widened—when she could have sworn he wanted to sweep her into his arms.

"Now you are glowing like a stoplight, Tanny. Why did you come over all rosy? What happened up there?"

"He ... he ... I just got the crazy feeling that he was strongly attracted to me. There was a time or two when he kind of abruptly moved away and then wouldn't look me in the eye. One of those times I swear we might have kissed if he hadn't done that."

"You were there only two days, and you felt that?"

"It was kind of like what my parents always warned me about, except it wasn't. Jeff even talked about respect and consent—"

"What? In less than two days?" Susan was astonished.

"Well, it was theoretical. We were joking about how Jacob and Eileen would assume we would have sex because there were no chaperones—"

Susan made a sympathetic noise.

"—and we officially promised not to seduce or molest each other, as a kind of way of being clear with each other and well, addressing the awkward reality of that generation's fears. Then Jeff said he was all about consent anyway. And that was a turn on.... He's really intriguing. I WISH I could have spent more time getting to know him."

"My, my. This is a remarkable turn of events," said Susan, her brown eyes sparking. "He's the fourth steward and in all likelihood, you will be spending a lot more time with him."

"But not for another three weeks at least. I actually have to be down here, moving, finding a job. I don't even know if I was just imagining the mutual attraction...." Tanny faded out. She did not make it up. "Oh, I don't know. I'm so desperate to find someone, and then Britt invited me up there in a dream..." The fire snapped, a log shifted and settled down again.

"She what?"

Tanny's gaze came back to Susan's. She described her vivid dream. She said, "I don't really take such dreams seriously, because they could mean anything, including 'a bit of undigested beef,' but it was so vivid. Britt said I needed to 'come find someone who adores me.' And then Jeff was right there. And he remembered me from so long ago. And he seemed ... he seemed ... so ... into me?" Tanny was struggling for the right words.

Susan made the sound from the twilight zone, grinning. Then she asked, "So, how did it end? Are you going to continue staying in touch? Did he ask for your number or anything?"

"Actually, I asked for his number. So, we did exchange contact information. But it is so deeply ingrained in me to wait for the man's initiative, that I keep stopping myself from reaching out. I feel like he should be the one to reach out first. Otherwise, it could be really awkward...." Tanny trailed off.

Susan said, "Nobody died from really awkward, Tanny."

"Are you sure?" Tanny asked, but she was grinning and looking intrigued. Maybe she would reach out to him....

As they enjoyed the crackling fire the conversation moved to the renovations at Cedar Haven, to Sue's adjustment to married life again and so many other things. Eventually Susan announced that she had to lie down. They said a warm goodbye, promising to do this again soon. Tanny slowly made her way back to her soon-to-go-away apartment. She was warm and happy to be back in touch with Susan. Haley twins! That would be amazing.

Nineteen

February 25 to February 28

Tanny let herself into her parents' mud room off the kitchen. She shed her boots and carried them through to the front. Her mom was in the kitchen and was glad to see her.

"Tanny," said Emily, wiping her hands on a towel. "We need to talk." She followed Tanny to the front door where Tanny left her coat and boots. Tanny felt a little trapped.

"If you are taking that job in Ben Kirk, you have two days to get ready. Jon and Stephen are driving down on Sunday afternoon, and I've asked if you could ride with them. You would be staying with Fifi Dunkirk-Jones in the Ben Kirk Estates. She's getting her hip replaced tomorrow, and her niece can only help her over the weekend. So, you'd arrive Sunday night, just in time."

Emily looked determined that this was the plan for Tanny. "I will hire some help and get your stuff moved to Jenny's and get Jenny moved in here, so you don't have to worry about any of that. I even hear that I can hire Barbara Millwood to help with unpacking and settling things. So, it will all be handled." She took Tanny by the elbow and led her to a seat on the sofa. "Your focus needs to be on packing and getting ready to be away for several weeks. You can rest assured that all your things will be moved with care. We'll even refund February's rent to help you."

Tanny was used to her mother's way of bulldozing her life. She had gotten used to artfully dodging some of her mother's "arrangements" and at other times just riding the wave. But she never ceased to feel sideswiped and derailed. Her mother's uninvited hyper-involvement in her life exhausted her. *But I want to help Susan. But I want to go back up to Cedar Haven. Maybe I could get a job in Bracebridge and live up there?*

"The Canadian dollar is not strong against the U.S. dollar right now, so your U.S. earnings will convert to a lot more," added Emily.

Tanny did have to face that her vet bills, her living expenses, and the cost of keeping Herman running were pushing her into a shell game with interest-free credit cards. She needed the money. She sighed and asked, "How long will this job last?"

Emily looked satisfied. She said, "Well, a minimum of one week, but it could last longer if you make yourself indispensable. Maybe you could take some classes at the college. Your dual citizenship makes it easy for you to stay as long as you like."

My mom wants to marry me off to some guy in the religion, in the US. That is her plan of salvation for me. I wish she would leave me alone!

Tanny sighed. "I'll think about it, Mom."

Emily said, "You don't have time to think about it. If you don't go, we will keep your February rent. This is an ideal chance. I mean, what do you have keeping you here when there is a lucrative position just waiting for you there? I pretty well assured Fifi that you'd be coming."

Tanny felt that grinding pain in her stomach that she often felt with her mom. *I have friends, family, history, belonging here. I have connections here. I have a potential male connection. I have Cedar Haven. She is forcing me to go with the threat of the rent bill.* She said, "Mom, I'm on the board of Cedar Haven. How can I do that from Ben Kirk? I don't want to go right now."

Emily looked thoughtful. She said, "You may only be there a week or two. I'm sure you could Zoom some meetings. When will your first one be, anyway? The will was read over six weeks ago."

"We kind of decided to let Jacob and old—um, Jeff keep running the place until Susan was married and the congregation finished the task. Life has been kind-of non-stop since then. But we do finally have our first meeting scheduled for March twenty-first-ish," explained Tanny.

"Then you have plenty of time. You might be back for the meeting, or you could use face-calling or something to join it, right? The stewardship position shouldn't prevent you from earning a living, should it?" argued Tanny's determined mother. Then she continued as if to herself, "That's if that foster-son doesn't move out west with his girlfriend. If that happens, you will need to find a replacement for him."

Tanny stopped breathing. *A girlfriend? There had been no sign of any girlfriend at Cedar Haven. There had been no pictures of a girl in Jeff's room or anywhere. How did she miss that?* Tanny felt nauseous. She wanted to run away, curl up in her bed, escape reality altogether. *Did he have a serious girlfriend and she just missed it?* Tanny put her hand up blocking Emily's face as she had done so many times before. "Give me an hour. I will tell you my decision then," and she ran, stumbling, down the stairs into her apartment and locked the door. But Tanny knew sooner than that. She didn't have any fight left in her. There was nothing holding her in Canada now. She had almost a month before the first stewards' meeting. She might as well go down to Ben Kirk and earn some U.S. money. It might be nice to get away from all the roadblocks and bad luck she was having here anyway.

Two days later, Tanny was climbing into Rev. Jonathan Haley's minivan. She took the passenger seat because Stephen had claimed the back bench for a nap. It was just after church, and they were hoping to get down to Ben Kirk before nine-thirty that night. Ben Kirk was the church's international centre, and the men would be in ministers' meetings for the next six days. Tanny had her Canadian passport ready and knew to say she was going to visit friends, not going for work. She was travelling as a Canadian. Her American passport had lapsed, and she had not gotten around to visiting the US consulate in Toronto to fix that. Her parents had fought to get "birth abroad" status declared for Tanny and her younger brothers based on Gilbert's U.S. citizenship. If any of them had wanted to work and live in the US, this would have been helpful, but none of them had so far. Meanwhile, the dual citizenship simply seemed to create a lot of extra work and expense at tax time.

It had been many years since Tanny had been down to Ben Kirk. She remembered visiting the enormous classes in the church-run elementary school. Tanny came from a mixed grade in the Cliffside church school with no more than twelve kids in the classroom the years she had attended. The classes were even smaller today. But the Ben Kirk elementary school classes had about fifty kids per grade. Each grade was divided into two sections. She had found it a bit overwhelming to visit, but fun. Still, she always preferred her small school.

Tanny had also opted out of attending the boarding high school or college though her mother had pushed her hard to go. She wanted to stay in Canada with her familiar school friends. Some of her church classmates had gone down for school, but Tanny never felt the need. Historically, many Canadian girls who went there to school ended up marrying an American and then never returned home. Sometimes a Canadian young man would bring an American bride back—but not as often. Always the wife followed the husband and not the other way around. Tanny was *not* interested in leaving Ontario.

Tanny's last visit to Ben Kirk had been for the wedding of a cousin about five years ago. When she was there it struck her like never before that the town was almost a wedding mill for young people in their denomination. Her entire peer group seemed to be getting engaged, or getting married, or having their first babies already. She found it both appealing and appalling at the same time. Was it necessary to marry so young? One of her friends had been panicked at age twenty-five when she wasn't engaged yet. Something about that desperation to marry disturbed Tanny, even as she felt it in herself. She wanted to belong. She did want to get married and have a family. But something about the young adult culture in Ben Kirk looked more like lemmings desperate to jump off the marriage cliff—desperate to find anyone so as to get married. Tanny wondered how much of that culture was a holdover from older times and how much was an ongoing ideological attachment to marriage as some sort of salvation. Barbara Millwood had called it "salvation by heterosexual marriage alone." Tanny had laughed out loud. That definitely described Tanny's mom's attitude!

Nevertheless, here she was, buckling up to go down to Ben Kirk anyway. At least she had comfortable travelling companions. Jon drove them out of Cliffside and on through the mushrooming housing developments towards the highway. Stephen was instantly quiet.

"Ja," said Jon gently, glancing back in the rearview mirror, "He works way too hard. I don't think many in the congregation realize how hard. Liz has been trying to make him cut down on his hours. But when he cuts his hours, he stresses about all the things he's falling behind on." There was a silence. "I'm happy to let him sleep and sleep," was Jon's conclusion. Tanny caught a look of affection and concern on Jon's face. She wondered if she ought to be worried about their strong and steady pastor. It had never occurred to her before.

They settled onto the multi-lane highway heading east toward Hamilton and Niagara, and the two chatted easily about his job, her lack of job, and Jon adjusting to married life and fatherhood all at once. Tanny remembered not to say a word about possible future children. The conversation then moved to Cedar Haven, its possible future, and the future of the congregation.

"Well, if there's one thing to jerk a congregation out of identifying with its buildings it is to lose its buildings," said Jon. "Most congregations don't have a strong enough sense of identity to survive that, which is too bad. What is it that we pastors are doing wrong, that our congregations lose their sense of identity once they have a building? Newly formed community churches who are nomadic—having to meet in school gymnasiums and libraries—tend to have great resilience and a strong sense of identity. They have high congregational involvement at that stage. But once they settle into a space, something big changes, and not always for the good. Buying a permanent building almost seems like a step backward. Once a congregation begins to take its existence for granted, they can begin to see their building and its maintenance as the most important thing, rather than serving others.'

"Oh, but Cliffside Chapel is so beautiful," Tanny objected. "I feel like its warm, welcoming space is part of our identity. I can understand being confused about what the point is without it."

Jon glanced over at her then back to the road. He said, "We need to ask ourselves if we actually are a warm and inviting congregation, or if it is just our space that is warm and inviting? Would we stay warm and inviting without our space, or would we discover we are insecure and lost without it? If we are insecure and lost without it, we have lost our center and purpose." Jon cut himself off. "I'm sorry, these are some of the thoughts that keep me up at night. Steve and I have had several conversations about the potential loss of the buildings due to Britt's will. For the congregation to survive, we have to establish or reestablish a sense of purpose and call in the world for the congregation. Who do we feel called to be today with or without our buildings? If the congregation doesn't figure that out, I'm likely going to be reassigned, and Steve will be doing grief management and a search for a rental space." There was a pause. "I don't think she intended it, but Britt's will is a time bomb."

Tanny sat in silence, the truth of Jon's words sinking in. Then she did some math. There were ten sets of puzzles and tasks, each spaced six months apart. The completion of each puzzle and task combination bought them another six months in their buildings and on their property. Then they had to do it all again every six months until … until … Tanny counted on her fingers, it would take four and a half more years. That's if they didn't fail on any of the puzzles or tasks in the meantime.

The first puzzle had been a real head-scratcher, but they had managed to solve it in the nick of time. The first task had been for seven elders to each complete seven hours in a soup kitchen. This was hampered by one extremely grumpy member (Conrad Knapp's father) refusing to be "bossed around by a dead woman". They had nearly failed in the soup kitchen task thanks to his stubbornness. They would have failed if it hadn't been for an act of God (well, that's how Tanny liked to see it). Tanny wondered how challenging the next set would be based on their first experience. It was entirely conceivable that they would fail on one of the puzzles or tasks before they ever got through all ten sets. If they failed, the property would be sold and the money donated to a congregation in Bracebridge. Jon was right. Aunt Britt's will truly was a ticking time bomb.

Tanny pondered this a while, staring out the window.

Jon said, "But there have been good outcomes, despite the disruption of the will. Folks are continuing to volunteer in the soup kitchens, with more congregation members trying it out."

"Are they really?" asked Tanny. She'd had no idea.

"I have heard from a few who are finding a real feeling of fulfillment from it. Joeline Dietrich says she's become fond of her fellow Monday afternoon volunteers at the Working Centre kitchen. She likes the range in age from students to retirees." Jon snorted, "Even Siegfried Schmidt, who resisted helping for so long has continued to go, even though he no longer has to. It warms my heart. Maybe Britt knew what she was doing after all."

Tanny was amazed to hear about the impact of Britt's first task. It was small, but definite. She had never doubted great Aunt Britt's intention. But she was beginning to question her wisdom. She didn't like that feeling.

The van had been cruising behind the same car for a long while. Tanny observed, changing the subject, "What do you think of these new license plates with the four letters instead of the three?"

Jon lifted an eyebrow. "It has been fun to watch the progression. They must have started with AA combinations. By the time I got my plate they were up to the AFs."

"So the people in front of us got theirs before you did."

They both contemplated the AERF plate that had been in front of them for many kilometers.

Tanny said, "That plate belongs to a Gaelic dog."

Jon's laughter made her grin. He added, "A Canadian dog would say, 'Arf! Eh?'"

After a pause Tanny added, "A medieval dog would say, 'Arfeth.'"

"Ja nee," chuckled Jon. "And the king of the dogs would be King Arfur."

"Noooo," moaned Tanny. She sighed, ending on a burp. It sounded like, "Fraurp," Which made Tanny giggle more.

"What was that?" Jon asked.

"That was a dog going backwards."

The next stretch of silence saw grins on both travelers' faces.

When they merged onto Queen Elizabeth Way—"the QEW" to locals—Tanny realized that her cell phone would stop working once they crossed the border in another hour. She had been teetering on the edge of reaching out to Jeff for the past few days. Now that she was just sitting, with little else to do, she decided to send him a text.

Hi Jeff. How's Mack? How's Cedar Haven? She hit send before her insecurity could stop her. She waited and waited, but there was no response, no wiggling dots representing typing. Her heart sank. Eventually she typed, *I'm going to be in the States for a few weeks and my cell phone won't work unless I'm on wifi.* She hit send.

She sat and thought some more. Then she typed, *I hope all is well. I really enjoyed my time up there and am looking forward to the stewards' meetings. See you in a few weeks.* SEND.

Was that too needy and forward? She couldn't ask him about a girlfriend. She couldn't even dream about getting to know him better if he was already taken. Why had she not realized that about him? Surely her mom hadn't made that girlfriend up.

Tanny heaved a deep sigh.

Jon turned down the playlist he had been humming along to and asked, "Do you want to talk about it?"

Twenty

February 28

"*H*mmmm," said Tanny. Now was the opportunity she had longed for and dreaded. She gathered herself. "I was wanting to ask you about waiting for Sue. You had to wait a long time before you found her. Didn't you get impatient? Didn't you wonder if you'd ever find anybody like Sue?"

Jon said, "I wondered every day. Sometimes every breath."

"How did you stand it?" breathed Tanny.

Jon chuckled. "Did I have a choice? What else could I do?" He thought for a bit. "By the time I met Susie, I was resigned to being a bachelor. I'd visited hopelessness so many times, I had just decided to live there."

Tanny knew that feeling. "I'm almost twenty-eight. I have waited and waited. There are all sorts of guides to finding the perfect person online. There are books on how to get a guy to marry you; there are YouTube how-tos, but they all feel so ... calculated. Some suggestions feel even deceitful or manipulative." She sighed. "Nothing works. But 'trusting providence' feels so passive. I mean, 'help comes to those who help themselves,' right?"

Jon shifted his shoulders a bit. He signaled to pass AERF, and moved into the next lane. He said, "I had the same struggles. It was very hard to wait and hope." There was a silence. "I truly believe that the more we trust providence, the easier the waiting can be. I *tried* to believe that, but it didn't always help. I trusted and felt peaceful for a while, but eventually I'd get impatient and struggle again."

They drove to the muted sound of Jon's playlist. At that moment it was James Taylor's, "The Secret of Life." Jon signalled to move back into the usual lane. Tanny indicated putting her feet up against the dash and asked, "May I?" When Jon nodded, she pressed her feet against the dash, her knees almost to chin height. It was comfortable and also felt a bit like a hug.

Jon continued. "It seems as though things just take as long as they take and go the way they go, and nothing we do can rush them along." He took a drink from his water. "Susan and I weren't *ready* to find each other until we were ready.

Thanksgiving dinner is no good if you take the turkey out of the oven before it is cooked. Babies don't thrive if they come out too much before their due date.

"I look back now, and, while the wait was excruciating, I wouldn't want anyone but Sue. I would wait again, knowing what was coming. The hardest part was the *not knowing*. I like to think I was trusting that God was handling things, but honestly, a lot of the time I just forced myself not to think about it. I got on with my life. I couldn't control when I would find the right woman, or even *if* I would find the right woman."

Tanny said, "I hate the idea of being single forever, and never knowing what it is like to make love with someone I genuinely love." There was a long silence as Tanny thought and Jon navigated passing a long line of transport trucks. Eventually she admitted, "A few years ago, I just went out and found somebody nice to have sex with—just to cross it off my bucket list. It was kinda weird, and kinda nice, and lasted a few months. But eventually it just felt empty. I couldn't make the relationship into something it wasn't. There was a sort of low-grade disappointment each time because it wasn't *real* or lasting. So, I ended it." She was silent. "Please don't judge me. I can't believe that my choice ruined me, because I don't feel ruined. Besides, I have so many friends who've experimented with sex and seem fine. Several are happily married now too."

"You are not ruined," Jon said without hesitation. "You might feel ruined because you have been taught that you are ruined. Sexual activity doesn't 'ruin' a woman any more than it does a man, or any gender in between. Our spiritual worth isn't ever about our outsides. It is about our insides.

"Women have been taught they are ruined for centuries because men wanted to be sure any offspring were theirs. There really aren't consequences for men who sleep around, but if a women did and got pregnant, she was often cast out, shamed and abandoned. She and her child were perceived as illegitimate, because no man had made her and her child legitimate. Very often she could not care for herself and her baby—hence the rules around waiting until marriage. There needed to be a guarantee that a man would provide for the impregnated woman and the child. It was a deeply ingrained social morality to protect the most vulnerable."

Tanny made a gesture by her head and an explosion sound effect. "My mind is blown. All our religious rules and morals, all the shame and judgment actually spring from pragmatic cultural protection of the weak?"

Jon shrugged. "That's my firm belief from my study. That's what makes sense to me. The social codes were designed to protect women from being used and discarded. Ironically, they have become a way to shame and control women, until 'controlling women and their bodies' is seen as religiously necessary, completely disconnected from the original values."

"Oh. My. Gosh," said Tanny. She dropped her feet back to the floor. They had cleared the tractor trailers at last and were looking at a wide, open stretch ahead.

"Think about it; the vast majority of young adults are sexually active today but are much more cautious about the full commitment. You might say they value marriage *so much* that they wait until they are quite sure. No one needs to rush to get married just to have sex anymore—besides, that rush to have sex makes a lousy foundation for marriage anyway. There are plenty of options for birth control; and a woman who might find herself pregnant today is often supported by her family and has lots of choices." He glanced over at Tanny's attentive face. "I'm going on and on."

"No. I LOVE this! I've never heard a minister speak like this, but it makes so much sense to me. So, the *original* moral rules were always about protecting the most vulnerable in society, NOT about *shunning* the most vulnerable if they were created. Amazing. We've gotten it exactly backwards!"

"Welcome to the human race, Tanny," sighed Jon. "History shows humans doing this again and again, starting with great values, and then eventually forgetting the reason behind the 'rules' and ending up judging and shaming each other for not following the 'rules' correctly. This happens in and out of religious bodies." He shrugged. "It's just what humans do."

They were getting closer to the border. Tanny shifted around to pull out her passport and checked her phone. Nothing from Jeff.

"In conclusion," Jon said in a grand voice, as if finishing a speech. He returned to his natural tone, "If everybody is experimenting sexually before settling down, then that's just the new normal. And where does the morality lie in this new norm? I think it comes down to mutual consent, emotional maturity, and personal responsibility. So much of sex can be abusive. But that wouldn't happen if both parties were respectful, thoughtful, and looking out for each other." Jon signaled to pass a giant motorhome towing a car. "If you feel fine about your choice to experiment, then you *are* fine. I honestly don't think ministers have any business in church members' beds anyway. Being a virgin *cannot* be the definitive factor in whether a marriage will succeed or not. I think it is ridiculous that we ever thought so."

"I know, right?!" agreed Tanny. "Jenny did everything right, she was a virgin and look what it got her. Her soon-to-be ex is a womanizer and sexual offender.

She's raising a child alone. So much for waiting until marriage."

Jon made a face and smacked the wheel. "What we do with our bodies simply cannot matter as much as what we do in our spirits. Spiritual life is shaped by our *inner* motivations and intentions. Am I using others towards my ends, or seeing them as of equal value? There are marriages in which there is disrespect and resentment and competition for control, as well as the lovely, healthy marriages. There are common-law and same-sex couples living in respect and mutual tenderness, as well as those who aren't. The outsides can never define the insides, but we humans love to mistake the outsides for the insides."

Tanny was thoroughly enjoying this discussion on religious thought. She felt like a responsible, capable human while talking to Jon. He never made her feel like she needed to be corrected or controlled. Jon wasn't telling her what to think. He was describing how he understood things and asking her to think about it for herself. His ideas resonated with her heart and seemed like common sense. After a time of silence she said, "That sounds like you think same-sex couples are okay? Is that true?"

Jon sighed. "I should hope we always remain open to the evidence of what is truly loving and wise. Otherwise, past perspectives become mistaken for timeless wisdom. If our old, 'Bible-based' values were still upheld, women would still be possessions of men; whites would still be assumed to be superior, slaves would still be subhuman; and all of this would be justified by the Bible somehow. That doesn't work for me."

"People used the Bible to say that whites were superior?" asked Tanny. "Really?! Where does it say that? I mean, if anything, Semitic peoples would be superior, right?"

Jon grimaced. "Tanny, to quote Reverend Lovejoy from the Simpsons, 'the Bible says a lot of things.' The Bible has been used to justify many inhuman things. Today is it being used to shame homosexuals and tell them that they are evil or perverted. But maybe we are wrong about those ideas the same way we have been wrong about women and slavery and white supremacy? It is our hearts and how we treat our 'neighbour' that matters, not specific things we do with our bodies in mutually consenting relationships."

Tanny sat with her jaw open. "I love this! My mind is continuing to be blown. So how do we know what to believe if we keep using the Bible to justify inhuman behaviours? How can we know what is true?"

"That's the ten-million-dollar question, Tanny." Jon chewed on his lower lip. He glanced at her with a raised eyebrow. "Look, as a minister I have never been accused of being orthodox. You could get me into a lot of trouble if you carried some of this back to the council of ministers. But for me, everything must go through a lens of lovingkindness, of the Golden Rule, of mutual human respect. The Bible is powerful. There will always be those who try to control and shame others with it. But the Bible also points to love and shows all the ways we humans hurt each other when we forget love."

"I can't even...." said Tanny. "A religion founded on lovingkindness, not rules and control and judgment. I guess I always thought that is what it should be."

Jon smiled. "Each religion points to respect, kindness, and compassion. I liked it when the Dalai Lama said that love and compassion are his religion. That is what resonates for me."

They had passed the motorhome at last. Jon signalled and moved back into the main travel lane. The kilometres moved steadily beneath them. It was overcast—nice conditions for driving.

After a while, Tanny asked wistfully, "So there's nothing you can tell me that will make my true love show up faster?"

"What sort of thing did you have in mind?"

"Oh, I don't know. Prayers? Parts of the Bible to read? Some kind of soul purification ritual to clean out what is blocking me from finding my true love...?"

Jon laughed. "Well, I can do that if you want—if it would make you feel better. But the truth is, I could have done all those things for myself ten years ago or five years ago, and I doubt it would have made me find Sue faster. In fact, much earlier, and she would have still been a married woman."

They were in the line for the border now. Jon called back to Stephen to wake him. When he didn't respond, Tanny had to crawl back to rouse him. When Tanny swatted his calf, Stephen's sleepy face appeared. "Are we there yet?" he asked, joking even as he returned to full wakefulness. "Ah. At the border." He sat up and dug around for his passport.

Tanny jumped back into the front and shut the door.

Jon pulled closer to the inspection window. They were lucky. It was a short line this day, unlike so many others.

Just before Jon rolled down his window he murmured, "These are not the droids you are looking for."

When Jeff got off his shift—a blessedly quiet one—he put his gear away and plunked down on the sofa, Mack's head in his lap. Rubbing the large ears he checked his phone. There were three messages. His face lighted up as he read. Then he checked his watch and sighed. She would be across the border by now.

He laid his head back as he scrubbed Mack's fur, thinking. Finally, he sat up. He typed, "May I call you?"

Twenty-One

February 28

*B*ack in Cliffside, Susan had taken the girls down to visit with their grandma, Kate Bender. It was not a long walk. Kate welcomed them into the simple, seventies-style ranch house that had been Susan's childhood home. Susan breathed in the long-familiar scent of the wood-burning fireplace, fresh bread, and house plants. The girls ran down to the basement playroom with its large dollhouse. Sue and her mom got themselves tea in the old kitchen and eventually settled themselves in the mid-century modern furniture around the fireplace. Sue loved the gently vaulted ceiling and spacious feeling in the living room.

Kate Bender, Susan's widowed mom, watched her daughter with kind eyes.

After some small talk about the girls and Jon's week away, Susan said, "Mum, when we talked before, you said you were kind of lonely married to dad. Are you still lonely? Have you thought of dating again? I don't like thinking of you as lonely."

Kate thought about that for a while, twirling a blanket fringe around her fingers. She said, "I actually have thought about it. Sometimes when Noah was alive, I dreamed about someone more emotionally present and warm—you know, when I was really unhappy in the marriage. I didn't want our marriage to end. I just ... sometimes ... felt better imagining that one day I might find a ... a *companion*, a heart-friend." Kate sighed. "That sounds disloyal to your father. I'm sorry." Kate bundled up the blanket and held it against her solar plexus.

"No, I think I understand," reassured Sue. "Dad was pretty quiet and reserved."

Both women sat, thinking. The fire crackled.

Eventually Sue said, "But he died, mum. Maybe now you *could* find a heart-friend."

Kate shrugged. "Yes, your father died. And I still miss him. But by then all my romantic dreams had died. I am worn out. I'm liking my quiet independence. And the thought of starting over with somebody new feels like a lot of work."

"Oh mom." Susan gave Kate a hug. Then she settled herself kneeling on the floor at her mother's knees—a position from her childhood and teenage years.

"I just want you to be happy. I want you to find a man who makes you happy. Like I have."

Kate smiled down at her daughter. "That's very generous of you, sweetheart." Kate smoothed Susan's hair. "But I'm making myself happy. I'm not looking for someone else to do that anymore. I'm content alone. I don't think—" the gentle face framed with the salt-gray ponytail smiled. "I don't want to share my space anymore."

"But mum...."

"Don't you worry about me; I'm very content. I can choose when to be with friends and when to be alone." Kate's hazel eyes were gently apologetic and amused. "I mean, what an upheaval to start all that negotiating and space-sharing and caretaking again. I'm too old for that."

Sue had never considered it that way. A silence stretched between them.

Finally, Susan said, "Well, if you do ever find someone, I am in full support." She gave her mom a squeeze and then returned to the sofa.

"Is that why you're here, Susie? To ask me why I haven't remarried?"

Susan went blank. Then she remembered and flushed. "Not really.... She looked slightly apologetic.

Kate grinned and tossed a stuffed doll at Susan. "Out with it."

Susan lifted and dropped her shoulders. Her wide eyes followed the chimney up to where it met the ceiling, and she sighed. She met her mother's eyes and said, "Jon and I, we kind of, blew it on our honeymoon." Her cheeks turned rosy red. "And I'm worried."

Kate was intrigued. "So, if I'm hearing you right, you experienced wild passion on your honeymoon and the problem is...?"

Sue twisted her hands around the doll. "Well, what if I'm pregnant?"

"Ohhhhhhhh! Well, could you be?" Kate wondered and counted on her fingers. "It's barely been two weeks. You haven't even had time to miss your period."

"It is due *today*, which doesn't mean anything yet, except I'm sore in my breasts, and I feel crampy and very tired. We used protection after that, but we did have that one time. Mom, I'm not ready to be pregnant."

Now it was Kate's turn to cross the room and hug her daughter. She sat next to Sue on the couch and held her close. "Dear me. Well, you'll know soon enough. And if you *are* pregnant, I'm right here. We'll get through it somehow."

Sue gave a shuddering sigh and rested her head on Kate's shoulder.

"It's going to be fine." Kate reassured her.

Like clockwork, the girls, ready for snacks, emerged from the door to the finished basement. "What's going to be fine, Mommy?" asked Andrea, her eyes wide.

"Filing our taxes," announced Kate. "It's a boring, grown-up thing."

"Are you boring grownups?" asked Alyssa, coming up behind her sister.

Once through the border, Tanny turned her phone off. No response from Jeff. And no more possible texts or data until she found WIFI. They were wending their way along the various highways on the outskirts of Buffalo, New York, starting their way down to the Philadelphia area in Pennsylvania.

"Can I ask you something else Jon?" said Tanny.

"Ja. Of course," Jon reassured her.

"So, how did you manage all the waiting to find someone? I'm finding it really hard."

Jon thought for a while. He scratched his beard. Finally, he said, "I tried not to think about it too much. I went on dates, but no matter how much I craved simply having someone to hold, I kept strict boundaries." He fiddled around in his pocket, finally finding his sunglasses and settled them in place. "In fact, there was a gal I became very good friends with in my first year in Ben Kirk. We would go to her parents' house, then cuddle and watch movies together in the basement rec-room just to stave off the loneliness. Nobody could see us to care. It was comforting and warm and completely platonic." Jon chuckled. "I think folks often thought we were a couple. And neither of us did much to disabuse them of that idea. It worked for both of us."

"But how did she handle that?" asked Tanny, bewildered. "Did you break her heart?"

Jon laughed. "She is one woman whose heart I could never break."

"Was she your sister?"

There was a moment's silence. Jon cleared his throat. "Not at all. But you see, Misty liked women, not men. It made her an excellent friend. No weirdage. No strings."

"Misty?" Tanny pushed back and looked at him. "Misty Merrick? Oh my gosh, that makes so much sense."

"You know her?"

"Not super well, but yeah. She came to Trillium Camp one year."

"The camp for teens?"

"Yeah. She was classic. Funny! Tough. A smoker. I never was great friends with the smokers. But she was whip-smart and kind."

"That's Misty all right. It worked for both of us. She dodged a lot of harassment by appearing to have a boyfriend. And I dodged a lot of husband-hunters."

Husband-hunters. Tanny wondered if she was a husband-hunter. It did not feel great to think about that.

Tanny said with some wilting optimism, "So I should find a cuddle buddy, not try too hard, and get on with my life, huh?"

"I'm not going to comment on the cuddle-buddy, but the rest sounds pretty good to me. I honestly cannot tell you better, except ..." Jon quirked an eyebrow, "that prayer can help. Prayer doesn't change God. It always changes us. And it often seems to help. It aligns our soul to follow and listen better. That's what I think, anyway."

Tanny sighed deeply in resignation. "Prayer." She made a farting noise. "It just seems so unscientific and impossible to tell if it is actually doing something." After a bit, she laughed and said with full self-disclosure, "I can't *control* God with prayer, you see? I want certainty. I want to put in my money and get what I'm ordering. That's what I want from God. I do my part, and He does His."

Jon was grinning widely, delighted by her honesty and humour. "I know, right?"

"Dumb God," Tanny continued, stifling her smile. "He just does what He wants, and we have to beg and often don't get what we want anyway."

The wheels hummed along the highway.

Jon said, "Something I heard that I rather like is this: God answers 'yes' to every prayer. It's just the timing we don't like. It's never 'no', just 'not yet.' I guess one has to believe there is a benevolent afterlife to be satisfied by that idea. My friend may die of cancer, but I will see him again, happy and healthy, in the life to come." He paused. "I certainly understand why lots of people aren't satisfied by that perspective. But it works for me."

"The answer isn't 'no', just 'not yet,'" Tanny repeated. "I think I can work with that."

After a moment of confusion while they made sure they got the right exit, Tanny thanked Jon. "You make it all sound so sensible. Honestly, I'm so glad you came to Cliffside, and into Susan's life. You are pretty great."

"You aren't too shabby yourself."

Tanny chuckled, "Do you have any brothers?"

Jon made a noise. "Two, and I wouldn't recommend either. They are both married with kids."

"Of course they are!" complained Tanny. "Besides, I am getting on with my life."

William Lyon Mackenzie King, otherwise known as "Mack" was becoming frustrated with his master. He would indicate they were going out, but then do something else. Once, they got into the moving cave, only to get out again and go back into the main cave again. His master kept looking at that thing in his paw. Mack had sniffed it and even licked it once, but other than tasting of his master's sweat, that small, hard thing was utterly uninteresting.

Mack could sense that his master was restless. He was not at ease, which made Mack feel uneasy too. Sometimes Mack would bark at him to get his attention, and usually a nice ear-rub followed, but other times his master just barked back. Mack did not like it when that happened.

Just now his master was sitting on the large soft rock, staring and staring at the small hard thing. Mack sighed and rested his head on his paws.

Jeff, with a slight feeling of guilt for delaying Mack's walk, waited and waited for a response from Tanny. But nothing came. He wondered when Tanny had crossed the border, and if she'd even gotten his response. His shoulders slumped as he realized that staring at his phone would not make her respond sooner. That woman had gotten under his skin in his teens, and she had never let go.

Was there any hope of a relationship? Jeff stood up and called Mack to prepare for a walk. This time they really did get out for a long exploration around the property.

Twenty-Two

February 28, evening

The twisting, narrow Pennsylvania roads shone dimly in the van's headlights and the very occasional streetlights as they approached Ben Kirk. Jon's minivan bobbed and wove between the fields, trees, and colonial style houses. Then came a swooping drop of their stomachs over a dip in the road. Tanny smiled when they all gasped at the sensation. Her childhood friends had called this road "Tickle-tummy Road." In only a few days, from a few times riding with any of them, they had taught Tanny to anticipate the sudden drop with joy.

A moment later they turned left, descending into what felt like the bowels of the earth. "Into Narnia we go," said Jonathan. With the tall trees and bushes on the right, and an increasing wall of earth to the left it felt like they were descending into a cave. They had to slow nearly to a stop at the bottom to make a hard right turn around an ancient stone mill. A tall stone retaining wall crowded against the road on the left, while the mill stood so close to the road on the right that Tanny often wondered how many cars scraped against it while trying to navigate that turn.

Past the mill, the sky opened up a bit. The tires hummed across a short metal-framed bridge. They passed an old post office on the left and a "Welcome to Ben Kirk" sign in a fork in the road. They climbed up the left fork which curved between large, treed properties. This road also forked, though Tanny knew that both directions joined back together on higher ground. They continued climbing gently along the right fork toward where stood the cathedral, schools, offices, and two castles.

Many of the old, old trees had been taken down and replaced with saplings here, and the wide sky became more and more evident as they passed the community park and reached the small highway that divided the cathedral and "castles" from the wide campuses of the secondary schools and college. The cathedral stood illuminated in the dark, drawing all eyes in its vicinity. Stephen sighed, looking at the graceful, soaring tower and spires. He said, "That never gets old."

"Let's get you settled at The Estates, Tanny, and then Steve and I will head off to our billets," decided Jon, turning left at the light. Soon the van was pulling in front of the low-rise seniors' home. The men helped Tanny unload her gear, and waited with her until she was buzzed in. She gave them both a hug of thanks and watched them go as the door swung closed and locked again. She then looked around the mid-century modern lobby with the vaulted ceiling. A man stood up from behind a counter and said, cheerfully, "Now who might you be?"

Tanny grinned and said, "I might be Tanny Smith, daughter of Frederick Smith and Emily Bender Smith from Canada. I've come to help Fifi Dunkirk-Jones...."

"Ah yes! Fifi told me to expect you tonight. I can take you down there. Would you like help with your bags?"

"That would be great," accepted Tanny. "I don't even know which way to go."

The gentleman came out from the small office and approached. He had sandy hair, glasses, khaki's and a "Mr. Rogers" sweater. He was probably in his sixties.

"I'm Kevin Bach—yes, Bach as in J.S. No relation that we can find—you can call me Kevin if you prefer. We don't stand on ceremony here." He grabbed Tanny's largest bag and said, "This way." As he lead Tanny past a dining room, he said, "I remember a Frederick Smith from Pittsburgh, but I really don't know the Canadians, except for those who have settled down here."

"My dad is from Pittsburgh; so he's probably the one you know. My mom insisted that they live in Canada if they got married, so he moved to Canada to marry her."

"Does that make you a dual citizen?" asked Kevin.

"It does, in fact. Dad jumped through all the hoops to get 'birth abroad' documents for all of us."

"So you can just move down here whenever you want."

"Yes. I could."

"Lucky girl."

Tanny didn't comment.

They passed a solarium with comfy looking chairs and then continued past a series of doors into residences.

"This is 'C' wing," said Kevin. "Past the lounge ahead is 'D' wing. That's where you are going."

Beyond a spacious lounge with large windows, tall, brocaded wingback chairs, a grand piano and its own entry, Kevin led Tanny to another corridor in which the residential doors were more generously spaced. Tanny was beginning to wonder how much farther when they came to a stop in front of the very last door on the left.

"Your new home," said Mr. Bach, and knocked.

A young woman opened the door and flashed a bright smile. "You must be Tanny. Great!" she reached out her hand in welcome. "Come in and we'll get you settled."

Mr. Bach and Tanny followed her into a well-lit, open kitchen-dining-living space. There was probably a lovely view beyond the two curtained windows. Instead, they turned immediately left down a hall where Tanny was shown into a moderate room with a single window. It had a single bed, a dresser, and a desk. The décor felt feminine and old fashioned. She dropped her bags on the bed while Mr. Bach parked her suitcase.

"Do you have a restroom?" asked Tanny.

"You mean a bathroom?" said the young lady. "It's just across the hall."

Tanny found a commodious washroom across the hall and had a much-needed "rest". She washed up, appreciating the Matisse shower curtain and matching towels. Everything was high-end and very pleasing.

She came out in time to wave goodbye to Mr. Bach, who had to get back to the front desk. "I'm Cecily," greeted the young woman. She had a blond, pixie-cut and wide blue eyes. She was slim and slightly taller than Tanny. "Are you ready to come meet Aunt Fifi? It's just that I really need to get going."

"Sure. Okay," agreed Tanny, slightly surprised by the rush. She would have preferred to settle in and catch her breath first.

Cecily led her beyond the washroom to the end of the hall and knocked on a door. In response to a peremptory, "Yes?" she pushed open the door to a sizeable master bedroom complete with a king-size bed, matching dresser and armoire, a sitting area, and a desk. It felt spacious even with all the heavy furniture. The tones were muted and tasteful. An imposing woman sat propped up on some pillows, with a walker ready near the bedside. Some slippers were arranged tidily by the bed.

"Miss Smith. Come in. Thank you for coming," commanded the well-preserved woman among the pillows. "You don't look a bit like your family," she announced after a long assessment of Tanny. "I don't see Smith or Bender in you. How odd."

Tanny didn't know how to respond. *I'm sorry?* She ran though all the various comments told her throughout her life about her looks. She was "all Bender." She was "all Smith." She was even "a definite Starkey," "a Millwood" (both from her father's side) and "a Neufeldt" (her mother's side). *Didn't she just look like herself?*

"Just now you put me in mind of Doris Allen. I wonder how that could be?"

Tanny's mother played the church genealogy game all the time, so Tanny knew that Doris Allen was her mother's first cousin though the Neufeldts. "She's my cousin on my mother's side. My mother's mother had a sister named Mildred, and Doris is Mildred's daughter."

"Ah yes," was Mrs. Dunkirk-Jones' satisfied response. She nodded in approval at Tanny. She seemed content now that she had placed Tanny somewhere in the great genealogical tree of the church. "Doris lives over in 'B' wing. You should go see her."

"Aunty Fifi, I really need to get going," inserted Cecily.

"Oh dear," sighed the regal old matriarch. "Well then, show Miss ... Smith where everything is and then you can go."

As the two women headed toward the kitchen, her imperial voice followed them. "I expect to see you back in here at nine pm, Miss Smith!"

Cecily's lightning overview of all Tanny needed to know regarding the locations of meds and devices, Fifi's exacting schedule, clothing, laundry, foods and much more left Tanny a little breathless. Before Tanny knew it, Cecily was cheerfully gone. Tanny stood in mild awe, grateful that there was a carefully itemized list in her hand, penned by Cecily. She looked at her watch. It was five minutes to nine. She just had enough time to gulp some water and down a granola bar before presenting herself before the grand dame of the unit.

Tanny wanted a shower. She wanted to unpack. She wanted to get on the W-FI—thank goodness there *was* WIFI—and let her mom know she had arrived safely, as Emily had requested. She wanted to see if she had any *other* messages.

Instead, she smoothed her hair and headed to the master bedroom.

Fifi Dunkirk-Jones commanded her room from a nest of pillows in her bed. She had volumes of soft, elegant white curls and a face that held a similarity to Cecily's. Her chin had a slight lift, that gave the impression she was looking down at Tanny, even from her bed. She smiled brightly and said, "You've arrived so late we won't have any time for niceties, though I would love to know more about you. That will have to wait until morning. Ah, I see you have Cecily's list." She barely stopped for a breath. "As you can see, at nine pm you help me do my toilet before bed. Cecily kindly got me in my nightwear, so all you have to help me with are the other things on the list."

The list included helping her sit up, put on her slippers, navigate to the bathroom with her walker, find particular meds and write them in a log once taken. Then Fifi did a complete facial cleansing and moisturizing routine, wanting her jars and bottles put back precisely so. She cleaned her teeth and needed help using the potty-chair. There was much moaning as she navigated seating herself and then rising later. Then Tanny was to change the bandages over the incisions, before helping Mrs. Dunkirk-Jones arrange her nightwear as she liked. Then Tanny guided a sore Fifi back to the bed again.

"Now, keep *this* pillow, and help me set the others over there." Together they moved the extra pillows to the empty side of the bed. Fifi sat herself down and kicked off her slippers.

"No, my slippers go precisely *there,* ready for me when I next rise," barked the sore senior citizen. Tanny recovered the slippers from where she'd tossed them out of Fifi's way.

"That's much better," approved Fifi. "Now help me put on my crown."

My crown?

Fifi's crown turned out to be a fine mesh structure that she fastened around her curls to "keep them tidy." Then Tanny was to help her lie down.

Once Fifi was arranged in the bed just how she liked it with the covers just so, Tanny anticipated some time to herself at last. But as she wished Mrs. Dunkirk-Jones a good rest, Fifi interrupted her.

"I want my grabber propped just here." Fifi smacked the edge of the mattress.

Tanny had to find "the grabber" and prop it up just so. She hesitated, waiting for the next command.

"All right then," said Mrs. Dunkirk-Jones, looking a bit impatient. "You can go. Thank you. Good night."

"Um," Tanny hesitated, "what would ... how would you like me to address you, Mrs. Dunkirk-Jones? 'Fifi' seems awfully familiar," asked Tanny.

"Oh no. Not Fifi. That is for my friends only. I think Mrs. Dunkirk-Jones works just fine." She thought a bit. "Though nearly all the young people call me 'Aunt Fifi' whether I know them or not. That would be acceptable."

"Good night then, Mrs. Dunkirk-Jones," acknowledged Tanny, not quite ready for "Aunt Fifi." "You can call me Tanny, if you like, rather than 'Miss Smith'."

"Leave my door open a crack, Miss Tammy, and yours too. I want you to be able to hear me if I call for you."

Tanny stopped herself from saying, "Yes, your Majesty," and instead said, "Of course," as she politely bowed herself out of the room. She got the Tammy for Tanny mistake all the time and opted not to press the point tonight. "I think I'll call her 'Queen D-J,'" she muttered as she returned to her unopened bags.

It was now ten pm. Tanny made sure to put her baby carrots into the fridge and wondered about a supper. She saw some bread and found some peanut butter, and dinner was decided. As she munched she found the WIFI password and finally got her phone capable of some communication. Immediately two messages came in; one from her mom, "Are you there safe and sound?" to which she replied, "Safe and sound."

The next was from Jeff, and her heart raced. *"May I call you?"* She looked at the time; it was after ten pm. She decided to answer, late though it was. "Yes. Of course. My schedule implies I have a break at noon tomorrow. How does twelve-fifteen-ish sound?" She started unpacking enough to at least find her pajamas and toothbrush. She opened the closet and dresser drawers to discover there was minimal room in the closet and only one small drawer available in the dresser. Her phone dinged, making her jump.

"Twelve-fifteen-ish tomorrow sounds great. I'll call you unless I hear differently. Sweet dreams."

Sweet dreams? Why did that make her heart curl up in a happy ball?

Suddenly feeling more energetic, Tanny rearranged the items in the drawers freeing up one drawer in the dresser and one in the desk. She still had several items in her suitcase after that, but it was a start.

It was not quite midnight by the time she had found all she needed, eaten, changed, brushed her teeth, refilled her water, and climbed into the slim bed. It was so padded, she felt she might roll off if she wasn't careful. So she set her back against the wall (at least one side was against a wall), and set her alarm for six-fifty a.m. as she was to start work at seven. Eventually she fell asleep. She only had one dream of nearly falling off a cliff.

Twenty-Three

Tanny's alarm woke her at 6:50 am. She nearly hit snooze until she remembered where she was. She had ten minutes to be up and ready and at Queen D-J's bedside. By one minute after seven she was dressed and standing ready for the regal senior.

Mrs. Dunkirk-Jones had managed to gather her pillows and prop herself up. She had removed her "crown" as well and presented it to Tanny to put away. Moaning from stiffness, Fifi got herself sitting on the side of the bed with Tanny's help, and Tanny put Fifi's slippers on.

"Okay chickee, let's go," winced Mrs. Dunkirk-Jones, and she rocked herself forward to grab her walker.

Tanny smiled at the "chickee" not certain if Fifi was cheering herself on, or Tanny. They arrived in the bathroom and got the pain-wracked old woman toileted. Immediately after, Tanny got the pain meds for Mrs. Dunkirk-Jones, feeling sympathy. She stifled the urge to rub Fifi's back in a comforting way. She didn't think that would be welcome.

Then, seated on her walker, the grand dame got Tanny to fluff her curls where they had been flattened by sleep. Tanny was impressed by how well the "crown" had preserved the orderliness of the elegant woman's coif.

Then came the morning skin care and delicate make-up. Eventually Queen Fifi was ready for her morning attire. The pain meds were doing their work now, and Tanny was comforted that her clumsy first efforts to help the woman dress didn't cause much discomfort. Tanny was astonished at the elegant outfit Fifi had chosen. The fabrics were of good quality, in muted tones, and draped in a lovely way. The woman even added an artfully tied scarf in dark greens, turquoise, and gold. Tanny now felt she needed to improve her own fashion game. If it had been her that was post-surgery, she would have just stayed in her pajamas.

Tanny got Fifi to the dining table, and began her first experience of cooking, serving, and waiting on her boss and client. Today the regal senior wanted oatmeal, decaf, and a special blended juice that Tanny was to make for her fresh every morning. Fortunately, the oatmeal was instant, but the juice required several different fresh and frozen fruits to be blended just so. Tanny's first try was deemed, "Adequate, but too watery." Well, she had at least four more tries to get it right.

Fifi also wanted to read the morning paper over her breakfast and was grumpy that it was late arriving at her door. She told Tanny she was welcome to read the paper after she was done with it. Tanny simply nodded in gratitude and carefully set the sections aside as Fifi finished with them.

Tanny grabbed herself some oatmeal and real coffee, sitting to eat when ordered.

"At seven thirty I must walk for fifteen minutes. You will time me. At seven-forty-five I must rest with my feet elevated and ice on my wounds. At eight thirty you will supervise me doing my exercises. Immediately after that I rest with ice again. At nine-forty-five I need you to walk me down to the solarium for my ten o'clock bridge club. It is my first time back since my surgery. I need you to stay in the room with me. Bridge usually runs until eleven-thirty, though I doubt I can sit that long. I will need to walk back and lie down before it is over." Fifi straightened her back and smiled optimistically. "I will do what I can do!"

"I'm sure you will," Tanny agreed. She appreciated the elegant woman's humour. Tanny was also impressed by Fifi's intention to stick to the tightly scheduled regimen she had drawn up for herself. It followed almost precisely the recommended activities and rest periods on the home care sheets from the hospital.

Tanny sneaked a peak at her cell phone, but Fifi said, "No. None of that at the table. Turn it off and put it away. You will have an hour to yourself once I am down for my afternoon rest, and you can look at it then if you like. Read the paper if you want something to do now."

Tanny was taken aback but did as she was ordered. She had never been a newspaper reader, so she poked through and found a crossword puzzle. It was a bit too hard for her. She gave up and finished eating. She checked herself before standing. "Permission to clean up breakfast?" she asked.

"Of course," said Mrs. Dunkirk-Jones, looking up from her paper. The old woman's eyes followed Tanny as she gathered dishes and carried them to the sink. "Tell me about yourself," asked Fifi, her chin up in that remarkable way.

"Well, I have a sister and two brothers. I had a beautiful golden retriever that died just over a week ago, that I miss terribly."

"I'm sorry about your dog. I still miss my Toby, my Cocker Spaniel, and it's been over ten years," commented Fifi. She finished her coffee and offered her cup to Tanny. "And your siblings, are they all married with kids?"

Tanny raised her eyebrows but continued loading the dishwasher. "No. Just my older sister got married. She has an adorable son that I babysit sometimes. My brothers are younger and still finishing school. Liam is actually graduating this year," Tanny added in surprise as the realization hit her.

"No girlfriends or fiancées as yet?"

"You are all about the romance, aren't you?" Tanny asked playfully, giving the elegant woman a look.

"I just like to see the young people settling down and starting families, as they should. It is comforting. And it ensures the future of the church." Fifi finished her juice and handed Tanny her glass. "It is nearly seven-thirty. I would like to start my walking now," Fifi brushed imaginary crumbs from her beautiful scarf and moved to reach for her walker. Tanny helped the older woman up from her chair.

Fifi walked the length of the "D" wing, leaning increasingly on Tanny as they returned to the apartment. Tanny realized that Mrs. Dunkirk-Jones was probably in a lot more pain than she was letting on. There was an occasional hissing intake of breath, or a barely concealed wincing around the eyes that alerted Tanny to the woman's courage and fortitude. Tanny's heart softened. She was more careful to watch for ways to ease Fifi's progress without removing her dignity.

"That's good enough," said an obviously struggling Fifi. "Now ice and bed." She gave a small moan as she lay back into her pillows.

Tanny checked the med schedule and saw it was too soon for more pain medicine. She ran to get ice packs and settled them around Fifi's tender joints.

Before Tanny left the room to finish the dishes, Fifi stopped her. "We are still doing my exercises at eight forty-five. You must wake me if I have fallen asleep."

"Yes, Mrs. Dunkirk-Jones," Tanny promised.

Tanny finished cleaning the kitchen (better than she had found it) and then managed a few more tweaks to her bedroom storage to accommodate the rest of her things. She hoped like crazy she would remember to put everything back the way she'd found it.

Eight-thirty came quickly, and Tanny knocked on the master bedroom door. Fifi was awake and ready for her exercises. Most of the exercises could be done lying down, which was a relief to Tanny. They involved ankle movements, knee bends, and several upper thigh strengthening calisthenics. Then Tanny helped Fifi stand at her walker and do several more exercises extending and bending her legs. Fifi was in clear pain but said nothing. When these were done Fifi insisted on walking to the kitchen with Tanny who returned the old ice packs and got fresh ones.

"The exercises plus this walk will count as my hourly walk," Fifi grunted as they progressed back toward the bedroom. Tanny tucked the ice packs around the tender hip incisions and joints, praying Fifi would rest. Fifi did, indeed, fall asleep.

At nine fifty-five, after a good rest and walk down the hall, Fifi was established at a table in the D wing lounge with her bridge ladies. The ladies were all very interested in who this new young helper was, so Tanny did her best to explain her lineage and relationships to the women. One of them was her not-really Aunt Doris who already knew of her. The second was "Mads" (short for Madeline?) Bradford, another moneyed widow who lived in the D wing. The Bradfords were from Pittsburg, so she viewed Tanny with favor. The third woman was June somebody from B wing. Tanny decided that only the wealthy women got fancy nicknames. Eventually Tanny found herself a wing-backed chair against the wall and settled down to wait until she was needed again. This was the first chance she'd had to sit since breakfast.

Tanny caught up on some texts and cleared some emails as she sat. She had butterflies in her stomach in anticipation of the call with Jeff. She couldn't seem to shake them. How she wished time would hurry past! She distracted herself with some solitaire on her phone. She couldn't help but overhear the conversation over the game of bridge.

"Aunt" Doris complained about the new assistant pastor and his conservative leanings. "Mads" thought he wasn't conservative enough, but it was all said in good humor. Mrs. Bradford went on to complain about the insurance on her third vacation home going up and how unfair it was. Tanny felt a little sick, remembering that she, herself, didn't even have one home. It made her dislike Mrs. Bradford and her tight curls and buttoned-up designer pantsuit. Had she no idea what it was like for some people? Tanny could muster no sympathy for the woman.

June whoever-she-was was sweet and vague—just pleasant and benign. Doris had a caustic and quick wit which kept them all entertained. Doris felt like family.

The gossip turned to a wealthy widower from Michigan who was wanting to buy into Ben Kirk Estates and was asking for some special consideration based on his years of donations and dedicated service to the church. When Mads dropped her voice to a whisper, Tanny gleaned that this was confidential information. She probably shouldn't be talking about it at all. "We all had to pay our full buy-in. Why should his buy-in be reduced or waived?" She dropped her voice even lower, causing Tanny to try to lean forward without looking like she was listening in. Maddy continued, "I get the impression that if he doesn't get his way, he will go somewhere else! The nerve! I'm glad we are standing our ground."

So even the super-wealthy bully each other, marveled Tanny. Somehow, she had imagined the upper class to be a monolith. She shook her head in disapproval, then realized she should probably have no opinion. She wasn't even supposed to be listening (how could she not?).

Tanny observed that the people in Ben Kirk Estates didn't just buy or rent their units, they had to put up a chunk of money ahead of time just for the privilege of joining. It boggled her mind. She wondered if they then owned their unit, or if they had to keep paying rent even after the membership fee. She wondered how much the buy-in was and how much the rent. It must be a pretty tidy sum if a wealthy widower was trying to negotiate it down or away.

I will always be a peasant. I will always be "the help," reflected the homeless, barely employed young woman. She resented that, but again, did she want the shoe to be on the other foot? Did she want to have all the money and treat others like "help"? *Would I treat others like "help?"* she wondered. Then she chuckled. *No, I would pay generously and help everyone until I had nothing left.* She didn't understand a world in which some people got a lot more and some people got less, and it didn't actually seem connected to greatness of character or altruism or genuine merit. It was often transferred wealth from parents. It was luck. It was luck that was called "shrewdness" and "hard work". It didn't take into account all the hard work so many were doing just to make ends meet. It made her grumpy.

Fifi's voice cut through Tanny's reflections. "I am tired and need to go rest Miss Smith! Please help me back to my apartment!"

Tanny jumped up and moved to Mrs. Dunkirk-Jones' side. "Absolutely, Mrs. ... Mrs. Dunkirk-Jones." Tanny had been about to say, "Mrs. Fifi," which struck her as inappropriate. At least she hadn't said, "Your majesty." She didn't feel great about the slight resentment that was growing.

Mrs. D-J was down for another rest with ice by eleven am. Tanny couldn't quite believe it was only eleven. She was tired, possibly from her stirred emotions about the rich/poor divide. But she moved Fifi's laundry, hanging up some delicates in the large utility room. Then she started lunch, which was going to be baked salmon with lemon-pepper and a spinach salad. She texted Jeff, realizing she might not be ready by twelve fifteen.

"I'm off today. Let me know when you're ready," came the response.

Tanny felt heat rise under her ears.

By twelve forty-five, Fifi was fed, exercised, medicated, and lying down again. She was watching Masterpiece Theatre and didn't want to be bothered for at least an hour.

It was time to talk to the baffling, attractive man in Bracebridge.

Twenty-Four

March 1, afternoon

It was agreed that Tanny would call Jeff when she was ready. She wasn't ready, however, for the way her heart skipped a beat at hearing his voice.

"Hello. This is Jeff."

"Hey. It's me," she said.

"Hi...." He drew it out, almost with relief. "It's good to hear your voice. Where.... What are you doing in the States?"

"It's good to hear you too. My mom found me a job in Pennsylvania. I'm helping an old woman recover from hip surgery."

"How did that come about? Why Pennsylvania?"

"Oh, it is from her connections to Ben Kirk."

"The captain on Star Trek?"

"Huh?"

"Ben Kirk.... Wasn't he a captain on Star Trek? You know, 'Captain Kirk'."

Tanny laughed. "No. Ben Kirk is a place. You are thinking of ... what was his name ... James T. Kirk. I think 'Ben Kirk' means something like 'Church on a Hill.' It is definitely not connected to Star Trek."

"I was wondering what Star Trek had to do with a job in Pennsylvania." There was a smile in his voice. "Come to think of it, Jacob and Emily may have mentioned that town before. It's connected to the religion?"

"Yes," said Tanny.

"Ben Kirk," Jeff mused, then asked, "How long will you be down there?"

"Probably a week. Maybe longer. It's good money."

"How are you liking it?"

"Well enough. My overlord seems fair."

Jeff chuckled. "Will you be coming back up here for the meeting?" *Was there a hint of hopefulness in his voice?*

"I plan on it," responded Tanny. "I don't see this as a long-term thing." She paused. "Will you be there for the meeting?"

Jeff sounded puzzled. "Of course. Why wouldn't I?"

Tanny hesitated. "Well, my mom said something about you moving out west."

"Why would your mom—?"

"She talks a lot with Aunt Eileen. I guess it's something Aunt Eileen told her?"

"Wow. The only thing that might have given her that idea is that I told Eileen about a coworker of mine that is moving to Edmonton and trying to talk me into joining her."

"Are you thinking about it?"

"Not at all. I have no reason to move." Tanny could almost hear his bafflement over the line. "Why would Eileen think that conversation was newsworthy?"

"Well.... My mom implied that your coworker is your girlfriend and that is why you were considering moving."

Jeff's laughter was fresh and contagious. "She is not at all my girlfriend. I think she might have leanings that way, but I don't return the interest. I told Eileen about it because this woman's proposal that I move to Edmonton was so out-of-the-blue. There is work in Edmonton, but her desire that I move with her is not founded in reality. I had to be careful how I said 'no.'" There was a silence. "It's odd that Eileen gave your mom that impression. I guess I have to talk to Eileen again about discussing my personal affairs with others."

Tanny snorted. "My mom has the same problems." She was actually trembling with relief to discover *there was no girlfriend.* "So, no girlfriend is about to whisk you away to a remote location?" she asked, smiling.

"Not the last time I checked," he said. "And that's something I'd check."

Something in his voice sent tickles through Tanny. He was flirting.

I want to move back home now. Today.

"Well then," she responded. "That's a relief. Without you at Cedar Haven we'd have to appoint a new steward. It would probably be a beaver or loon, as the new one ought to have some interest in the property, and then we'd never get anything done. The beaver would chew up all the paperwork, and the loon would never shut up." She was grinning.

Jeff's laughter curled over the connection. After a comfortable silence, Jeff asked, "Do you have an opinion about the future of Cedar Haven?"

Tanny had to think about it. She realized that she had indeed developed an opinion since her recent time there. She said, "Honestly? I wish it didn't have to be given to the church *or* sold. I wish we could keep it in the family and run it ourselves."

Jeff barked with laughter. "That's exactly what I wish! Except, I'm not really family. So, though I *feel* like family, I have no real stake here except a feeling of belonging. I have a job as caretaker until Cedar Haven's fate is settled, then I have no stake at all. It's a strange feeling. I *feel* like family with Britt, Jacob, and Eileen. But nothing was ever legitimized."

"But aren't Jacob and Eileen your foster parents? Doesn't that make you family?"

"I've been looking into it. I think Britt's intent was that I be part of the future of the place. But Jacob and Eileen stopped being my legal guardians the minute I turned eighteen. Though they treat me the same, they never adopted me, so I have no legal standing in the family. I guess I didn't really think about it until Britt's death, when it sunk in that I am not legally part of the family at all, so I have no rights."

Tanny felt a flare of indignation. "Of *course* you are family! How can you live with and be raised by Jacob and Emily and Aunt Britt for—how many years—?"

"Legally twelve years. Physically twenty-two years."

"—*twenty-two* years, and not be considered family? *I* say you are family!" championed Britannia Suzanne Smith with fierce determination.

Rolling chuckles rumbled over the phone. "That's very kind of you, but I don't think that would hold up in court."

"Why didn't Jacob and Eileen ever adopt you?"

"Mmmm. You'd have to ask them. But I suspect it might be because my mother was Cree."

"So? Wait. That's kind of cool. But what difference would that make?" Tanny was considering Jeff's half first-nations lineage and finding that it made him more appealing.

Jeff said, "You'd have to ask them. But since starting to research my ancestry, I discovered a lot about historic racism in Ontario. There might have been stigma attached to adopting me."

The impact of Jeff's statement left Tanny outraged. She said, "That's just stupid. People can be so stupid! I'm sorry, Jeff. I had no idea. I know so little about your background."

Jeff continued, "I'm half Dutch Canadian and half Cree. My Dutch grandparents threw my father out when they discovered he had gotten my mother pregnant. They had forbidden him to see her. They said they didn't want a mixed-blood grandchild, then cut him off completely. So, my teenage parents ran away and got married, and shortly after, I was born. I remember feeling loved, and that they loved each other. But I remember sleeping in a lot of different places. I remember them fighting about money. I know now that they were constantly struggling to find employment and housing. Racism against their mixed marriage was a big part of their struggles—it was back in the sixties."

Tanny made a noise of sympathy. "I'm only now learning just how badly the indigenous have been treated. I feel awful."

Jeff grumbled, "Depending on how you look at it I am half victim and half racist."

Tanny was dumbstruck.

"My therapist is asking me to see myself as a blessing—as a representation of when love unites different cultures."

"I like your therapist," enthused Tanny. "I much prefer that perspective to seeing yourself as the product of racism."

"Well, exactly. Yet I live with racism in my own bloodstream. I feel guilty that I prefer Northern European culture to life on the Res. When I was a kid, when finances and housing were really tough, we went to mom's family on the reservation, and they took us in. They took care of us because we were family. That's beautiful. But I think it bothered my dad's pride. We were welcomed on the reservation, but he always seemed uneasy there. I loved having so many cousins to play with, but I was used to my tiny family. On the Res there were many people who all seemed to know me. I wasn't used to that. I was passed around among people who were 'looking after me.' But I felt abandoned when my parents 'dropped me off with the relatives.'

"Anyway, my parents never stayed more than a few months on the Res. I think my dad wanted to support us by himself. I preferred when our family was just the three of us anyway."

"I can't even imagine," sympathized Tanny. "So, how did you end up with Aunt Eileen and Uncle Jacob?"

"Ah. As I got older, I became aware that my parents were drinking. They first lost custody of me when I was five because of their drinking. At the time they were renting an apartment in Bracebridge, and they were arrested for petty theft and driving drunk. I think they were already alcoholics by then. That's when I went to Jacob and Eileen the first time. My parents were sent to rehab. They had to sober up and stay clean, and both hold down jobs for six months and have a decent place to raise me before they could ask for me back. My parents did win me back after about a year. Eighteen months after that they died in a car accident driving drunk, so I went back to Jacob and Eileen for good. I was seven and a half. Though I had an uncle and many cousins on the Res, the system wanted me in my current neighborhood and school, with Jacob and Eileen who knew me already and loved me.

They have been my family since then. I didn't go back to the Res to visit until I was able to drive. I have some connections with my cousins there, but I don't feel like the reservation is my home. The only place that has felt like home is Cedar Haven."

Tanny was deeply moved by these heart confessions. She said, "Thank you for telling me all this. I feel honored."

There was silence on the line. Then Jeff said, his voice rumbling with emotion, "Thanks for being someone safe to talk to about this. I used to be able to talk with Britt. I've stopped trying to talk to Jacob and Eileen about what I'm discovering. They keep changing the subject. With Britt gone, it has been hard."

"I'm always happy to listen," said Tanny, meaning it. "It's a lot that you are processing. I admire your honesty and strength."

There was the sound of throat clearing.

"And I'm thinking I'm going to give Jacob and Eileen a hard time about never adopting you."

Jeff's laughter was infectious. "Look, I'm not looking for pity. I don't want you to bother Jacob or Eileen about adopting me. It's way too late. All of this was meant to be about the future of Cedar Haven. I want to find out what 'stewardship' means, and what the scope of our roles really is. I'd like to make sure my own longings don't interfere with what Britt appointed us to do."

Tanny was being newly impressed with this man's integrity when her alarm went off.

"Darn it, Jeff. My time is up. I'd love to keep talking, but I have to get back to work."

"Understood," he said. "Thanks for your time. This was great." After a hesitation he asked. "Could we talk again tomorrow? I promise not to monopolize the conversation this time."

Tanny made a double fist pump, phone and all. Then she brought the phone back and said, "Of course! Depending on the fabulous Fifi's schedule, I'd love that."

"Might we do a video chat this time?"

It felt like tickle-tummy road. "Sure. Yes. We can do that." It would be *great* to see his face again. Maybe her big reactions would settle down once she saw his ordinary self. He seemed to have grown in importance and meaning since those few days in Bracebridge, despite her mother's bucket of cold water. Tanny had not realized what a philosopher Jeff was. And he was in therapy! Her curiosity just grew.

"Okay, bye!" she said.

"Goodbye for now," came his response. And the connection dropped.

Tanny stared out her bedroom window at the grassy meadow beyond and thought and thought.

"Miss Smith!" came the peremptory call for the other side of her door. "Five-minute warning!"

Returning to the present, Tanny finished tidying up and gathering herself. Then it was back into the fray.

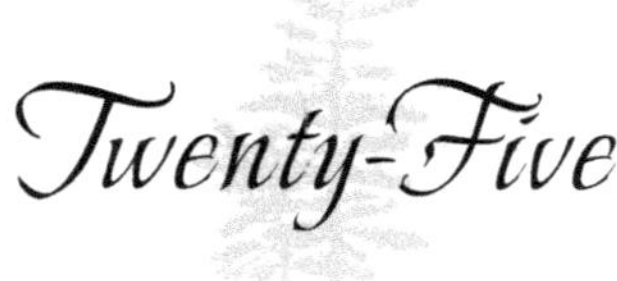

Twenty-Five

March 1, afternoon and evening

Mrs. Dunkirk Jones was sitting on her walker outside Tanny's bedroom. It had not been quite the uninterrupted hour Tanny had expected, but Fifi was the boss. Tanny asked for time to use the washroom and then presented herself to her royal employer for next instructions.

Fifi's pain meds were working, and she was ready to do more planning and talking. They sat and reviewed the afternoon schedule. The nurse would be coming at three to check Fifi's progress. "She will probably change the bandages, which lets you off the hook," explained Fifi.

Tanny was struck by Fifi's voice. It had a decided vocal fry, yet it sounded nothing like the latest generation of young women. It sounded like her voice was well-worn. It had sounded like this the whole time, but for some reason Tanny just noted it.

"I want you to write that down," continued Fifi.

Tanny realized that she had missed something important. She tried replaying the sound of Fifi's voice in her head, but was pretty sure "Make the flounder for Mimi to dinner" was not what Fifi had said. Tanny grabbed a pen and paper and clicked the pen open. "Could you say that again please?" Tanny asked, hoping to cover her loss of focus. *I really should get tested for ADD.*

"We must remember to take the flowers to dinner to give to Mimi. We cannot forget!" said Mrs. Dunkirk-Jones with some impatience.

"... to dinner," said Tanny as she wrote it out. Yes. Fifi had been telling her about the community dinner in the dining room that happened on Mondays and Thursdays. They needed to head down there by five and remember to bring a bouquet of flowers that Fifi had forgotten on Thursday. The flowers looked only a little tired. Tanny decided to try to spruce them up if she had time. Perhaps the recipient had poor eyesight.

Once the planning was done, Fifi needed help toileting. Fortunately, the pain meds were still working well, so the disrobing and sitting were not as uncomfortable as at other times. Still, Tanny's heart expanded in sympathy at the indignities involved in toileting the elegant woman. Fifi seemed to bear it with grace and a certain matter-of-factness that prevented some of the awkwardness.

Tanny realized that she wanted to do nothing but talk about Jeff. Fifi would probably be interested, but she would want all the details so she could dispense judgment and advice, not listen like a sympathetic girlfriend. *No thank you.* Tanny scoured her brain for someone to call when she had another moment to breathe. *Susan!* Of course!

The afternoon progressed with the walking exercises and the icing and rests, and then Tanny being asked to dust and vacuum while Fifi was with the nurse.

"I cancelled my usual cleaner for this week, because I realized that you could just do it in your spare time." Fifi seemed satisfied with her clever idea for saving money. Tanny wondered how much the usual cleaning people counted on that income. She also wondered how much money Fifi was "saving" by not paying Tanny for the added work. Apparently Tanny's "spare time" wasn't considered "spare" at all. Did Fifi's level of privilege really make her incapable of imagining the impact of her "cost saving" workarounds on those less privileged? Mrs. Dunkirk-Jones didn't seem malicious. Nevertheless, she seemed unaware how Tanny felt at being told that her free time should be spent doing more work for Fifi than was originally agreed upon.

So Tanny dusted and vacuumed instead of doing any self-care. There always seemed to be another task that Fifi expected of her when she was still for a moment. Tanny sighed. Maybe she could write in her journal at bedtime. It didn't seem like there would be any time to talk to Susan in the foreseeable future. She was deeply grateful for her *almost* hour after lunch. That might be her only window for communication with Jeff. What about talking to her family? Or other friends? She hadn't even notified her few Ben Kirk friends to let them know she was in town.

At least Fifi let her use the washroom without question. Tanny sent off two texts when in there, one to Susan and one to Lauren Anderson—first cousin on her Smith side—who lived in Ben Kirk. She didn't know when she'd have time to talk to either, but she had to believe she would.

The afternoon went by. Tanny had to spend the anticipated break when the nurse was there housecleaning and learning about wound care.

By five o'clock Fifi and Tanny were arriving at the dining room, flowers propped in the basket of Fifi's walker.

Visitors as well as residents were welcome to this meal if they paid. The large, big-windowed, carpeted room with the vaulted ceiling was filling with incomers, many of whom looked at Tanny with curiosity. Except for the few helpers like Tanny and some of the wait-staff, it was a sea of comfortable, Caucasian seniors. Fifi presented the flowers to one of the ladies as they passed. "Happy belated birthday, Mimi," she offered. The woman nodded and smiled gratefully. She did not look like one of the wealthier residents.

Tanny wove through the tables behind Mrs. Dunkirk-Jones until they came to a table of Fifi's choosing. It sat four, and it became evident that the other three chairs were for Fifi's usual dining companions. Tanny had to find an open seat nearby.

She found a table with only three others, so she grabbed the fourth seat. But as she sat, a woman in many tribal shawls pressed a hand on her shoulder and said, "You don't want to sit there, dear. Come sit with us."

Scooped up by the elbow, Tanny was taken to another table with two other women already there. She sat, curious about her bohemian rescuer. She whispered as she sat, "Why didn't I want to sit there?"

"Oh dear, Homer can't keep his hands to himself. He feels completely entitled to any young woman and can get unpleasant when rejected. We all make sure that only his sister or other men sit at his table."

It was said with such matter-of-factness that Tanny stared. What nastiness had she just avoided thanks to this woman?

The humming in the room was dulling as people found their seats.

Tanny introduced herself to the table, again playing the genealogy game. The three ladies all seemed to know her ancestors, but she had no idea where they all fit in, though they told her their connections as if she would know everyone they named.

The shawled woman, who made Tanny think of a chubby Professor Trelawney without the glasses (Tanny loved the Harry Potter books) introduced herself as Fawn Love. *You're kidding,* thought Tanny. *Did she mature to fit her name, or was she born a hippy baby and the parents named her accordingly?* She seemed warm and motherly. The other two were Mimi Schmidt (of the wilting flowers) and Evelyn Andover. *Seriously? Evelyn Andover? Maybe she was Evelyn Something-else and married an Andover.* They were all warm and felt like they would be great to get to know.

Soon an older man stood up and clinked on a glass for silence. He greeted them and announced that it was time for the blessing. "Let us bow our heads in prayer," he said in an Australian accent. After a short pause he said, "Ohhhh....."

"—give thanks unto the Lord..." joined the entire room, reciting the quote from Psalms that most of them had used since childhood. Tanny recited along with them, having been raised in this religious culture.

As soon as it was over Fawn murmured, "We seem to have landed the bishop himself tonight." She winked at the table, and her friends smiled. Then, rising from her chair and tipping her head toward the buffet she added, "Shall we?"

Several of the residents were now rising (or struggling up) from their chairs to approach the buffet table. As Tanny made her way to the line with her table mates, "Mads" Bradford from the bridge game tapped her shoulder. "Don't worry, June is getting a plate for Fifi, so you don't have to."

Tanny thanked her for the information but was left wondering if she should have known to get Fifi a plate. It seemed there were customs and rules that she was simply expected to know. She was glad she hadn't gotten in trouble over NOT getting Fifi her food. She would have done it happily if someone had told her how things worked here.

Once in the line, a few people were indeed leaving the buffet table with two plates, as if this was a common thing in this dining room. Tanny was touched by how the residents looked after each other.

The buffet had a few choices of items with a wait staff ready to provide whatever was requested. Tanny felt uncomfortable realizing that most of the staff were people of colour. It just seemed a bit on-the-nose to have these young, obviously not white people serving this crowd of wealthy all-whites. She accepted her serving of beef tenderloin and gravy, mashed potatoes, and perfectly steamed broccoli with thanks.

As she returned to the table where the other three ladies were already seated Fawn was saying, "I wonder if the ministers find this turn saying grace for us bothersome. I used to assume they couldn't wait to serve as ministers on every occasion. Now I wonder if having to show up and lead us in grace every single meal is like yet another ribbon-cutting for a politician—a necessary but tedious part of the job."

"Somewhere back in time the church leaders decided that we couldn't move or breathe or think without a minister presiding," said Evelyn. Tanny noted a tang of bitterness under her voice.

"They didn't want us to fall into 'falsity,'" agreed Mimi with a twinkle in her eye.

"Now they're stuck having to show up for every single unimportant thing to say a blessing or read some Scriptures. I guess it's too late for them to change their minds," agreed Fawn.

Tanny liked these ladies. They didn't seem afraid to discuss possible problems in the church, something Tanny had felt was unwelcome with her parents and other church members.

Tanny said, "Like, how come single people can't just be *people*, and not just someone-who-isn't-married-yet? Maybe people have worth without being married. Some people don't even want to be married." She stuffed a forkful of gravy-covered beef into her mouth.

The table went silent. Tanny lifted her eyes to see all the women looking at her. She lowered her fork, chewing like mad.

"Where did you find this one?" said Evelyn in delight, patting Tanny's shoulder. "You have a knack for finding the good ones."

Mimi Schmidt said, "I've been saying that for ages, but nobody listens to me!"

Tanny's eyes were wide with wonder. *Other, older people had been thinking about this too? Why had nothing ever been done to remedy this problem?* She grinned, her heart rate recovering from what she had thought was an enormous foot-in-mouth situation.

"You don't have the right genitals, dear," said Evelyn.

"Or gobs of money," added Fawn.

Tanny was a little shocked by the casual ease with which these ladies were discussing church politics. She was also shocked by what they were saying. *The leaders favour those with money? They do? Isn't this a church?*

Tanny had her criticisms of her childhood faith, but she felt uncomfortable to hear these observations. She wanted to believe the leaders were sincere and genuinely trying to follow the Lord. But according to these women, corruption in the leadership seemed to be a given.

Fortunately, the conversation turned to lighter matters; who was the latest resident to have to go into memory care, who really *ought* to be in memory care but their partner was trying to keep them at the Estates, and what they thought of the young men coming up for ordination in June.

The young men. Tanny thought. They still only let men be ordained as ministers.

The dessert course was served and Tanny checked in with Fifi to see how she was doing. Did Fifi want dessert?

Fifi had somehow already gotten her dessert. She said she would finish up and be ready to leave momentarily. So Tanny returned to the table with her dinner companions to say goodbye. They all agreed they should dine together again, and Tanny returned to Fifi's side.

As she waited for Fifi to finish, an old woman just sitting in the aisle in a wheel chair said, "You are reminding me of an old friend." She had a British accent. Tanny smiled absently.

"Britannia Bender"

Tanny turned and looked at the speaker. She was a stout old thing, obviously wigged, sitting up in her chair. She was studying Tanny.

"Yes...." She said in satisfaction. "You could be her granddaughter." She looked intensely at Tanny. "What's your name?"

"Tanny—er, Britannia Smith. I'm named after her."

"Are you indeed? Now how could that be? 'Smith'? No, that isn't right...."

My mother was ..." Tanny stopped in confusion, corrected herself, "is ..." she stopped again, "well, *was* Emily Bender," she finished. "She's married, not dead. She's David's daughter."

"David's daughter..." the old woman murmured, brow creased.

"David was Aunt Britt's brother. I'm Britt's great-niece."

The woman continued to assess her. "Mmm. Well, you've certainly got the look of Britt about you, though the colouring's all wrong. She was very dark. Almost like an Indian." The woman had gone into herself. "Headstrong, she was. There was no telling *her* what to do."

Tanny grinned. "That's Aunt Britt, all right.

The woman asked offhand, "We lost touch. Did she ever have any children?"

"Aunt Britt? Oh. No. She never married." Tanny chuckled. "She never found a man she could stand well enough."

"Oh yes she did," said the woman in the wheelchair.

"Miss Smith," came Mrs. Dunkirk-Jones's peremptory voice right in her ear. Tanny jumped.

"Oh, hello Grace. You're looking well." Fifi greeted the woman in the chair. Then she said, "I'm ready to go now dear," and turned Tanny by the elbow.

Tanny spun back and looked urgently into 'Grace's' face. "What do you mean? Aunt Britt loved someone? Who was he? What happened?" Tanny begged.

"Miss Smith! Are you coming?"

"Grace's" eyes were gazing off somewhere. "Nearly broke her heart, he did."

Tanny wanted to shake the woman. "Mrs... Miss..." *What is her name? I can't just call her "Grace"!*

Somebody came up behind the chair and took the handles. "Ready to go, Mrs. Evans?"

"Mrs. Evans," Tanny urged. The eyes refocused on her.

Grace smiled and stroked Tanny's cheek. "Very like her, yes. That's why I thought perhaps..."

"Britannia Smith!"

Tanny stamped her foot. "I'm coming! Just a minute!" She looked at Britt's friend. "Mrs. Evans. Who? Who nearly broke Britt's heart?"

Mrs. Evans had turned wistful. "I'm the only one who knows, you see. Scandalous, it was. But she had to confide in someone. I would have been the maid of honour."

"Britannia Smith, I am waiting," came Fifi's voice, not sounding pleased.

"Look, I have to go. But can I come visit you? Please? Tomorrow?"

"Certainly, dear. Certainly."

"Thank you!" Tanny gave the gentle woman an impulsive kiss and spun round, nearly knocking Mrs. Dunkirk-Jones into her walker.

"Great heaven's girl! You're like a bull in a china shop!" declared her highness.

Twenty-Six

March 1 to March 2

On the way back to Mrs. Dunkirk's apartment, Tanny asked her employer about Grace Evans.

"She moved in about eight months ago. She has lived in England most of her life but wanted to be here once her husband died. I don't know her very well, but she seems pleasant. She isn't in my circle, you see."

Tanny knew that "isn't in my circle" probably meant that Grace wasn't a wealthy woman. The Estates did have a lot of mixing of the upper classes and the "lower" classes. Still, Tanny had learned that a person had to put up one-hundred thousand dollars just for the privilege of moving into the Estates, after which you were expected to pay a monthly rent; so "lower" class wasn't very low in this case. Tanny definitely identified with the lower classes—the ones who wouldn't ever be able to afford to move in at all.

Once back in Fifi's apartment Tanny helped Fifi get a sponge-bath at the bathroom sink and prepare for bed. Tanny assisted the older woman to settle back on her pillows. Fifi put her hair-protecting helmet on and had taken all of her meds.

Tanny said, "Mrs. Dunkirk-Jones, may I take part of tomorrow afternoon off to go visit Mrs. Evans? She knew my aunt back during the war. She knows things about her that I have never heard before."

Fifi huffed and asked Tanny to bring her the day planner.

Tanny returned with it and Fifi looked it over. "I was meaning to give you Wednesday afternoon off. Tomorrow, I have the physical therapist coming at ten am." She thought for a bit, frowning.

Fifi handed the planner back to Tanny and said, "You could see if she can see you tomorrow at ten am, or you'll have to wait until Wednesday afternoon."

Tanny thanked her employer and finished settling her for the night. She crossed her fingers that Mrs. Evans could see her tomorrow at ten. She was desperately curious to hear about the man that nearly broke Britt's heart.

It was barely nine pm. so Tanny called her mom. Emily was delighted to hear from Tanny. She wanted to hear how much Tanny loved living there and that Tanny had found a nice church man to go out with.

"Well, mom, I'm kept pretty busy with my job. I don't meet a lot of nice young men in this retirement home. But I did meet a friend of Britt's from the war. I'm hoping to visit her tomorrow."

"Why would you do that? Britt's dead now, honey."

"Because I'm curious about her life, mom. You did name me after her. I've always been curious about her."

"Okay, sweetheart. Do what you want. Are there any ministers around in the Estates? Surely some of the unmarried seminary students have duties there?"

"Mom. I'm sure you are right. I have not seen any, and if I do see one, I'm not about to lie down in front of him waving a handkerchief to get his attention. It's just not done anymore."

"Oh sweetheart, please be serious. You know you want to get married. You are in 'marriage central' right now! Just get out there. Someone's bound to snap you up."

Tanny reflected just how far apart her mother's focus and perspective were from her own. Then she had a mischievous thought. "Actually, mom, between you and me, I do have my eye on someone." She really hoped her mother would assume it was someone in the church.

"Who is it? Is he from a good family? Is he a theologue? Is he a Dunkirk descendent? Or perhaps a Bradford?" Her mother had taken the bait.

"He's from a great family, mom. He's working in medicine. But we haven't even had a date. We've just talked a bit. So, I don't know...."

"Who are his parents? What is his name—"

"—Mom, I have to go," interrupted Tanny with some urgency. "I'll call again when I can. Love you!" Tanny hung up, her heart racing. She had told no lies.

Then Tanny texted Susan, hoping she would be able to talk.

But there was no response from Susan.

Tanny texted Lauren Anderson next, who replied that she couldn't talk just now, but what about meeting tomorrow some time? They agreed to go on a walk on Wednesday afternoon when Tanny was free.

It was nearly nine thirty, probably too late to call Mrs. Evans, even if Tanny could find her phone number.

Tanny texted Jeff. "Hey Jeff, I loved our talk today. I'm looking forward to talking tomorrow." And then because he had said it to her earlier, she added,

"Sweet dreams."

"Sweet dreams, he replied. "And a slobbery kiss from Mack."

Tanny fell asleep, grinning.

Tuesday morning started smoothly. Tanny was accustomed to Fifi's routine now. Fifi seemed to be healing without incident, and it was just a matter of keeping up the exercises and ice, rest, and medications. Shortly before ten o'clock, Fifi got a phone call from a friend, so Tanny used the time to look up Grace Evans' number in the Estates Directory and call her. She was delighted when the woman answered, and even more thrilled to learn a visit at ten would be welcome.

Tanny stayed to see the PT in and then sprinted down the three long halls to get to Grace Evans' unit, which was in "B" wing. She started out sprinting but soon had to restrain herself to a speed-walk, as her hastiness seemed to upset the residents in the halls.

"My goodness! Slow down, girl!"

"What is going on? Is there a fire?"

"Inappropriate!"

Tanny realized that running was not appreciated in these corridors. Still, she didn't slow when Kevin called from the front desk asking what was wrong.

Tanny called back breathily, "I'm visiting Grace, and I need to hurry."

It seemed like quite a distance from the end of D wing, past C wing, through A wing (the one with the main entrance), to partway down B wing. She had traveled almost the entire length of the C-shaped structure. But she arrived outside a unit marked with the name "G. Evans" and knocked.

"Goodness, child, you are out of breath!" welcomed the woman from her wheelchair. She rolled herself backwards to let Tanny in.

Grace's unit was sweet and small. The layout was similar to Fifi's but with less generous proportions and only one bedroom. The kitchen was small and the living-dining area a little cramped. But Grace seemed content and had decorated it with a decidedly British feel – knick-knacks and chintz and doilies.

Grace welcomed Tanny to sit on the flowered sofa and offered to serve her tea. Tanny wondered how Grace would manage the kitchen with her wheelchair, but relaxed when she saw the bewigged lady rise from her wheelchair to hobble around the kitchen, using the counters to support her weight.

Tanny wanted to offer to help but had a feeling that could take away the dignity of her host. She said, "Let me know if there's anything I can do, Mrs. Evans."

"Oh, I'll be just a moment," replied Grace. She had placed a kettle on to boil and was placing teacups and saucers and small plates on a tray. She added a small pitcher of cream and some sugar. As the kettle began to hiss, Grace placed some packaged digestive biscuits onto a plate.

Tanny watched Grace "hot" the pot in true British teamaking style. Though Tanny had become lazy in her home tea brewing, she had learned all the little tips to brewing the perfect cup of tea as she grew up. Grace was following all of the best practices. Tanny realized that she was looking forward to a great tasting cup of tea. Grace dropped the bags of a popular British tea brand into the pot.

The kettle sang, and Mrs. Evans poured the water into the teapot. She then set a timer and began to transfer the tray and cookies down the counter towards the table.

"If you would please..." said Mrs. Evans, indicating the tray and plate.

"Of course," said Tanny, rising to carry the tray and cookies over to the table pressed against the side wall. Though small, it was covered in a clean, lacy tablecloth. She went back for the pot of tea. Grace lowered herself into her wheelchair with a small grunt, then pulled herself over to the table using her feet.

"Now then," Grace said, and handed Tanny a small plate, indicating the biscuits. Tanny selected two. They waited for the timer to ding, at which point Grace promptly removed the teabags from the pot. Once that was done, the British gentlewoman poured two cups of tea into the elegant cups. She first handed Tanny her saucer, then her cup, then a spoon. "There is sugar and milk, if you like," she offered.

Tanny was enjoying herself. Impatient as she was for information, she was enjoying this old-fashioned ritual. She knew to add a bit of milk and a bit of sugar for the best experience. It was just like her best memories of having tea with her grandma Smith from Pittsburgh when Tanny was little. It was lightly sweet and rich without any bitterness. Tanny dipped her tea biscuit in her tea and then bit off the soft cookie penetrated with tea.

"Now, I understand you want to hear about your great aunt, Britt," began Mrs. Evans.

"Oh yes please," encouraged Tanny, covering her mouth as she chewed and swallowed. "You said she fell in love with someone? Who was he?"

Grace sat back in her chair and smiled, looking inward. "We were both in the war effort, you see. We met during training as communications officers in England and formed a close friendship. The training was tough, but we would laugh and keep each other's spirits up in the evenings. We just understood each other. We knew we were going to be posted to the continent soon, which we found both exciting and frightening.

"Finally, our postings came, both in France it turns out, but we didn't know that at the time. She was sent to a small village not far from Nantes. I was on the outskirts of Paris. Over time, we figured out where the other one was and managed to send innocuous letters to each other as frivolous young French girls. We would have been disciplined and pulled out of service if our supervisors ever found out. We were so foolish! But we thought we could bend the rules and get away with it."

What happened?" asked Tanny, eyes wide.

"Oh, well, we *did* get away with it, but it was sheer dumb luck," replied Mrs. Evans, her eyes showing her astonishment. "We were so naïve and foolish. If we had gotten caught, we could have put many other operatives in danger. But we felt lucky and invincible." Grace shrugged her lacy shoulders. "Or we were just so skilled at our deception we never got caught; but I don't think that was really it."

"Britt's love interest?" Tanny prompted.

"Yes. So, Britt was embedded with a rural family who had a son and a daughter. It turns out they were all active in the underground, and that is why Britt was sent to them. They kept their heads low and acted subservient when the occasional German patrol stopped to check on them. The son, Lucien, eventually fully joined the maquis, but before he did that, he had to hide when German troops came snooping. The LaRoches made it look like their son was long gone. To the Germans, it appeared it was just the parents, the daughter, and Britt, "the cousin," working the farm. They even had to be careful to keep the son's rooms looking long abandoned.

"Lucien?" asked Tanny. "That's the same name as Britt's godson." The hairs were rising on Tanny's arms.

"Aha, yes, Britt's 'godson,'" responded Grace Evans with a twinkle in her eye. She chuckled. "Britt's godson. It was brilliant and tragic."

"What?" demanded Tanny. "You have to tell me!"

"You see, Britt had fallen in love with Lucien LaRoche. Oh, he was a handsome one! Britt and Lucien snuck in visits whenever they could. But he was often away fighting, and she had to travel a lot with her work. They set a date to be married in February, nineteen forty-two. Britt wanted me there—were we such fools. I was attempting to find a way to join them when, on New Year's Eve,

Lucien was killed."

Tanny gasped in sadness.

"I have never know such a strong woman. Britt could have asked to be extracted. She could have asked for leave, but she stayed on, risking her life every day. I suspect she wanted to die except—"

"Except what?" urged Tanny, her skin tingling.

"Except Britt was carrying Lucien's child."

"The 'godson,'" whispered Tanny.

"The godson," confirmed Grace.

Twenty-Seven

March 2

Tanny sat still as the full confirmation hit her. Britt gave birth to a child in France while working with the French resistance. She had not been able to marry the father before he died. So, she left the infant in France.

"But who took care of her baby? His last name is not LaRoche...?" she had to ask.

The sister, Justine, and her sweetheart pretended he was their baby. His name was Etienne Boucher—"

"Yes. Boucher!" Tanny remembered.

"They raised him as their son. The family resemblance through Justine was enough that no one questioned his parentage. Besides, in France during the war they weren't so concerned about premarital sex and children born before a marriage. And so, it made sense that Britt left her only child with family in France. She hid well how desperate she was for the few letters and pictures they sent about his growth. I am the only one outside of his French family that knows. Even little Lucien might never have been told of his real birth parents. There has been no sign he had ever saw Britt as his birth mother."

Now Tanny wanted to get back to Cedar Haven as soon as possible to look more closely at Britt's pictures. She wondered if there was a diary anywhere, or other evidence of Britt's time in France.

Tanny said, "But Britt always said there was no man alive that she couldn't live without." Then it struck her – *alive*. "No man *alive*...."

"No man alive," repeated her British hostess. "Because her one true love had died. Ironically, she managed to live without him anyway. She had no choice, poor dear."

"Aunt Britt...." Tanny's heart ached for the woman whom she hadn't known as well as she thought, and for the child who never knew his real roots. Tanny wanted more than anything to reach out to her newly discovered "uncle" in France and wondered if there were any cousins her age.

Grace Evans said, "I got to meet him, the wee one. He had a shock of dark hair, and eyes that looked like they might go brown, like Britt's. They named him Lucien, after his father, and David, after Britt's father." Using her feet, Grace wheeled herself across the room to a secretary desk. She fished around in it and pulled out a faded, black and white photo. She held it out to Tanny.

In the picture, a much younger Britt was holding a tiny bundle with lots of dark hair.

Tanny made a noise of endearment as she looked at the faded image. "May I take a copy of this with my phone?" she asked.

"I think you should keep it," Grace said. I don't need it anymore. I think Britt's family should have it."

"Oh, thank you," was Tanny's sincere response as she looked at it more closely.

"In fact," continued Grace, "I think you ought to have these...." Pulling her chair along with her feet, Grace took herself to her bedroom. "Follow me," she called. "I'll need you to reach...."

Tanny followed the woman to the bedroom where Grace was pointing at the folding doors of a closet.

"On the top shelf, in a box. Please lift it down for me."

Tanny had to determine *which* box, but eventually an old bankers' box sat on the bed as Grace rummaged through it. "Here they are," she said at last. She held up a small stack of letters, tied together with twine. "These are the letters Britt wrote to me during the war and after. Some of them may not make much sense because we had to use codes, but you can see her handwriting and get a sense of who she was from them."

Tanny took them gingerly, not believing what she was holding.

"I probably shouldn't have kept them at the time, but I couldn't see what the Gestapo might get from them should they find them. I still don't. None of these letters held war-related information. I want you to have them." Grace's hand shook a little when she delivered them to Tanny.

"I don't know what to say," whispered Tanny. "This is amazing! I will take very good care of them."

"You are more than welcome, my dear," smiled the sweet woman with the delectable British accent.

As they traveled back to the table Mrs. Evans said, "I believe I have more pictures for you around here somewhere, but I won't look for them now. I will just have to have you over for another cup of tea!" she smiled sweetly as she returned to the table.

Tanny was itching to look at the letters but instead began asking Mrs. Evans about her own time in the war and her husband. Any children—? But the alarm on Tanny's phone cut her off.

"Oh dear! I have to go already?" Tanny finished her second biscuit and then gulped her tea. "Thank you SO much, Mrs. Evans. I look forward to visiting again!" She took the soft, wrinkled hands and pressed them.

"Do come again, little Britt. It is almost like seeing my Britt again, visiting with you."

Tanny laid a kiss on the silky cheek and ran for the door, clutching the photograph and letters. "We will do this again," she called. "Thank you!" and she again ran—no, speed-walked—back to the far end of D wing, entering a minute before eleven am.

"There you are, miss Bender," announced Fifi with satisfaction. She was sitting in her living room as the physical therapist was finishing her notes and packing up. "Right on time."

"Yes! Hello, Mrs. Fifi. I'll be right with you." Tanny deposited her new treasures on her bed and returned to help her wealthy employer get lunch, then settle in bed with ice, awaiting Masterpiece Theatre. It was time to call Jeff again.

Tanny's heart beat faster as Jeff's face came up on screen, and Tanny saw that he was on the couch in front of the fireplace. His hair was growing back in a bit. It was a solid layer of golden stubble now.

"Hey there," he said. "It's great to see you."

Tanny felt her heat rise. She grinned over it and said, "It's good to see you too. You are starting to have hair."

Jeff ran a hand over his scalp. "Yes. This stage is always a bit strange. It feels like a beard on my head. But it doesn't last long. How's the work going?"

"Ohmygosh, Jeff! I just had the most amazing visit with an old friend of Britt's. She has so much information about Aunt Britt that I never knew." And Tanny filled Jeff in about Britt's French lover and their out-of-wedlock child. "In those days, an unmarried woman with a child was such a disgrace in Canada that Britt had to give him up. He was adopted by the father's sister who pretended he was theirs. Britt had to leave her infant in France and return home to Canada. She never told anyone the truth about him. We believed her when she said she had a godson."

"The pictures on the mantel," Jeff said, and he moved over to look at them. "So, these ones of her godson are really of her *son*?"

"Yes!" Tanny confirmed. "Hey, could you photograph them and send them to me? That would be awesome."

"I can do that," agreed Jeff.

"Mrs. Evans also gave me some of Britt's letters from the war. I can't wait to read them."

"I wish you were here. I'd love to read them too. May I see them when you get back?"

"Of course!" agreed Tanny, still a bit dazed from the recent revelations.

Jeff said, "I don't think Jacob and Eileen know anything about this."

"I don't think anyone in the family does," said Tanny.

"I'm trying to decide if Jacob and Eileen would be interested by it or embarrassed by it," speculated Jeff, running his hand over his stubble as he thought.

"I'm pretty sure my siblings and cousins would find it rather romantic, not scandalous. I wish I could meet Britt's son."

"I would like that too." There was a silence as they both digested the news. Then Jeff said, "Do you know when you'll be back?"

"Well, my first plan was to ride back with Jon and Stephen after their meetings, this coming weekend."

"Your first plan?"

"Well, probably my only plan. My mom wants me to stay down here working until I find a husband."

"Really? A husband. Down there? Is that what you want?"

Tanny loved the way lines creased his cheeks when he half-smiled. And he could do that cocked-eyebrow thing that was darn cute. "I don't think it's likely to happen. I just want to come home. But I also need an income desperately. If another senior wants me to help them and will pay decently, I might stay on another week or two."

"Well, I vote for you coming back to Canada this weekend. You've got a ride arranged and everything."

Tanny felt her cheeks warm. "And maybe I'll get lucky and find work up there." *He clearly wants me back!* Her insides were squirming. "Besides, I have to be back for the Cedar Haven Stewardship meetings, so I might as well come home soon."

"I think you are very smart."

There was another silence between them as they gazed at each other, so many layers of meaning humming between their spoken words.

Tanny couldn't stop herself from grinning.

She had no idea what her dimples did to Jeff's insides.

After a bit Jeff said, "Look, I can't talk at this time tomorrow or Thursday. But we could look at Friday. Does that work for you?"

Tanny tried to hide her disappointment. "Of course. Is it your work?"

"Yes, I've got two long shifts coming up. I have no control over my availability, but I'll text when I can." He looked apologetic.

"We'll make it work. Besides, I'm way behind on my calls to family. And by Friday, I may be about to head home."

Jeff's masculine grin unfolded Tanny's stomach.

"I will look forward to that, then," he said.

All too soon it was time to hang up, and the two of them finally managed it.

Tanny sighed and rested her head back against the wall.

She was *definitely* enjoying this man and looked forward to their next contact. Were they headed into a serious relationship? Things were looking that way.

The rest of the day ticked by on schedule, and once Fifi was settled Tanny was able to get Susan on the phone.

"Hi Susan, how are you? I've missed talking."

"Hi Tanny. I'm sorry. Last night I was so tired I went to bed at eight. I saw your text this morning."

"No problem. Are you okay?"

Susan gave a light chuckle. "Well, the home test came back positive that I'm pregnant."

"You are!" Tanny was about to burst into happy praise but remembered Susan's fears about being pregnant so soon. She said instead, "Wow. How do you feel about that?"

"I still have to go to the doctor and get it confirmed. I told Jon yesterday on the phone. He wanted to head back here immediately." She laughed again. "I've told Jon and mom and you. I'm going to wait until Jon is back and we have confirmation before we tell anyone else. Can you please keep the secret?"

"Of course I can. But, if you are pregnant, how are you feeling about that?"

"Jon's excitement pretty much washed away my fear. And I do know that not all pregnancies are as hard as my first one was. The idea is growing on me. I mean, there's a new being swimming inside me that is part of Jonathan and me. That tickles me tremendously. I'm pushing away the memories and fears from the twins' pregnancy and trying to accept that this is what's happening. So ... I think I'm getting used to the idea."

"Susan, I'm so happy for you. I plan on supporting you all the way through if this is real. I'm coming back with Jon on Saturday."

Susan laughed out loud. "You are such a darling. I do have a lot of support, with extended family and Jon and neighbors. I just hate asking for help."

"Let me move into your basement apartment, and I will be steps away!"

"If we had it finished, that would be great!"

"I will be living in Jenny's house before it is sold, so I'll still be close."

"Yes, you will. Oh, hang on—" There was the sound of one of the girls asking a question. Susan returned with a sigh, "Tanny, I guess the girls aren't down for the night after all. I have to go sort out some dispute about the blankets."

"That's just fine. You're a momma first. I'm glad we got to talk."

"But I didn't find out how you are doing," apologized Susan.

"No worries. We'll do me next time, okay?"

"I love you, Tanny."

"Love you too. Bye!"

Tanny sat back. *Wow. Jon and Sue are having a baby.* Tanny did a wiggly, happy dance where she sat.

Next, she called her cousin Lauren. She was checking to see if the walk was on still.

"Yes, of course! I want to see you, no matter what we do," agreed Lauren with enthusiasm. "The weather is looking a bit iffy, so we could just hang out in my house too. I'm still setting it up. If it's too gross for a walk, maybe you could help decide where to hang my art, or where my printer should go?"

"Absolutely," said Tanny. "As long as it's with you. But if the weather *is* bad, could you pick me up?"

"Of course!" Then Lauren suggested treating Tanny to dinner too.

"Awww, thanks. But I have to be back by five to start Fifi's dinner."

"On a first name basis, are we?"

"No. It's just that Mrs. Dunkirk Jones is such a mouthful. I'm lazy."

"I knew I liked you," said Lauren.

Twenty-Eight

March 3

*F*ifi's morning regime moved by smoothly and soon Tanny was anticipating her afternoon with Lauren. She made her way to the entrance so she could watch for Lauren through the large glass windows there. The sky beyond the big Pennsylvania trees was grey with scudding clouds.

Kevin was on duty again behind the desk. He greeted her and said, "It's looking stormy today. They are promising rain, possibly mixed with snow."

"Oh yeah?" replied Tanny with genuine interest.

"It's frightfully cold out there. I nearly froze making my way in from my car," continued the kind gentleman.

"What's the temperature?" asked Tanny, thinking surely the rain would freeze if it was so cold. It didn't look cold, but years of Canadian springs had taught Tanny that looks could be deceiving.

"The thermometer says thirty-five. Brrrrr," shuddered the grey-haired man in his sweater vest.

Tanny contemplated the friendly man as he moved papers in the office. But "thirty-five" Fahrenheit was well above freezing. How cold could it really feel when it was a balmy thirty-five? Tanny knew it didn't get truly uncomfortable until several degrees below freezing. Maybe these Pennsylvanians weren't as tough as southern Ontarians. Tanny shrugged. She said, "There must be quite the wind."

"And damp," said Mr. Bach. "The damp makes everything feel colder."

Tanny could agree with that.

Soon a dark blue sedan was pulling into the covered drive-through. "That's my ride," announced Tanny.

"Stay warm!" encouraged Mr. Bach.

Tanny stepped outside and into Lauren's car. It was brisk and windy, but not unbearably cold to her. She grinned and reached across to hug her friend and cousin. Lauren had brown eyes and long brown hair, pulled back in a scarf today.

"How are you?" laughed Lauren, as Tanny buckled herself in. "It's been ages!"

"I know! But it's like no time has passed. I love that about our friendship."

"Me too," agreed Lauren as she shifted into gear and pulled out of the drive-through onto the long driveway. She took them out past the old stables and ice rink, past the fancy new sports field and community gardens, and past the several million-dollar remodel of the church college. Tanny had to admire how attractive the new building looked, swallowing the award-winning brutalist concrete building in a covering styled after a grand English country home. It was fieldstone with a steeply pitched grey shingled roof. At least, that's what Tanny saw. There were definite variations on that theme throughout the complex of buildings, all funded by the Dunkirk, Lindgren, and Bradford fortunes. Tanny sighed.

Lauren had married a Dunkirk descendent, so she was very comfortable financially, but didn't seem to show it. She stayed accessible and warm and ... down-to-earth. She drove them down the winding college drive, past all the dormitories, then off the campus towards the elementary school. She and Garth had just purchased a home on one of the several no-exit roads across from the elementary school.

Tanny had never been able to keep all of these roads straight. Each had a personality, and several were defined by the wealthy family in the final property. Some of these wealthier families had split their large plots and given pieces to their children, such that the end of one road might end in a conclave of sibling dwellings.

But Lauren drove Tanny to a road that had two modest homes at the end. Both properties could look out onto the woods and the stream that had defined the no-exit status of all of these little roads. Garth and Lauren had purchased the old nineteen-forties home on the left. It looked cozy from the street with its few gables.

The cold air swirled around them as they ran from the car to the house.

"Come in! Come in!" laughed Lauren. Tanny entered. One step down to the right was a sunken living room (probably an addition). It was a large square room with a big window looking out onto the woods. It had a beautiful fieldstone fireplace.

Tanny patted at her wind-whipped hair as Lauren shut the door firmly. Tanny said, raising a finger, "I would just like to draw attention to the fact that my hair is amazing today."

"It is indeed," grinned Lauren, taking in the nearly erect frizz on Tanny's head.

Lauren led Tanny straight ahead to a modest dining room with a set of wood stairs climbing to the second floor. Beyond was an interesting kitchen with a table looking out onto still-bare trees and gardens.

Lauren stopped here and indicated a chair at the kitchen table. There were unpacked boxes tucked in corners of the dining room and kitchen.

"Shall we start with some tea or coffee?" she asked.

"Absolutely," said Tanny. "One can never have enough coffee." She was finger-combing her hair, trying to get it to lie flat again.

"Excellent. How does butter pecan flavour sound?"

"Like I died and went to heaven."

Lauren went about grinding and brewing the fragrant blend while Tanny scoped out the interesting mix of styles in the quirky older home.

The stairs had a unique look. Instead of the usual spindles up the stairs, there seemed to be a solid piece of wood that had curved geometric openings carved in it. It was painted white with a natural wood railing top.

There was a fireplace in the dining room, interestingly.

Lauren saw Tanny absorbing the house layout. She said, "Apparently, that room used to be the living room. The original house was a tiny, postwar design. Where you are sitting was the original dining room and this side was the kitchen."

"It was so small!"

"It was. Just a square, yet with three bedrooms upstairs. Later someone added that glorious living room that you saw. And a different family added the giant playroom off the back here."

Tanny walked through the kitchen and saw off the back a generous room running the length of the original house. "Wow," she exclaimed.

"I know. It's a funky place, but I love it already. There is a giant bedroom and full bath above that playroom. It looks out onto the woods—just gorgeous."

"Amazing," Tanny enthused, returning to the kitchen. The coffee maker was burbling, filling the kitchen with a wonderful scent. Tanny gave Lauren a hug. "This seems like a great house."

Lauren indicated a chair and told Tanny she would bring her cream and sugar once the coffee was poured. Tanny sat. Soon Lauren had set a delectably yummy smelling mug of coffee in front of Tanny. Bringing cream and sugar and coffee for herself, Lauren sat down too and sighed. "We are hoping to put a screen porch off to the side back there," she said. "So far, this place is a bit of a money pit, but we are looking forward to bringing it up to modern standards. There's still an oil furnace in the basement. We are looking into geothermal, or solar panels. It's just that the trees are so big around here, we'd have to have some cut down to make sure the sun can reach the panels, and I hate to cut down trees."

Tanny reflected how nice it must be to have married into the Dunkirk wealth. Lauren and Garth could take their time and have quality renovations and upgrades done to their home. They could shape it into something they loved. Tanny had watched her parents struggle to keep their home barely in repair. There had never been money for upgrades., except the basement apartment, which was also about bringing in more money.

"But catch me all up!" asked Lauren.

Tanny wondered where to start. "Well, I just lost my job and my apartment, and my dog died...." Tanny was annoyed to feel her eyes fill. "And I need money, so my mom found me this gig down here with Fifi."

Lauren had risen from her chair and extended her arms. Tanny rose reluctantly but accepted the embrace and found herself weeping. She let the tears come, not realizing how much she had needed this.

"Aww, honey," came Lauren's gentle reply.

Lauren's soft words and tightening arms invited deeper release. Tanny's tears became sobs. "I miss Charm so much." It felt good just to be held and supported as she wept. The tears came and came. Her dog, her apartment, her job, even her dying car—months of grief and anxiety—came pouring out in the kitchen. Eventually Tanny's sobs became snuffles, which then became sniffs. She reached for some tissues and said, with raised eyebrows, "Wow. I had no idea that was there. I really needed that."

"I can only imagine," sympathized Lauren as they both sat down again.

Tanny chuckled as she mopped herself off. "I get so busy coping and managing, I don't realize how much I'm holding in."

"So, if you need more work, what are your plans after Fifi?"

Tanny took a sip of her coffee and practically slid out of her chair to the floor. Once she had recovered, she thought a minute and a slow smile spread. "Honestly? I want to move up to Britt's old homestead and help the hunky guy who oversees it. I want to get any old job up there—waitressing, maybe—and see if that relationship keeps growing the way it has been—"

"Hunky guy who oversees it? What's this?" Lauren asked with sparkling eyes.

"I haven't been able to tell anyone yet," responded Tanny, wistful that Susan had been too busy to confide in. "Aunt Britt left her big home to be looked after by four people: Susan, me, Uncle Jacob, and Jeff. Jeff is Uncle Jacob's foster son. Jeff has been looking after the property while its fate is decided.

"I met Jeff years ago, then forgot all about him. I didn't realize that the 'Jefferson' person listed in the will was that young man until I went up there for a few days. Instead of an old geezer friend of Britt's, I ran into this full-grown man I had known only when we were in our early teens."

"So, what's he like?"

"Where to begin?" Tanny filled Lauren in about the shaved head, the tattoos, the paramedic position, and the conversations about consent. She shared about the magnetic pull she felt when she was around him. "And he has a big dog named Mack. I enjoyed snuggling with him on the couch. It comforted me to snuggle with him—the dog, not Jeff. I miss Charm so much."

Lauren's eyes spoke of warmth and empathy. "And do you think your feelings for him are reciprocated?"

"Definitely! That's in part why I want to move to Bracebridge." Until she had said it out loud, Tanny had not realized that she truly planned to do this. But she really did. "I want to see where this goes. It's too hard to know where it is going over video chats."

"Do you have a picture of him?"

"I don't, except for this," Tanny held out a screen shot of Jeff's face that she had taken when they were video chatting.

Lauren leaned in and took a look. "He has an openness about his eyes. I like the look of him from this, anyway."

Tanny gazed at it. "He's not exactly handsome, yet he is so attractive!"

Lauren took a pull at her coffee and grinned. "Then I'm going to have to make the most of this visit, because soon you are going to be even farther away than Kitchener!"

The two cousins smiled at each other.

Tanny swooned through another swallow of her coffee.

Lauren said, "I will pay you to help me unpack while we visit. How does that sound?"

Tanny said, "Just give me another cup of this and I will do anything."

Once the coffee was drained to the last drop, the two women got to sorting and unpacking the kitchen utensils and teas, linens, and paraphernalia. It turned out Tanny was good at this, making some commonsense suggestions that seemed intuitive to her, yet surprised and intrigued Lauren.

When bending down to place some pots in a low cupboard, Tanny shrieked and jumped when a loonie-sized spider leapt from a dark corner.

"Cheeses!" Tanny squeaked, hugging herself as Lauren whacked at the spider with a cookbook. It moved no more.

"That scared the bejeebers out of me!" declared Tanny, a little breathlessly. She then added, "I am now empty of all bejeebers."

"So, you are now bejeeberless?" asked Lauren, scraping up the mess that was once a large spider.

Tanny shuddered and looked away. She said, "Yes. I have been de-bejeebered."

"How does one get re-bejeebered?" wondered Lauren.

"More coffee?" asked Tanny.

By four pm and more cups of butter pecan coffee later, all of the kitchen boxes had been unpacked.

"You are really good at arranging things," Lauren observed as she and Tanny washed their hands and did some final tidying. "You might want to talk to Ventnor's wife, Barbara, about organizing. I'm pretty sure they moved to Kitchener to live. She's been doing that quite successfully for several years."

"I actually have spoken to her. I hadn't seriously considered doing what she's doing, but maybe I will if the waitressing thing doesn't work out. I'm sure she could give me some tips. And in Bracebridge I wouldn't be competition."

"Or maybe she'll give you some work while she trains you. You never know."

They ran out to the car, garbage bags held above their heads to avoid the worst of the pelting rain.

Once they were safe in the car a big sigh escaped Tanny. "I'm both excited and terrified about the future."

"Of course you are! Just remember how many people love you and are rooting for you."

A loud siren started up, and Tanny remembered that this little borough had its own volunteer fire company. She didn't know how the residents got used to the strident alarm that could go off at any time, day, or night. Apparently, they were so used to it they barely noticed unless it interrupted their conversations. The route back to the Estates took them quite near the fire station. Tanny pressed her fingertips into her ears. A small sedan with a flashing blue light on the roof raced by them on its way to the firehouse. Tanny reflected on how many sirens there were in this town compared to the sleepy part of Kitchener where she lived—er, sort-of lived.

Finally, Lauren slowed to a stop in front of the Estates' front door. The siren had quieted. She put the car in park under cover of the drive-through.

Tanny was pressing her fingers into her right eyelid. It had started twitching, probably due to all the coffee.

Lauren cocked an eyebrow at her and said, "Is your eye okay?"

"Oh, yeah. It just does this when I'm over caffeinated," explained Tanny, pressing and stretching the skin where it was twitching. "It was completely worth it!"

Lauren laughed and reached over to hug her. She said, "Thank you for all your help. It was SO good to see you." She pressed an envelope into Tanny's hands. "This is for all your help today and a good luck gift as you face so many changes....

Tanny started to object but Lauren unbuckled Tanny and gave her a gentle push. "You will take this with my love and blessing. And next time you come down here, I hope you will consider staying with us. We have lots of room."

"Thank you," Tanny said with sincerity. "I'll keep in touch." She exited the car and waved as Lauren drove off. As she walked inside, still pressing against the tiny spasm, she peeked in the envelope. There were five one-hundred-dollar bills inside.

Twenty-Nine

March 3, late afternoon

Tanny was blinking back tears as she returned to Fifi's apartment. She entered and moved quickly to her room to drop off the envelope of money.

She was wiping her eyes as she returned to the kitchen to start dinner. Fifi was sitting in her bright living room with "Mads" Bradford and a woman Tanny had never met. Tanny greeted Fifi and Mrs. Bradford.

Fifi introduced the new woman. "Tanny, this is Mrs. Mary Flint, wife of Rev. Jeremiah Flint."

Mary Flint was stocky with beady eyes. She had a pleasant, almost childlike face, belying the hawklike assessment in her expression. Tanny shook her hand.

"Tanny is my help while I recover. She has been doing a very adequate job," Fifi continued, addressing Mary.

Mads and Mary nodded approval even as Tanny flinched inwardly at being called "the help," and "adequate."

Fifi continued, addressing Tanny, "The ladies will not be staying for dinner. You may go ahead and cook for the two of us."

Tanny retired to the kitchen area of the open concept space and washed her hands. She looked at the day's schedule and found the evening's selected meal. She started preparing.

You said her name is Tanny? What kind of name is that?" asked Mary Flint, wife of a minister. It was clear she was asking Fifi, not Tanny herself.

Fifi responded. "I know. It is an odd name, but it has grown on me. It is a nickname made from her real name, 'Britannia'."

Mary didn't quite cover her snort of derision. "Who names their child Britannia these days?"

I'm right here, thought Tanny.

"Do either of you remember Britannia Bender?" explained Fifi. "She was down for two years of college in the late nineteen thirties. She was a few years older than I am, but I was very aware of her when she was here. She was a real stir-paddle.

My parents discussed her at the dinner table several times. She was all for women being in leadership."

Tanny chopped perhaps more aggressively than necessary.

Mads exclaimed, "I was born in nineteen thirty-eight; of course I don't remember her."

"As was I," chimed in Mrs. Flint.

"She made a reputation for herself and that's a fact. I suspect she was a lesbian. She took herself back to Canada after college and we never heard of her again. I'm pretty sure she never married, though."

All the women nodded sagely, as if everything was explained by Britt's Canadian status as well as being a lesbian.

Tanny nearly blurted out, "She was NOT a lesbian!" But choked it back. Simply saying that would both invite questions and attention Tanny did not want, plus it would imply that being a lesbian was a bad thing, which was not what Tanny was intending to communicate. Instead, she stirred the sauce with extra vigour. She wondered if steam was coming out her ears.

"But this young lady," Fifi continued, indicating Tanny, "was saddled with her great aunt's name, poor thing. I think 'Tanny' is a delightful accommodation."

"I wonder what her middle name is?" asked Mrs. Bradford, thinking she might solve Tanny's 'problem' by suggesting she go by her middle name.

Tanny hated her middle name. She suspected it was because it was only ever spoken when she was in trouble: "Britannia Suzanne Smith! Would you get down here this minute!" *No thank you.*

"So, this Tammy—er, Tanny is Canadian?" asked Mrs. Flint with curiosity. Apparently Tanny's citizenship was the salient point to her. "I suppose you are paying her in cash?"

"Why do you ask?" returned Fifi.

"It is all about the taxes. I don't think she's allowed to earn money here, so the only solution is to pay her in cash."

Tanny's skin was crawling with all the discussion about her while she was *right there.* The meat and vegetables were cooking; the sauce was coming along nicely. Tanny started some biscuits to go with the meal.

"Speaking of which, did you go to Richard's session on taxes? He had more clever ideas about how to send money overseas to keep it out of the government's hands."

Tanny froze. This "Richard" was teaching how to commit tax fraud—*avoiding* paying taxes—when the government needed the money to *run the country*?

Did they not see this as stealing from their neighbours? Tanny had heard that some people, mostly the very wealthy, *who had more than enough,* were especially adept at doing this. It was just the opposite of how Tanny and many Canadians viewed paying taxes. They were a nuisance but so was paying for car repairs and rent and groceries. If the citizens who have more won't chip in proportionately, how does the country provide health care, or university educations, or services for those in need? Tanny shuddered even as the women continued to share strategies for keeping their money away from the government—as if it was a game. You 'won' the game to the extent that you kept back taxes for yourself, depriving the nation of the portion they *ought* to be contributing.

Tanny tried not to let her outrage show on her face.

Fifi boasted, "Also, I now have a handicapped placard because of my surgery. I'm so looking forward to being able to use it once I am more mobile."

"Fred Behlert has one of those because his wife was so ill," added Maddy Bradford. "He keeps using it and loans it out to friends. "It's great when I am in a rush, or it is raining."

"We might as well use them if we have them," commented Mrs. Reverend Jeremiah Flint.

Tanny willfully unclenched her teeth. These ladies seemed to revel in a sense of entitlement without any thought to the wellbeing of others. Tanny was increasingly disillusioned with the people she was meeting in Ben Kirk.

But it wasn't her job to comment. She turned down the heat under the sauce and lidded it. The biscuits were browning beautifully, and the sautéing meat would be done in another several minutes. "Dinner will be ready in about ten minutes," she announced with calm professionalism.

"I guess that's our cue to go," sighed Mrs. Flint and she struggled to get up from her soft chair.

"Oh, don't rush," reassured Fifi. "I'm sure Tanny can keep it warm until we are done."

But Mary Flint was up and not looking like she wanted to sit down again. "No, I should go and start cooking for Jeremiah."

"How is Jeremiah?" asked Maddy.

"Oh, you know. Retirement just freed him up to write more papers for the council of the clergy. He is presenting one tomorrow on the dangers of the liberal slide in the culture's thinking. The laity are pushing for the admission of women into ministry, and for accepting homosexuals without conditions, as if allowing and condoning their perversions isn't then *supporting them* to do harm. We must *never* let our children think that perverted and disorderly behaviours are 'just fine.' They should be allowed to feel their innate disgust at such perversions. We must reinforce that innate disgust with our church's Divinely inspired morals just to fend off this evil cultural trend!"

Mary clearly agreed with her husband's theology. Tanny glanced and noticed that while Fifi was nodding, Mads was looking a bit stiff around her smile. Tanny wondered if she had a family member that was suffering because of the church's teachings.

"So, he keeps himself very busy," Mary Flint finished. "He's still working for the Lord."

Is he? wondered Tanny.

Madeline Bradford rose as well and the two ladies moved towards the door. Fifi used her recliner/lift chair to get herself up to use her walker. She followed them to the door.

"Just don't get me started on the golf-course fiasco," said Fifi.

"Great heavens, no, though I think we'd all be in agreement," returned Madeline.

They said their goodbyes and Fifi returned to Tanny. "All set?" she asked.

"All set," Tanny said, and began serving the meat, vegetables, and biscuits onto their plates. She drizzled some of the sauce on the sauteed meat and vegetables and brought the rest in a gravy bowl. They settled themselves to eat. After the usual, "Oh, give thanks..." they began to eat.

Tanny asked, "What's the golf course fiasco?"

Fifi made a noise of disgust. "Michael Nelson proposed turning all that unused farmland back behind here," she indicated in the direction of the view, "into a golf course. He's a big golfer, and his property backs onto it, so he's the main proponent. But a lot of people love the idea—the Bradfords, the Lindgrens, and many of my family all would use it. It seems ideal.

"But," she continued, "there's a large group of people objecting to the idea." She took another bite of dinner. In a bit she continued, "The group that's objecting want to see affordable housing put in back there. They say they want to live close enough to the schools for their kids to walk. They say they want to be 'part of the community.'"

Tanny thought that sounded reasonable. Surely more housing for the lower income people would greatly benefit the whole community. Certainly, Tanny would have to live in a rental unit if she wished to live around here. She could never afford a home in this neighbourhood!

"But when we did a survey, nearly everyone said they'd rather own than rent. So why put up a string of rental properties when people would rather own? Besides Michael doesn't want a bunch of poor people on his doorstep."

Tanny's chewing slowed as she processed this. Of course, people would rather own than rent! That doesn't mean they don't want affordable rental homes when they *can't afford to own.* Did anyone ask them if they'd rather rent than live so far away that it was a great burden to get their kids to the school? They already had to pay for their kids to attend the church school. There were no busses for the private Christian school. This meant that the parents had to undergo long drives two or more times a day, just to participate in the school and community. Tanny thought renting *in* the community to save all the driving and disconnection might make a lot of sense. Plus, wouldn't someone be making money off the rentals? The "poor people on Michael's doorstep" boiled Tanny's blood. She knew of this Michael Nelson. His mother was a Dunkirk, and he'd done well with his mother's money. Tanny had even seen a helicopter coming and going from his property across those fields. Just how did he line up his Christian beliefs beside his unwillingness to allow the low-income church members to have housing *near him*? Was he completely unaware of the optics of putting a golf course right in the center of this supposedly Christian borough when so many young families were doubly burdened trying to keep their kids in the school (which they were expected to afford) while there were no housing options for them anywhere near? She wondered how many families stopped bringing their kids to school simply because of the financial burden. Public education was free, and Tanny knew the school districts surrounding the borough were excellent.

"So, it looks like there will be no housing *or* a golf course, thanks to the protesters," concluded Fifi. Why do they keep using their resentment of our wealth to block us from having the luxuries we can afford? And besides, it would be so much more pleasant to look out at a golf course," Fifi indicated the pastoral view, "than a bunch of tightly packed townhouses and apartments. It would be crawling with people back there!" She shuddered. "So, Michael may not get his golf course, but neither will they get their housing," finished Fifi, as if this was poetic justice.

Tanny had lost her appetite. Fortunately, Fifi was not at all curious about Tanny's silence. Tanny asked permission to begin to clean up, and Fifi grudgingly agreed, as she was nearly finished.

Tanny moved through the cleanup efficiently and silently.

Fifi made some comments about watching Wheel of Fortune and Jeopardy and returned herself to her special chair. "But I want to see you out here promptly at eight to put me to bed."

When the kitchen was spotless, Tanny got herself to her room. She felt so impotent and irrelevant when she was around such conversation. She felt alienated from her church if this was the dominant thinking among the wealthiest. Did money and influence actually shape the doctrine of her church instead of fundamental Christian teachings, such as, "treat others the way you would want to be treated?" She felt sick to her stomach. Was *this* the actual face of the church to which she had been so loyal? Then she thought about Lauren Anderson. Lauren was young and monied. Maybe the younger generation would be able to return the church to its basic good-heartedness and Christian orientation. Maybe there was hope for change, and that not all members thought like those three older women.

Besides, she had been given a generous gift, she remembered, seeing the envelope on her bed. Plus, she still had Britt's letters to read! At first, she was shocked to find them all in French, then realized that the two women of course had to maintain their covers at all times, especially in written communications that could have been examined by German officers at any time. Fortunately for Tanny, she had done quite well in French studies and could understand most of it.

Darling Lisette,

Lisette? Wondered Tanny. *Who was Lisette?*

Sometimes the quiet in the countryside makes me forget there is a war. When the weather is so lovely, and I'm not hearing bombs or troop transports, and when little Luke is nursing at my breast, I gaze at the wonderful shapes of the clouds in the blue sky and feel sure that Luke's father will come round the bend in the road whistling cheerfully, as he always did. Surely all will be as it ought to be.

But alas! I try not to think what the future holds. My little man deserves a beautiful life, yet he is born to an unmarried mother in a country at war. I know he will have a loving family to care for him, but I cannot bear the idea of leaving him behind.

I long to return to my work yet never wish to return. I'm sure you understand.

How are you? Are you staying safe? Are your hatchlings developing nicely? Have they grown and become strong? I pray it is so. Those darn Germans keep taking them from you. But you deserve a healthy flock so you can survive during all these hardships. How about that gander of yours? Is he servicing your flock as well as ever? Oh, what a harsh year it has been! Even our troupeaux d'oies are dying, as well as the Allied troops.

But not today. The sun is warm. The air is sweet. The clouds speak only of rest and peace. Today there is no war for me.

Sending all my dearest affection, and a lock from my dear Lukie's head, so you know he is real.

Louisa

Louisa? Who was Louisa? Was this the right letter? Or maybe ... these names were aliases to protect their real identities? Censors surely read these letters. Tanny searched "troupeaux d'oies" and it meant flocks of geese. Were they actually discussing the health of "Lisette's" fowl, or was this an inquiry into the spies she was constantly recruiting to work for the French underground? Tanny wondered who the "gander" was and what he provided. How clever it was of her to refer to the actual troops alongside the 'flock of geese,' though it seemed risky. The meaning was so transparent to Tanny, and yet, nothing important was being said.

Tanny quickly picked up another.

My dearest and brave Lisette....

Thirty

Tanny had to fumble with her alarm and stop herself from hitting snooze again. She had stayed up much too late reading letters from Britt to Grace. Her imagination was full of her great aunt's life behind enemy lines, woven from the truth Britt described about her "ordinary" life in the French countryside and the obscure references to Grace's "family" and "geese" and adventures on a poultry farm where "Lisette" worked.

At first, Grace's life seemed to be on the outskirts of Paris while Britt was at a city called Port Nazaire. At least, this is what Tanny surmised from the addresses on the envelopes, the day-to-day descriptions of Britt's life, and her questions about Grace's life. Britt was employed in a flower shop somewhere around Nantes. (Apparently, even during war in France, the French raised and sold flowers, though it was mostly German officers who bought them.) The letters were genuine communications between two friends. They were not carrying any top-secret information, though Tanny suspected that some of their more cryptic sentences were cloaked references to their undercover efforts. "Two weeks ago, during one of my rambles, a pack of feral dogs decided I looked tasty and gave chase. I was so very lucky to have my bicycle and a head start. I knew the area well and managed to get well ahead of them. Eventually I made it to a village and the house of a friend. The dogs must have lost interest by then. Perhaps they lost my scent?" *Was that actually about dogs?* wondered Tanny.

Shortly after the dog story, Britt abruptly moved to a farm south of Bergerac. That is where the LaRoche family lived. As near as Tanny could tell, Britt was sent there after a "thorn" tore her calf. *Had Britt been shot?* She said she was visiting relatives and getting farther away from the Germans. And that is where she met Lucien. Six months later she was pregnant. Seven months after that, Lucien was killed by the Germans while trying to sabotage a bridge on a main highway.

The stories made Tanny immensely curious about what really happened during the German occupation of France. She only vaguely remembered her history classes; none of the material had seemed relevant at the time. She had memorized well for tests but had forgotten much of the lessons through the years.

She did remember hearing that Britt had been a "radio operator" in France. She had not thought much of it, picturing Britt sitting in a truck near troop encampments, working the radio. Her surprise as she discovered what World War Two radio operators *truly* did, turned to fear for Britt and gratitude that she had survived. The risks Britt had taken! Tanny's great aunt had been insanely brave and lucky to have survived. Perhaps the pregnancy had been part of the reason she survived? Tanny was more determined than ever to get herself back to Cedar Haven to dig about for any diaries or other related documents that Britt might have kept.

Notwithstanding, Tanny was expected in Fifi's bedroom in minutes, so Tanny launched herself out of bed to splash cold water on her face and wake up. There was no time for a shower.

Once breakfast was over, Tanny was clearing the dishes when Fifi asked her to sit down with her in the living room. Tanny wondered what it was about. She found a seat on the sofa and faced her employer.

"I understand that you have been doing your best work this week, and I am content. Indeed, you have made a good impression throughout the building, despite your habit of running in the halls.

"Now, the family of Eleanora Christie is looking for someone to attend to her care tomorrow afternoon while they scout out a new placement for her. She has finally lost her marbles completely and needs more care than the Estates can provide. So, I have offered to loan you to them for tomorrow afternoon. She is in unit five on the "C" wing. Cecily has agreed to attend me at that time, so I will be in good hands while you are there.

"You are to report to Eleanora's unit at noon tomorrow, where the family will meet you. They will relieve you at dinner time. And don't worry, I will pay you your full wages through Friday afternoon, regardless. No doubt Eleanora's family will give you something too." Fifi announced all of this without any invited comment from Tanny.

Tanny thought a moment. Was there any reason not to consent? It irked her that she had been volunteered without consultation, but did it really matter? She would be paid, regardless, and she got to go home on Saturday, no matter what. She said, "All right. I can do that."

Fifi continued, "I believe they will continue to want you for several days after, and I assured them that you needed the work. They have a spare room and are most grateful."

Tanny bit back her immediate refusal. After a deep breath she decided that it would be far easier to apologize to Eleanora's family than to try to convince Fifi that she was not interested. Stephen and Jon would be picking her up just after breakfast on Saturday to head home. Forget the money. There was no way she was staying behind! She needed to get back to Bracebridge to pursue ... things. Tanny simply nodded her head and got back to work.

Fifi had another visit with the physiotherapist in the mid-morning, so Tanny started a load of her laundry, already planning her packing. She sent a text off to Jeff, asking him how things were going and announcing her return to Canada on Saturday. "I'm hoping to come stay at Cedar Haven shortly after that. I'm going to look for a job up there on the assumption that I have a place to stay at least for a little while. What do you think? Feel free to say 'no.' I'm sure Aunt Eileen and Uncle Jacob would be more than happy to host me." Jeff and Tanny had been exchanging short and funny texts on and off since his shift started, and she definitely wanted him to know of her plans.

Before she knew it, Tanny was knocking on the door of C 5 the next afternoon. Her things were mostly packed already. All she had to do was babysit this woman, sleep, and she would be heading home!

The door was opened by a bright-eyed and energetic woman. She was older than Tanny and welcomed her in to meet her husband as well. It became clear that this was the son and daughter-in-law of the occupant, Candy and Mike Christie. They brought Tanny over to meet Eleanora, who was sitting in an easy chair by the window.

"Mom, this is Tanny Smith. She's going to keep you company while we go out shopping for you."

Eleanora looked alert and intelligent. It was hard for Tanny to imagine she was hampered intellectually.

"Hello there! It's nice to meet you," greeted Tanny.

Eleanora put down her crossword puzzle. "Smith, you say. I know your father. He has been helping me with my investments."

Tanny was about to correct Eleanora when she noticed Candy shaking her head and mouthing, "Just agree. Don't bother," from behind Eleanora's chair.

Tanny said, "Yes. Of course," and smiled.

Eleanora lost interest and Candy brought Tanny back to the kitchen.

"She has a peanut butter and raisin sandwich for lunch every day," said Candy, opening a cabinet to reveal the location of these items. "The bread is in the fridge. She also likes a full glass of milk and a cup of tea, though she rarely touches either. We've just gotten used to dumping milk down the drain every day."

Tanny's mind jumped to how there were people in the world (and even in North America) who were starving but shut those thoughts down. She would not be solving any injustices by pointing that out. She simply nodded.

"Here is the schedule for her meds," continued Candy, indicating a calendar-like paper on the fridge. "She used to take her meds at all sorts of hours, sometimes several times over, and sometimes not at all, so we have to hide the meds and administer them on a schedule. The meds are in here." Candy opened another kitchen cupboard that had a child-lock on it. Inside were carefully labeled meds with times and amounts clearly marked, matching the schedule on the fridge. "Her next dose is with lunch, see? And then she has a different set at three pm."

"Yes. I see," agreed Tanny.

"We recommend that you take her to the washroom after each dose. She often doesn't notice that she needs to go until it is too late, so we use Depends and also take her every few hours. It reminds me of potty training my kids, except in reverse," was Candy's wry observation. "Don't worry. She will not fight you on this or take exception to being treated like a child. She only gets anxious when she is left alone and can't figure out what is going on. Stay in her sight most of the time. She might want to talk. But she might just read or sleep. If someone calls for her, let her talk to them if they are friends. Don't let any professional or salesman talk to her. We have power of attorney. They have to go through us now."

Tanny felt a niggling of doubt at this but also knew it could be completely legitimate. If Eleanora truly was losing her touch on reality and was made anxious by the unknown, a call from a telemarketer could confuse her. *Who needs telemarketers anyway?* thought Tanny, with some grumpy feelings.

The Christie's looked at each other. "Maybe we should just turn the phone off and have it go straight to message," suggested Mike.

"Brilliant idea!" agreed Candy and did exactly that.

"With any luck we will have decided on a place by tonight and not need you for more than the weekend," finished Mike, addressing Tanny.

"Oh! About that. I can't help you after today. I'm going home tomorrow. I'm sorry Fifi gave you the impression I was available after today."

The Christie's both looked dismayed. Candy said to her husband, "I guess one of us is sleeping over again tonight. It also means I can't help tomorrow at the fair."

Mike returned, "You take tonight, and I'll take tomorrow so you can help at the fair."

Tanny saw the disappointment on Candy's face and wondered if sleeping over AND helping at the fair were not her first choice, but Candy said nothing. Tanny was not going to step in and rescue them, despite her sympathy. She knew without a shadow of a doubt that she needed to get home.

Once the Christie's had accepted their ruined plans, they gave Tanny final instructions and headed out the door.

Tanny moved to sit beside Eleanora, who looked up and smiled at her.

Tanny asked her if she was ready for her lunch.

"Lunch? But I never had breakfast yet, or my medicines! Can you bring me my medicines?"

Thinking on her feet Tanny said, "Of course! Your breakfast and medicines! Coming up right away. You rest easy. I'll get them right now."

Tanny headed to the kitchen and Eleanora seemed to settle right down.

Tanny put the kettle on and then got out the bread and peanut butter. She layered a nice coating of the protein-rich spread on one slice before reaching for the raisins. The container was nearly empty, but she scattered a thick layer of the dried fruit across the peanut butter, pressing the raisins in so they wouldn't fall out of the sandwich so easily. She sliced the sandwich, got a glass of milk, and poured the tea for Eleanora. She put it all on a tray and took it to the sprightly-looking woman.

"Oh no!" said Eleanora, and Tanny's stomach plummeted. The older woman continued, "I always take my meals at the table, not in my chair!" and she got herself up to move over to the table.

Relieved, Tanny set the meal out for Eleanora at the table and found her a napkin. The woman settled down happily, without any comment that this was not what she ate for breakfast. Tanny decided to make herself the same sandwich. She went to scatter raisins on her peanut butter and noticed something amiss. The raisins in the bottom of the container seemed to be moving. On closer inspection, Tanny realized that the raisins were riddled with weevils. She jumped back, shuddering, and then threw the container in the garbage.

Looking up to warn Eleanora, she saw the older woman munching away happily on a second bite of her weevil infested sandwich. She hesitated. *Would the weevils actually harm the woman more than snatching the sandwich away? How many days had Eleanora already eaten weevil-ridden sandwiches without realizing it? Maybe the weevils could just be considered extra protein?* Tanny took what was possibly the cowardly route, though she liked to see it as pragmatic, and simply let Eleanora finish her sandwich. Tanny made her own with honey and joined Eleanora at the table.

After she had given Eleanora her lunchtime meds, Tanny encouraged the older woman to have some milk, which she did, obligingly. Then Tanny dumped out the tea and the rest of the milk.

Eleanora said, "Last Tuesday.... Was it last Tuesday?" She paused. "I think it was last Tuesday.... Was it last Tuesday? *Maybe* it was last Tuesday." There was another long pause. "Maybe it was last Tuesday. Anyway...." and she continued with a long tale about driving down "the Schuylkill expressway (with a bunch of unrelated side-observations including the President's choice of suit) and onto River Drive...." Tanny stopped trying to follow after a while, unable to find a point or direction to the narration. She was also certain Eleanora hadn't been driving for quite a while. Instead, Tanny just nodded, smiled, and made listening noises upon occasion while dreaming about going home. She thought, *I am being paid to stand here and listen to Every. Single. Unimportant. Detail.*

Then Tanny jerked to attention.

Eleanora was saying, "I had a bit of a bowel movement in my underwear. I went to the bathroom and there was already a bit of ... ... bowel movement in my underwear. Then I did a load in the toilet and put on a depends. Then I went and looked for the Imodium because I thought I had some and so I looked and sure enough I had some and...."

Tanny, realized with relief that this story was not in real time and tuned out again. She wondered if she would also be so unfiltered and uninteresting when she lost her marbles.

Eventually Eleanora had said her fill and settled down. She picked up a book, so Tanny began cleaning up. Tanny reflected that aging was rarely a dignified or kindly thing to go through.

When the Christie's got home they were elated. They had found a memory-care placement for Eleanora for a week from Monday. The family just had to manage Eleanora's care through the next week and weekend. Tanny had to stand strong in the face of their imploring looks. She did suggest asking Lauren, hoping

Lauren wouldn't mind. Candy eventually shifted from stress to gratitude and paid Tanny fifty dollars for the afternoon, thanking her.

"It was my pleasure," assured Tanny. She had been happy to help.

As she was on her way out the door she warned them, "You will need more raisins before lunch tomorrow."

Once the door had closed, she heard a text come in. "It is definitely not a 'no'."

Tanny practically danced down the hall.

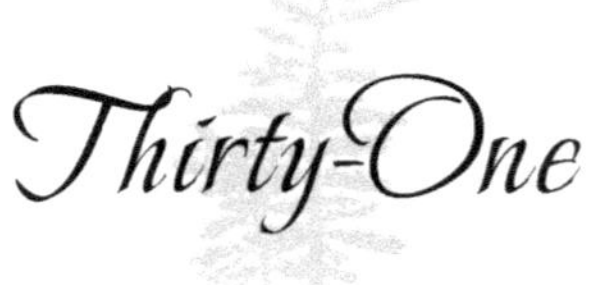

Thirty-One

March 5

$\mathcal{I}$t felt like the plane was attempting to land on a city street. The skyscrapers emerged much too close as the plane descended through towering buildings. Tanny realized with dismay that she had forgotten to pack a suitcase. She had come to Amsterdam without any luggage. How had she managed that? She comforted herself that at least she had her purse and clutched that leather item close.

After disembarking, her group was taken straight to the hotel by shuttle. As they were being led to their rooms Tanny was mentally itemizing all that she would need to purchase in clothes and toiletries when the complete emptiness of her hands brought her up short. No purse. She had left her purse on the shuttle! She was in a foreign country, without identification, passport, or any banking cards. She had no way to prove who she was in order to get replacements.

Tanny started sprinting back towards the hotel entrance. She had to find her purse! Maybe it was still on the shuttle, or had been turned in. She thought of the five hundred dollars in cash that was sitting in her wallet, and her heart sank further. She found an agent and was about to ask for help when she thought, *this is ridiculous! Why did I go to Amsterdam without any luggage, and without even remembering to pack? And then I lost my purse? Even I am not that scatterbrained. This must be a dream.* As she struggled to wake up the agent was taking her hands. Aunt Britt was the agent, comforting her, and telling her she had everything she needed already. Britt opened Tanny's hands. Looking down, Tanny saw money and resources, images of people she loved and places where she was welcome blossoming out of her hands and spilling all over the floor. She felt amazed. She felt disbelief and hope in equal measure, even as the world began vibrating gently and something was poking her head.

Tanny started awake with a stiff neck. She straightened up to see Stephen and Jon chatting in the front seat. The vibration was the hum of the road. She rubbed her head, realizing that a seat buckle had been digging into her scalp as she slept.

"What time is it?" she asked, then dug around to find her phone. It would have the time.

"Uhhh, it is eleven forty-five," answered Jon, turning around to greet her. "You haven't missed much."

They had left Ben Kirk promptly at nine am. Tanny asked for the back seat and had fallen asleep immediately on the way to the turnpike. She had not slept well at all for the excitement to get home.

"I was just in Amsterdam," observed Tanny. "My plane landed on the city streets. It was all quite normal."

"Welcome back to reality," said Stephen. He was driving, and Tanny could see mountains rising around them as they whirred along the highway. "We've been making good time. We're in New York already."

Tanny loved the sight of the gently rolling mountains even with their leafless trees. The highway seemed to be following a river valley, sharing the way with both the river and a set of train tracks. Sometimes the two routes were fighting for the little space left by the river. Other times they had ample room in a wide plain. Nearly always the highway and train tracks were elevated. Tanny noticed how high the river was running; trees were undercut along the banks and there were large swathes of water standing in the fields. She recognized that engineers had specifically designed the routes to remain safe even when the river flooded.

"Stephen is taking us by his favourite short cut," Jon added.

"This route angles us up through Corning and brings us out at Batavia. It's a lot more scenic and not so heavily travelled," added Stephen.

Tanny wished she could look at her maps app. But her phone was useless; she couldn't afford the exorbitant Canadian roaming rates. She was so tired of having no money.

As she gazed out at the mountains rising one after another from the river-valley, she sighed with deep appreciation of the beauty. The empty branches made a soft grey wash across the hillsides, interspersed with boldly green evergreens and the occasional homestead. There were the merest hints of pale green and pink among the soft grey of the many branches. Spring was on its way.

Tanny found herself imagining arriving home to her basement apartment. Then she remembered that she no longer lived there. There would be no Charm to greet her, and she was instead returning to a disorganized and abandoned marital home. Her "home" was Jenny's and Will's now. All of her stuff would have been put in the MacGregor house. An ache set up in her stomach when she remembered that. She wasn't really going home at all. She still had to set herself up in Jenny's house. And that space was only temporary. Dread filled her. Where would she go? What would she do? Her mind leapt to Cedar Haven and a life in Bracebridge, and suddenly she was filled with hope and excitement. She would make a fresh start somewhere new. *And with someone new?*

The three travelers traded positions at the next rest stop. Tanny took over driving; she loved to drive. Stephen went to the back again.

"How did the meetings go?" Tanny asked Jon as she pulled back onto the highway.

"The same as ever. The conservative faction continues to fight for control. They have most of the money, so they usually win. If I didn't love the teachings so much, I'd be looking for another job. My faith in the council of ministers is at an all-time low." He sighed. "However, my theology degree qualifies me to do nothing else than work in our denomination. I suppose I could find work as an organist somewhere, but that can be pretty low-paying and precarious."

Tanny glanced at Jon, then back at the road. "I had no idea you were considering leaving the ministry."

Jon's laugh was wry. "I've only been at it three months, and it's nothing like I expected. I love the people. I love the teachings. I love teaching and comforting. I don't love how much of it comes down to politics and the fight for control."

"But we're all about trusting God's leading and avoiding the urge to control," puzzled Tanny.

"EXACTLY," said Jon with surprising energy.

"So ... the leaders aren't living by their own teachings?" Tanny was appalled.

"I don't know why I expected differently. I just somehow thought our denomination was above all that," reflected Jon. There was frustration in his voice. "I can't say much more, but I worry for the church. If the conservative backlash continues, it may choose a path that I can no longer follow." There was a silence. "Except now I have a wife and family to support."

There was another long silence. Then Jon said, "I'm sorry. I shouldn't tell you any of this. I should pretend I'm happy and delighted with the direction the Council is headed. You're the parishioner, and I'm the leader, and I should display loyalty and faith. But not telling the truth about the problems feels hypocritical and ... and enabling."

Tanny's heart went out to Jon. "You can say anything you want to say, Jon. You know me. I've seen problems with the church for a long time. I'm just sad to hear how bad it is for you. I simply can't imagine how hard it must be to keep working for an organization that has lost your loyalty and trust."

"It has indeed lost a lot of my trust. I am remaining as loyal as I can. Soon we will be picking a new Bishop, and that could mean the start of a new era, or a swing into even more conservative control. I'd like to think that our teachings will lead us out of this latest crisis without major fractures in the organization. I'd like to think we will rise above the need to control."

Tanny mused, "I don't know. Maybe major fractures would be good. Let the one group go off and be all controlling and leave the rest of us to get on with living the way we were taught to live—in lovingkindness."

"You might be right. It would ease a lot of tensions but create a whole new set of problems." There was a silence. "Anyway, one *very good* part of the meetings was a required special session about recognizing and avoiding pastoral abuse. I thought I knew what I needed to know, but I didn't. It really spelled out the clear boundaries between the pastor and the parishioners he serves. Any and all boundary-crossings are *the fault of the pastor*—the fault of the one with power-over. No pastor can blame a church member when there is sexual abuse. They can't claim, "I was seduced," no matter how aggressive a congregation member might be. It is always the duty of the one in the power position to hold the boundary. It makes absolute sense to me now. But I had never been taught this perspective, nor seen the great harm that can come to parishioners who are abused by their leaders. It was a really sobering class."

Jon took a breath and continued, "Technically, me even telling you my experience at the meetings could be seen as an abuse of my power."

"It definitely could be," came a grumble from the back seat.

"But how?" asked Tanny. "How on earth can you being honest about your feelings be an abuse of power?" She was indignant.

"You see, by giving you an inside scoop on my feelings, I'm elevating you above the other parishioners to special status. You are now a confidant with inside information. That essentially gives *you* power over the other parishioners. I'm not supposed to do that with anyone. I think the only person I'm allowed to talk to is Susan. Even telling Stephen can be dangerous in case he wants to 'out' me with the denomination."

"Because that's the sort of thing I would do," came Stephen's declaration from the back, oozing sarcasm.

"I am lucky to be working with you, Stephen!" called Jon.

"It's mutual. Now talk about something less interesting, please. I want to sleep."

Jon chuckled. He dropped his voice to just above a whisper. "I really blew it with Susan, it turns out."

Tanny glanced toward him, worried. "What? What did you do? Is she okay?"

"No! I mean, yes. She's fine. I'm talking about the morning after I met her, in November, not recently."

Tanny rested back into her chair in tremendous relief. "So, she's fine. She's okay." Just in those few seconds Tanny had imagined the marriage failing just as Susan was pregnant with another child. Tanny would consequently have had to murder Jonathan. She kept her eyes on the road but took a deep breath.

"She is great. Things are very, very good between us right now," continued Jon.

"Sleeping!" came from the back.

Jon dropped his voice again. "You see, I kissed Susan the day after we met."

"You what?" exclaimed Tanny.

"SLEEPING!"

Tanny continued in a fierce whisper. "You kissed her that fast? The second day? Did she slap you?"

"Not ... exactly." Jon felt his cheeks flush. "The thing is, I was WAY out of line in doing that. It didn't matter that she ... participated. MY duty as her pastor was never to allow such a thing to happen."

"Technically, *I* was her pastor. You were the new guy." This was from Stephen who was sitting up in the back seat, his arms resting on the seat back. Apparently, he had given up.

"It just feels rotten to discover that I crossed that boundary so egregiously right out of the gate. I had no idea at the time. But it's no excuse."

"And look how terribly it turned out," was Stephen's comment.

Jon seemed angry. He turned back to Stephen and said, "My brother, I thank you for your defense. But I think I need to feel the weight of this. I clearly forget the power my position gives me. I just see everyone as equal and forget about these hidden boundaries. I had no idea how much harm I could do."

"You see everyone as equal because you do not seek power or control, my friend."

"But I could have destroyed Susan's feeling of safety in her home congregation. What if she had not fallen in love with me? Would I have known that I should have taken full responsibility and left immediately? I doubt it. Every parishioner deserves to feel safe in their congregation. My staying—any abusive leader remaining in power—would be a profound betrayal to the ones he supposedly serves. It wouldn't have mattered that I was ignorant. The harm would have been done."

Tanny watched Stephen in the mirror. It looked like he wanted to crawl forward to support his friend.

"Jonathan. You are blessed in ministry in so many ways. And luckily, no harm was done. Please don't be hard on yourself about this. It looks like you have learned what you needed to learn. Just go forward from here. Cliffside needs you. I need you."

Tanny felt like she was on sacred ground. She was witnessing a moment of great intimacy between these two colleagues. The depth of their affection and respect for each other left her in awe. She also realized her privilege in a way she never would have before. She had been witness to a great deal of vulnerability between these two leaders. She had an obligation to keep this exchange confidential. She felt protective of these dear men.

"Thank you, Stephen. The only thing I can do is go forward. But I shudder to think—"

"Then stop thinking. Stop fretting. Nothing bad happened. And now we all know better." He balled up his coat and lay down again. "And I'd really like to get some sleep."

"Sleep, Stephen," murmured Jon. He turned to face front. He had a twinkle in his eye. "Tanny, look at that building. I think the paint is drying nicely."

"Oh, yes," joined Tanny. "The paint on that billboard is being very slow to dry though. We could watch it for a long time."

"The blue paint."

"And the red paint."

"Perhaps the green paint will dry a bit faster?"

"And the pink—oh! We can't see it anymore," sighed Tanny.

"The sky now, is that painted?" asked Jon.

"I think the blue sky-paint takes such a long time to dry that it sometimes drips and mixes with other colours."

"Oh, look over there. That hillside is covered in sheep! How many are there? One. Two. Three. Four. Five."

Tanny's voice was full of laughter. "Six, seven, eight, nine, ten, eleven...."

Stephen slept until the car stopped at the Tim Horton's in Batavia.

Thirty-Two

Tanny had the men drop her off at the door to Jenny's house. She let herself in with the key and sighed. It looked like someone had tried to arrange the living room for her. That was a comfort. She kicked off her boots and found the thermostat. It was set to a chilly twenty degrees centigrade. Tanny set the thermostat to a warmer twenty-three and padded across the cold tile floor to find her furniture set up in the first bedroom. She dragged her cases onto the carpet and looked around.

Tanny was struck with how well laid-out the room was. There were even clean sheets on the bed. Her eyes stung with gratitude. She dug her slippers out of her suitcase and headed to the kitchen.

In the kitchen she found the fridge stocked with some soup, bread, and fresh half-and-half for her coffee. She started warming the soup and flipped on the kettle for tea.

She called her mom.

"Hi mom. Just wanted to let you know I'm home safe and sound."

"Hello darling. So, you came home right away. I thought you would stay longer."

"The money is great to have, mom. Thank you for that. And it worked out perfectly to travel with Stephen and Jon. But I want to be here, figuring out my future *here*. My future isn't down there. It's here. I feel it."

Tanny's mother heaved a big sigh. "Okay. Well, I tried. And there's part of me that is glad not to lose you."

Tanny was surprisingly touched. "Thanks for saying that, mom. That means a lot to me."

Emily got mumbley and changed the subject. "Jenny is all settled in here with Will. I think it is very good for them to be out of that space and near family. Jenny brings Will up almost every morning and we have coffee together."

Tanny was struck by how much sense it made that both Jenny and Emily would welcome the close contact and time together. Tanny, on the other hand, had done as much as she could to live independently from her parents—especially her mom. One of the big irritants between Tanny and her mom was that Emily sought out Tanny for company while Tanny just wanted to be left alone. She felt smothered by Emily. Jenny welcomed their mother's attention.

Tanny admitted how much better this new arrangement would be for Jenny and her mom, even as she grieved the loss of her home. She felt she was on the outside of the family looking in, feeling glad for *them* but wondering where on earth her own, warm place of belonging was. She immediately imagined Cedar Haven and got a glow of hope and optimism.

Tanny said, "I'm so glad that is working out for you both. It was a good idea." She pushed down the lump of anger she still felt at how her mom had manipulated the whole thing. Even if the swap was a good idea, Tanny resented being maneuvered into surrendering her home without real consent.

Emily said, "I hired your cousin Barb to set the place up for you a bit. It was so helter-skelter when Jenny left. I hope it felt homey for you when you got in."

"Thank you so much, mom. It made a real difference." Tears sprang to Tanny's eyes. "That was really thoughtful." How could she stay angry with her mom?

"I'm glad to have done it. You should talk to Barb about organizing. Maybe you could work for her. She charges an awful lot. You could get wealthy easily. Then you could pay me back." Emily chuckled.

Tanny wondered if the price commentary was meant to inspire obligation to her mom. Didn't her mom realize that it didn't feel like a gift if she was asking to get the money back? Tanny now felt like a financial burden, not a loved child worth supporting. But she wouldn't play that game. She'd appreciate the good actions and ignore the passive-aggressive words. "I was considering asking Barb about organizing," she replied.

Emily started to ask Tanny about working for Fifi Dunkirk-Jones, but Tanny cut her off.

"I'm really tired, mom. I'd be happy to tell you tomorrow or whenever I see you next. But I honestly need to unpack and get to bed. I just wanted to let you, and dad know that I'm home safe."

"Thank you for that, sweetheart. I will be sure to tell Gilbert. He will be happy to know you are home."

They said their goodbyes. It was nearly seven in the evening, but it felt later. She checked the soup and added more time on the microwave. It looked like a creamy chicken broccoli. She sliced off a fat piece of bread and popped it in the toaster.

Then, leaning her back against the sink she checked her messages. She had texted Jeff the minute the van had crossed the border just to let him know she was back in town. He hadn't responded yet, but she knew he was often away from his phone. She hadn't heard a text come in, but when she looked again, there was a response from him.

"It's great to know you are back in the country! I'd love to catch up when you have a chance. Let me know when it is a good time."

Tanny's midriff felt like it was full of baby rabbits. She replied, "I could talk in fifteen minutes. I'm trying to get some dinner right now."

"Fifteen minutes it is. Let me know when you are ready."

Tanny's toast popped up just as the microwave dinged. She slathered some butter across the thick wholesome bread and carried it to the table with her soup.

The warmth in her tummy was as much from the texts as the delicious soup, she suspected. Nevertheless, she took her time to enjoy the meal before wiping away the crumbs and checking herself and her teeth in the mirror.

"Ready," she sent.

Soon the screen was lighting up with a picture of Jeff. She accepted the call and there he was. He had heavy stubble and his hair showed another week's growth. It was starting to show the buttery goldness she had seen in the photos of him. He looked so good, stubble and all.

"Hey..." they both said at the same time, then laughed. Jeff's eyes were alight with a look that made Tanny's neck heat up. She felt the need to swallow.

"It's really good to see you, Tanny," Jeff greeted. Mack pushed his head into Jeff's space, with a small whine. Jeff chuckled and said, "I think Mack misses you too." He dealt with the eager shepherd-mix. "Down Mack. Come on. Settle down. Thaaaat's a good boy. Yeah."

Jeff's face came back into the frame. "How was your trip back? Good weather?"

Tanny told Jeff about the uneventful drive. She described coming home to a place that had not been her home when she left. "But my cousin really made it cozy for me. I will have to thank her."

"When do you think you will get up here again?" was Jeff's next question. Tanny's tummy rabbits started hopping again.

"As soon as I can," was her prompt reply. "I will need a timeline from Jenny for when she wants this place on the market. They are letting me stay here rent-free so long as I prep it for selling, so I need to be here to be getting that done. But there's nothing stopping me from coming up for short stays." She paused. "Besides, we need to get going on our stewardship responsibilities."

"I'm not even sure what they entail, and I think I'm already doing a chunk of what I imagine is involved. But I guess we should spell it all out."

Tanny asked, "Have you gotten any paperwork from Uncle Jacob?"

"I haven't seen anything official. I just assumed I was doing what I was meant to do."

"I asked him to email me what I needed. But I haven't seen anything from him," replied Tanny. "I guess I need to ask again."

"Let me know what he says."

"I will."

Jeff described his last few days at work. There had been the usual handful of heart attack symptoms that weren't heart attacks, the one that *was* a heart attack but survived, and the one that also was but hadn't survived. "He was only forty-two."

"That's so sad!" Tanny exclaimed. "How awful."

"It never gets easier," responded Jeff. "It's especially hard when the family is right there, suffering in real time. That's when I wish we had a ride-along chaplain."

"Of course you do," sympathized Tanny.

"Then there was the three-year-old with the Lego figurine up her nose," added Jeff, lightening the mood. "The mother was very upset, but the child wasn't suffering at all. We were able to get it out with the usual tricks. We ended up giving the mother a lollipop to calm her and recommended she put away everything nostril-sized for a while."

This made Tanny grin. She wasn't sure she could manage being a paramedic. She said, "I am thinking of coming up next weekend, unless I am needed here. I mean to look for a job if there is any work to be found up there."

"You are looking for work up here?" Jeff's face lit up.

"Well, soon I will have nowhere to live as well as no way to pay for my life," explained Tanny. "Maybe a fresh start somewhere new would be the way to go. I can waitress anywhere."

"I will keep my ear to the ground," offered Jeff.

Tanny asked, somewhat diffidently, "What should we charge me to rent a room there? I mean, as a Steward, do I get a discount?"

Jeff's eyes twinkled. "I'm sure we could arrange something. We'd just have to win over Susan and Jacob."

"Susan would say yes," Tanny supplied.

"Maybe when you're up here, you could do a lot of baking for Jacob to win him over. He does love a good rhubarb pie."

"Maybe I could pay someone to bake a pie and pretend it was me?" laughed Tanny. "I am not much of a baker."

"I won't tell."

They smiled at each other a while. Tanny could hear the crackle of the fireplace over the phone. She wished she was there with him, talking to him, learning about him, discovering the potential between them. Then she remembered that she had a tendency to jump "all in" to relationships, only to discover there were major mismatches down the line. What were the mismatches she had yet to discover with Jeff? Her heart sobered.

She sighed. "Well, I need to get to bed," she announced.

"Thanks for letting me know you are back," Jeff said, smiling. "I wish you all good luck figuring out your schedule."

"Thanks," said Tanny, her heart warming again.

"Sleep well," he said.

"Good night."

Tanny put her dishes in the dishwasher and made her way to bed.

Tanny was up with the sun the next morning. She showered and got her coffee and checked her social media. There were a few funny memes that she liked. She took a yogurt over to the table and ate it out of the package. She fired off an email to her Uncle Jacob asking again for the stewardship paperwork.

Next, Tanny texted Jenny. "Hey dearest. How are you liking the new place? It's pretty cozy. I miss it. When were you thinking of selling this place? I want to know how fast I have to work to get it ready. Where would you like me to start? I want to do some travelling but don't want to delay the work here too much. Let me know when you have time. Love you."

Jenny called back almost immediately.

"Hey, Tanny! Welcome home! How was your trip?" After the niceties and updates, they got down to business. Jenny said, "I have no idea where you should start. I don't want to think about it. I completely trust you to use your judgment and do your best. Please don't ask me to make any decisions. It hurts just to think about it."

"Aw, honey. Okay. I hear you. Mom and I will handle it."

"Thank you. You can get Barb to help, too. She's been great."

"It will be good to have someone to bounce ideas off," Tanny agreed.

There was nothing else for it. Tanny would have to call Barb next.

She texted first to see if it was a good time to call. It was. Barb was knocking on her door a half hour later.

The tall brunette blew in on a swirling gust when Tanny opened the door. Barb's thick brown hair was blowing in her face, but finally the door was shut and her face emerged. The area around her nose was red and she apologized for having a cold. She did an air hug motion so as to keep any germs at a distance.

"Sorry, I think it's just a head-code, but better safe thad sorry. Want be to wear a bask?" She sounded a lot like she needed to blow her nose.

"Naw," said Tanny, making sure the door was secure. I will wash my hands a lot and stay away from your face. I think we're good."

Barb removed her boots and coat.

Tanny said, "Take a look around. We are supposed to get this place ready to sell. While you walk through, I'm going to go finish blow-drying my hair. I am realizing it is too chilly to let it air dry."

"Whed you're dud, I deed to blow-dry by dose, too," laughed Barb, honking into a tissue. She used sanitizer on her hands before heading off on her inspection.

Together the two women drank a lot of coffee and hashed out a plan for the place. They were going to deep clean the whole house and paint several of the rooms. Barb knew about "staging" and suggested bringing in some plants and decorative items to add flair and beauty to the spaces. "They also distract the eyes away from any problebatic visuals. If we put a large Ficus here, for exapple, you doe longer see the udattractive padel. The eye goes to the pladt and the padel essedtially disappears." Tanny was translating Barb's stuffed-up pronunciations without too much trouble. "Padel" was "panel."

Tanny realized she could learn a lot from Barb even though Barb said she was "a datural."

"Hey, do you think you could train me to do what you do?"

Barb looked at Tanny. "Absolutely I could. Are you idterested?"

"I think I am," said Tanny, realizing she really was.

Thirty-Three

March 8 to March 9

Over the next two days, Tanny worked closely with Barb on Jenny's house. Emily and Jenny came when they could. Tanny was surprised in how comprehensive the transformation was becoming.

"Who knew cleaning and painting could make such a big difference?" marveled Jenny, brushing her hair from her eyes with the back of her wrist. She was finishing up a fresh coat of white paint on some baseboards. The carpets had been steam-cleaned, which had meant Tanny was sleeping in the finished basement while they dried.

Emily thoroughly scrubbed the bathroom tiles, making several years of slowly accumulating mildew stains and soap scum disappear.

Barb had brought in some plants and art to help with the staging, teaching Tanny a bit about design, colour "conversations", and Feng Shui.

"A lot of what I do is instinct," Barb told Tanny on a sunny afternoon when it was just the two of them. Tanny was holding a picture up against a wall as Barb looked at it with tilted head. "A little to the right," she instructed. "Yes. Hold it there." And the professional organizer approached with a pencil.

Once the picture was hung along with two more in a collection, they both stood back and contemplated the grouping.

"That looks really nice," Tanny decided, impressed. "How did you know to hang them that way, just there?"

Barb shrugged with wide eyes. "Time? Experience? Gut feelings?" She tipped her head to the other side and smiled in satisfaction. "I suppose that with years of trial and error I've developed a kind of sixth sense. Success with trying things out and finding when they work has taught me to trust my instincts." She turned her bright eyes on Tanny. There was a light in them—a light of satisfaction and pleasure. "It's really fun."

She kept on teaching Tanny as they worked, trying to put words on why certain arrangements worked better than others. They talked about flow and eye-line and "feel." Barb taught that the use of colour could make the eye travel from a piece of art, to a similarly coloured throw, to a complementarily coloured piece of ceramics on the mantel. Tanny found it was true. It had always been true, but no one had ever taught her to notice it or understand what her eyes were doing. Once she learned this trick, she started right away to experiment with it herself.

Then she learned that she needed to take into account textures, styles of art, and periods of furniture. Not all things of similar colour would go well together, because a texture was wrong, or the styles clashed even if the palette was right. It wasn't so much that Tanny was learning strict rules as that she was learning the explanations for why some things "felt right" and "worked" while some other things didn't. There were so many variables to take into account.

Tanny had found a chair in the basement rec-room that seemed as though it belonged in the front right bedroom. It was a golden colour that picked up the gold colouring of the mirror frame and some tones in the bedspread. After dragging it up and setting it in the corner she called Barb with excitement. "Look what I found. Doesn't it go perfectly in that corner? Look at how nicely the colour matches."

Barb tipped her head and squinted her eyes. "I see what you are trying for," she said. "But something isn't working. Can you feel it?"

Tanny was deflated. "It seemed like it works to me," she said, confused.

Barb eyes lit up. "Wait! I think I know what to do." She pulled the mirror off the wall and carried it out of the room. She came back with a streamlined, more modern mirror from another bedroom and put it up. It had a slim frame, which had the merest, gentlest hint of gold. Then Barb moved the chair to the other side of the little reading table and centered them.

Something clicked for Tanny. "Oh! That's amazing! How did you do that?"

Barb screwed up her eyes, thinking. "So, that chair is a perfect find for this room, first and foremost. Well done! It just needed to go closer to the window," she began. She went back out and returned with the ornate and heavily framed mirror and set it on the dresser in front of the replacement. "I think the addition of the gold chair somehow made this frame stand out. My eye was drawn to the ornateness of this frame, which felt out of balance. It changed the feeling in the room, giving the elaborate frame too much power, or something. The chair *did* work. But it showed that the frame was a mismatch for the feel in the room. By adding this understated mirror in its place, the energy settles down again. Can you see that?" She moved the ornate frame away again.

Tanny saw it.

Barb put a hand on her shoulder. "You did something brilliant. I am praising you for your find, and grateful that it highlighted the misfit of the mirror, which I hadn't seen until you added the chair." She looked thoughtful. "Your instincts will only get better over time. When I first started organizing, I would not have understood why the mirror felt wrong, I simply would have felt compelled to change it. All these years later I am beginning to understand *why* things work or don't work, which helps me teach new organizers."

"It's so much more than putting things in boxes," mused Tanny.

"Yes. Yes, it is," agreed Barb.

Tanny got a call on the morning of the eighth inviting her to join in honouring Pastor Stephen Shantz's birthday the next day during the school's lunch period. This call reminded her with shock that she had arrived at another birthday herself. She was turning twenty-eight. Tanny had a long tradition of celebrating her own birthday with a small gathering, but this year, with the travel and changes, it had completely slipped her mind. She had been painting in the living room when the call had come in. Barb wasn't there, stuck at home waiting for a repair man. Jenny would not be arriving until Will was down for his nap.

Tanny stood alone in the partially painted room. Her playlist had just ended, and the chilly overcast light did nothing to lift the spirits.

Tanny felt out-of-step and caught off guard. Usually, she was excited to plan her annual gathering with her best girlfriends. But this year she had wanted to spend her birthday with Jeff. She had no reason to want that other than the compelling attraction and curiosity about their possible future. Now she wanted a gathering with her best friends *and* Jeff, which she knew was impossible.

Tanny sat down hard on a tarp-covered chair and felt ... she felt ... FRUS-TRATED. She made a sound that was half-growl and half scream. "I'm really pissed-off, God!" she protested into the room. "Why am I so overwhelmed and scattered? I don't feel like I'm coping at all. I'm stuck in this house, cleaning and painting for my sister who is even more overwhelmed than I am. I can't even resent her for marrying a jerk, or having a son that isn't quite right, or suffering from depression! None of that is her fault, yet *I'm* the one losing my apartment and preparing her home for sale." The frustration converted to tears and Tanny sat alone in the chilly room and wept. Eventually she had to struggle to put her paint brush somewhere safe and wipe her hands before she could find a tissue and blow her nose. "I'm really mad about all this!!" she whined.

There was a knock on the door and Barb poked her head in. "Hey. I thought I heard weeping and gnashing of teeth." She shed her coat and boots and came over to hug Tanny. "The repairman cancelled. So, I'm here. What's going on?"

Tanny explained her frustration. Her birthday was the next day, and she had forgotten. She had no plans, and she felt, she felt ... lost in the shuffle. "Everybody else's needs are more important than mine," Tanny complained. "I feel like I'm being bull-dozed under other people's agendas, and I don't know how to stand up for myself without looking like a selfish jerk."

Barb made sounds of sympathy. "I know the feeling," Barb murmured. "I call it 'nice girl syndrome.' As a girl I was so well-schooled in being 'unselfish' that I never learned what my own needs were. I felt punished whenever I expressed my own needs or said 'no.' To survive, I shut off awareness of what I needed and wanted—I became completely focused on serving and helping others—until, after many years, I was absolutely exhausted." She took a breath. "At least, that's one of my pet peeves and something I've been struggling with. I can't say for you if that is what is going on. It just looks like it from the outside."

Tanny started laughing. She was nodding and laughing. She started to speak a few times, but her giggles would overtake her.

Barb watched her, delighted and baffled.

Finally, Tanny, a finger raised, said, "Lucy van Pelt," and kept laughing. "You know, when she's leaning on the piano, and she says, 'That's IT!' so loud that Schroeder flips over several times? That's what I pictured as soon as you said that. Oh my gosh." Tanny wiped more tears from her eyes. She lifted her finger again and said, "That's IT!" and kept laughing.

"Glad I could help," chuckled Barb.

"I like to think I'm good at knowing my boundaries," protested Tanny, "but clearly I'm still feeling stepped on or what you said would not have resonated so strongly." She continued mopping her eyes.

"Better tears of laughter than rage," sympathized Barb. "So, it's your birthday tomorrow?"

Tanny wilted. "Yes. The big two-eight. Usually, I plan a fun gathering with my best women friends. But I completely forgot this year. And besides, where would I hold it? Here? Amid the buckets of paint and drop cloths?"

"Maybe not such a good idea," agreed Barb. "Let's let it percolate a few hours and see if some great idea doesn't come up, eh?" suggested the resourceful cousin. "Maybe we could do something at my house?"

Tanny loved Barb's "woo-woo" optimism. Barb often said things like, "Let's see if this picture tells us where it belongs," or "the solution will show itself," about organizing a challenging room. And so far, the answers had appeared each time. Tanny wondered if her own life would work better if she started saying "woo-woo" things like that. She could say, "My new career will reveal itself." She doubted that would work.

When Tanny had her video call with Jeff that night, the heartache came out. She talked about "nice girl syndrome" and how hard she had to fight to hold any boundaries.

Jeff grinned at her. "I would never have expected you to have trouble expressing your needs."

"Maybe I don't have trouble *expressing* them, but it sure seems like they are ignored or silenced, or I get shamed for having them."

Jeff looked troubled. "I hope I don't do that to you. Have I ever overridden your needs?"

Tanny's funk lifted. "You? No. No, you never have." She grew silent. "Maybe it's a church thing. Maybe it's the church culture that is that way. Good grief. I'm being so whiny and sorry for myself. What a charmer."

"Whine away, Tanny. You can have bad days. Don't beat yourself up for struggling sometimes. With Jacob and Eileen as foster parents, I'm no stranger to the judgmental nature of the church. Eileen is far too hard on herself. And I wish she'd stand up to Jacob a bit more often. Please keep being feisty and standing up for yourself. Especially if I'm a jackass to you."

Tanny let the implications of that statement sink in. Was Jeff putting himself in Jacob's shoes and her in Aunt Eileen's? Was he asking her to stand up to him ... once they were married?!

Jeff seemed to have realized the way his words had come out too, because he coloured and suddenly gave Mack a lot of affectionate scrubbing, hiding his face.

"I can't imagine you being a jackass," murmured Tanny.

"Just give me time," assured Jeff, mostly into Mack's fur.

The conversation turned to the possibility of listing Jenny's house by the weekend, and Tanny asking, "So, can I come up there and hide out from the peering and prying Realtors?"

"There's plenty of room here," agreed Jeff, his face coming back into view. "What do you want to do about Jacob and Eileen?"

"I will be twenty-eight. I can manage my own life without their opinions. I really need to stop caring what the older generations think of my choices. I must assert my independence and adult status."

"So long as you are sure. I will be happy to have your company."

Tanny's heart warmed. "I know I can trust you not to molest me."

"I have no interest in molesting anyone," Jeff agreed.

Tanny spent a minute imagining a fully consensual interaction between them and then had to hide her face too. "How's the work on the apartment going?" she asked. Jeff had switched a lot of his attention to getting it insulated in the last week.

"It's almost fully winterized," he said, proudly. "If we do go to a Bed and Breakfast model with Cedar Haven, I will have a fully separate living arrangement in plenty of time."

"I really like the idea of running it as a Bed and Breakfast," Tanny warmed. They had talked about this before. "That main floor office could be for the business, and the rest of the house could be for the guests. We could hire a cook, or I could advance my breakfast skills."

They spent the next hour discussing Bracebridge news, possible ideas for Cedar Haven, Jeff's work, Tanny's possible careers, and everything else. They had to make themselves get off the phone. Jeff had an early shift.

No sooner had she hung up than Tanny's phone was ringing in her hand.

"Hey Tanny, how are you? I'm sorry I've been so hard to reach," said Susan Haley.

"Hi Sue! How are you feeling? How are you doing?" asked Tanny with enthusiasm.

"It's a bit of a bumpy ride so far, but Jon has been amazing. I think the girls might suspect. They seem to know what morning sickness is. Except I have "all-day" sickness, so we're still working with the 'Mommy has a stomach bug' for now. But we'll have to announce pretty soon, or it will be one of those secrets everybody knows but is pretending not to."

"Oh, my," breathed Tanny. "Well, I can't wait. I support you, whatever you need."

"Look Tanny," said Susan, "I know tomorrow is your birthday. If you don't have any plans yet, could we host a little something here tomorrow night? Say, seven o'clock? We'll invite all the usual suspects."

"That would be amazing!" agreed Tanny.

Thirty-Four

March 9, evening

Tanny's birthday arrived with bright sunshine. After a morning of satisfying room staging, she and Barb walked up to the school to sing happy birthday to Stephen with the children. Some of the children put on a skit in which a seventh grader played Stephen, mimicking Stephen's voice patterns delightfully. Angus Kinloch even captured the way Stephen would lay a hand on his heart when he was saying something particularly deep. Angus had the room weeping with hilarity as he clutched at his sweater and said, with a fair imitation of Stephen's voice, "Thanks to God's Divine Providence, the cake will now be served."

Barb and Tanny walked back to the house in good spirits, each trying to copy Angus's tribute. Clutch. "I think it is important that we have coffee." Clutch. "I don't need gifts; these children are my gifts," followed by stumbles and knocking together with laughter.

The carpets were dry and Tanny could sleep in her chosen bedroom again. The living room and halls were staged as well as the main floor bathroom. Even the garage sparkled. The master bedroom and the third bedroom were almost finished. But the kitchen and finished basement still needed a lot of work.

Barb suggested a coat of paint and new hardware on the kitchen cabinets to update the look without too much expense. They had a lot of scrubbing to do to prepare them, which became the afternoon's task. Ultimately, they realized the walls could use new paint as well. She had researched the latest trends in paint colours and picked a rich dark blue for the cabinetry and white for the walls and trim. "This kitchen gets a lot of light, so the dark blue cabinets will add depth and coziness."

"And class," marveled Tanny.

"I know the paint seems like a big expense," Barb continued, "but the updated appearance really helps the prospective buyers imagine themselves in the space. The house is much more likely to sell quickly and at a better price with this fresh paint than if we sell it 'as-is.'" Barb chuckled, "Several clients have commented that they think about keeping their house once we've cleaned and staged their places. The home becomes a place they want to stay in. Just a little TLC can go a long way to making a house feel welcoming and homey." She continued, "I'll bring over my bread-maker when we are ready for showings. I can cook a loaf or two a day to keep that fresh bread smell permeating the house."

Tanny wondered if she could help eat that freshly cooked bread with some melty butter.

Barb chose brushed nickel drawer pulls and cabinet handles, "To pick up the white from the walls."

"How did you learn how to do interior design too?" Tanny asked, amazed.

Barb laughed. "I did, if you can believe, a correspondence course. I knew it was very basic, but it taught me enough to lay a foundation. I just love watching redecorating and home makeover shows. I pick up a lot through them. I'm no expert, but I keep learning."

Tanny liked that idea: to be a constant learner.

After a dinner of stew and fresh rolls, Tanny bundled up to walk over to the Haleys'. She'd chosen a cozy lavender sweater with a cowl neck, dress slacks, and her dress boots. The evening was chilly, but Tanny was loving the slow return of the light as the earth approached the equinox.

Tanny noticed a surprising number of cars as she hiked up the sloping drive. She opted for the formal front door instead of the casual side door. It looked like there was already a crowd.

Susan pulled open the door and welcomed Tanny in with a bear hug. "Hey, welcome! I'm so glad this worked out. Come see how many people made it!"

Entering the warm living room, Tanny was greeted by many Bender relatives. There was Meghan Bender, throwing her arms around her with her delightful southern drawl, "Happy birthday, Tanny!" Meghan was an outgoing, gregarious, and beloved family member. She had met Tanny's quiet and brilliant cousin Samuel when they both attended college in Ben Kirk. Everyone called Samuel "Brains" as he was a near-genius and wildly successful as a computer programmer. Meghan had adapted well to the northern climate but never lost her Atlanta drawl.

"Brains" was there too and gave Tanny a hug with his signature chuckle.

Shelley was there with her wide smile and mischievous eyes. She was even sporting a camera and was getting shots of the gathering.

"Because twenty-eight is such an important birthday?" Tanny asked her.

"Because all of your birthdays are important," grinned Shelley.

Stephen and Liz pushed over to greet her. "Happy birthday!" hugged Liz. "We can't stay long, but we had to come by."

Tanny thanked person after person as she was drawn into the cozy living room with the crackling fireplace and teal sectional.

Jon shoved a mug of coffee into her hands saying, "Susan thought you might like this." It was raspberry chocolate coffee from Second Cup.

"Oh, yum!" Tanny exclaimed.

Suddenly Tanny was face to face with Conrad and Gary. Tanny grabbed them with wide-open eyes and mouthed, "Oh my gosh. It's great to see you here, to-geth-er!" They were both grinning, and Tanny's heart warmed. Her eyes stung with tears as she recalled their support when Charm died.

"We couldn't stay away," assured Conrad. "Jon insisted we come; both of us, together."

Gary leaned in for a hug. "Happy birthday. I'm really enjoying meeting so many of Conrad's crowd."

The two of them weren't holding hands, but they clearly emanated "couple" energy. Tanny was delighted.

It was quite a while before Tanny could find a seat. Alyssa and Andrea had to compete for "best hug." Peter and Laura Bender were there. Tanny's mom and dad brought greetings from Jenny who was home with Will.

Finally, the greetings settled down and Tanny was looking around at the large gathering. So many cousins and school friends had either come or sent greetings.

Tanny had an aching wish that Jeff could meet these people. Then, to cover her ache, she suggested a round of "This is a Cat; This is a Dog," and after a few false starts the game was underway with confusion and laughter on all sides.

The doorbell rang as things were coming to a head, but Tanny was too engrossed to see who had come. Susan had stayed out of the game to play hostess and mind the girls, so she answered the door.

When she had a second, Tanny threw a quick look over her shoulder, and her eyes met Jeff's. Everything stood still. She barely heard the, "This is a cat," from her left, nor the, "This is a dog" arriving simultaneously from her right.

Jeff is here...?. . . !

Conrad, on Tanny's left insisted, "This is a cat," waving a wooden spoon at her. Meghan Bender on her right waved her spatula and insisted, "This is a dog." Tanny came to her senses and said, "A what?" to Conrad and "A what?" to Meghan, and leapt up from her seat. "You got this," she reassured Conrad and Meghan and broke through the circle to greet Jeff.

Her approach was tentative but became an enthusiastic launch.

"Jeff!" she exclaimed. "What are you doing here?" Her arms were around his neck with her face resting in the cold puffiness of his coat. She dropped back to the floor as they both felt the impact of that contact. They both seemed a little breathless. Their arms held on a little longer.

Jeff realized he had just held Tanny in his arms again; something he'd wanted to repeat for a long time. He said, "Jon called last night. We realized I could make it down after my shift. I wanted to come." His eyes drank up her rosy cheeks and dancing eyes. He had loved the feel of her soft sweater.

There was so much Tanny wanted to ask the surprise guest, but she was increasingly aware of all the eyes watching them. Somehow the cat and the dog had gotten lost in the interruption.

Tanny turned to her group of friends and family. "Everyone, this is Jefferson VanGalen from Bracebridge. He's Jacob and Emily's foster son, and he's the caretaker at Cedar Haven."

"Oh my gosh. A foster-cousin," said Meghan. "Great to meet you."

A host of other greetings sailed toward Jeff as Jon took his coat. Tanny watched dumb struck as Jeff folded into the chatty group.

Susan was at her elbow. "He has a lovely energy," she said. "We've invited him to stay the night in the spare room, so he doesn't have to drive back tonight."

Tanny spun to look at her. "That's brilliant! He's ... he's meeting everyone...." Her eyes followed him as the EMT squatted to greet the twins, then rose to chat with Conrad and Gary.

Tanny realized that, while she wanted him to know her world, she also wanted everyone to leave immediately so that she and Jeff could be alone. It felt strange to have him so near, and to feel so emotionally close, when they'd not actually spent that much time in each other's physical presence. How did she explain why he was even there?

"So how do you know Tanny?" she heard Paul Bender ask.

"I got to know Jon and Susan when they were arranging their honeymoon stay. Tanny and I are both Stewards of Cedar Haven. Susan is also a Steward; and Jon and I have really hit it off. They all feel like family," was Jeff's response.

Paul exclaimed that he had been barely aware of Jeff's existence, and he was sorry not to have met him sooner.

As Tanny pushed back into the crowd, that became the common thread: Jeff was family and was a Steward with Susan and Tanny. It was weird for Tanny. She had wanted Jeff to meet her friends and vice versa, but the narrative that was arising left out what Jeff and Tanny were to each other. What were they to each other?

Eventually Jeff found his way back to Tanny's side. He grabbed her in a one-armed hug and kissed her temple a little fiercely. "Surprise! Happy birthday." His grin was wicked.

Tanny's world righted itself immediately. "I'm delighted you came. How did you know it was my birthday?"

"Susan and Jon told me last night. With the invitation to stay over, I had to come."

He looked around the room and back at her. "How much longer will these wonderful people stay?"

Tanny's face warmed at the intense look in his eyes.

Susan came up to them just then and said, warningly, "If you are not an item, you need to stop those smoldering looks immediately."

Jeff dropped his arm from Tanny's shoulders and cleared his throat.

"Susan, could you decide it is time for everyone to go home by nine-thirty? You know, 'school night' and all that?"

"I could absolutely do that," agreed Susan.

The group eventually attempted to resurrect the game, and they stumbled to the final, "A cat! A dog!" with whoops of triumph. Jeff had decided to sit next to Tanny and quickly picked up the crazy rhythm. Their bond increased with each laughing, "A what?" communicated down the line.

Soon Susan was shutting down the gathering, looking genuinely peaked. Jon helped folks find their coats and Tanny thanked everyone as they departed. Susan clearly needed to lie down and did so as soon as the last person exited the door.

Jon started to clean up, and suggested Tanny and Jeff go to the guest room to visit as the open concept layout offered them no privacy.

The guest room was tiny and doubled as an office. It had a large sliding door to the back yard as its only window. The two of them sat on the bed and looked at each other grinning.

Jeff was the first to speak. "May I hold your hands?" he asked.

"Of course!" said Tanny laying her hands in his large, roughened ones. It felt like they belonged there. His hair was still quite short yet showed a hint of gold which matched his golden eyes. Absurdly, Tanny asked, "What is the colour of your eyes? I've never heard of golden eyes before."

"I've often been teased about them," Jeff said. "I like to think I'm a 'Witcher,'" he added with a twinkle in his eye.

Tanny laughed. "They are amazing. They are not brown or green.... Are they a version of hazel?"

"Eileen tells me they are amber or golden." He waggled his brows. "She said that golden eyes signal supernatural powers and special wisdom. I think she made that up to comfort me."

Tanny grinned and moved her face closer to look into them deeply. "I think they are an amazing colour." She wanted to add, *I think you are amazing* but didn't.

Jeff's pupils widened until his eyes looked almost black. "I ... I would like to kiss you." Was his husky comment. "May I?"

Tanny felt a rush of awareness, not having consciously intended to invite a kiss. But she said, "Absolutely," without a second thought.

Jeff's hands encircled her face, and his kiss was gentle, asking for consent.

Tanny's response was immediate and complete. Her arms were around his neck, and she opened to greet him. The room began to swirl. Her heartbeat and breathing accelerated as she tasted the salt and coffee of him. She dimly realized, for the first time in her life, how a couple could get "carried away." *Oh my God....* She never wanted the kiss to stop. She wanted to explore more and more about this man.

They both pulled back at the same time, and rested with their foreheads touching, breathing heavily. Tanny felt like she had a firecracker in her low belly.

"Wow," she breathed.

"Hey," he chuckled. "I've wanted to do that since I was fourteen. That was every—" he panted, "—everything I dreamed of...."

Tanny closed her eyes and soaked up the incredible confession. He had desired her all the way back then? This wonderful man, that she had completely missed, had loved her since they were early teenagers? And he hadn't changed his mind now that he knew her? It blew her mind. How was this possible? Nobody— she took a gulp of air—nobody had ever valued her like this. She felt a great gulf opening beneath her. What if she accepted and welcomed this love, and it went away? How would she ever manage?

Tanny looked into his eyes again, and saw longing and respect, hope and trepidation there. He was afraid too? Afraid to lose her? Her!? She sucked in air as she realized she was willing to risk a broken heart for this man. She trusted him to be kind. She trusted his integrity.

Jeff saw the change and realization in Tanny's eyes, and was struck with amazement and joy. "Oh, you are so doomed," he murmured and pressed into her with such hunger that soon they were lying back on the bed. Her hair, her lips, her soft skin, her smell, her soft sweater. Oh, to continue deeper and deeper....

Jeff stopped himself. They had only been getting reacquainted for two weeks. They were guests in someone else's home. It was much too soon to go where he wanted to go, no matter how willing and responsive Tanny seemed.

So Tanny and Jeff lay together, looking into each other's eyes and touching each other's faces.

Jeff chuckled. "So, does this mean we are seeing each other? May I consider you my woman-friend? Are we 'dating'?"

Tanny twisted her mouth and looked up to the side. "Hmmm," she said. She acted like she was mulling it over even as her insides were doing jumping jacks.

She sat up and smoothed her hair. "Okay," she announced.

Jeff sat up too and grabbed Tanny's arms, looking intently into her eyes. "Are you sure?"

"Is there something you're not telling me?" Tanny asked in mock alarm. "Are you actually a Witcher or a vampire or something?"

"May-be," Jeff responded.

"You're a goof! Let's go with a hard, 'YES,' and take it from there, Witcher or no."

A long, savouring kiss followed this.

"Will you go out to breakfast with me before I drive back?" Jeff asked when they came up for air.

Tanny was still reeling with the abrupt change in their relationship. Each wave of comprehension hit like an electric shock.

"I'd love that. What time?"

"Pretty early. Say, six thirty? It's a good three hours back to Cedar Haven. I'd like to be back by one."

"What if I stay the night?" she asked.

At Jeff's look of shock, she put up her hands. "Fully clothed. No hanky-panky. Just holding each other." She paused and said, "Well, no shoes in the bed."

Tanny could see the hesitation and questions in Jeff's eyes.

"Jon and Sue will be fine with it so long as I explain the circumstances. And so long as you can control yourself." She grinned. "Full consent or I go back to Jenny's and see you in the morning."

Something unwound in Jeff then. "I would love that, if you are willing." So Tanny stayed in her clothes and crawled under the covers with Jeff. They settled into the spoon position, Jeff's arms around Tanny's waist. Tanny felt amazingly safe. She slept like she had won the lottery.

Thirty-Five

March 10

Tanny awoke in an unexpected room with arms around her waist and a warm body pressed against her back. Her heart sang. It did something amazing to her nervous system to feel Jeff at her back, to hear his slow, even breathing. She smiled so hard and soaked up the marvelous sensations. *It's like somebody has my back,* she thought. *Jeff has my back.*

Tanny sighed in happiness. She noticed every detail in the room as her pulse thrummed with the delicious feelings. Jeff stirred. Tanny wasn't sure that she wanted him to wake up just yet, because it would mean that they would probably change positions. But she also needed to pee.

"Mmmm. Good morning," Jeff murmured in her ear in his deep bass. He nuzzled a bit in her neck. "Did you sleep well?" He didn't seem to want to move either.

"I slept wonderfully. How about you?" she asked, her hands pressing his where they rested on her belly.

"I can't complain," he chuckled.

Tanny understood that he meant it had been as delightful for him as it had been for her.

"I don't want to get up, but I really need to pee," Tanny complained. She began to wiggle loose from Jeff's hold.

He made a noise of unwillingness and pretended to hold on to her.

Tanny hopped into the attached half-bath and did some washing up as well as relieving herself. She searched the bathroom cabinet. *Yes!* There was a spare toothbrush and a tiny toothpaste. She cleaned her teeth and sniffed at her breath. It seemed okay.

When she came out, Jeff was holding a robe and some toiletries. "I'm going to check if the shower is free," he said.

When Tanny followed him out of the room, looking for coffee, Andrea and Alyssa were there in the open concept living-dining room reading books.

"Hi Jeff!" they each chimed up. Then Andrea said, "Aunt Tanny? What are you doing here?" Both girls ran over to her for hugs.

Thinking quickly Tanny told them, "Jeff is taking me out for breakfast, and so I'm here really early."

Alyssa took her hand and lead her over to the sectional. "Will you read to me?" Alyssa settled into the cushions and held up a book.

"Me too," complained Andrea. "Read my book too."

Tanny felt that pinch of annoyance she sometimes felt when children demanded things of her that she wasn't in the mood to give. But then she realized that this was precious time with nieces she loved, and she really had nothing better to do. Of course she would read to them!

Tanny proceeded to deliberately change the stories in small ways and then look at the girls with confusion. The girls knew the stories so well they would call out things like, "Hey! That's not how it goes!" and "Tanny, get it right!" They proceeded with giggles and the occasional tickle until a shaved and robed vision of masculinity walked back through the room toward the guest room. He even smelled good.

"He's leaving today," informed Andrea.

"He came for your birthday party," added Alyssa.

Tanny's heart warmed as the realization hit her again. "Yes, he did. That was super nice of him." Tanny felt herself blush.

Andrea cocked her head. "Are you in love with him?"

Alyssa leaned into Tanny, looking into her face. "Are you going to marry him?"

And he is hearing every word of this, thought Tanny. She felt warm from her head to toe. She said, "Well, I think I *am* in love with him, but that's a secret for now. It is a brand-new secret and we aren't ready for everybody to know. So please only talk to your mom and Jon about it and not people at the school. Can you keep that secret for me?"

Both girls nodded with enthusiasm.

"Thank you so much," said Tanny, wondering how long until the news was out. "And as for marriage," she added, looking directly at Alyssa, "there is usually a lot of time between dating and deciding to get married. We *just started* dating. So, we won't know for a while if we will get married."

"You should get married," announced Alyssa.

"Only if they want to," said Andrea.

It was a relief when Jeff appeared, ready to go to breakfast. He had all his stuff packed and ready for the car.

The girls ran over to him and hugged his legs, nearly throwing him off balance.

"I think you should marry Tanny," announced Alyssa.

"You'd better be good to Tanny!" said Andrea, "or you'll have me to answer to."

Tanny had so many feelings at once that she just wanted to grab Jeff and run out of the house.

Bur Jeff said in his friendliest voice, "I will take that into account, Andrea. I want you to know that I have only gentlemanly intentions toward Tanny. Thank you for defending her so beautifully."

Alyssa said, "I am defending her too!"

Jeff looked at Alyssa and said, "Yes you are. Thank you as well. I don't know if we will get married, but right now I like the idea very much."

Tanny was sidling closer and closer to the coat room.

"Now I need you two to let me go so we can be on our way."

The girls released him, and he followed Tanny to the coat room. "Please thank your mom and da-, I mean, Jon, for a wonderful stay."

A voice came from beyond the kitchen. "No problem, Jeff. Susan's still asleep, but I am glad not to have missed you," came Jon's morning-gruff voice. "You two are getting breakfast? You know we can feed you here if you like."

Jeff set down his bags to give Jon a brotherly hug. "Thanks, man. I know. But I think we want this time together before I head back."

Jon lifted one eyebrow. "I am seeing that." He grinned and gave Jeff a swack on his shoulder. "Safe travels. It has been a treat to meet you face-to-face, my brother."

Jeff escorted Tanny out to his truck and helped her in, throwing his gear behind the seats.

Tanny's head was spinning. Her heart was full of effervescence at Jeff's, "right now I like the idea very much," about marrying her. None of the girls' pressuring had thrown him.

"How did you learn to be so good with kids?" she asked as they drove away.

"*Little* kids are great; it's teenagers that frighten me," Jeff corrected her.

"Really?" said Tanny. "I'm impatient with little kids and generally love teenagers."

Jeff gave her a brief glance of amazement. "Are *you* kidding?"

"Yes! I mean, I'm not kidding. I love teenagers. They have minds. I can have great conversations with them. I love to hear how they are seeing the world. I love to hear what they are struggling with. They can be very authentic, you know. And they just want to be seen and heard and validated. I find that easy and it feels good."

Jeff was looking thoughtful as they proceeded along the convoluted route of back roads to get to Homer-Watson. He asked, "Hey, where shall we go? I almost always go to Tim Hortons when I'm down here, but I bet you know some nicer places for a real sit-down meal."

"How much time do we have?" asked Tanny.

Jeff made a low squeaking noise indicating 'not a lot.'

"Okay. Country Boy it is." Tanny responded with a smile. She directed him to turn right on Homer-Watson and then left on Manitou.

They settled into a booth, right by the big table where the wedding party had gathered. She commented on that.

"Wait. So, Jon and Sue took everyone out for breakfast after the wedding?"

"Yea, they did. It was nice. They saw it as a sort of reception, and then they drove up to Cedar Haven for their honeymoon."

The waitress delivered menus and asked if they wanted coffee, tea, or maybe orange juice. They both ordered coffee.

Jeff continued, "I was down here at that time. That is why I never met those two until last night."

"You were *here*? Why?"

"I occasionally take Paramedic courses at Conestoga College to advance my skills. Some courses are online. But I happened to have a required in-person set of classes that week. So, I was down here at a course when they were up there. It worked perfectly."

"What would you have done if you hadn't had a course?"

Bunked in with a co-worker or asked Eileen and Jacob."

"Huh. So, Cedar Haven is your home, unless you get kicked out by guests."

"Yep. Those are the terms of the Stewardship agreement as it stands, so Jacob tells me."

Tanny's brow crumpled. "I really want to see those documents. I wonder if we are allowed to amend them and how open they are to interpretation. As it is, the terms seem awfully disruptive for your life."

Jeff shrugged. "Eventually I will have an apartment in the barn for when guests want the house to themselves. Until then, I must bunk other places."

The waitress brought their steaming coffee as well as glasses of ice water. They weren't ready to order so she went away. Jeff put cream in his coffee and poured some for Tanny too when she smiled her yes. They busied themselves over the menus until they had each selected their meals.

"Where do you sleep when you come down for classes?" Tanny asked.

"There's a hotel down by the campus."

"But you have so much family here!"

Jeff made that same, uneasy squeaking noise and said, "Do I? I have never seen myself as part of the extended family. Except for that one summer, I've never been included in any family gatherings. I don't think Jacob and Eileen saw me as family, really. I was a project, and a Christian act, and maybe the child they never had. But I also felt that they were ashamed of me. I felt their judgment of my parents for not being able to keep me. I felt less-than, because of my parents' addictions and my mother's indigenous heritage."

Tanny made a noise of exasperated sadness. "But that's terrible. Those things aren't your fault. And native heritage isn't even a fault! Surely white people aren't still looking down on indigenous people?"

Jeff just looked at her. Tanny remembered all the reports of missing indigenous women in many provinces. She paled. "I'm sorry. I guess because I think all races deserve equal respect, I believe everyone else thinks that too." She put her hand on Jeff's. "Please help me understand. I don't mean to be an ignoramus."

Jeff took her hand in his warm, callused one.

"I love you just the way you are, Tanny."

The waitress came just then to take their orders. The declaration hung between them as Tanny stumbled through her order. Tanny wondered if Jeff knew the impact of his words. She felt warm all over. She wanted to grab him across the table and kiss him fiercely.

She cleared her throat and looked at him once the waitress had left. "I ... I .... Are you sure? You don't know me that well yet. What if I'm a secret, uh .... What if I cheat on my taxes, or beat my old parents, or yell at other drivers in my car?"

Jeff just looked at her with a twinkle in his eye.

"I actually ... do ... yell at other drivers when I'm in my car," Tanny admitted sheepishly. "But they can't hear me."

Jeff laughed out loud. "Let's just say that for now, I love you just the way you are. I can't help myself. I have loved you since I first met you. It feels deeper than reason. It feels ... spiritual?" His amber eyes begged her to understand. "Like destiny? I hope that doesn't frighten you. It is okay if you feel differently." He squeezed her hand.

Tanny was speechless. How did she get so lucky? She felt as if destiny *had* made them for each other too, even though she didn't believe in such things.

"Jeff, I ..."

Misreading her feelings Jeff released her hand and held his up in a sign of surrender.

"I'm sorry. I didn't mean to make you uncomfortable—"

"No, Jeff!" Tanny reached for his hand again. "I love what you are saying. I just can't believe it. It doesn't make sense to me. But I *feel the same*. I do. It just ... frightens me."

Jeff returned her grasp, and his gaze became intense. Tanny's insides squirmed with excitement. She felt her cheeks flame.

"I don't want to frighten you. Please consider what you are frightened of, and when you know, tell me, if you can. I will never hurt you."

Was this gorgeous man for real? Where did he learn such emotional intelligence?

Tanny took in a big breath. "I will see if I can figure it out. I'm kind of baffled by it myself."

Jeff leaned back, grinning in relief. "Take your time. There's no rush. As long you feel completely safe."

Tanny had the image of herself as a frightened puppy cowering before a big, gentle lion. *A close-shaved lion,* she thought, and grinned.

Their meals arrived and they settled down to eating.

Eventually Tanny said, "Jeff, I think you should be treated as a full family member. I think you always should have been welcomed and included." She paused. "Unless you prefer to stay apart. Do you prefer to be apart? I mean, separate, not 'A Part'. Funny that they sound the same: 'A part' and 'apart'." Her hand gestures indicated the separated words.

Jeff sat in a morass of unexplored feelings. If only she knew how desperately he had wanted to belong in the big, interrelated Bender family. Britt had treated him like a full grandson. Jacob and Eileen had treated him like ... like ... a pet? They were loving and close sometimes and kept their distance other times. But here was this magical girl from his youth, now a vibrant woman, welcoming him with open arms to the family and to her heart. It was his turn to feel shaken and afraid. He trusted Tanny and felt completely at ease with her, but .... Now it was his turn to realize that he had some unexpected fears to explore. Thank goodness he was seeing his therapist soon.

"I ... I kind of decided I was my own safe space. *I* had my back, and I decided that was all I needed," he said. "But once I had met you and your siblings, I realized

I longed to belong to a big family. I wanted to be a Bender, like you. But nothing ever came of that, and I made my peace with being alone."

"Well, you are not alone now," said Tanny. "You've got me." She extended her hand across the table again, and he took it. They managed to finish their breakfasts without letting go.

Tanny asked, "Why do you think Uncle Jacob is being so slow to give us the documents for the stewardship position? How can we get him to cough them up? I feel like we must go to his house and stand there until he gives us our copies."

"We might have to do that," chuckled Jeff. "I think he has liked being the one in complete control and doesn't want to give that up. But who knows?" He scooped up the last few bits of hash browns on his plate.

Tanny set her fork down. She was done. "When will I see you again?" she asked.

Jeff gave her a twisted smile. "When you come up for an extended visit?"

She grinned. "Would it be okay if I moved into the house with you? It's a big place. We wouldn't necessarily be 'living together.' We'd be 'housemates.'"

Jeff's eyes crinkled over his last sip of coffee. He said, "You are welcome anytime. We can be whatever status feels comfortable to you." He took her hand in both of his and added, "But just for the record, I think I'd like to live together, if you should want that." His eyes twinkled devilishly.

Tanny would have fallen into his arms if there hadn't been a table between them, but she said, with some cheek, "One step at a time. We only started dating last night!"

As they rose to get their coats Jeff murmured, "I started dating *you* the moment we met."

Jeff paid for the breakfast as Tanny wondered if she had been meant to hear that. It made her heart pound. *Was it selfish to love someone just because they loved you?* No, she loved him for his character, for the way he lived, for the way he treated others.

Jeff had to take Tanny back to Cliffside before he could head north, and Tanny knew he was cutting time short. She offered to take a bus home so he could get going, something which he adamantly refused to consider.

Jeff followed her into the MacGregor house for a quick look at where she was living. Then he pulled her into a powerful kiss. They were both in their winter coats, and the puffiness was both a protection and an added coziness as the kiss lasted and lasted.

Jeff finally pulled away saying, "Damn!"

Tanny watched from the porch as he strode out to his truck, every fibre of his being radiating resignation about his need to leave.

Tanny waved as he backed his truck down the drive. His eyes were sombre. But as he drove off, he waved out the window until he was out of sight.

Thirty-Six

March 11

Jeff sat in his truck outside his therapist's office. He had yet to drive away, as he was pondering and pondering what they had uncovered. They had opened up ways his childhood traumas could booby-trap his relationship with Tanny. He had been made to sit with raw and old feelings of abandonment. To sit with them. To just keep feeling them and emote as he needed. It was terribly hard. He felt shaken and bruised. But he felt a little freer and more hopeful.

His therapist was half Anishinaabe, just like him, and Jeff trusted him completely. Dr Eagletree frequently asked him to get out of his head and be with his feelings—something Jeff believed in but found much harder than it sounded.

Jeff had told Dr. Eagletree about his complex feelings when Tanny wanted to include him in the family. Jeff both wanted to belong but also wanted to whisk Tanny away and not share her with her huge family. Jeff was used to going it alone and only relying on himself. The idea of truly belonging to any group brought up terrors from his childhood abandonment. His parents had said they loved him and were often loving but then would leave him on the Res for weeks or be unavailable even when they were around, due to their drinking. Eileen and Jacob were steady and firm and had provided good boundaries but often treated him as though he were second class. This had built in him an almost pathological inability to trust or rely on others. He hadn't seen or felt this until this session.

Jeff loved the idea of being part of a big family, but he saw himself as quite separate and was more comfortable being separate. Dr. Eagletree described it as intimacy adjacent. Jeff liked the idea of belonging but needed to protect himself from further neglect and abuse. His wounds could make him find non-inclusion even when it wasn't there. After all, if he didn't rely on anyone, no one could let him down.

This defence pattern could absolutely hurt Tanny if he did not acknowledge it and stay alert to when it was triggered.

Jeff had liked to see himself as well-adjusted and trustworthy, and it hurt to see his vulnerabilities. It hurt to realize he couldn't necessarily protect Tanny if his fear of abandonment got triggered. Even his desperate longing to bring her into his life sprang in part from his wounds. His subconscious had decided she would never abandon him, perhaps because she had been so completely inclusive all those years ago. No wonder he wanted her so completely. His inner child believed she would be the loyal defender he never knew.

Jeff felt shaken to his core. Tanny could abandon him. Heck, Jeff would just need his subconscious to decide she was abandoning him for him to go into a very bad place. Thank the Great Creator that Dr. Eagletree led him to these realizations. And Dr. Eagletree was there for him, should his demons overtake him.

Meanwhile, Jeff would continue his focus on service, courtesy, and respect. He would use deep breathing when he felt the terror creeping in, and he would bury himself in his work and woodworking on those weeks when the anxiety persisted.

Dr. Eagletree also encouraged him to confide in Tanny about his struggles with abandonment and anxiety. That was a step toward deep trust and intimacy— the things Jeff both longed for and avoided.

Jeff started his truck. He took a slow, deep breath and headed out to the road back to Cedar Haven.

Meanwhile, Tanny dropped in on Barb Millwood to discuss a future in organizing. Barb had made them both coffee and they were sitting at her old-fashioned wooden table in her kitchen. They looked out to the back yard through the sliding patio doors. Beyond the deck, the grass was still crushed and yellow-looking. The trees were leafless against a grey sky.

"I had forgotten how slow spring is to come up here. In Ben Kirk, the grass would be greening, and buds would be on the trees. The early flowers would be sprouting.

"Here, nothing."

Tanny waved a hand towards the greyed treeline. "No, look at the beautiful greys and browns and subtle mauves and golds."

"The what?"

"Well, that's what an artist friend said to me when I was complaining about how ugly nature could be. I think she wanted me to see my birth-month as beautiful. It kind-of helped. But mostly I am impatient for the greens and warmth to return."

"Yeah. I hear we might get snow tonight," commiserated Barb.

"Speaking of your birthday," she continued, turning her brown eyes on Tanny, "Did you enjoy yourself last night? Jeff seems like a solid guy. He's got that charisma that makes a man very handsome. I mean, I think I'm not supposed to comment on his physical appearance any more than we like men assessing us for our bodies' features or lack thereof...." Barb wavered and stopped.

"No. But I want to hear what you were thinking," encouraged Tanny.

"Well, it reminds me a bit of my brother. He's not bad looking, but he's not model-handsome either. Yet there's something about his physicality. There's humour and aliveness in his eyes, and his body just radiates ... masculinity? And suddenly his man-dimples are gorgeous, and his physicality is just so ... attractive—not that I find him attractive in that way!" she scrambled to finish.

Tanny laughed and felt her cheeks warm. "I love that you put that into words. Since meeting Jeff, I've realized how creepy my sense of entitlement to a 'handsome' man has been. Jeff is intensely attractive to me, but it is everything about him." Tanny stopped abruptly, realizing her mistake.

"His presence transforms him into a very handsome man," Barb agreed, with an assessing look at Tanny. "And you find him 'intensely attractive'? Are you saying what I think you are saying?"

Tanny buried her face in her hands. She said between her fingers, "It's brand new. It's a secret. But I think I am I love with him." She looked up, her eyes begging her cousin not to get over-excited.

Barb took a sip of her coffee. "Well, that's fun!" Her eyes twinkled. She held up her hands and imitated Sergeant Shultz from Hogan's Heroes, "'I know nothing! NOTHING!'"

Tanny laughed. "Thanks Barb. The party was lovely, but I was knocked-flat by Jeff's arrival. I hadn't realized just how much my feelings had grown for him until he walked in. I was a bit of a scatterbrain once he arrived."

"Well, I didn't notice that, but I definitely noticed the electricity between you two. I hope everything works out for you. You so deserve some stability."

Tanny took a deep breath. "Thanks. Me too! Speaking of which, I came here to ask about organizing. How do I become an organizer like you?"

Barb sighed. "Well, when I started, I asked another organizer. She asked me whether I compulsively lined up pencils or tidied things. She said it sounded like I was a natural, and to just start doing it. I did, and it worked out well for me.

"But these days there is a board certification you can get. I don't have it yet, but plan to get it, just to cross all the t's. It looks like it teaches a lot about proper conduct and ethics, which all came naturally to me. The prohibitions certainly show all the terrible things organizers have done or tried to do! There wouldn't be prohibitions if nobody had ever tried to do some pretty clueless things!

"But I would say you can go ahead and start. If people ask if you have your certification, just tell the truth. Tell them you are working toward your certification. Hours organizing help toward your certification. But I recommend that you eventually get the certification, because you will probably learn some things, and it looks much better to have it these days."

Just then a black and white cat jumped up onto the bench beside Barb. Tanny's cousin gave it a diminutive pat and pushed it off the bench. "No. You are in disgrace. I haven't forgiven you yet." A trail of airborne hair floated behind it. "Honestly a person with mild OCD shouldn't have cats," Barb muttered. She grabbed a handheld Dyson and started trying to capture the hair before it landed.

"I have just had to embrace the chaos," Barb commented, as if reminding herself. "Hair in the fridge. Hair in the butter. Hair all through the laundry." She vacuumed away. "Oh look! Hair in my coffee." Barb set down the hand vac and tried to scoop the hair out of her beverage.

"May I come with you on some organizing gigs and observe? I'd like to start right away."

"Of course!" said Barb, still fishing for the evasive hair. "Any time! I must get consent from my clients, but most should be fine with it."

"Great! Let me know when the next one is, and I'll ride along."

Barb had finally pulled out the hair. Her nose was scrunched as she wiped it off into a napkin. "I will probably put you to work too. Once the client has made some decisions or made her wishes known, there can be a lot of lifting, carrying, and sorting to do. Other times, there is a lot of waiting, listening, and encouraging as the client makes decisions."

Tanny's thoughtful cousin sipped her coffee. "Sometimes they like to tell stories about the things we are sorting. One woman came across her husband's death certificate. Talk about emotional heavy lifting! I sat with her as she talked and grieved. Then I coached her through ways she could store it and keep track of it. She picked her method, and we set that up. She's the one who got through three inches of paperwork and was still down on herself 'for not doing enough'. I had to remind her just how much hard work she had done. I encouraged her to be proud of herself, and to see if she didn't feel much lighter about that pile of papers going forward. I think it hadn't even occurred to her to congratulate herself for what she had done. To her, the whole place wasn't perfect yet and 'all we had done was a little stack of papers.' That's how clients block themselves. They see a giant mountain ahead, not progress already made."

Tanny said, "It sounds like we give a ton of encouragement."

"It is so easy to give! I have seen so many spaces transformed and so many lives made easier, I KNOW it is possible to get them there. But they can't see it. So, we believe FOR them until they begin to see the shifts happening."

Barb downed the rest of her coffee. "I'll teach you as much as I can. I will tell stories about my experiences, because there is no way to imagine what you will encounter out there. My stories will help you have frameworks and solutions for things you may encounter."

That night, Tanny was curled up on the couch, ready for Jeff's call. The realtor had been through the house and liked the improvements and staging so far. They planned to get the house listed by Saturday. Tanny planned to be in Bracebridge during much of that next week, so as not to deal with the endless strangers.

Jeff's face popped up on the screen with an incoming call announcement.

Tanny's heart skipped a beat and she picked up.

"Hey!' they both said in unison and then chuckled.

They checked in with each other, both still marvelling at their confessed attraction. Jeff told Tanny about his shift, work he was doing on the property, and Mack's antics. Tanny told Jeff with excitement about the house being listed soon, and her opportunity to start training with Barb.

"It won't be a steady income by any means, but it could eventually become one," Tanny explained.

"Good for you! I'm sure you'll be great at it. And anytime you want to tackle Britt's things in the attic you'd be welcome. The estate could use your help. I suspect a lot of the stuff in the attic is from before Britt had the house," offered Jeff.

"My great-grandparents' things? Cool! That should be interesting."

"Depending on how it goes, I think the estate could pay you for your time. We'd have to look into the legality of that—you are a 'steward' after all. Don't tell Jacob and Eileen you've been doing it for free though, or they might decide you should continue doing it all for free—something you may or may not want to do."

"I never thought of that. I mean, shouldn't I do it for free?"

"Whatever feels right to you. It's just easy to be taken for granted, and I would hate for that to happen to you. If you become a professional organizer, you deserve to be paid for your expertise."

Tanny laughed. "Oh. I have SO MUCH expertise!"

Jeff grinned. "You know what I mean. Just keep it in the back of your mind. The second you begin to feel resentful for doing the work, consider asking to be paid. Okay?"

Tanny wondered what experiences Jeff had had to lead him to these conclusions. It made her uncomfortable to think of him being taken for granted.

Soon they were talking about Tanny coming to Cedar Haven. She had decided to drive up Saturday morning, hoping to avoid the real estate traffic through the house. "I can't believe how soon that is. I will go on a gig with Barb tomorrow, but then I start packing. Would it be okay if I stayed though the next week until the stewardship meetings?"

"Of course, Tanny," Jeff said, with warmth. "It will be good to have company, especially in figuring out exactly what our duties are."

"Still no documents from Jacob?"

"No documents from Jacob. Whenever I raise the topic, he changes the subject or suddenly must take care of something."

"This doesn't feel good," said Tanny.

"It's beginning to bother me," agreed Jeff.

"Could Eileen send us copies?" Tanny wondered, watching Jeff's movements as he patted Mack.

"I've tried that," Jeff responded, loving the way Tanny twisted her hair around her finger when she was thinking. "She says Jacob keeps his copy in a safe."

"I thought Jacob said he has electronic copies."

"He does."

"So, it would be easy to just email us copies," Tanny said with a bit of irritation.

"Yes. That's what isn't making sense."

They both sat in silence.

Finally, Jeff said, "I wonder if the lawyer who handled Britt's will would know how we could get our copies."

"Just do an end-run on Jacob?"

"I don't see why not. It can't hurt. I'd really like to see the documents before we meet."

"I know, right?" agreed Tanny. "I'll ask him one more time, and then we will see what the lawyer says when we are up there."

"Sounds like a plan," Jeff agreed.

After they had hung up, Jeff realized he had completely forgotten to talk to Tanny about what the therapist uncovered. He twisted his mouth. Freudian? he wondered.

Thirty-Seven

March 13

*I*t was Saturday morning, and Tanny was pulling into the well-ploughed drive-way of Cedar Haven. It had indeed snowed on Thursday night and kept snowing lightly right through Friday. Bracebridge had clearly gotten more snow than Kitchener. The drifts along the roadsides indicated that they had gotten about thirty centimetres recently. Fortunately, the sun was shining brightly, making the world gloriously bright. The closer they moved to Spring, the less likely it was that the snow would last as long on the ground. The increasing light helped with the melt-off in the sunnier areas.

Jeff's truck was parked outside the garage, and Tanny pulled up beside it. Jeff was coming around from the front of the house to greet her. He must have seen her coming along the drive.

"Hello there!" he said and pulled her in for a kiss. "Mmm, you taste like coffee," he commented.

"Well, duh," Tanny responded. It was just after noon. Tanny had had several coffees on the drive up to help her with warmth and alertness. "You takes your chances when you grab me for a kiss without checking."

"I like coffee," he said, grinning.

"Help me get my stuff inside and then I need lunch," Tanny said, dodging his attempt to nuzzle her neck. But she was smiling all over. It was so good to be in Jeff's presence again.

The two of them got Tanny's gear inside and up to her room. Tanny had packed a lunch, not sure if Jeff would have anything in the house, but there was a big pot of chili on the stove and cornbread in the oven.

"You can cook?" Tanny asked in wonder.

"I've been cooking for myself since I was six. My parents weren't always able to cook for me. Later, Britt taught me many of her recipes. This is her chili and cornbread."

"Eileen didn't teach you?"

"I think she felt like it was her duty to feed me. She didn't even want me in the kitchen when she was cooking. I don't think she ever knew I could cook—well, mostly eggs and cereal back then. I'm not even sure if cereal counts as 'cooking'."

"You continue to amaze me."

As they ate together, Tanny observed that the chili and cornbread recipes must have been passed down through the family, as they tasted just like her mom's chili and cornbread. "I've never found a cornbread I liked better," Tanny said, munching away. "There's just something about this recipe that is perfect."

"I'm glad of that because it's the only way I know how to make it."

Tanny wondered if that meant that Jeff planned to help with the cooking. That made her realize how programmed she was to assume that she had to do all the cooking simply because she was female. She gave a little shake, not liking that sign of internalized sexism. She had assumed she would cook without question. She didn't mind the idea of doing the cooking, but it felt great knowing that Jeff didn't just expect her to cook all the time, simply because she was the female.

Tanny listed some of the steps and ingredients to the chili, and Jeff responded with, "Yes. Yes. Yes."

"It's definitely a family recipe," they said in unison, and chuckled.

A bit later Jeff said, "I've had to swap shifts around with my fellow paramedics to get next weekend off. It means I will be away much of the next few days."

"No worries. I'm sure I can keep myself busy."

"How did your organizing gig go yesterday?

"Barb is a genius. I can learn so much from her. She has a partial degree in psychotherapy, and it showed as she worked with the client. I just wanted to grab the obvious junk and throw it away. But Barb had a way of asking questions and drawing on the client's dreams for the space, that made them see they wanted to release the stuff." Tanny's eyes showed amazement. "I realized that the cleared spaces would stay clear longer and mean more to the client if we get the client *ready* to release things. That the clearing wouldn't last if we up and take their stuff away before they are ready. Barb says that we can kick off a power struggle with the client if we just take charge and make decisions. They can end up feeling coerced and resentful. Instead, it's about gently handing ownership of the space to the client. When they feel forced or coerced—when they feel their things are being removed without their consent—they often cling more tightly and see the organizers as abusive. They are less likely to 'own' their spaces, because they are too busy defending themselves from feeling judged and having their things ripped away from them."

Tanny shook her head. "I have so much to learn."

"It sounds like Barb uses psychology with her clients. She's not just a deep cleaner."

"You said it. At least here at Cedar Haven, I don't have to worry about power struggles with Britt."

"No," Jeff said, "But you might want to keep in mind that other family members could feel attachment to the Bender heirlooms. Other family members might want pictures or journals or furniture."

"Right...," Tanny replied, looking into Jeff's eyes but not seeing them. She thought for a moment in silence. "I know. I can photograph everything and make a spreadsheet online. Then I can invite family members to look through in case they want something."

Jeff raised his eyebrows. "That sounds like a lot of work."

Tanny finally focused on his eyes. A small jolt of electricity went through her when their souls touched that way. She looked away but was smiling. "Yes. But it could work, especially with family scattered around Ontario and beyond."

Then she realized, "Journals. There might be journals! I hope I find some!" She rose as if she was going to go look for them right away.

Jeff took her wrist gently. "Maybe finish dinner first?"

Tanny caught herself, laughed, and sat down. "Sorry. I'm a bit like a puppy." She arched her hands forward in front of herself to symbolize paws and said, "Ooh! Squirrel!" and started moving her paws like she was running.

Jeff chuckled and just soaked up the vibrantly alive, entertaining, adorable presence that was his longstanding and new love. Her cheeks were flushed. Her eyes were sparkling with excitement while also showing bemusement at her own impulsiveness. He couldn't help himself. Jeff pulled Tanny into a kiss that lasted and deepened. Finally, he released her and said, "I adore you."

Tanny was rosy. She let go of him with reluctance. "I'm a scatterbrained airhead, and you adore me." She shook her head, her mouth twisted in humour. "I don't understand, but I'll take it."

Jeff murmured, low and slow, "Oh. You are so doomed."

The moment crackled, and Tanny wondered what "being doomed" meant in Jeff's mind. She squirmed and looked away from him, delighted by his funny choice of phrase.

Once the dishes were washed, Jeff followed Tanny up to her room, Mack tagging along behind. Jeff took up a seat in an armchair to watch Tanny unpack.

"So, I just checked and still no word from Uncle Jacob," Tanny informed Jeff. She lifted out some shirts and went to hang them up in the old wardrobe. The house was so old, none of the rooms had closets.

"I called him this morning. He said he would send the documents, but I've not seen anything," responded Jeff, enjoying the curve of Tanny's back as she hung her things.

"Shall we try the lawyer tomorrow if still nothing shows up?" asked Tanny.

"Tomorrow is Sunday."

"Oh! Right!" Tanny returned to her suitcase, opening a drawer in the dresser on her way back.

Mack whined. Jeff said to him, "I know. It's time for your walk."

Tanny stopped what she was doing. "May I come too?"

"Of course!"

Tanny sped through the rest of her unpacking, leaving some tasks until later.

Soon the two of them were walking the grounds, with Mack bounding away and then back, his snout often covered in snow. Jeff described aspects of the land, the various concerns, the fences that needed mending, the bushes that were being devoured by the deer, and so much more.

Tanny held his hand as they trudged through the occasional drift to see certain areas, finding her curiosity growing and growing. She had had no idea how much was involved in caring for a large patch of mostly undeveloped land.

Jeff told her about Jacob's plan to build small cottages around the property for vacation rentals. Tanny wasn't sure how she felt about that. Apparently, Jacob hoped to start clearing the land in the late spring.

They walked in silence as they absorbed the natural beauty. It seemed neither of them liked the idea of developing the land.

"But Jacob insists it is the only way to make the property pay for itself. The taxes are just getting higher each year because we have so much waterfront," explained Jeff.

Tanny had walked the land before but had never seen it through the eyes of expense and maintenance. Clearly there were significant costs just to keep the property the way it was. Now it sounded like the family could lose the property simply by being priced out by the taxes. That seemed incredibly unjust, and she felt an overwhelming sadness.

"But I know Britt had a plan. I assume it is in the paperwork that Jacob has.

It is so frustrating not to be able to see the papers and read them ourselves."

"Let's go to the lawyer on Monday, first thing if we can," was Tanny's fierce response.

Jeff started a twenty-four-hour shift at midnight.

"Your shifts are twenty-four hours long?" Tanny asked, only now putting it together.

"Well, sometimes, yes. But that just means we are on-call for those twenty-four hours. When we aren't on a call we are sleeping, eating, talking, cooking...."

"Oh! I get it. And you all live together at the station in case a call comes in," Tanny said, realizing how sensible that was in a rural area.

"Yes. It would take us all far too long to get to the station to leave for a call. We need to be ready to leave immediately. All the rural companies need their teams together and ready, so we stay at the station."

"You must be tired when you get home."

"It depends on the shift. Occasionally a shift is crazy, with almost no down time, but those are rare. Usually those are due to big weather events like extreme heat or a nasty ice storm. But the average call rate is ... maybe six calls in a shift? So, it really depends on the shift."

Well, I hope you have an easy shift," Tanny said, and kissed him.

It took a while for Tanny to fall asleep, alone in the big house. But Mack's presence was comforting. Once he leapt up onto the bed, she was able to fall asleep with his big, warm body under her hand.

Tanny awoke to a world blanketed in a fresh, new covering of snow. Tanny loved how beautiful everything was but grumbled when she stepped outside with Mack. The steps and walk needed to be cleared. Mack got in his morning romp while Tanny shoveled the new snow up onto the already high piles beside the walkway.

It was nearly Spring, but that did not mean the end of snow in Bracebridge. April snow was still possible, though it usually didn't stay on the ground for long. And all the time, the light was growing every day.

Tanny tidied her bedroom and then began to look around the house. Jeff had taken the bigger room. It was at the top of the stairs and right next to the bathroom. Tanny's room was across the hall from his, also next to the bathroom. Both rooms looked down the sloping property to the water.

There were two more bedrooms, each looking out on the barn and greater yard of the property. Tanny visited them. They were chilly and still had the old feeling from longer ago. One even had one of those four-posters. Everything was covered in sheets in these rooms, something that had never been true in Britt's day. Saddened, Tanny went back downstairs to the warm, bright, newly redesigned family space. She made a second coffee and sat by the fire, looking through Britt's guestbook.

There were Jon and Susan's signatures and comments. The entries were sporadic, and had names she didn't recognize as well as some she did. Tanny felt deeply close to Britt as she perused the comments—nearly all of which mentioned serenity or healing or beauty. Abruptly her hand flipped back several pages. Tanny had the weird sensation that Britt had turned the pages for her. The first signature before her eyes was that of the musician, Linda Worster. Susan and Tanny's good friend, the musician from Massachusetts had spent time at Cedar Haven after the death of a very dear friend. Linda had spoken of her time there with deep gratitude. Cedar Haven had been a place of healing for her. In her comments Linda said, "The pain is breaking. I have a new song forming in my heart thanks to your healing lands. I hope you investigate the connection your lands have with the Anishinaabe people. I think you may be onto something about the land's healing energy."

Tanny sat back and thought. The land might have healing energy? Certainly, that had been an affectional description Britt had often used. Tanny had thought it was just Britt's whimsy, or the simple healing qualities of nature itself.

Then Tanny was struck by the information that the Bender Homestead might be on Anishinaabe land. Tanny felt afraid of what it could mean that the land was originally part of First Nations' culture. Would they have to give the property back to the Anishinaabe people because of the unjust way the European settlers had appropriated the land? But she loved Cedar Haven! It held generations of her family's history! She had so much to learn about her heritage and Cedar Haven.

Tanny was struck by the irony of her feelings. As if the land hadn't held generations of Anishinaabe history before the English government sold the land to the first Bracebridge Bender. Her insides pinched. She wanted justice for the badly treated Indigenous, but this made it personal. This possible loss of their heritage home affected her directly, and now she understood how hard reconciliation work really was. The thought of losing Cedar Haven really hurt!

Had Britt wanted her to find this information? What did Britt want her to do about it? What else did Britt want her to find?

Suddenly Tanny was eager to get started on the attic. She grabbed a piece of cornbread, refreshed her coffee, and put on her coat to head up to the unfinished attic.

Thirty-Eight

Sunday, March 14

The steps to the attic were enclosed, probably as another protection against the cold. Tanny opened the old door, noticing that someone had insulated the inside of the door and the walls up the steps. The chill struck her, and she realized just how well the insulation was serving the second floor.

Tanny had been up in the attic a few times as a young teen. The week that Jeff and her siblings were looked-after by Jacob and Eileen at Cedar Haven was one of them. They had pretended they were runaways hiding in an attic, stealing food from the kitchen and being incredibly clever in how they snuck around without being seen (by the imaginary house residents. They didn't count being seen by Britt or Jacob or Eileen, who were decidedly unimpressed by their games).

There in front of Tanny were the boxes and old pieces of furniture that she remembered. They were moved from their original places, possibly as part of the insulating efforts. A television, a broken recliner, and many more items had been added to the jumble since those earlier days of childhood adventure.

Tanny's eyes saw the magical refuge and adventurescape from her youth alongside the clutter-clearing challenge that lay ahead. Why did anyone bother to drag that large, broken chair up here? she wondered. Was it going to repair itself as it gathered cobwebs? Its only value in the attic was possibly to children who would claim it as a bed in a game of runaways.

But there were no children coming to this house anymore. Did Britt have plans for this space? Tanny wondered if she should wait to do much sorting or organizing until after the meeting, when she would know what was intended for the space.

Tanny wandered around the dusty belongings, hearing her siblings' voices echoing in her memory. She saw Jeff dragging flannel nightgowns from a chest deciding they would be his bed, as the other possibilities had been taken. She remembered helping him find more soft items and even an old pillow for his "bed." She and Liam had claimed the old double mattress, and Eric grabbed the oversized stuffed ottoman as the only other raised, bed-like surfaces. Jeff hadn't even realized that claiming beds was required before he was maneuvered out of all the good ones. Tanny helped him create something that was usable.

Was her small kindness part of what had drawn him to her? If so, Tanny was indebted to her past self. Her life was being irrevocably transformed by Jeff's unswerving love.

A particularly old chest caught Tanny's eye. It was about two feet high with a slightly domed lid. Tanny remembered using it as a chair when they had played. She even thought they might have hidden "treasure" in it. She pulled over the ancient, dusty ottoman, sneezing, and sat down to open the trunk.

The latches were in good shape and not locked. A flood of memories greeted Tanny when she lifted open the heavy lid. Right there, on top of the original contents was a small collection of "treasures": a shiny knob, some jacks, an old wooden spool, some playing cards, a Barbie hairbrush, coloured beads, and several other odds and ends. The feelings of their adventuresome game surrounded her, and Tanny smiled. She put the small treasures in her pocket to show Jeff later.

The chest had a divided tray that sat in the top, designed for smaller items. There was an old, beaded bag, a pair of gloves, some hair combs, and what seemed to be silk stockings. Tanny reached out to feel the stockings, but to her dismay, the fine material disintegrated at her touch. She felt terrible and wondered if she had just destroyed a precious heirloom.

There were papers under the stockings, but Tanny dared not disturb the stockings any more just now. Instead, she gently lifted out the entire tray and set it to the side.

The inside of the trunk was full and had been disturbed. Was this where Jeff had found the nightgowns? She suspected it might be. She had to pause and sneeze again as she began moving the items around. There were blouses and skirts and undergarments, and down at the bottom among the shoes were seven books that looked like diaries.

Tanny lifted out the little volumes, pressing the rest of the trunk contents back into place. The books were filled with Aunt Britt's handwriting, except it looked sturdier and less wobbly than Tanny remembered. Perhaps Britts' hand had been affected by her aging? This handwriting was fluid and strong and quite beautiful.

The page Tanny opened to said, "... has stopped talking to me altogether which is decidedly satisfactory. What an uncomfortable ordeal this has been!"

Tanny flipped to the previous page which ended in, "Now Heinrich ..."

Was Aunt Britt writing about Heinrich Knapp? Ooh! These journals could be full of juicy history!

Tanny sneezed. The accumulated dust was getting to her. She sneezed again, her eyes watering. She put the opened journal down and returned the divided tray to the top of the trunk, closing the lid. More dust flew up when the lid was dropped back in place causing Tanny to sneeze violently three times in a row.

Tanny grabbed all seven journals and took herself down the attic stairs. She was required to change her clothes and shower before her watering eyes and sneezing settled down enough for her to continue reading. She knew she had a dust allergy, but never had she felt the effects so completely. Would that be a problem for a professional organizer? *I will have to ask Barb.*

Tanny took herself down to the living area and emptied the coffeepot into her mug. She heated up some chili, ready for an early lunch after the sweet cornbread breakfast.

Now, which volume had that been? Tanny wondered, wanting immediately to discover what the "uncomfortable ordeal" had been. Unfortunately, she was not able to get any of the volumes to fall open to that page again. She spent considerable time digging for it, only to be frustrated. The diaries seemed to be set during Britt's twenties and thirties. Giving up, Tanny sorted the books into chronological order and began reading.

The earliest journal entry was dated in June 1928. Tanny counted on her fingers and decided that Britt had been about fifteen. The entries were youthful, including gossip about her peers and opinions about the church leadership. Tanny pieced together that Britt was living with her Aunt Serena and Uncle Henry Faulhaffer in Kitchener, Britt's mother having died when Britt was only seven. Britt's father and two older brothers had stayed in Bracebridge leaving Britt with her female relatives.

Britt had developed a good friendship with her cousin, Grace Faulhaffer, three years older, and a Joanna Neufeldt whose parents were part of the small Swedenborgian group in Kitchener.

But within a year, Joanna was engaged to marry Britt's oldest brother, David. Britt bemoaned the loss of her friend, thinking that seventeen was far too young to be marrying anyone, especially her dumb older brother. But Joanna seemed very happy.

Tanny looked out a window. David and Joanna Bender were Tanny's grandparents! Tanny hadn't realized how close Britt had been with her grandma Joanna. No wonder Britt seemed to favour David's kids. David and Joanna would go on to raise Noah, Susan's father; as well as Uncle Jacob; her own mother, Emily; an Uncle Ivan who died in WWII; and Aunt Peggy Frost, mother of all the Frost cousins.

Tanny loved learning about Britt's history. Suddenly Britt was no longer an older, wise great-aunt, but a teenager and then young woman struggling to earn an income, just like Tanny.

Tanny got up, walked around, and decided to take Mack for a stroll. The sky was looking leaden, like snow was coming soon. When she and Mack came back, their coats smelling fresh with winter air, she was ready for more reading.

Tanny moved onto the next volume. A July 1929 entry described gossip about a John AIDEN Hill who had survived the measles. It was sensational because John's two older brothers, both named John Hill, had died—one after only six days and the other of the Spanish flu when he was nine. Those boys had both been named 'John MCKELLAR Hill.' The rumours were suggesting that the name change to John AIDEN might have saved this boy from his brothers' fate.

Tanny sat back and dug into her memories. She had heard the stories but had not paid much attention to the details as a child. They were tales for her parents and not very interesting to her young self. But now she found it astonishing. Back then if a child died, they just named another child the same name! Tanny couldn't imagine anyone doing that today.

Tanny reflected that Jenny's father had been from the very Hill family Britt was discussing. There was something more about the Hills besides the deaths of the two John McKellar Hills that was niggling at Tanny's memory, but Tanny couldn't recall what it was.

Tanny read on. "It looks like Beryl Hill might outlast her husband this time, unlike her sisters. Can you imagine? Three sisters, all named after jewels, all marry the same man one after the other. That sort of thing wouldn't happen today! First there was Opal who died giving birth to the first John. That John died six days later. Then the husband, also named John, marries Opal's sister, Ruby. Ruby has three kids, two girls and another try at a John McKellar Hill. But Ruby and that young John died of the flu, so then the old man married the third sister! I can't imagine being wife number three after a man had killed off my two sisters. No, thank you!"

Tanny sat back again. That was what she had forgotten. The three McKellar sisters had all married the same man, one after the other—Opal, Ruby, and Beryl. *You couldn't make that stuff up!* she thought. Tanny did know that the third John had indeed survived and had children of his own, Jenny's father included. Susan's mom, Kate was a Hill too, but Tanny couldn't remember how she was related to the other Hills.

Britt concluded, "But Aunt Serena says that there were not a lot of men after the war, and there weren't a lot of options for women's lives besides marriage. Well, I am deciding today that I am never going to be dependent on men, starting now! I will find a way to support myself and only get married if I really want to."

Was this where Britt's fierce, lifelong pursuit of financial independence started?

Tanny got back to reading. Britt mentioned a very obnoxious boy who was always getting into trouble. "That Heinrich is such a little bully. But Uncle Henry says that Heinrich's own father was a cruel man before he died in the war. Heinrich's mother has been trying to raise the children all on her own since then. Uncle Henry says she likes 'the bottle' too much, so no one will help her. The children run wild."

Tanny was outraged. Seriously, a woman's (admittedly cruel) husband dies in the war, and yet no one will help the struggling widow because she turned to alcohol to ease the pain? *No wonder Heinrich has issues,* thought Tanny. And the entry she had just read was dated ... August 1929. Wasn't that getting close to the Great Depression?

Tanny moved onto the next volume, sometimes skimming, sometimes reading more deeply. The Depression indeed struck, bringing tremendous suffering. Uncle Henry lost his job and had to travel to find work. Grace's only surviving brother was much older and already married with a new baby to feed and house.

Britt found work in an ice cream shop and at a tailor in Kitchener, doing whatever she could to support her Aunt and cousin Grace. Aunt Serena hired herself out as a housecleaner and Grace was a nanny for a wealthy Kitchener family. Together they managed.

Tanny skimmed and skimmed. Joanna had a new baby and named him Noah. Susan's father. Grace married a fellow named Jack Carling and moved to London, Ontario. Britt missed her terribly. Britt sent herself to secretarial college, graduating and quickly finding work in a Kitchener law office. Meanwhile Britt's peers were all marrying, annoying Britt to no end. "If I had a nickel for every man who has asked me when I'm going to settle down, or every woman suggesting that I am unwomanly for wanting a career—if I had a dime for every hint that I am hurting my chances for marriage because I like my job, I would be a very wealthy woman!"

Tanny opened another volume and kept looking for names to jump out at her. But aside from comments on marriages, births, and deaths, there was very little of interest and no more comments about Heinrich Knapp. Instead, the entries contained rumours of another war in Europe. Britt, even with her lucrative job, began researching how to contribute as a woman in the war effort. Canada had started manufacturing weapons. It was nineteen thirty-eight.

Then Tanny found something. "Heinrich has been hanging around me after church. I make my usual rounds, talking with family and friends, spending time looking after my nephew, but Heinrich sticks to me like a burr. He doesn't take any hints. I often must hide in the ladies' room. He is seven years younger than me, and I have zero interest in him, but he seems determined to hound me."

Skimming further Tanny found, "Heinrich finally cornered me behind the church. He wouldn't let me pass until I heard him out. Then the fellow proceeded to tell me how much he loved me and wanted to marry me. Oh, my head! I finally had to interrupt his claims of profound love to assure him that I had no interest in marrying him, and would he please stop hounding me. I think I said I released him to find someone else.

"I have never seen a man get quite so red in the face. I thought he was going to hit me! After he had stopped protesting that he was completely serious—after he finally realized I was having none of it, do you know what he responded? He said I would be lucky if anyone ever married me. He said I was homely and old and 'dried up' and no one would want me, so I should be grateful to him for offering! So, this is what I said: I said I was glad he had realized his mistake, and as nobody indeed would want such a homely, old, dried-up wreck as myself, he must be relieved not to have saddled himself with me. I congratulated him on his escape. I promised I would tell no one of his error in judgment, and he should go away quickly so no one would see he had even been speaking to me."

Tanny laughed out loud, her eyes full of delight. Way to go, Aunt Britt!

"Heinrich was so befuddled, he stared at me, tried to say something, and then stumbled off. I guess he realized he couldn't come back from such ghastly insults when I agreed with him and congratulated his escape. Joanna and I had a good old laugh together about it later. She is enormous with her second child, but she found time for me. Good for her for waiting ten years before cranking out another child. I didn't ask, but I wonder if they waited for David to find a good, solid job before conceiving again?"

Tanny sat back again. She noticed that it was getting dark and that she really ought to get some supper. Mack was ready for another romp as well. So maybe Tanny hadn't found the quote she was looking for, but this proposal from Heinrich could easily explain the remarks Tanny had seen on that first glance. Tanny set aside the journals and went to make supper.

It was snowing rather steadily when Tanny and Mack emerged from the big house to stretch their legs. The flakes fell swift and thick. Tanny hoped that Jeff was having an easy shift. After doing the dishes and settling the house for the night, Tanny tucked herself into bed, her mind whirling with Britt's stories.

Sometime after midnight, Tanny felt Jeff's big frame slide into bed behind her, molding to her shape. She sighed in contentment and fell fast asleep again.

Thirty-Nine

Monday, March 15

Tanny awoke to a scratchy chin nuzzling her neck. She moved and stretched, enjoying the feeling.

"Good morning," rumbled Jeff's low voice near her ear.

Tanny could tell that Jeff was aroused, though he was not making it obvious to her. She made a purring sound and rolled over to kiss him.

Jeff rolled above Tanny, pressing her back. He slowly kissed her neck and cheek and mouth. But when he realized Tanny was keeping her lips tightly closed, he pulled back. "Nothing is happening now unless you want it, Tanny," he promised, eyes concerned.

Tanny made a face. "It's just that I really need to pee and I probably have terrible breath."

Jeff's rugged face broadened into a grin. He laughed. "By all means." He released her. "Go pee! Brushing your teeth is optional."

Tanny vaulted from the bed toward the bathroom. She heard Jeff call after her, "Would you like me to shave?" Tanny paused and thought. Then, grinning she said, "No. I like your sexy stubble." Then she disappeared into the bathroom.

Jeff took himself down to the main floor to freshen up. His body was taut with desire, but he took slow breaths and made himself practice intention over his drive. If this happened, this would be the first time he felt a genuine, whole-spirited love for his partner. He would do nothing to ruin this. If she changed her mind, so be it. He looked at his stubbled face in the mirror and said, "You've got this."

Tanny was shivering with realization as she relieved herself. Was this happening? She asked herself if she was ready. She had only started the pill on Wednesday, so she knew she wasn't safe yet. She reminded herself that full penetration didn't need to happen today. It didn't NEED to happen ever. But she certainly hoped it would one day.

Tanny washed the sleep from her eyes and brushed her teeth thoroughly. Now all that was needed was for her to return to the room. Her body was vibrating with excitement. She absolutely wanted this with Jeff. But she was nervous. She heard Jeff returning upstairs, two steps at a time. She knew he wanted her, which filled her with desire. And she trusted him, absolutely. She opened the door.

Jeff was waiting inside the bedroom. Tanny's eyes skipped over the evidence of his sexual readiness. His pyjama pants hung from his hips, just showing the arrow-tip of his pubic hair. It was dark blond, just like the hair on his broad chest and arms. He was ripped! Tanny's knees almost buckled.

Jeff cocked his head. "Are you still interested?"

Tanny said something incoherent and went into his arms.

Jeff was tender as he removed Tanny's top. It went up over her head, and she stood there, bare breasted in front of him. She resisted the urge to cover herself.

"Gorgeous," he almost whispered in reverence. "May I touch you?"

Tanny nodded and shivered when the slightly rough hands first held her and shaped her.

"Tanny, I want you so much," came Jeff's husky voice. "May I make love to you? God, I want you."

Tanny nodded. The look in Jeff's eyes had already wiped away any final reservations.

"I am going to use protection. I insist on it," said Jeff.

Jeff's lovemaking swept Tanny past overwhelming bliss more than once in their time together. At first Tanny was delighted to let Jeff lead, as he was incredibly skilled. She was ready for him to enter well before he did. Finally, her inner tigress pushed him onto his back and she mounted him, unwilling to wait any longer. She had little experience, but it didn't seem to matter, for it was not much longer after she mounted that he came, with a sound like growling triumph. Tanny had already climaxed twice, and she collapsed over him, feeling like she had given him something in return.

When she went to slide off him, Jeff reached for some small towels he had handy, giving her one and keeping one for himself. It seemed to be all he was capable of. Afterwards he lay still, panting, sweat gleaming on his gorgeous body.

Tanny soaked up his beauty, then tucked herself into his side, her head on his shoulder and her hand on his chest. She pulled a sheet up to cover them against the chilly air.

Tanny had never felt so ... fulfilled? Complete? Content? Safe? It was a much richer feeling than 'happy.' She rested, soaking up Jeff's presence and warmth.

This sense of deep connection and trust was nothing like what Tanny had imagined love to be. She didn't have to fight to "deserve" or keep Jeff's attention. He simply adored her whether she "deserved" it or not. How had she gotten so lucky?

Tanny wondered why she had been unable to imagine this level of trust and safety in a relationship before. Why had she always imagined love would include an anxious struggle to keep the man interested? She frowned slightly. What was that about?

Tanny's eyes had been following the lines of the ceiling as she rested. She lifted herself on an elbow and gazed down at this man that was already so precious to her. She gently traced her fingers through his chest hair, loving his energy and warmth, loving his beauty. His face was in full repose, and she delighted in the lines of his eyebrows, the shape of his mouth, and that sexy stubble that had left slight feelings of abrasion on her in several places. A thrill went through her at the meaning of those feelings. Jeff had been kissing and nuzzling her there. And there. And ... *there.*

Tanny grinned and leaned down to press a kiss into his stubbly jaw.

Jeff grinned. "Good morning," he said again, his eyes still closed. "Will you marry me?"

The minute Jeff said this, his eyes flew open, and he turned to Tanny, pulling away a bit, his hands up in defence. "Never mind I said that. I'm sorry. Please just let this be whatever it is. I don't want you to go...." His eyes were full of fear and longing.

Tanny was speechless. Had he just proposed? Did he then instantly take it back? What is happening?

She said, her hands also up, "Jeff, it's okay. Did you just propose? Did you not mean to?"

Jeff got out of the bed pulling a sheet corner to cover himself. "Tanny, please don't go. This can be whatever you want it to be," he said. "I love you, and ... I do want to marry you one day, if you'll have me. But if not, I really don't want to lose what we have."

Tanny got up and rounded the bed to him, not covering herself. She put a gentle hand on his arm (those biceps!) and said, "Why would I go anywhere? You have made me happier than I have ever felt in my life. Why would I leave you?"

Jeff's eyes were only half-seeing her. "Please ... stay," he said.

"Of COURSE I'm staying!" Tanny almost shouted. She changed her tone to something lighter and gestured with her hands, "I mean, I always imagined a proposal with you on one knee and we're both fully clothed, not with us both buck naked having just made love, but hey. I like novelty—"

Jeff dropped to one knee, clasping her hand. "Tanny," he rumbled. "Tanny, I meant what I said. I want to marry you. I want to be with you and near you and have you in my life for the rest of forever. I love you. Just, please, if it's 'no,' it's okay. Just stay, on your terms."

Tanny felt a thrill almost as physical as her moments of climax. She wiggled and jumped and squealed, pulling Jeff up to standing. "Yes. Yes. YES!" she cried and threw her arms around his neck. "I would love to be your forever partner."

Jeff's arms encircled her, his prickly chin tucked behind her shoulder. He crushed Tanny to himself.

Tanny realized Jeff was sobbing.

As from instinct, Tanny remained silent. It hit her that this was something profound and deep for Jeff, and she wanted to give his response all the time and space it needed. Eventually she whispered, "Yes. YES. It's a hard yes from me. I'm not going anywhere."

These words renewed his tears, and his arms tightened again.

Every fibre of Tanny's being treasured this man. She could wait to hear what his tears were about. She wondered why she wasn't crying too. It had been only a month since she was certain she would never find someone as wonderful as Jon Haley. *Jeff was ten times better.*

Had they only been reacquainted for three weeks? It felt like so much longer. He was someone she had met many years ago, and miraculously, someone who said he had loved her ever since.

How can I be so certain that this man is the man for me? Is this too rushed?

But try as she might, Tanny felt no hesitancy. Each beat of Tanny's heart only felt more certain of her answer. Maybe I should re-examine things when I'm not naked in his arms, she speculated. Nevertheless, she was deeply at peace and deeply curious about this man's easing sobs.

Jeff gathered himself. He thanked her and found his T-shirt to wipe his tears and blow his nose.

"We ... have tissues," Tanny said, realizing it was too late. She couldn't help but wince as Jeff tossed the used thing back on the floor. Was he going to expect her to wash that? Then she realized, Wait. Who says I have to do his wash?

They had a whole new world of negotiating their joint life ahead, Tanny realized. She prayed there would not be worse surprises down the road.

Jeff dragged a hand over his face and looked at Tanny sheepishly. "Is it still yes after that display?" he asked.

She took his hands. "Especially after that display," Tanny reassured the big man. Then she grimaced, "Except for the snotty T-shirt on the floor, part. We need to talk about that." Tanny was laughing now. Then she gentled and looked into his face. "I'd love to hear about those tears some time, if you're willing to tell me."

"Some time" Jeff agreed. "I'd like that." He cradled her face in one of his big hands. "You have made me happier than I knew was possible, Tanny. I can't believe you are here, saying yes."

Tanny nodded and smiled, finding herself tearing up. "Yes, Jeff. Yes."

They kissed again, long and tenderly, both realizing the change in their relationship, which just deepened and strengthened their mutual exploration.

Finally, Jeff pulled away. "So, future wife, I need to shower and get breakfast, and ... I have some wash to collect." His foot indicated the crumpled small towel on the floor with the bit of shriveled condom showing, along with the snotty T-shirt.

"Thank you," Tanny agreed, meaning it about the dirty wash. "Go get your shower. I'll put on some coffee and start some eggs."

Tanny dressed, thinking she would shower later. Honestly, for such a big house, how was there only one and a half baths? Then she remembered Cedar Haven's age and realized that both bathrooms had probably been added well after the house had been built. And if they were thinking of turning this into some sort of retreat centre, they would need to add a bathroom for every bedroom, wouldn't they? That would be a lot of work and expense! *What is in those documents?* Tanny wondered again. Well, it was Monday, and they could reach out to the lawyer now.

Over coffee and some scrambled eggs, the two lovers alternately basked in their new promise, and started planning the day. Tanny would call the lawyers to schedule a meeting while Jeff walked the property line with Mack. (Jeff had shut Mack in his bedroom just in case lovemaking would happen, knowing the dampening effect a curious large dog could have on an intimate moment. Now Mack was clearly making it known he wanted out.)

They agreed that they wanted to keep their engagement quiet until they, themselves had gotten used to it. Somewhere in the back of Tanny's mind she realized that there was so much she didn't yet know about Jeff, and there could be some behaviour she had yet to see which would make her call things off. But she simply couldn't imagine that to be true. The shivering thought came to her that many, once happy, battered wives had described those same thoughts. They had never imagined.... But Jeff was so respectful!

Jeff and Tanny waited to be shown into Lynn Ruch's office in a cozy, old Bracebridge home renovated to be a law firm. Snow fell lightly outside the window. The light was grey-white. Jeff and Tanny held hands, smiling and nervous.

A Helen Hunt look-alike came down the stairs and greeted them. "Mr. VanGalen and Miss Smith?" Her eyes flickered over their clasped hands. "Is that correct?"

"Yes. That's us," Tanny assured her as they both rose to greet the lawyer.

"Come on up to my office."

Tanny appreciated the character of the old home. The steps creaked and the dark wood panelling rose beside them as they climbed. She was glad the law firm hadn't covered everything in drywall and modern art.

Once they were seated in the gracious bedroom-turned-office, Ms. Ruch indicated they sit while she took the seat behind a grand wooden desk. She gazed at them and said, "How can I help?"

Jeff and Tanny explained the trouble they were having getting copies of the documents from Jacob. Ms. Ruch frowned.

"All four of you should have copies. Jacob has not distributed you your copies? It has been over a month." The lawyer looked puzzled when they shook their heads. "So how have you been making decisions about the property's management?"

"We haven't," said the new lovers in unison. "We are scheduled to have our first meeting with Jacob this weekend," finished Tanny.

"Excuse me," said Ms. Ruch, rising from her chair. She exited the office, leaving Jeff and Tanny gazing at each other in curiosity. Their gazes were just shifting to mutual adoration when the lawyer returned.

"Please, pardon me. I have just asked my secretary to make up copies for all three of the other stewards. You should have them in your hands shortly."

"Thank you!" cried Tanny. "That's amazing. It was that easy?"

"You all should have had your copies as soon as the will was read. The fault is mine. I gave them to Jacob, trusting that he would distribute them. I will have to have a sharp word with him." Ms. Ruch gazed at them with apology in her eyes. "Do you have any other questions for me?"

Tanny wiggled in her chair and then asked, "Susan, the fourth trustee? She's having some pretty intense health issues. She is wondering if she can step down from her role. What happens if she does?"

"Typically, the three remaining stewards choose the replacement together. But it will all be spelled out in your copies of the Stewardship documents."

There was a knock at the door and an older woman in a beige cardigan entered. She handed a stack of papers to Ms. Ruch.

"Thank you, Edith," said the not-actually Helen Hunt. "And be sure to mail the third copy to Mrs. Rennie."

"Absolutely," said the competent, besweatered woman. She flicked a smile to the clients and retreated.

Ms. Ruch handed the documents to both Tanny and Jeff. "Here you are. Be sure to read these through carefully. And if you have any questions, don't hesitate to call. Britt clearly wanted four minds making the decisions together. If Jacob gives you any more trouble, do get in touch."

Jeff and Tanny thanked the lawyer and headed out, pondering Jacob's apparent betrayal.

"But we now have the documents!" Tanny brightened as Jeff helped her into his truck. The flurries swirled around them. "Now we can see what is expected of us and how everything works."

They drove home through the old town and down the long road toward Cedar Haven, both eager to get home and start reading.

Forty

March 15, afternoon

"Okay, so, there will be four stewards, appointed by Britt, to oversee the maintenance of the grounds and buildings, including such improvements as Britt outlines ... somewhere else...." murmured Tanny, snuggled in the sofa near the fire. The snow was falling steadily outside. "I want to skip ahead. But I think we need to take this paragraph by paragraph."

Jeff was next to her, Mack at his feet. He reached for his coffee on the coffee table. "Here is where it says how to replace a steward: 'If any steward cannot fulfill the rights and responsibilities of the position, they must be replaced with someone of the same gender, to be selected by the one leaving or by the remaining same-gendered one.'" Jeff took a sip. "You can tell this was written before we recognized more than two genders."

"So, Susan selects, and if not Susan, I select. Huh. I'll call her and see what she thinks."

There was silence as the two of them read on.

"Look at this," said Jeff. "For all decisions about the property maintenance and upgrades, three of the four stewards must agree." Jeff sat back, looking thoughtful. "I have been working on building an apartment using one corner of the barn. Britt approved that before she died, and I have just been carrying on with it. I wonder if I need to get the remaining work approved or if I can continue until it is finished."

This refers to ongoing plans for upgrades, according to the blueprints as drawn up by the architectural firm of Bell and Simonetti."

Jeff looked over her shoulder to where she was reading and said, "Ah, yes. Both of the Simonettis are women. Britt wanted to use women architects. You know Britt! Plus, she wanted quality. Bell and Simonetti are one of the best firms around."

"But there are no plans here. I'd like to see those plans. Where are they?"

"I think Jacob has them," said Jeff. "He's been handling everything since Britt died, except for the hands-on property maintenance that I've been doing."

Tanny looked at Jeff. "I think we should have a set of plans here, on the property. I'd certainly like to see them before we meet! Can one make photocopies of blueprints?"

"I'm sure we could get more copies from the architects, but we'd probably have to pay for them." Jeff sat thinking. He brightened. "Maybe we should drop in on Jacob and Eileen today. We can take them some goodies from Big River Baking and see if we can get the copies. Shall we go now before the bakery is sold out?"

"Let's do it!" agreed Tanny, rising.

The two of them bundled up and invited Mack into the truck with them. There was already an inch of snow on the driveway.

"Come in! Come in!" welcomed Eileen Bender. "Oh! Hi Mack!" Eileen ran off to get a towel for Mack's wet paws.

Jeff and Tanny stepped into the generous kitchen, stamping snow from their boots and preventing Mack from exploring. Tanny fluffed the snow from her shoulders and hood before hanging her coat. She carefully removed her boots before tiptoeing away from the ice-strewn entry. Eileen came back with a towel. Tanny gave Mack's paws a good drying before releasing him to explore. Jeff handed the box of pastries to his foster mother who hugged him and kissed him on the cheek. He shrugged off his coat and dropped his boots by the door, following Tanny to the large wooden kitchen table.

"I told Jacob you are here," said Eileen. She offered them tea.

When Jacob rounded the corner into the kitchen Eileen told him, "They brought us cookies, croissants, and a big loaf of sourdough."

"Oh! That's great," said Jacob, rubbing his hands together.

Jeff rose and grasped Jacob's hand in greeting. Tanny managed an actual hug from the dapper man.

Eileen put the electric kettle on and started unwrapping the sourdough. "I don't know about you, but I'm in the mood for warm, chewy toast." She got out a cutting board and started slicing through the crusty loaf.

"What brings you over?" inquired Jeff's bespectacled foster father.

"It has been a while since I've been over," replied Jeff, "I figured we were due a visit. Also, Tanny and I have some questions about our responsibilities as stewards."

"Ahh," said Jacob, a smile crinkling his eyes. "You have nothing to worry about there. We'll cover all that on Saturday."

"Well, I'd really like to see the blueprints before then, Uncle Jacob," piped up Tanny. "I want to know what we are looking at. You shouldn't have to wait while we get all caught up on the contract and architectural plans on Saturday. It just makes sense that we see everything ahead of time."

Jacob tugged at his earlobe. He rubbed the back of his neck. "I'd have to look around for them. I'm not sure where they are."

Jeff reached for a thick slice of warm, buttered toast just as Eileen set some on the table.

"You always loved your sourdough toast," smiled Eileen at her strapping foster son.

Tanny could see the affection in Eileen's eyes and wondered again why this couple had never adopted Jeff.

Then Eileen said, "I think I know where the blueprints are. I'll just go get them."

"Eileen, it's okay." Jacob called to her retreating back. "Don't worry about it." He rose to follow her. Mack followed them both, attracted by their energy.

Tanny looked at Jeff, eyebrows lifted. She reached for some of the buttery, crusty toast and rolled her eyes in pleasure after one chew.

"I know, right?" said Jeff, grinning at her.

There was a bit of a commotion upstairs, and then Eileen came hustling down the stairs, blueprints in hand. Jacob followed, nearly tripping over Mack. He looked annoyed.

"Come over to the dining room table," said Eileen, spreading the large, rolled documents across the lacy tablecloth. "Wipe your hands first." She found a salt and pepper shaker, a napkin holder, and a heavy mug to hold down the corners.

Tanny and Jeff approached the table and saw the professional blueprints outlining extensive renovations to the place. The complete redo of the living and dining room were there as well as several changes to the bedrooms, plumbing, and electrical.

"As you can see, Britt got almost all the first stage done before she died. We saw it through to completion since her death."

Jeff was nodding. "I did a lot of bunking in here during the worst of it."

Tanny was struck by something. "Jeff, why didn't you come down to Britt's memorial service? We held a service for her, and you weren't there."

Jeff dragged a hand over his face. "I was in the Netherlands researching my Dutch heritage."

Eileen added, "We didn't tell him Britt was dying. We wanted him to be able to complete his research."

"I still wish you had told me," murmured Jeff.

"We held a memorial for Britt up here in the United church which she attended with all her Bracebridge friends and family. We waited for Jeff to get home for that one." Eileen patted Jeff's shoulder. "Your remarks were beautiful."

Jeff's face had closed, and Tanny began to understand the complicated relationship he held with his foster parents.

"Anyway, you have seen the blueprints," assured Jacob, and reached to gather them up.

Tanny planted her hand on them. "Wait, Uncle Jacob. I want to understand them further." She leaned over them. She lifted the top pages to look underneath. "What's this?" she asked, pulling out a smaller drawing separate from the main ones.

"That's stage two!" said Jacob, "the attachment of a granny flat or separate apartment off of the southern wall."

Jeff moved forward to look. "I've never seen this before," he said. "I thought the master bedroom or adding bathrooms was stage two."

"Well, Eileen and I think this should be stage two."

Eileen did not meet Tanny's eyes.

"Wait," Tanny said. "But Jeff is building a whole apartment out in the barn. It's almost finished. Why do we need another?"

"Can you have enough guest accommodations?" asked Jacob. "This addition lets the caretakers live right by the house and not need to go out in the weather to service the house. It makes much more sense. Your apartment can be for guests who want an entire private suite to themselves."

Both Jeff and Tanny were puzzled. Jeff said, "That apartment is for me, so I can live on the property as caretaker and not be in the way. It's not for guests."

Jacob waved his hands airily. "You see? This is why I wanted to wait until Saturday, so we could discuss all of this then."

Tanny pulled up a dining room chair and sat down. "No, let's discuss this now. I'm sure we'll need all the time we can get on Saturday. Why is this granny flat suddenly stage two? Jeff wasn't aware of it. Please, help me to understand."

Jacob heaved a great sigh and pulled up a chair as well. "My dears, who wants to trek across the yard in the snow several times a day to service the house? This addition has been designed in the same architectural style as the original house and will look like a natural extension of the original. It will have direct access to the kitchen area but also allow for complete privacy for the couple who are looking after the property. It makes perfect sense." He smiled at them as if they must see his perspective.

Jeff had caught the detail though. "Couple? What couple? I thought Britt intended me to look after the property until its future was settled. I don't remember Britt naming anyone specific as caretakers beside myself."

Eileen had the tiniest smile of satisfaction as Jacob blustered a bit.

"Well, as her blood nephew, I assumed I could take on that role. Eileen and I could sell this place and finish our days on the family property."

Jeff was taken aback. "But as the role of permanent caretaker has yet to be decided, and will be decided by all four of us, I think this decision needs to be made by the collection of stewards. I was not ... none of us had any idea of this addition."

"But I'm sure Britt would have been happy with this!" insisted Jacob. "This is a brilliant plan. It makes so much sense!"

Eileen remarked, "Jacob has already scheduled a ground-breaking for the new addition in early April."

Jeff rose. "Now wait a minute, Dad, you can't do that by yourself. The decisions must be made by all four of us. Nothing can happen without the approval of three out of four of us. The agreement says that clearly. Plus, now we need to find a fourth steward, because Susan is stepping down."

Jacob was shaking his head looking frustrated. "Do we really need to bother with all of that? Why not just have three stewards? Doesn't that make it simpler to make decisions?"

"No, Dad, because that is not what Britt wanted. It was Britt's property to dispose of as she wanted. Our job is to execute her wishes to the best of our ability. And she wanted decisions made by a team of four, perhaps to keep any one of us from trying to control the outcomes."

Tanny was looking more closely at the plans for the addition. The date on the document was January, well after Britt's death. She said, "Who had these plans drawn up? They are dated almost two years after the date of the original drawings."

Jacob stood up and turned his back. He said nothing.

Eileen said, "Jacob commissioned them. He likes the idea of us living out there and running the bed and breakfast ourselves."

Tanny asked her, "Is that what you want? I mean, surely, we can consider that as a possible outcome. But it must come from all of us, and we would need to see the costs involved in this addition." Tanny looked at Jacob's back. "Did Aunt Britt budget for all of the renovations on the original plans?"

Jacob nodded.

"But I assume then that no funds were allocated for this addition?"

Jacob murmured, "She had buckets of money. Surely, she could make sure that her nephew and his wife could be comfortable in their older days."

Tanny was stunned. So, this is what Jacob had been hiding. He was trying to wangle a home for himself and Eileen on the family property. He was trying to use his position to push this plan under the door before any of the stewards became aware that it was not actually part of Britt's will.

Tanny walked around to face her uncle and Jeff joined her. "Uncle Jacob, are you in trouble? What's wrong with the house you have? What's going on?"

Eileen said, "We've had some setbacks with investments. But we'll be fine. We'll manage. Jacob still has a few accounting clients and I have found part-time work at the library."

Jacob said, "It simply makes sense. I am the only relative in my generation willing and able to look after the family property. The job should go to me."

Jeff said, "Isn't that a conflict of interest? How can you be a fair trustee when you have a personal agenda about the outcomes?"

"As if you don't have an agenda!" said Jacob with a raised voice. "I'm sure *you* want to keep your position just the way it is, even though you're not a blood relation, so YOU have a conflict of interest too."

Jeff paled. "Of course I'd like to keep my position. But if the group of stewards comes to a different solution, I will abide by it. I'm not trying to, trying to ...." Jeff stopped himself. He knew any further words would only lead to entrenchment.

Jacob said, "It just makes so much sense. What is wrong with this solution?"

It was Eileen who answered. "Because, my love, you tried to manipulate the truth. You have been lying and withholding information. It's deceit. It's a kind of cheating."

Jacob winced and then made a growling noise, half anger, half defeat.

"Whatever. I will see you all here on Saturday," he said, and he stomped off towards the stairs.

Eileen turned her warm, grey eyes toward the young people. "I'm so sorry, my dears. I wasn't sure what to do. It didn't feel right to come to you directly. I guess I just hoped you'd figure out what he was doing. Between you and me, I don't want to move out to the property; I like being right here in town. But Jacob has his heart set on it."

Jeff said, "It feels terrible that this doesn't surprise me."

Eileen rested a hand on his sleeve, rubbing gently. "I know, son. I know you are aware of Jacob's ... flaws. I'm so sorry."

Jeff looked at his foster mother. "What are we supposed to do? We are already missing one of the stewards and now Jacob turns out to be untrustworthy. What are we supposed to do?"

Eileen raised her eyebrows in sympathy. "Jacob should be much more compliant, now that he has been found out. That is my observation after thirty-eight years of marriage. I recommend you find another steward before Saturday."

"But how do we do that? Who should we ask? You?" wondered Tanny.

"Heavens no, dear! Definitely not me. But I was wondering about Bet Giddings, Britt's long-time friend and confidant."

"Bet! Of course!" agreed Jeff. "We can reach out tonight and ask. Then I guess we vote her in on Saturday?"

"I'll call Susan and see what she thinks," said Tanny.

The young couple thanked Eileen, gathered Mack and the blueprints, and headed home in the snowy evening.

Forty-One

March 15, evening to March 16

Tanny had called Susan once they had returned to Cedar Haven. Susan was tremendously relieved and blessed whatever choice Tanny made for her replacement. She confirmed her pregnancy. She was utterly exhausted. They were still keeping the pregnancy a secret.

Tanny then looked up the number for Bet Giddings and put through a call.

"Hi, Mrs. Giddings," greeted Tanny when the woman picked up. Tanny explained the situation to Mrs. Giddings, who insisted that Tanny call her "Bet." "Bet" was delighted to to be asked to help. She was retired, only retaining a position as a church organist. Yes, she was available to attend the meeting on Saturday. Bet said she could hear a bit of Britt in Tanny's voice and looked forward to meeting in person. Tanny loved Bet's conversation and energy.

Jeff approved the replacement. He said he could drop the paperwork off at the Giddings' on his way to his shift that night.

Jeff had walked Mack, checked the property, and plowed the driveway. The two of them enjoyed a simple supper by the fire. Over dinner, Tanny showed Jeff the "treasures" she had found in the attic trunk, and they had a wonderful moment sharing memories. Their smiles were free and open, no longer needing to hide their mutual attraction. They saw their childhood friendship through different eyes now that their futures were entwined.

Jeff held Tanny's hands soberly. "I want to get you a ring. I want to get you every meaningful thing that marks my promise to you." His eyes twinkled. "Would you like me to send a horse to your parents?"

"A horse to my parents? Why would you do that? Why not send *me* a horse if you are sending horses to people?" Tanny was laughing.

"I don't even know if that is Anishinaabe tradition. I just know that the horse can be a sort of dowry in some First Nations' cultures. Would a horse make your parents happy?"

"I doubt it!" Tanny laughed. "But I think I'd love a ring."

"A ring it will be then. Do you want to help pick it out, or do you want me to surprise you?"

Tanny gazed into Jeff's golden eyes, reflecting. Finally, she said, "I think ... I'd like you to surprise me. And please know that I don't need it to be extravagantly expensive, just ... from you."

Jeff rested his forehead against hers. "Okay then. I will find something that represents my love for you." He kissed her tenderly. The kiss deepened.

Eventually Jeff heaved a great sigh. "I have to get ready for my shift. I'm sorry to leave you alone again." He thanked Tanny for taking care of Mack for him while he was at the station. "I usually take Mack with me, but C-shift frowns on having Mack around." Jeff had switched from his usual A-shift rotation to C-shift in order to have the coming weekend off.

"I have a lot of reading and research to do," replied Tanny with enthusiasm. "Besides, I have Mack for company."

Tanny waved goodbye out of the window as Jeff's taillights faded away down the driveway. Mack whined and Tanny agreed with him, giving his thick fur a good scrub. She let him sleep on her bed, drawing comfort from his warm presence, the way she had done when Charm was alive.

Tuesday morning dawned wonderfully sunny after so many days of greyness and snow. The light sparkled from every dripping evergreen. The mid-March sun packed new intensity, and the snow would melt quickly if the sun kept shining. Tanny listened to the weather report and discovered a warming trend was indeed in the works.

Tanny's heart soared as she walked around the property with Mack. There was the slightest smell of earth and pine needles in the air, and the sound of dripping, promising the coming spring. She felt elated that she and Jeff had managed to get copies of the stewardship documents and a look at the blueprints. Tanny definitely liked this Bet Giddings who would be coming onto the board on Saturday.

Tanny also had more of a sense of the motivations behind Jacob's secretive behaviour. Why he had felt compelled to lie and manipulate his way into a solution rather than just ask for help was beyond her. Was that what toxic masculinity did to a man? It taught him to hide mistakes and never ask for help? Was that as true in her generation, or worse in the older generations? In her feminist campaigning she had eventually come to realize how badly *men* were harmed by sexism. Sexism hurt EVERYONE, not just women.

Thank God that Jeff seemed to have dodged a lot of the effects of the toxic masculinity that pervaded their culture. Perhaps he would have more insights into how to work with her uncle since the man had raised him. Perhaps aunt Eileen could help too. Tanny hated the idea of having to "manage" another person. It would feel terrible to find out others were trying to "manage" her, so why do it to another person? Her mother had often tried to "manage" her. It felt awful.

Tanny and Mack came across an old fence-line. As far as she could tell, it was not along the property boundary. She wondered what it had been intended to do. But the bush got quite thick as she followed it, making her unable to continue. She would ask Jeff about it later.

Jeff. Jeff was a miracle. Tanny felt wonderfully at home with him. She felt safe. She admired him and was baffled by what he saw in her. But he saw *something,* and she loved that he loved *her.* Was that selfish? Did she *just* love him because he loved *her*? She thought about it as Mack romped ahead, somehow finding mud despite the snow.

Tanny remembered Jeff's respect and concern at every step. She thought of how well he fit in with her friends at her birthday party. She admired his calling as a paramedic. He went to a therapist for goodness' sake! She definitely loved, admired, and respected him well beyond the detail that he adored her.

Joy burst in Tanny's heart. She wanted to shout her love to the heavens. She also wanted to keep the whole precious truth a deep secret, in case there was pushback from her mom and dad. She wanted to tell Susan most of all, and Jenny, and Conrad....

Just *not her parents.* She even suspected that Jacob and Eileen wouldn't be thrilled by the news either. Why did she assume that? She would talk to Jeff about a timeline for revealing their new commitment.

For now, she had a Jeffless stretch of hours ahead of her, with documents needing more study and journals to read.

Tanny decided that a complete re-read of the stewardship contract took top priority. She alternately read the documents and paced the house, thinking. She read at the big harvest table; she read on the couch; she read at the kitchen counter while coffee brewed. She took Mack on another romp after lunch, not wanting to waste the glorious sunlight.

It helped her to say aloud what she was processing, "Britt's top priority was that Cedar Haven remain under the oversight of her stewards. Sale of the property is a last resort. Britt's next greatest wish was that Cedar Haven become a 'centre for healing, resting, and spiritual pursuits,' whatever that means. So, our next question will be HOW to offer *that* without going bankrupt. I wish I had a copy of the financials, so I could see what sort of runway we have before we MUST balance income with expenses."

Tanny continued this outward monologue until she and Mack reached the house. By the time they entered the front door, she was explaining directly to Mack, "There is no indication of an addition to the main house for managers or overseers anywhere in Britt's instructions. So, Mack," Tanny shut the front door and reached for the towel for the muddy paws, "how do we navigate those rough waters with Uncle Jacob? I'm really hoping Mrs. Giddings will help us vote to follow *Britt's* instructions and not Uncle Jacob's revised plan. I'm just feeling so uneasy about it all. Theeeeeeeere you go." She released Mack into the space. "I appreciate your good advice," she called to the waving tail.

The hazel-eyed, pony-tailed woman decided to bury herself in the diaries for the afternoon. It was less than an hour later when she found, "Now Heinrich has stopped talking to me altogether which is decidedly satisfactory. What an uncomfortable ordeal this has been!"

Tanny lowered the book to her lap and stared along the harvest table and out at the snowy yard. So, Heinrich had proposed to Britt all of those years ago and she had snubbed him, unequivocally. Heinrich in turn had cut Britt off. Had Heinrich continued to be so negative about things related to Britt because of that event so many years earlier? This added a layer of understanding to Heinrich's antagonistic behaviour. *If he is still holding a grudge after all these years....*

Tanny shook her head. *Heinrich had proposed to Britt.* She couldn't even imagine the two of them together. They were opposites! But Heinrich's pride had been wounded and apparently, he had never gotten past it. *Yikes! If only more people would get therapy!* Tanny thought. She sat a moment. *Pigs would fly, but the world would be a much better place.*

Tanny sat back in the chair and contemplated another coffee. There were still several more journals to go through, but much of it was tedious. She decided to see if Bet Giddings had time to meet and discuss the plans going forward.

Bet agreed to meet Tanny at Oliver's Coffee near downtown. After they had ordered their drinks, they sat near a window and gazed at each other. Tanny was struck by the golden-hazel of Bet's eyes. She almost commented, wanting to talk about Jeff's eyes, but decided not to. Instead, after the greetings and niceties, Tanny began describing the stewardship situation as she understood it, pointing out statements in the stewardship documents and describing the addition Jacob had ordered of the architects after Britt's passing.

Bet shook her head. "Jacob is a good man in so many ways. He can be very sweet and is an excellent accountant *for others.* But as Britt's confidante and a friend of Eileen's, I know he got in some big trouble several years ago, which Eileen, with Britt's help, managed to hush up so he wouldn't lose his accounting license. After that, Eileen kept a close watch on their finances, needing repeatedly to stop him from throwing money at 'investment opportunities.' If my suspicions are correct, Jacob managed to do it again, just recently, and lost a significant amount of their retirement income."

"Oh, Uncle Jacob!"

"I think it is like an addiction. The lure of the imagined wealth is just irresistible. Eileen has tried to get him into Debtors Anonymous, but his pride is too wounded at the idea."

"I wonder if Britt knew this when she appointed him a steward," mused Tanny.

"Of course she did, but we thought at the time his compulsion was behind him. Eileen had done such a good job of keeping him from gambling away their savings, we all thought the problem was in the past."

"So, what are we to do?"

"Well, I think we have the information we need to steer the decisions towards Britt's plans. Jacob is just one voice out of four. We must show him the respect he deserves without wounding his ego."

Tanny sighed. "Honestly. Why do we have to spend so much energy tiptoeing around men's fragile egos? Isn't it codependent to change our behaviour out of fear of someone else's emotions?"

Bet smiled gently at Tanny. "Unfortunately, we all have to *live* with each other's emotions. And women have egos too."

"I know, but honestly!"

"We'll be fine, Tanny. I've got your back. We will guard Britt's wishes while letting her nephew be part of the process. You may be surprised by the better parts of Jacob's nature."

I've got your back. Why did that phrase feel so wonderful?

Tanny reflected that Bet was a brilliant choice for steward. Her years of experience of Jacob and Britt—and just generally of Bracebridge history and politics—was much needed on the board. With Bet they had two older members, two younger members, and three Bracebridge residents. Tanny knew very little of Bracebridge "common knowledge" or whose toes not to step on. Tanny knew she could stomp into a situation with her social justice opinions and alienate people without meaning to. If she wanted to be a valued part of this community going forward, she needed to *listen* for the undercurrents and patterns of Bracebridge and be guided by Bet.

For the next hour the two women got to know each other better. Bet was organist at the church Britt had frequented. She and Britt had served on several committees together.

"She was like a big sister to me," explained Bet, who was closer in age to Jacob than Britt. "I admired her spirit and outlook. I was never as forthright as she could be. She could beard any lion in any den." Bet paused. "I suspect you are a lot like her." She smiled. "It's almost like having her spirit back among us. Too bad you live in Kitchener. Will you be up often?"

Tanny revealed to Bet her intentions of finding a job and staying.

"Oh! How delightful! This coffee shop is even hiring. What sort of work are you looking for?"

Tanny described professional organizing but expressed interest in the barista position in the meantime.

"Professional organizing sounds amazing," observed Bet. "I will pass that information around. Do you have a place to stay yet?"

"Well, I'm staying at Cedar Haven right now. I think I might like to stay there until we figure out its future."

"With the handsome and eligible young Mr. VanGalen," observed Mrs. Giddings, waggling her eyebrows.

Tanny felt her blush rise and wished with all her life it hadn't.

"Oh dear. I've stepped in it, haven't I? Are you in love with him?"

"Mrs. Giddings...."

"Oh dear. I thought I was 'Bet'."

Tanny lifted and dropped her shoulders, releasing a great sigh. She leaned towards the hazel-eyed woman and said, "Bet, it's still a secret. But Jeff and I are engaged."

Bet simply raised her eyebrows and her eyes twinkled. "My lips are sealed. You've got yourself a good one, there. May I be the first to congratulate you? That is simply wonderful."

Tanny appreciated that Bet had kept her demeanour calm and her voice low. Only Bet's eyes sparkled her delight.

"Thank you," said Tanny, sotto voce. "It seems strange that you are the first to know, but I've been bursting to tell someone. It means the world to me that you see Jeff as a catch. I can't believe how lucky I am."

"Oh, I suspect he has gotten a catch too." Bet radiated warmth and delight. She said, "Shall we move on to dinner? My treat. I know a place where we won't have to worry so much about being overheard."

Bet introduced Tanny to El Pueblito, a Mexican restaurant close by. It was tiny, but they got a table near the back, and the ambient noise covered anything they had to say. Bet and Tanny continued to bond, discovering more and more in common, particularly spiritual beliefs and general outlook.

And Tanny was able to tell Bet the whole saga of her love story with Jeff. She expressed her amazement at the swift movement of her love from barely remembering him to deep belonging.

Bet's eyes sparkled. "Jefferson helped us when Richard had his heart attack. He was so professional, and yet so comforting. He was almost pastoral in his care. He came around the house twice after Richard was home again, just to check in on us. It was very dear." She chuckled. "That's a small town for you. You tend to be aware of each other as town members as well as professionals. He often attended church with Britt, so I knew him a little from church before he ever turned up at our door to save Richard."

As Tanny waved goodbye to Bet from the restaurant parking lot, she mused about how lucky they were to have her coming onto the board. She looked forward to seeing Jeff again and telling him all about Mrs. Giddings.

Jeff crawled into her bed after midnight and fell instantly to sleep. Tanny hugged his heavy arm to her body where it rested across her waist. They spooned well together. He slept, but she lay awake awhile, filled with wonderful feelings of safety and comfort.

There was something about Jeff being at her back, "having her back," that made Tanny's anxieties grow quiet. *I have your back,* as Bet had said. What a powerful saying. Tanny's whole nervous system calmed, and she slept.

Forty-Two

March 17

Tanny was awakened by Jeff's nuzzling behind her ear. She could get used to waking up like this. After quick trips to the washroom, the lovers reveled in the playful exploration of each other again. Tanny could not get over how delighted she was in Jeff's whole being: his energy, his voice, his physicality, his thoughtfulness. She desired him more each day.

Jeff was enchanted by Tanny's sensitivity and responsiveness. His lightest touch could send her shivering. Making love to her was not only his heart's deepest longing, but delicious beyond anything he had known before.

They lay together afterwards full of smiles, Tanny tracing patterns in Jeff's chest hair as she snuggled into his shoulder.

"I suspect people will be able to tell something is going on soon," Tanny mused. "I suspect I will start looking incandescent if I keep feeling such joy."

Jeff's well-muscled arm tightened and released. "Even my work colleagues said there was something different about me, and they aren't my usual team. Put me back in my own shift, and they will harass me mercilessly until they find out what's going on," murmured Jeff.

"I guess I should tell my parents," sighed Tanny.

"And we should tell Jacob and Eileen."

A long silence stretched as the sun moved along the bedroom floor.

Another sigh from Tanny. "I will call my mom today."

"If you do, I think we should drop in on my folks as well. These announcements should happen close together, or they will be on the phone telling each other before we get the chance."

"Ha!" agreed Tanny. "I will call my folks from the driveway of Jacob and Eileen's. Then as soon as I'm done, we can knock on their door."

"I wish I didn't dread this," mused Jeff.

"I'm right with you," commiserated Tanny.

After a quick breakfast and checking that it was okay to drop by at Jacob and

Eileen's, Jeff and Tanny parked just down the street from his childhood home.

Tanny had her phone on speaker when her mother answered. Emily greeted, "Hello sweetheart! It's nice to hear from you. I was needing to talk to you today anyway, so this is perfect."

"Oh yeah?" Tanny asked. "What did you need to call me about?"

"There is already a hard offer on Jenny's house. We can't believe how fast it moved, but there it is."

"Oh! Well, that's great! I'm so happy for Jenny!" enthused Tanny.

"Yes!" agreed Emily. "But it means that you will be needing to move your stuff out by the end of March. The new owners want it by April first, if everything works out."

"Okay...." Tanny felt again that sense of being kicked out without consultation. She had known this would happen. She just hadn't expected it so soon.

Tanny saw Jeff gesticulating, indicating that she could move in with him. Her tummy swooped and rose, and she had trouble catching her breath. *Of course! How perfect!* She said to her mom, "No problem, mom. I will be fine. I'll be sure to get my things out before then."

There was a pause in which Emily made noises of satisfaction. Then Emily said, "Were you just calling to check in?"

Tanny's heart beat faster. "Um, no, Mom. Could you get Dad and put the phone on speaker phone?"

"Okay...." said Emily with hesitation in her voice. Eventually Gilbert was sitting near the phone too and they were listening.

"Mom, Dad, I want to tell you that Jeff and I are engaged to be married. I'm over the moon with happiness. He's wonderful."

There was a notable silence on the other end of the phone.

"Who's Jeff again?" said Gilbert to Emily in a whisper.

"Well. That seems sudden. Are you sure?" asked Emily. They heard Emily mumble to Gilbert about "that boy that Jacob and Eileen had taken on" and about him being at Tanny's birthday party.

Gilbert said, "Oh! He seems like a nice enough fellow. But isn't he your cousin?"

Emily said, "We don't even know him. How can we approve when we don't know him? He ... his parents.... Are you sure you want to get mixed up with that sort of person?"

He's listening to this, Mom. He's right here. He just heard what you said, Tanny thought.

"Well, why don't you say hello to him now, Mom and Dad? He's right here."

As if coming on the line just then Jeff said, "Hello Mr. and Mrs. Smith, I am the luckiest man alive. I will treat Tanny with all my love and respect. Thank you for raising such a wonderful person." There was another weird silence and Jeff made faces at Tanny. He said, "I know this may seem rushed to you, but Tanny and I have known each other since your trip all those years ago. This romance has sprung from deep roots, I can assure you. I promise to treat her well. I love her very much."

"Well. Well," said Emily, while Gilbert said, "We would like to meet you again before we can give our blessing."

"Of course," said Jeff. "I will come down with Tanny sometime next week, after the stewardship meetings, if that works for you."

"Yes. Okay then. We look forward to meeting you properly," said Gilbert.

"Thank you, sir," said Jeff, as Tanny hid her face in her hands.

"Goodbye then," said Gilbert.

"Goodbye," said Jeff.

"Bye, Daddy. Bye Mom," said Tanny.

"You're not staying there, are y—" said Emily, but Tanny had already hit the end button.

"Oh dear...." said Tanny.

"I thought that went quite well," said Jeff, his grin betraying his true feelings.

They stared at each other a minute. Then Jeff started the car and they headed up the street to Jacob and Eileen's little Victorian place.

"Oh, how surprising!" exclaimed Eileen. Jeff and Tanny were holding hands, having just announced their intentions. "How ... wonderful!" Eileen's positive words seemed heartfelt, if a bit hesitant. Jacob approached and shook Jeff's hand. "Congratulations, son. What do Tanny's folks say about this?" he asked.

"We will be going down to visit soon to let them get to know Jeff better," supplied Tanny.

"I should say so," smiled Jacob. "I mean, how long have you known each other?"

Tanny felt a flush of shame. *Had they rushed things?* It felt terrible that none of their parental figures shared their joy. *It isn't like we are sixteen!*

"Technically we have known each other since that summer when you watched us all together at Cedar Haven," responded Jeff. He looked at Tanny with affection. "I never forgot her."

But I forgot him, thought Tanny. *Well, technically I didn't* forget *him, I just didn't think of him very often. Why does this feel like lying?*

"So, you will be even more a part of the family, Jeff," said Jacob, indicating that they take seats at the table.

Eileen had put on the kettle. She got out some of the goodies from the bakery and laid them out. "We still have sourdough," she said with a note of happiness. She began slicing it.

"So where do you plan to live?" asked Jacob, reaching for a cookie.

"We haven't thought that far ahead," said Jeff, looking at Tanny. His arm was over the back of her chair, and they sat close together. "Maybe we share the apartment in the barn until Cedar Haven's future is decided. Then, I guess we find a place in town somewhere."

"So, you plan to move up here?" Eileen said, smiling into Tanny's eyes.

"Yes," agreed Tanny. "I've just lost my job in Kitchener anyway, so I'm going to find work up here. I do love Muskoka."

"Well, it will certainly be very nice to have you around," assured Eileen. She was spreading melty butter on the sourdough.

"What sort of work are you looking for?" this was from Jacob.

Tanny said, "Well, I can look and see if any of the vets need assistants. But I'm hoping to start an organizing business up here." Tanny explained what an organizer did, and right away Jacob and Eileen mentioned people who might want her services.

"I will spread the word," said Eileen, her grey eyes sparkling.

The phone rang, and Jacob went to answer. He said, "Ah yes. They're just here." He looked at Tanny and said, "It's your folks."

Of course it is, thought Tanny.

"Yes. Yes. They've just told us," Jacob spoke into the old-school land line. "Well sure, we can talk later. Yes.... Yes. Okay then. Okay. I will. Bye!" Jacob hung up and explained that Tanny's folks didn't want to interrupt the visit and sent their love.

Tanny bit into some buttery sourdough, determined to stay positive. It helped that Jeff was right beside her, strong and warm. It helped that these two people had raised him and loved him, even if they had not been perfect. Tanny decided to ask them for stories of Jeff's childhood, and they spent a companionable hour revisiting Jeff's mishaps and misbehaviours, to Jeff's pretend discomfort. But the stories delighted Tanny and told her even more about the man she was marrying. He had tried to rescue every wounded animal just the way she had, from baby robins to snakes to chipmunks. It was a comfortable and easy conversation. Tanny *wanted* to like and trust them.

My aunt and uncle will be my in-laws, sort of, Tanny reflected. *This is weird, but kind of cozy too. I mean, I already know them.*

A text dinged on her phone. It was from Jenny.

"Well, the news is out now," she announced to the room. Jenny was asking about "some news" Tanny was going to tell her. She would call Jenny soon.

This is real. She looked at Jeff and felt contented and excited.

Jeff and Tanny spent the rest of the day making phone calls. They wanted as many friends as possible to hear the news from them and not through the grape vine.

Tanny enjoyed a long heart-to-heart with Susan, who was beyond happy for them.

"I really like Jeff. I like his energy," said Susan. "And he and Jon hit it off immediately. That speaks volumes about Jeff's character. He must be awesome if Jon likes him." Susan was laughing.

"I think they both have great taste in friends," agreed Tanny.

Susan told Tanny that they would be announcing the pregnancy when they successfully reached eight weeks, which would be mid-April. "Though anyone who knows me at all well will probably have figured it out by then. 'Mrs. Haley, why are you throwing up all the time?' Honestly, if it was any worse, I'd need to go to the hospital for intravenous food."

"Oh, honey. I'm so sorry. And now I'm not even going to be down there to help much," apologized Tanny.

"So, you are going to move up there?"

"Well, yes. Jeff has a job here and I'm unemployed. I can look for work up here. And I can live with Jeff, as I now have nowhere to live."

"You'll be 'living in sin,'" remarked Susan, with absolutely no judgment in her voice. Tanny could practically hear Susan's eyebrows waggling in pretend shock.

"Yes. Well. That's if we are having sex, and it is rude for people to assume that," responded Tanny. Then she added, "They'd be correct, but it still is rude for people to assume that, and judge." Tanny felt a swirl of nervousness confessing this to Susan in case Susan would judge.

"Just don't get pregnant," said Susan with some emphasis. "You need some time to be a couple."

"I hear you on so many levels, dear one. Are you doing okay?"

"I live with chronic nausea, and I don't have much energy for housework, but if I stop worrying about that, everything is fine. So, what if there's cat hair in the fridge, and woven into our clothes, and gathering under the furniture?"

"Oh, but pets are so worth the extra cleaning," supported Tanny. Jeff and I are coming down sometime next week. I will do a round of housecleaning for you!" offered Tanny.

"Will you need a place to stay? You are welcome here if you don't mind cat hair on your blankets."

"That would be so great, Susan, thank you! Now I'll clean *twice.*" The women laughed together.

Tanny turned to Jeff. "We have somewhere to stay in Cliffside."

"Now I just need to find a gap in my work schedule," mused Jeff.

The next two days went by in a happy daze. Jeff had one more twenty-four-hour shift to serve and then his weekend was open. Tanny started looking for work and set about designing a name for herself as an organizer. "Tidy with Tanny" was a possibility, or perhaps "Serene Spaces?" "Free-Your-Life Organizing"? No. Too many words.

Tanny read on through the diaries. There was no more mention of Heinrich Knapp. The entries became more sporadic as World War Two approached but were filled with speculation and commentary on various leaders' and countries' responses. *I wonder if some of this would be valuable to historians?* Tanny wondered. Once Britt enlisted, the entries ran out. Tanny supposed the letters from France were the only records of what transpired in Britt's life once she became a spy. "A radio operator in France" was another word for a spy working behind the lines, helping the resistance. It still blew Tanny's mind. Tanny wished she could tell everyone about how amazing Britt was, but wasn't sure she would be allowed to, even still.

Tanny knew she needed to keep on exploring the attic and deciding what to clean out, but her attention kept coming back to her desire to move in with Jeff and start her life up here.

Saturday morning dawned. It took a phone alarm to waken the two lovers. They had been up late, talking and planning and making love. They had to scramble to get breakfast, look after the property, and get over to Jacob's house where their Stewardship meetings would begin.

Forty-Three

March 20

$\mathcal{J}$eff and Tanny arrived at his childhood home a few minutes before ten. They were greeted by the smell of coffee and happy compliments from Bet and Eileen as the two women were catching up. Jacob was in the dining room arranging papers on the table. The sunlight streamed in the windows, promising an unusually mild day for March in Bracebridge. Tanny and Jeff greeted their hosts and Bet and got their coffees.

Soon the four were seated around the dining room table and Eileen had taken herself and Mack on a walk.

"I am calling this meeting to order," said Jacob, using a little wooden hammer on a small wooden base. He grinned. "I got this just for this purpose," he said, indicating the gavel in his hand. "I think the first order of business is a show of hands on whether we accept Bet Giddings as the fourth steward, replacing Susan Rennie Haley. All in favour?"

Three hands lifted and Bet smiled happily.

"The vote carries." Then Jacob continued, "I understand that I am not the elected chair of this group. As my final act as the transition head, I invite us to vote on our first chair. Who will be the head of this committee? I offer my services. Discussion?"

Tanny looked at Jeff and then at Bet and Jacob. "I think I want to nominate Bet. Bet, you are the only non-family member. You were also quite close to Britt. I suspect that that makes you possibly the most objective. What do you think?"

Bet looked surprised, then thoughtful. "Well, hoping that the position doesn't eat me alive, I would consider that." She looked at Tanny, gentle eyes thoughtful.

"Is that a yes?" Tanny asked her.

Bet said, "Reserving the right to step down if it becomes too onerous, that's a yes."

Jacob, looking stiff, said, "Are there any other nominations? More discussion?

I point out my ten years of experience as chair of the Bracebridge Rotary Club."

"I didn't know that about you," said Tanny. "Well done, Uncle Jake."

When silence followed that Jacob said, "Okay then, by a show of hands, everyone in favour of Jacob Bender as chair?" He raised his hand. After a pause he put his hand down and said, "Everyone in favour of Bet Giddings as chair?" Three hands went up. "It is decided," he conceded, tapping the gavel. "Bet Giddings is the new chair of the stewardship committee in charge of Cedar Haven." He then said with a twinkle, "Secretary, did you make a note?"

The rest of the team looked at him blankly as he shoved the gavel and base over to Bet.

Bet said, "I guess we need a secretary and treasurer. Do we have volunteers for either position? Jacob? Would you be willing to be secretary?"

Tanny wondered if this was a clever move on Bet's part to avoid having Jacob continue to oversee the money. She then felt terrible for mistrusting her uncle around money. But hadn't he *embezzled* money earlier in his life? It was probably better that someone else be treasurer. That left herself or Jeff.

Jacob said, "I would be pleased to be the secretary." He pulled up some unused paper and a pen and started writing.

Bet looked at Jeff and Tanny. "Are either of you inclined to take on the role of treasurer?"

Tanny thought a bit, looking at Jeff. "I have a lot more free time than Jeff right now, so I guess I can take the position. I've just never been treasurer of anything, so you'll have to help me along the learning curve."

Jeff smiled at her, "Of course we will."

Bet said, "Thank you, Tanny. We are all here to help and support each other."

Jacob said as he wrote, "Britannia Suzanne Smith, also known as 'Tanny' is accepted as treasurer."

"Okay," said Bet. "I think we should review what our duties are, what Britt's intentions were, and if there are any updates we need to make to the current system we have been using to run Cedar Haven on behalf of Britt."

The four heads bent to the work. They agreed that it worked well to keep Jeff on as the caretaker. Jacob raised the possibility of conflict of interest with Tanny moving in with Jeff, as their opinions were likely to dovetail. He suggested replacing Tanny with someone less closely involved with another steward. Tanny kept her temper down, trying to see Jacob's point. She abstained from voting, as a way of showing neutrality. Jeff suggested that they replace him instead of Tanny— that it could be either of them that was replaced. After much discussion, Bet and

Jeff voted to keep the status quo for the time being. Bet suggested they revisit the question in a year, and it was agreed.

Jeff said, "We should be married by then, and both of us on the board could be seen as nepotism. I think I speak for both of us that we would be happy for one of us to step down at that point." He looked inquiringly at Tanny.

Tanny's insides were jumping at hearing the words, "We should be married by then," coming out of Jeff's mouth. She felt a little lightheaded. "Absolutely," she agreed, gazing back at him. Her cheeks were warm with pleasure. "I almost wish there were five of us," she added, "as then there would always be a tie breaker."

Bet observed, "I believe our lawyer is our tie breaker, if needed." Bet skimmed the paperwork, flipping pages. "Yes. Here it is." She indicated the paragraph where this was stated.

Tanny resolved to read and re-read the stewardship documents so that she wouldn't suggest a solution for something already solved again. And at least until she found work, she had the time.

The discussion moved to Britt's plans for the renovations. Jacob made a concerted effort to promote the apartment on the south wall of Cedar Haven. He said it was a brilliant idea going forward. But ultimately, he was voted down in favour of starting renovations on the north side bedrooms as Britt had instructed. Those bedrooms would have the windows and insulation upgraded and closets built. A new bathroom would be inserted between the generous bedrooms, as well as laundry facilities. The bathroom at the top of the stairs would be connected to the right-hand bedroom so that both rooms would have dedicated bathrooms. While the plumbing was being added upstairs, a bathroom and closet would be built for the main floor office (in case it, too became a guest room). The powder room on the main floor would be upgraded as well. These main floor additions would eat up a metre-wide swath along the inner wall in the office, turning the fourteen by twelve-foot former library into an eleven by twelve-foot bedroom or office. They would save as many of the built-in bookshelves as they could. They would also continue adding the framework for central air. Up until this point they had been using window units. The vent work for the rest of the main floor had been finished during stage one.

All of this work would require a major upgrade to the septic system.

"What's all of this going to cost?" asked Tanny.

Jacob flipped open the treasurer's binder and slid it over to her. He indicated a line on the page. "We have quotes of between fifty-six thousand and eighty thousand for the stage two renovations. The company that quoted sixty-two thousand is the one we used for stage one. They were good communicators and stayed very close to the budget. I recommend we go with them again. The new septic will cost an additional twelve thousand dollars," he added.

"Wow. That's a lot of money," mused Tanny, perusing the information. She flipped pages until she found the number for the current financial holdings. "Ohh-hh-kay," she said when she found them. "I guess we have nothing to worry about."

Jacob looked enigmatic, while Jeff and Bet were clearly wondering what she was looking at.

Tanny said, "This says we have over eleven million to work with. That's two million more than the lawyer said at the meeting in January."

"The original will was written in 1995," Jacob said. "Our investments have done well since then."

Tanny flipped through the binder some more. "I like that we are using a credit union and not a bank." She smiled happily and started uploading the app for the credit union.

"I will need to go with you to the Credit Union to add you to the account," Jacob offered.

Bet considered. "Jacob, I would like to come too. Tanny should have primary access to the accounts, with a co-signer for big expenditures. I suggest that I am co-signer as chair."

Jeff said, "I like the idea of a back-up person having access to the accounts in case Tanny is down south or sick, and as a co-signer for big expenditures. And I don't think it should be me or Jacob. I agree that it should be you, Bet, or the lawyer."

"The lawyer will cost us money," grumbled Jacob.

"Do we trust Bet to have back-up access to the money?" Jeff asked, looking around.

There was no objection, and so it was voted into policy.

Bet supplied, "I recommend that we set a relatively low expenditure limit—say, two thousand dollars—which the treasurer can withdraw without pre-approval. Any expenditure above that amount should require both signatures on the account and pre-approval from the board. Every expense will be recorded in the treasurer's books. That is fairly standard procedure."

Tanny looked at Bet with gratitude. This woman had clearly been on boards before.

The group voted and it was agreed.

Jacob suggested they call the company with the good reputation and middle bid for the renovations to get that underway. He also suggested that they hire the septic tank company and get them started as soon as possible. They all agreed, and he put in the calls.

Then there was discussion about expenses on the apartment, with Jeff providing a sheet of expenditures so far and explanations for his choices. He was praised for repurposing the old cabinets from Cedar Haven's kitchen. His carpentry skills had saved them a lot of money too.

The group broke for a light lunch provided by Eileen.

As they served themselves and sat at the kitchen table Jeff said, "We'll have to move the office up to the other south bedroom. At least we can make sure we put one of the better window units in there, because that room and mine get pretty warm in the summer."

As he and Tanny took seats at the table he murmured, "And you'll have to move into my bedroom." He quirked his eyebrow in suggestion.

Jeff said aloud, "I had better get that apartment finished soon, as Tanny will need the one remaining bedroom in the house."

Jacob said, helping himself to some soup, "How much more do you have to do?"

"Once the ground is thawed, I can have the small septic tank and heat pump installed. I have insulated the pipes and provided heating cables for year-round use. Fortunately, the water line to the barn is still in good condition and has enough capacity. The water-heater is on order. It is mostly just finishing the walls and trim after that and furnishing the place."

Eileen said, "That should be simple with so many pieces sitting in the barn from the first renovation. Plus, if we must sell our house, we may have some pieces you can take. I doubt we will end up in such a big place as this."

"Thanks, Mum," said Jeff. "We'll cross that bridge when we come to it."

"When do you think the barn renovations will be done?" asked Jacob.

"It should be ready within a month for basic living," said Jeff. "The bathroom and kitchen plumbing are ready to be hooked up, but there is no hot water and no septic to receive the waste yet. I can use the outhouse in the meantime. I can use a space heater to keep warm until the heat pump is in. The insulation is in, and the trimming and finishing can happen for months after I'm living there. I just want to finish the walls first, so I can put furniture up against them. It's too crowded otherwise."

Jacob said, "Well, the builders said they can start in about four weeks, so you want to push along. You'll need to be out of there by then. Tanny, you can move in with us if the construction dust and noise is too much."

"Oh. Thanks," said Tanny.

There was a short silence which Bet broke by asking Tanny, "Might I hire you to help me with my attic? I have a bunch of stuff that came to me from my parents' estate. I just stuffed it all into the attic because I couldn't manage it at the time."

"Oh! I'd be happy to try," agreed Tanny.

"Excellent. I will talk to you later to set up a time," smiled Bet.

Tanny sparkled at Jeff. *My first gig!* she mouthed.

The afternoon portion of the meeting covered more of the nitty-gritty. They discussed the taxes on the property and how they would be affected when they changed the property designation to a bed and breakfast.

Remembering, Tanny asked, "I noticed that there are some old fence lines in the middle of the property. Most of them are overgrown, but I wondered what they were for."

Jacob said, "Grandpa had horses when we were children. He still liked to use a wagon in the summer and a sleigh in the winter even when everyone else had switched to automobiles. Sometimes the horses came in very handy, especially before we got most of the roads paved in Bracebridge. The mud in the spring could be terrible. His big draft horses pulled a lot of trucks and cars out of the mud and rescued some folks in the winter when their cars couldn't handle the snow."

"I suspect you have found some of the fences that surrounded the pastures or paddock," Jacob continued. "A lot more of the land was cleared back in the day. The bush has reclaimed most of the old pastures. Pa wasn't interested in keeping horses. We had some goats for a while, and some pigs. But there hasn't been livestock on the land for many years."

"Britt had an old rescue horse when I joined the family," Jeff added.

Jacob looked at him. "That's right. He was a retired RCMP horse, living out his days."

"I remember the day she had to put him down," mused Jeff. "It broke my heart."

Tanny looked at the two of them, marveling at all the history she never knew.

"That must have been before you babysat us there, Uncle Jacob," she said.

"Well before," said Jacob. Jeff nodded.

There had been horses at Cedar Haven. Tanny *loved* horses. She wondered if the barn was in good enough shape to house more rescues. Perhaps that could be part of the appeal of the bed and breakfast?

The meetings wrapped up in the mid-afternoon. Tanny set a time with Bet to organize the attic in the following week. Then the two lovers headed home with Mack.

Forty-Four

March 21 to March 22

Jeff and Tanny decided to attend the United Church with Jacob and Eileen on Sunday. Bet Giddings was the accompanist there, and this had been Britt's chosen congregation. Surprisingly, the speaker was a guest up from Kitchener—a professor from one of the Waterloo seminaries. The regular pastor, Rev. Heidi, was travelling for meetings with the regional council.

The talk was about religious architecture, ritual, and pageantry, covering how the shape and decoration of a space evokes feelings. Some worship spaces point to the mighty power of God and God's lofty wisdom, such as great stone cathedrals, which dwarf the visitor. Some evoke more of an intimacy and warmth, inviting the congregation to feel community as they worship. Tanny reflected that Cliffside Chapel was of the latter, with its warm wood tones and semi-circular seating. She had never thought about worship spaces in this way before.

Sitting next to Jeff and holding his hand, Tanny learned that most Western worship rituals were born in theatre. "With the costumes and pageantry, special music and smells, and the theatre-like spaces, the leaders sought to weave a spell, inviting the worshippers from their everyday lives into the Divine Presence—a realm where the mystical and sacred dwelt.

"Today we may see all those fancy robes and bells as symbols of a dying and out-of-touch culture. But never forget that outward symbols, spaces, garments, and music, have power to affect us. Ritual is important. Our rituals don't have to be yesterday's rituals. We can craft important and meaningful rituals that speak to us in our modern context, which is what we must do to keep moving forward with relevance.

"Remember, rituals are anything we do with regularity. Whether someone is religiously observant or not, music has power, clothing has power, physical spaces invite feelings and moods...."

The service invited everyone to become more aware of the effect of rituals, garments, music, and sacred movements in their lives. It wasn't anything like an explanation of a Bible verse, but Tanny liked being called to a greater self-aware-ness regarding her own rituals, habits, and worship expectations. It also softened her to understanding how other worship cultures could feel so "wrong" to her but still be just right for the worshippers accustomed to them. She hadn't even realized that she looked with a little contempt on worship cultures that were not what she was used to. That realization made her uncomfortable, but she was glad to spot it in herself so she could stop.

The coffee hour introduced Tanny to several local community members and professionals. She met the local "osteopathic manual practitioner"—a certifica-tion which Tanny had never encountered before. Tanny liked Katrina Hawkins right away and hoped she might be a new local friend. They agreed to meet over lunch some time to discuss what Katrina did and generally what to expect of life in Bracebridge.

Though the United Church worship ritual was a bit different from Cliffside Chapel's, Tanny realized that the culture of community and service felt like some-thing she wanted to join. The generally inclusive and non-judgmental feeling at this church felt amazing, and she was grateful to see more than one obviously same-sex couple in the congregation. Why couldn't Cliffside be like this? She didn't like feeling disloyal to her childhood denomination. But its flaws were be-coming more obvious to her.

On Sunday afternoon and evening, Tanny sat down with Jeff to plan when and how she might move up to Cedar Haven. They looked at Jeff's work schedule and decided to go down to Cliffside the upcoming Wednesday. Susan's mom, Kate, was happy to put them up, to avoid questions from the twins or others. Kate was still in Susan's childhood home with several bedrooms.

Tanny called her mom to let her know and immediately had to disabuse her mom of her assumption that Tanny would be staying in her childhood bedroom. "Aunt Kate has several bedrooms, and we have been invited to stay there, Mom. We have accepted. But thank you for the offer." Emily wasn't happy and cited "time with your sister and nephew" as an argument for Tanny to come home. But Tanny reassured her mom that she would make time for Jenny and Will while she and Jeff were in town, and they would be staying with Kate.

"It feels like lying," Tanny complained to Jeff after the call. "I guess it *is* lying.

But I'm protecting myself from her judgment and control. I'm protecting every-one from feeling like they belong in our business." She heaved a sad sigh and walked into Jeff's sympathetic arms.

"I'm sorry sweetheart," Jeff comforted, holding his beloved. He wanted to protect her from every cruel, prying, and judgmental eye in the world. It wasn't fair and she didn't deserve their judgment.

Jeff reflected wryly that no one was judging or controlling *him*. It was all aimed at Tanny. Jacob and Eileen had been actively uninterested in his own love-life. He had liked it that way. But now Tanny was being put through the wringer simply because she was a woman, and from a religiously conservative upbringing. "We will get through this, sweetheart," he said. "And once we are married, it will all go away." They held each other in somber silence. "Shall we just get married next week?" he added.

Tanny looked up at him considering. "There's nothing stopping us from pulling a Jon and Sue: getting legally married now and having an official cere-mony later."

The lovers looked at each other in speculation.

"I want time to think about that," said Tanny, gazing at her beloved. Jeff's hair, at five week's growth, was over an inch long now, showing itself to be golden brown, like his eyes. He put Tanny in mind of a big, kind lion. He did what he could to get it to lie flat, but some of it still stood up, fighting gravity. Tanny loved running her fingers through it. It was soft and thick.

Jeff had a twenty-four-hour shift starting that night at midnight. The two lovers retired in the early evening to Jeff's bedroom. Now that there was full con-sent, they were in a honeymoon-like state. They were increasingly enjoying each other's responsiveness, learning what each one wanted and enjoying giving and receiving pleasure. Jeff introduced Tanny to tantric lovemaking practices. She was so inexperienced, she was a sponge to learning everything she could. Both had a learning curve and were excited to practice. After this session, they fell back, pant-ing, sweaty, and happy.

Jeff, with one arm lifted over his head turned to her and said, "How does August sound for a wedding month?"

Tanny, still floating said, "August? It sounds hot."

"Okay, May?" invited Jeff, eyebrows lifted. He kissed the fingers of her hand.

Tanny lifted up on one elbow. "May?! But that's much too soon! I couldn't possibly get ready in time!"

"I want to get past all the public scrutiny and judgment. I want you to be my wife so we can sleep in the same bedroom without raised eyebrows."

Tanny rested her lower arms on his broad chest and looked into his amber eyes. "That means a lot to me, Jeff. But I also want to have a chance to create a meaningful service unique to us, and have our friends present. You heard the minister this morning, 'rituals matter'!"

Jeff placed his hands on Tanny's upper arms, rubbing gently. "Okay, my sweet. When would you like to have this ceremony? And where?"

"Hmmm," reflected Tanny, looking off in thought. She brightened. "How about in late September or October? The colouring up here will be gorgeous by then, and maybe enough of the construction will be done to hold the ceremony and reception here?"

Jeff's eyes glowed. "I would love to hold the ceremony here. If the weather is good, we can hold it outside, and if not, there's always the barn."

Tanny scrunched up her nose. "Not the barn. I guess I was imagining a smaller gathering; that way we could fit it in the great room if the weather was poor."

"We will make it work, no matter what," assured Jeff.

"What do you think of asking Jon to do the ceremony?"

"I'd like that very much," agreed Jeff. "But if he's not available, I'm sure Rev. Heidi would be happy to help us."

"A woman pastor! That would be something for my family to see." After a pause she added, "And who cares what people say? Let them speculate and gossip. They can knock themselves out, if that's what they want to spend their time on. I know I love you. We are committed to each other." Tanny settled back down, snuggling her head into Jeff's shoulder. "Whether we do a quick legal ceremony soon or save the official marriage until October, I feel a kind of peace I haven't felt, well, ever? I feel like I've come home."

Jeff's arm tightened around Tanny, deeply moved by her words. He felt like he was home at last too.

Eventually Jeff had to rise and get ready for his shift. Tanny decided to stay and sleep in his bed for the night. She would have to move all her stuff out of her chosen room anyway, as it was one of the ones destined for renovation. Jeff headed off into the night, leaving Mack with her. He would be telling his coworkers of their engagement now that everything was decided.

Tanny arrived in Herman at Bet's house the next morning. Bet welcomed her in, and they sat down over coffee to discuss what Bet wanted. Then Bet took Tanny up to the attic to show her the jumble of possessions piled up there. The attic was bright and spacious, and well-lit, but the space was impassable, blocked by a solid wall of piled possessions. Though it was insulated and ventilated, the area had never been partitioned, so the belongings were wall to wall. Bet left Tanny to get started. She had to go run errands but would be back in about ninety minutes to see what had been accomplished.

Tanny had brought graph paper and a pencil. She looked at the space and envisioned aisles, with items in categories and easy access. Then she set to work. She played some of her favourite tunes and sang as she worked. It was a little like solving a Chinese puzzle box. There was only so much room to work in, so she had to do a lot of shifting items this way and that. Soon the chaos began to be sorted into categories and the aisles began to take shape. After ninety-five minutes, she had most of the items in categories and several aisles opened. She was drawing a map to what she had done including labels for the areas containing different categories—rolled carpets, linens, artwork—when she heard Bet arriving home and ascending the attic stairs.

"Oh, my goodness!" exclaimed Bet when she saw the transformation. "You've made everything accessible! I can get around up here!" Bet moved into the space, looking all around. "This is tremendous."

Tanny grinned and showed Bet the map, made so that Bet could find specific items quicker by knowing where to look.

"You are a miracle worker," continued Bet. "Now I can *think* in this space. I have ideas now on how to begin offering items to family members, and it feels easier to see what can immediately be donated. Like this." Bet lifted an unremarkable lamp. "And these." She grabbed some throw pillows.

Bet announced, "Let's get lunch," and started marching down the stairs, lamp and pillows in hand.

Over lunch, Tanny explained her thinking, and reasoned that another half an hour should let her complete the sorting and organizing.

"You must be exhausted," declared Bet, her hazel eyes full of wonder.

But Tanny felt excited and energized. "This little break will have me ready to get back to work in no time," she said.

Bet shook her head in amazement. "I think you are really cut out for this work. I'm astonished by how much you've gotten done and how helpful your map will be."

"After lunch I can finish my reorganizing or help you start hauling things out for donation, whichever you like," Tanny added.

It was decided that Bet would begin pulling things out of the categories for donation while Tanny finished the sorting, categorizing and mapping. Another hour went by, with Tanny completing the map and helping Bet to load up things to be donated. As they had worked Tanny talked about how excited she was to be moving to Bracebridge.

"But won't you miss your family and friends?"

"Well, I'm sure I will, but it's only a three-hour drive. Besides, I am already feeling lonely and homeless down there. There isn't a lot for single people in the church to do. My best friends are married and many have kids. It's like they have moved on to another dimension without me. I can't be part of their conversations about child-rearing or marriage or in-laws or anything. I have loved the church so much. But now I feel like there isn't really a space for me. *This* move feels like I'm moving towards a future designed for me. I can't see what my future might be in Cliffside, going forward, anyway. Not with everything—" Tanny's voice caught, and tears sprung to her eyes. "Gosh. Sorry," she apologized.

Bet put down her armful of items and came to lay a hand on Tanny's shoulder.

Tanny was wiping at her eyes feeling disconcerted. "It's just that I kind of lost everything all at once: my dog, my job, my home...." Her eyes stung and she fought to hold back her tears.

"Good grief!" sympathized Bet. "Even your dog? How awful!" She rubbed Tanny's back. "No one should go through all that at the same time. That's just cruel."

"I know, right?!" Tanny cried and laughed at the same time. "It ... it su-ucks...." The laughter quickly dissolved into tears.

Bet pulled Tanny into her arms and rubbed the young woman's back as she wept.

When Tanny had recovered somewhat Bet said, "You are astonishingly functional for someone who has been through so much. I never would have known." Bet's gentle eyes were luminous with compassion.

"I guess I ... I just haven't had time to process any of it. Everything just keeps coming at me, thing after thing. All I can do is respond to and cope with each thing before the next thing hits," said Tanny. She gave a small shudder, as if even that small acknowledgment allowed her body to express some of the pent-up trauma.

"We have some good therapists in town," offered Bet. "I can get you some names if you are interested."

"Therapy?" asked Tanny, feeling slightly insulted. She felt vulnerable and exposed. Then she reflected that Jeff was in therapy, and she admired him for it. Did she think therapy was good for everyone *besides* her? Abruptly she recognized that she had no money to pay for therapy anyway and felt doubly disappointed. She was upset that someone thought she could use therapy, and upset that she couldn't afford it, even if she should decide to access it.

Tanny swallowed and said, "Sure. I'd like those names." She was partially placating Bet and partially feeling like she now *did* want to get therapy if she could ever pay for it.

Bet seemed to see Tanny's inward struggle and became gentler. "You've got more support here than you know, honey."

This made fresh tears spring to Tanny's eyes which she fought back.

Bet lifted her head with a sigh of satisfaction. "Well! You've gotten a lot done for me today! Do you feel like we are done? I feel like we are done. This has been amazing, and I'm going to tell everyone how helpful you have been."

Tanny grinned, and thanked Bet.

Bet continued, "I think I can drop the donations off by myself. So, how much do I owe you?" After hearing Tanny's low-ball request, Bet wrote a check, doubling the amount. "You deserve to be paid what you are worth," she declared, tearing off the check.

Tanny cried all the way back to Cedar Haven.

Forty-Five

March 23 to March 24

Tanny awoke in Jeff's bed, with Jeff asleep behind her. His heavy arm was resting across her, holding her as he slept. He had fallen asleep shirtless, and Tanny could look again at the snake tattoo that twisted up his left arm. That tattoo had made her so nervous the first few times she had glimpsed it. Tanny had been taught to see snakes as evil and representing evil, so why would anyone put such a symbol on their body?

At first Tanny only occasionally noticed Jeff's tattoo due to winter weather and long sleeves; but as they'd spent more time together, he'd roll up his sleeves to wash some dishes, and she'd seen the serpent winding up his lower arm, seeming to move with his flexing muscles.

Because of the positive things she was learning about Jeff, Tanny had chosen to overlook the tattoo. But eventually she had worked up the courage to ask him why he had a snake tattoo on his arm. Jeff had pulled off his shirt to let her see the completed art. Tanny had caught her breath a bit at his bared chest, but made herself look upon the whole tattoo, with the tail pointing to Jeff's palm and the head at his shoulder. It was a benign-looking head—no fangs or tongue—but she still felt alarmed by it. Tanny thought of Adam and Eve and the corrupting snake and had to ask Jeff what he had been thinking.

Jeff spoke of his desire to be a healer, and of the symbolism of Asclepius' rod and snake representing medicine. He also had learned that snakes in many cultures represent healing, transformation, and wisdom—all qualities he desired to embody. And so, Jeff had found an artist that helped him envision the bones of his arm as the rod of Asclepius and made the snake wrap around them. Jeff was proud of the tattoo, and it clearly held great meaning for him. That had been an important moment for Tanny. She realized that she had judged him for having an "evil" symbol on his arm, when in Jeff's mind the snake represented healing and transformation.

Tanny heaved a deep sigh, remembering how Jeff's story had shifted her fear and superstition into admiration and respect. Now she loved the tattoo, because of what it said about her lover.

Jeff was deeply asleep, so she slipped out from under his encircling arm and went to relieve herself. Tomorrow they would be driving down to Cliffside to visit Tanny's family. They would also rent a truck and bring all Tanny's belongings up to Cedar Haven. It would be a trick finding places to store things, with the barn filling up with furniture from the emptied rooms. Perhaps she would drop many of her things off at Goodwill instead. Most of her furniture was second hand anyway. There was already plenty of furniture at Cedar Haven for her to use.

Tanny dressed and took her slippered feet down to the kitchen to make coffee. She saw Jeff's keys and papers scattered on the island along with the remains of a meal. *It must have been a rough shift.* Jeff usually tidied up after himself and tucked his dishes in the dishwasher. She left the coffee brewing and tiptoed up to gaze at Jeff. He had a careworn look around his eyes even in sleep. Tanny drew the drapes more tightly, darkening the room a bit more. Mack had followed her out earlier, so she closed the door to prevent Mack from waking the weary paramedic.

It was almost noon when Jeff made his appearance.

"Heeeeey," Tanny said, and folded her arms around him. He rested his tousled head on the top of hers but remained silent.

Eventually Tanny asked him, "Rough night? There's coffee." When she went to move, Jeff's arms tightened.

"Wait," he said. "Just stay a minute."

Tanny stayed tucked in his arms. Eventually Jeff lifted his head, and his arms loosened.

"You had a rotten shift, didn't you?" Tanny asked him, not moving away.

Jeff nodded; eyes weary. He pinched the bridge of his nose, closing his eyes. "I watched a child die last night, despite our best efforts." He heaved a shuddering sigh and looked into Tanny's eyes. "I've never watched a child die before."

"How awful, Jeff; I'm so sorry!" exclaimed Tanny. She moved deeper into his arms, hugging him more fiercely.

Jeff welcomed Tanny to him, cradling her head against his shoulder, as if she were the child and he was saving her. "I'm sorry. I shouldn't burden you with this. It's just ... my first ...." He pressed a kiss into her hair. "Thank you for holding me."

They held each other for a long while. Then Jeff said, "I'm going to see if I can move my therapist appointment up to before we leave. I hope that's okay."

"Of course. Of course, Jeff. Whatever you need."

Jeff moved to get some coffee. "They say you never forget your first one.

I always knew this was coming. But to watch that toddler go from breathing and alive to still and lifeless—no amount of lectures and promises of support can ever.... I just want that child to be ALIVE again! I want to hand that child back to her parents, breathing and living." His voice cracked and he set down his coffee.

Tanny went to him and held him as the sobbing shook his frame.

"I'm so sorry!" Tanny wept with him, her own imagination providing more than enough for her to feel something of his trauma. "I'm here. I'm here," she reassured her beloved.

Eventually Jeff was ready to become present to the day ahead. He did manage to contact his therapist and was relieved to learn a spot was open for him the following morning thanks to a cancellation.

"I'll let everyone know that we will be later than we'd planned," Tanny offered.

Jeff went about the day with a somewhat sluggish, distracted manner, but together Tanny and Jeff managed to consolidate things in the barn and move some of the north bedrooms' furniture out there. Tanny's idea about aisles from Bet's attic helped her think to create aisles in the barn rather than stacking things deeper and deeper.

The next morning, Jeff was up and gone to his therapy appointment early. Tanny continued packing and preparing to be away for several days. She gave Mack a nice long walk, and began poking along the old fence lines, to see if any usable fencing remained for possible future horses.

When Jeff got back, he looked wrung out and had clearly been crying. But there was a lightness about him too, which brought Tanny comfort. Tanny insisted that she drive so that he could rest. Jeff ended up stretching out on the second seat with Mack, and almost immediately fell asleep.

So Tanny made the drive in silence, watching the pines and rocks roll by. The road curved around bodies of water in some places and played peekaboo between the trees with the lakes in other places. She counted down the trip by the landmarks, passing the Gravenhurst exits, crossing the Severn River, and skimming alongside the sixteen-mile-long Lake Couchiching. She passed Webers, a restaurant on Highway Eleven so famous for its fresh and juicy burgers that they had to build a parking lot on the far side of the road and a walkway over the highway to prevent accidents and deaths from tourists trying to cross the highway on foot for the burgers.

Then she passed Orillia, and just north of Barrie followed Highway Eleven as it flowed into the massive Highway 400. When she was just south of Barrie, she decided to take the back route to Kitchener instead of the massive highways and headed off to zig-zag along country roads towards home.

Tanny loved southern and central Ontario with all her heart. She loved the big skies and acres of farms, the rolling hills and quirky museums, and she loved the ubiquitous Tim Hortons that smelled the same no matter where she stopped.

Jeff slept through all of it only stirring as they were passing Elora.

"Hey sleepy man. We've got another thirty minutes or so to go."

She saw Jeff's golden-topped head pop up in her rear-view mirror. Mack was wriggling to sit up beside him.

"Mack stayed with me the whole time?" he mumbled. "It felt like he never left my side."

Tanny assured him, "No. He wouldn't leave you. Even when I needed to stretch my legs and pee, he refused to come with me."

"Wow." Jeff shook his head as if to shake the sleepiness off. He addressed the panting shepherd mix. "Thank you, my man. I couldn't ask for a better friend. Are you ready for a walk now?"

Mack whined a little. Jeff gave his dog a hug while Tanny pulled off to the side of a road near a wooded area.

In no time, Jeff and Mack were back, both relieved, and Jeff looking much restored. The paramedic climbed into the front seat next to Tanny and reached over to kiss her before she started up again. "Want me to drive?" he asked.

"Naw. I got this," Tanny smiled at him. She put the truck in gear and off they went.

Jeff gazed at his miraculous fiancé, adoring her light freckles, sparkling eyes, and swinging ponytail. She was strong and capable and so loving. He considered himself the luckiest man alive.

After some quiet time had passed Jeff said in an offhand manner, "Oh. My therapist wants me to tell you more about my childhood."

Tanny looked mildly surprised and then said, "Okay. Shoot. I'm listening."

Jeff was at a loss. He rubbed a hand through his hair and said, "I didn't mean right now. I meant, 'some time'. I wanted to tell you—I wanted to tell you about this *now* so I wouldn't forget." He didn't add "again."

"Oh! Okay," shrugged Tanny. "I'd be happy to listen and love you completely, whenever you want to do that."

"Well, thanks," Jeff said, a man-dimple winking in one of his cheeks. He felt bemused. His therapist had praised him for going to Tanny with his recent trauma and pointed out to him that the outcome of that vulnerability had been loving support. Jeff's first impulse was *not* to seek comfort from someone else because traditionally for him his "someone else's" had been unavailable, or in a worse state than he was, or verbally abusive. Therefore, his default coping mechanism had been to go numb and disassociate during trauma. Yes, Britt had begun to change that, but then she had died, and he had fallen back on his old coping mechanisms.

And now Tanny was in his life.

It was new behaviour for Jeff to allow himself to fall apart in the presence of a loved one again. Dr. Eagletree had encouraged Jeff to stay present and breathe through the memories of the latest trauma. Jeff sobbed and shook, and then would abruptly start talking about something else, distancing himself from the feelings. He would intellectually discuss helpful medical procedures only loosely connected to the trauma. The therapist gently called him back to his feelings. Once Jeff talked about noticing that his one leg was falling asleep as he lay on his belly on the roof of the tumbled car, supporting the suspended head and shoulders of the toddler as his teammate struggled to cut the straps of the car seat. He had popped into noticing odd details to avoid the impact of what they were struggling to do.

"You are safe, Jeff. You are strong. You are doing everything you can."

Then more sobs would come. Dr. Eagletree had burned sage and sweetgrass to cleanse the room and Jeff's spirit at the close of his session. Jeff did feel clearer and stronger. And he wanted to give Tanny a heads-up about what habits he turned to in the past when his PTSD got triggered.

But not right now as they were driving.

By the time they pulled into the sleepy church community, Jeff was feeling able to be present and perform socially, even if the trauma was still fresh. He had boxed away the trauma for now, allowing him to show up to normal life with greater presence of mind.

They pulled first into Kate Bender's driveway, when they arrived in Cliffside. They gave Kate a warm greeting and dropped off their bags. Then they had to go to Tanny's childhood home.

Emily came to the door before they could knock, possibly alerted by the sound of the truck doors being closed. Emily drew Tanny into a warm embrace and offered Jeff a stiff handshake. "Gilbert! They're here!" She called into the house. Then she backed away to let the couple enter.

Tanny made a face at Jeff as they removed their coats and hung them in the entry closet. The smell of roast beef filled the house.

"Come in; come in!" Emily encouraged them and led the way to the kitchen where Gilbert met them on his way out of the office.

Jeff saw a stocky man with once dark hair going silver throughout. He was an inch or two shorter than Jeff, though not a short man. Tanny's father stood with his hands on his hips and looked Jeff up and down. "So, you are Jacob and Eileen's foster son, are you?" His tone was neither hostile, nor overly friendly.

"I am, sir," Jeff found himself saying as he shook the proffered hand. Gilbert's grip was firm, but not aggressive. He watched the assessment moving behind his potential father-in-law's eyes. "And you are Tanny's father?" he returned with a hint of playfulness.

"That I am," Gilbert responded, with a light behind his eyes.

Emily was pressing wine glasses upon them. "Don't drink any yet," she said. She opened the door to the basement and hollered, "Jenny! They're here!" down the stairs.

Tanny heard, "Da Heeah!" from the basement.

"I assume Jacob and Emily raised you in the church?" Gilbert was asking Jeff.

"They did indeed," Jeff responded.

Tanny sucked in a bit of air, knowing that her dad had meant the *Swedenborgian* Christian church, where Jeff had assumed the generalized Christian church. Jeff hadn't understood the nuance in the question and had responded truthfully, if not accurately. Tanny had no inclination to correct the misunderstanding.

Besides, at that moment, Jenny was coming up from the basement with Will leading the way. Tanny went over to greet Will and Jenny. Jenny's eyes were sparkling. "Congratulations! I'm so happy for you!" she said. Jenny pulled Will up onto her hip and hugged Tanny saying, Ooh! So happy!"

Will, apparently following her lead leaned over to hug Tanny too. "So eppy!" he said.

The sisters both laughed and Tanny thanked Will.

The small kitchen was quite crowded now. Tanny introduced Jeff to Will and Jenny while Emily pushed a wine glass into Jenny's hand.

"And now, a toast to the church," Gilbert announced, and the four family members burst into song: "Our Glorious Chuuuurch! Thou heav'nly briiide...."

Tanny gave Jeff a pained and sympathetic look as the family sang. Emily hitched a concerned eyebrow at her potential son-in-law who was not singing.

Jeff stood there bravely, his wine glass aloft.

Will got increasingly agitated, trying to take his mother's wine glass, and then making begging motions with his hand. He squirmed and whined until Jeff let

Will hold his wine glass with him. The now happy Will "sang" along with the somewhat dramatic song, until it was done.

"To the church," said Gilbert and Emily in unison and reached to clink their glasses around the group.

"To the church," murmured Tanny and Jenny, clinking in return. Jeff followed suit, letting Will join in the clinking with Jenny's help. Then everyone drank, and Jeff did too once he had carefully extricated his wine glass from Will's grasp.

Tanny's plump, dark-haired sister gave Jeff a grateful smile for his help with Will.

"Jacob and Eileen didn't teach you our toast?" Emily asked Jeff.

"I'm afraid not," responded Jeff.

Emily made a face and murmured something about Eileen falling down on the job.

Meanwhile Gilbert had moved toward the dining room. Emily shooed everyone after him except Tanny, whom she expected to help with the serving.

Jeff offered to help too, which surprised Emily. Something softened around her eyes even as she insisted he take a seat.

"I haven't had such good roast beef in a long while, Mrs. Smith," Jeff sighed in gratitude as the meal wound toward an end. Jenny had left the table already with Will who had finished early. She had to give Will a bath as his head was covered in gravy.

"Well, thank you, Jeffery," said Emily.

Tanny wanted to say, "It's Jefferson," but stopped herself.

Emily continued, "I am so glad to hear that you were raised in the church. If you are going to marry Tanny, that is very important."

Tanny squirmed and tried to change the subject.

"Jeff is a paramedic in the Bracebridge area," she said.

"Is he?" asked Gilbert and then began telling Jeff a story about serving in the Ben Kirk volunteer fire company when he had been a young man.

Tanny just wanted the dinner to end. She wanted to get back to Kate's to unpack and go to bed.

Emily signaled for Tanny to join her in the kitchen on the pretext of starting the dishes. Tanny braced herself.

"He seems nice enough," observed Emily, sotto voce. "But are you sure you want to *marry* him? So quickly?"

"Mom. I appreciate your concern, but I *am* twenty-eight. I know what I'm doing."

"I'm just worried about his background, sweetheart," continued Emily. "Those types come with hidden problems. I don't want you dealing with an alcoholic husband."

Tanny reflected on the rampant alcohol dependency and alcoholism in her parents' generation and found the comment ironic.

"I'm not sure what 'type' you mean, Mom," replied Tanny. "Employed? Stable? Kind? Respectful?"

"You know. 'Troubled.' His parents were drug addicts and who knows what all," Emily said. "Those early childhood traumas can leave scars for life. Are you sure you want to be saddled with that?"

Tanny had so many responses (most of them sarcastic) spring to her tongue, that she couldn't respond at all. Finally, Tanny sighed and said, "Mom. Thank you for looking out for me. I understand that your concern is your way of saying, 'I love you.' But I am one-hundred percent sure I want to marry Jeff. I *choose* Jeff. He is good and kind and respectful, and I love everything about him. If I *am* making a mistake, it is mine to make. You don't have to worry."

"He's a *foster* kid! His parents were teenage alcoholics!" Emily said, forgetting to keep her voice down.

"His parents are also Jacob and Eileen, your brother, and his wife. I think Jeff is a remarkable human being despite a rough start, mom. I *love* him. We are getting married."

"Would you even *consider* talking to Stephen about true marriage and how to prepare?" Emily asked. "He has some time available tomorrow. I checked."

Tanny felt a roar of rage building in her chest. She took a deep breath and had to wait until she could be civil. "Tomorrow, we need to pick up the moving van and get my things out of Jenny's house. That will probably take most of the day. I just don't think we will have time." Then, to pre-empt Emily's imminent objection she said, "But we will see if we can fit that in on another visit."

Eventually Tanny and Jeff were able to extricate themselves from the family home and head off to Kate's to unpack and get some rest.

Gilbert and Emily's approval seemed ambiguous, but as they had not openly disapproved of Jeff, the young couple was taking the encounter as a positive sign.

They had a brief visit with Kate over herbal tea. Tanny appreciated again how gentle and thoughtful her aunt was. Then, once they were finally alone in their room, Tanny buried her head in Jeff's chest and growled in frustration.

Jeff chuckled. "It wasn't *that* bad." He rubbed her back.

Tanny glared at him. "It was too!" she said. But Jeff's mischievous grin and hug helped her let go and laugh too. They unpacked and fell almost immediately to sleep.

Forty-Six

Jeff and Tanny managed to get the moving van loaded up by three in the afternoon. Conrad was able to come help as well as Jonathan Haley, and the four of them got the job done. They were very lucky in the weather. It was overcast and chilly, but the forecasted rain/snow mix never materialized. Mack helped by getting underfoot and barking.

Conrad was warm with congratulations on Jeff and Tanny's engagement. Jon invited them all back to the Haley household for dinner that evening. Jeff, Tanny, and Conrad headed off to donate a bunch of her furniture and tie up the remaining items securely in the truck. They took and donated some of Jenny's furniture too, as she didn't want any items that reminded her of her soon-to-be ex-husband. Finally, they locked up the empty house and gave the keys to Jenny. Jenny was almost rid of the place.

Then Tanny and Jeff turned up early at the Haley's to do the promised housecleaning for Sue. Jeff assigned himself to vacuuming and mopping the floors while Tanny did the bathrooms, kitchen, and dusting. Jon ran ahead of them tidying, while Susan, at everyone's insistence, sat with her feet up in an easy chair. Even the twins got into the spirit of it all by cleaning their room and selecting toys they were ready to donate. Mack had to be left in Kate's care as he and the Haley's cats had not been fully introduced.

They had a mix of music playing with something for everyone. "What a Wonderful World" by James Taylor and Paul Simon came on the mix, and Jeff stopped near Tanny so they could sing the duet together as they cleaned. Jeff's voice was warm and resonant, if not always on key. Everyone was grinning as the song came to an end, and Jeff gave Tanny a long-lasting kiss.

It was nearing five thirty when the cleaning was finally done and the new lovers headed back to Kate's for showers.

Tanny was full of energy and joy. She loved her new life. At last, she had a feeling of purpose and belonging. She was wonderfully comfortable with Jeff, and he fit in with her friends as though he had always been part of the group.

Over pizza the three couples shared their news, dreams, and hopes. Jeff and Tanny had asked Jon to perform their ceremony, and Jon said he'd be delighted. With the ceremony set for October, there was plenty of time before the arrival of the Haley baby.

Jon worried aloud about Stephen's overwork. Gary and Conrad discussed the worship at the UU congregation—how it was different and how it was the same compared to Cliffside services.

"But they are not Swedenborgian!" Tanny exclaimed in mock consternation. "You will be swept into falsity and endanger your immortal souls!" She reached for another slice of the Canadian pizza, with its mushrooms, bacon, and pepperoni.

"I can't believe I ever thought that way," said Conrad. "Doesn't Swedenborg say God is present in all religious systems and provides all that is needed to everyone on the planet in their contexts?"

"Yes, but somehow, if you've been raised Swedenborgian and don't stay Swedenborgian, you're worse off than someone who hasn't heard of Swedenborg," concluded Tanny. "At least, in my family it seems to work that way."

Gary clicked beer cans with Jeff saying, "I guess we are safe because we weren't raised Swedenborgian."

"Don't tell my dad that," added Tanny. "He thinks Jeff was raised 'in the church'."

Jeff looked confused. "But I was...."

Tanny asked Jeff, "What church did you attend as a kid?"

Jeff said, "Jacob and Eileen took me to the United Church, where Britt attended. They made sure I was there every Sunday."

Tanny nodded. "When my dad asked you if you had been raised in the church, he meant the *Swedenborgian* church. That's what my parents are all about. Jacob was raised Swedenborgian, but I don't think Aunt Eileen was."

Jeff considered. "I was aware that Britt and Jacob were connected with another Christian denomination; I just thought they didn't attend because there wasn't a church nearby."

"There isn't," said Jon. "There are only three Swedenborgian churches in Eastern Canada."

"Three?!" asked Jeff and Gary in unison.

"Three—" said Jon, "—split between two divisions. Cliffside is with the more conservative division. There's another Swedenborgian church here in Kitchener, but it is with the more liberal division."

"Huh," said Jeff. "And this whole community here is Swedenborgian?"

"Pretty much," said Susan.

"Except a few homes that have been sold out of the church, which makes some church members very grumpy," explained Tanny.

"The conservative branch likes to run schools, a lot like Catholics. They tend to form communities or enclaves of members around the schools," added Susan.

"It lets us brainwash the kids starting early," remarked Tanny. She dodged and laughed when Susan swatted at her. "I mean, there's a lot that is good about having a community."

"So, that song that your family sang last night, was that a Swedenborgian song?"

Tanny hid her face in her hand. "Yes," she said from behind her palm. "We burst into song at the drop of a hat."

"I like how musical we are," said Susan.

"Me too," said Jon, squeezing Susan's hand. "But then, I get paid to be musical, so that works well for me."

"I guess I should take you to a service some time," Tanny said to Jeff. "You can then at least hear the hymns sung in four-part harmony."

"I'd be open to that. I'm genuinely curious about what makes Swedenborgians different from other Christians. I guess there are a lot of different kinds of Christians, and I'm not sure why any of them are different from the other," mused Jeff.

Tanny looked expectantly at Jon, the minister in the group.

"Oh, no," said Jon. "That's on *you*, Tanny. *You* tell Jeff what is different. That will help you learn what you do and don't know about Swedenborgianism. Better yet, tell him what you like and don't like. Then you can compare notes. I will stand ready to answer any questions. But the process will help you both discover what you believe as a couple, and where you might want to raise any kids, if you choose to have kids."

Jeff studied Jon with growing respect. "That is about the wisest advice I've ever heard from a minister."

Gary whispered to Conrad, "What do you think of *him* marrying us?"

Conrad whispered back, "I think he would lose his job. He needs to pay for a wife and kids now."

Gary frowned. "Imagine that. A church that fires you for following your conscience."

"I know, right?" said Conrad. "I don't hold it against him. He's kind of trapped."

The evening wound up pretty early as Susan needed to get to bed shortly after her daughters, and the other Kitchener residents all had work the next day.

There were warm hugs all around. Jeff and Tanny expressed how much they would love to have them all up to Cedar Haven when the renovations were done.

"We could have a couples retreat!" said Conrad, his arm tucked tightly into Gary's. There was a mischievous light in his eyes.

Jon swiped a hand over his face. "Let's just call it a vacation. I get enough weird rumours about me as it is."

"It will be a while before the renovations are completed, but I *love* the idea," Tanny concluded.

The rest of March rolled into April as Tanny settled into Cedar Haven. Good Friday and Easter passed, with Tanny and Jeff joining Jacob and Eileen for worship and an Easter meal. Tanny was growing in comfort worshipping in the new setting and culture.

Tanny also had to get used to giant plastic sheets intersecting hallways and covering doors, supposedly blocking construction dust. Even with these protections, fine plaster dust and mystery dirt got into everything, which spurred her to help do the finishing work in the barn apartment.

With both Jeff and Tanny working on it, that apartment moved closer and closer to completion. It was beginning to feel like *their* place—*their* home as a couple. They made joint decisions on finishes and furniture placement and decorations that helped the place feel like it was theirs, and not just Jeff's construction project. With luck they could move out there full time by the end of April.

Meanwhile Tanny got another organizing job via Bet's word of mouth—a recurring client in a higher-end home. Stephanie Veitch was dealing with a sudden chronic illness and needed help keeping up with her many projects. She also needed help adapting her home to accommodate her more limited mobility. Tanny had quite a few moments learning how to navigate clashes between her own ideas and the new client's ideas. She had to swallow her opinions and bow to Stephanie's ideas on several occasions—something that she found exceptionally hard. Tanny could *see* what really needed to happen in the re-organization, but Stephanie insisted that she knew best. *Why couldn't her client see what she saw and trust her?* Tanny had to realize that even if she did have the better idea, she could only move at the client's pace and readiness. These experiences helped her grow in interpersonal skills and in self-awareness. And she could take her frustrations home to Jeff, who listened with empathy and support.

Mrs. Veitch hired Tanny for a few hours every few days, which gave Tanny a somewhat steady income and helped her grow in confidence. Despite the occasional disagreements, Tanny genuinely liked Stephanie, and wondered if her struggle was in part because their personalities were so alike—both strong-willed and opinionated. This certainly gave Tanny pause to reflect on where her own blind spots might be.

Tanny missed her peers from Cliffside more and more, so she reached out to Katrina Hawkins, the osteopathic practitioner she had met at church. They were of a similar age, and young professionals, but it wasn't the instant-kindred-spirit connection she was hoping for. Tanny wanted a new best friend in town besides Jeff *now*, but was having to accept that it takes time to build up friends in a new town, no matter how impatient she was to do so.

Tanny was also able to get a part-time job at Oliver's Coffee, which helped her move closer to supporting herself, and did enable more networking in the community. She suspected that a few of her coworkers there might become good friends given time.

In her free time, Tanny dug some more through Britt's journals. She eventually struck upon the years when Britt's unhappiness with the culture at Cliffside Chapel was coming to a head. Britt found fault with several "pillars" of the church and their apparent insular and entitled attitudes. Britt thought these leaders felt superior to those who were not in the church and treated many others with contempt. She also was increasingly frustrated with the unacknowledged alcoholism in the membership. She wanted the pastor to speak up about it and insist on behavioural and cultural changes in the congregation. But after several sessions speaking to the pastor, she decided that Reverend Geoffrey Walters was too invested in the status quo himself to dare to rock the boat.

Tanny knew that right before Britt moved away from Cliffside (selling her home to newlyweds Susan and Duncan Rennie) she gave an impassioned speech for "God and kindness and common sense" to prevail in her beloved congregation. But her desires fell on deaf ears, and she had settled in the family homestead in Bracebridge instead, never to return.

Tanny found pages of Britt's unhappiness with the church before her big move written in the pages of her journal. Britt's complaints resonated strongly with Tanny's own struggles, surprising Tanny, and dismaying her that the church seemed to have made no progress on any of the issues in the more than twenty years since Britt had begun voicing her concerns.

Britt struggled to be taken seriously as a single woman. Britt kept being treated as someone "who wasn't married yet" and as a threat to the marriages that did exist. "As if I'd have anything to do with the husbands of other women!" Britt objected. Britt felt ignored and invisible by virtue of being female, being single, and being childless. She felt like "an annoying loose end."

But Aunt Britannia Bender had had a whole career and had even been a spy (though no-one could know that then). Instead, she was gossiped about as a possible lesbian, due to her single status.

Tanny was outraged on Britt's behalf, reading all of this. *So what if she had been a lesbian? Wouldn't that make her less of a so-called threat to all those apparently fragile marriages? Apparently same-sex attracted people were also a threat to marriages somehow.* It made Tanny wonder what the church's obsession with marriage was about.

Britt also bemoaned the lack of social life there was for singles, including widows. Any activity that did happen for the singles seemed mostly to be an attempt to marry them off to each other, "Like in a Gilbert and Sullivan musical."

It made Tanny's heart ache. She didn't want to find fault with her childhood denomination, but the older she got, the more problems she saw in it.

Early in the second week of April, Tanny had another dream about Britt.

In this dream, Britt was walking in a Muskoka setting. She was wearing Indigenous garb, and Jeff was walking at her side, also in First Nations attire. They looked like they belonged to the landscape and the surrounding nature.

Then suddenly Tanny was kneeling beside a box in Cedar Haven's attic. She saw her hand reaching out to open this particular chest. Suddenly Tanny's mother started demanding her attention, and started pulling on her other arm, trying to drag her away. Britt wanted Tanny to open the box, but her mother was doing everything in her power to prevent her.

Tanny jerked awake. Jeff slept peacefully beside her, not at all in leather or buckskin.

The feeling of urgency to open that attic box and the feeling of being tugged away was still strong. Tanny felt immensely curious to know what the dream meant. She looked at her phone. It was two in the morning. She decided to go see if the dream box was actually in the attic as pictured. Donning a robe and slippers against the chill, Tanny ascended the stairs up into the dusty, cluttered space.

There was no box sitting where it had been in her dream. Tanny realized that the chest she had already explored was near where the dream box had been, but she didn't think the one represented the other. She poked around in the space, looking for anything that looked like the dream's box. But nothing seemed even close to what she remembered. The more she poked around, the sillier she felt as the dream receded. What was she doing?

Still, the urgent curiosity had not abated. Tanny felt certain that there was something she was supposed to find up here. But what?

She wandered over to the other end of the attic, where there were mostly old furniture items—a rocking chair missing some spokes in the back, an age-fogged mirror, a dresser with half of the drawer-pulls missing. Tanny tugged at one of the drawers and found inside a small strongbox.

The strongbox was the very shape and colour of the dream chest but was many times smaller. Tanny tried to open the box, but it was locked. She felt around inside the drawer and then spent quite some time trying to wrestle open all the other drawers, but there was no key to be found anywhere.

As she searched Tanny wondered why people kept broken things. Did they imagine they would get around to repairing them? How long had this dresser been up here, housing some ancient window coverings, stained bedsheets, and a strongbox? Other than the strongbox, this stuff was junk (unless somebody wanted to repair the dresser).

Tanny lifted out the metal, shoebox-sized lockbox and carried it back downstairs. She slid it under the bed, climbing into the warm bedding while trying not to shock her sleeping fiancé with her chilly fingers and toes.

The morning found both Tanny and Jeff searching through Britt's desk drawers and collections, trying to find a key that fit the tiny lock.

"I mean, we could take it to a locksmith or simply cut the thing open if we have to," suggested Tanny, after several unsuccessful hours of searching.

They were seriously considering these options when the phone rang. It was Tanny's mom. "I wanted you to know that Stephen Shantz is in the hospital," she said. "He has had a massive heart attack. He's alive, but we don't know the prognosis yet."

Forty-Seven

April 10 to April 13

Three days had passed, and Stephen was not responding to treatment as well as could be expected. The medical team had gotten to him just in time, but everyone was whispering that the terrifyingly titled "widow maker" heart attack he had suffered had only a twelve percent survival rate. Stephen received a stent in the nick of time, which increased his survival rate to a whole twenty five percent. Tanny felt sick. She thought of Liz and their six children and felt at a loss for ways to help.

With Stephen out of commission, Jon was having to pick up all Stephen's duties including the weekly preaching. This passed the organ duties back to pregnant Susan. How would Susan manage now, having to play the organ for church along with Jon being overloaded with work? When Tanny talked to Susan, she heard the exhaustion behind Susan's cheerful front. She remembered Susan's nonstop nausea when she carried the twins and wondered how she would cope. (What a rough start to such a great marriage!) At least the twins were of an age where they could be somewhat helpful.

With this new development, Jon and Susan went ahead and announced the pregnancy. The twins were delighted to learn of the new baby, and became extra solicitous of Susan, which helped a lot.

Susan mentioned that old Rose McKellar was willing to take the organ every other Sunday for a while. Rose had been around when Susan had carried her twins, and remembered how sick Susan had been for that pregnancy. So, though militantly retired from the role of organist, Rose had been willing to come back part time. There was also Zanna Shantz who was adept enough at piano to fill in for church if neither Susan nor Rose could manage it.

Tanny knew that Liz was tough. But as there was still no guarantee that Steve would survive, Tanny was having a hard time imagining how Liz could be bearing up. Liz's older sister had flown up from Florida to support her, allowing Liz to spend more time at the hospital with Stephen in any case.

If Stephen rallied and recovered well, he might be able to resume his duties by early June. But things were not going particularly well for him so far. The word was that if Stephen was facing a prolonged recovery, the leadership in Ben Kirk would pull someone out of retirement to come fill the post while he recuperated. The responsibility of serving as main pastor was too much to put on the brand-new Jonathan Haley.

Meanwhile, at Cedar Haven, the "haven" part was not in evidence. The demolition and construction noise—the tramping in and out of workers day in and day out—was getting very tiring. The dust and debris, despite the hanging tarps, got into everything. When Tanny wasn't out organizing or taking a shift at Oliver's, she often took herself out to the barn apartment simply to enjoy the quiet as well as to work on the finishing. But the heating out in the apartment came from the one kerosene heater, and April in Bracebridge could be very chilly. There wasn't even hot water out there yet, and there were tarps draped on most of the furniture which had to be pushed aside if she wanted to sit. There was also no WIFI out there yet, and Tanny's cell signal was spotty. So, she'd often return to the main house to warm up and reconnect.

Jeff brought her home a pair of sound-cancelling headphones after one of his shifts. They helped a great deal in drowning out the noise, and Tanny could now curl up on the couch by the fire to work or read without suffering from the constant din. There were only the drafts from the front door opening and closing as the workers carried materials in and out.

Tanny considered returning to Cliffside temporarily to help Susan and Liz. She talked the idea over with Jeff who was in full support. Tanny was undecided. She could remain in Bracebridge, keeping her shifts at Oliver's (there were not many organizing gigs yet) or go stay at Kate's in relative clean and quiet. But how much could she do to help? She could do laundry and cleaning and cooking. She could watch the twins when they were not in school. But Kate and many of the other women were getting those things done for Liz as well as for Susan.

At Susan's advice, she stayed in Bracebridge, and she worked on advertising her organizing. For now, she was calling her business "Tidy with Tanny," but she was looking for something with a little more pizzazz.

Jeff and Tanny had taken the strongbox to a locksmith in town who had succeeded in opening it. Inside were many black and white photos of Tanny's Bracebridge ancestors, with some in front of the original cabin before it had burnt down. While Tanny was happy to find these photos, she had no idea why they had been in a locked box. And why would Britt lead her to this box in a dream?

At loose ends one day, Tanny sat down on the sofa with her headphones on and opened the box again. She decided to lay out all the pictures on the coffee table, grouping them by similar faces. There were a bunch of Great Grandpa Bender and his Inquist wife. In some, he was wearing a big, furry hat and animal-skin coat, probably because he was one of the first settlers in the area and had to keep warm with what was available.

But there were other pictures of Great Grandpa in a nice suit with his pretty wife next to him. This Inquist woman had a sweet and likable face. What was her name again? Tanny looked on the backs until she found the names David and "Ingrida". Ingrida sounded right. But something niggled at her consciousness. She thought the founding Bender had been named something else, not David.

Tanny separated the fancy-dressed pictures from the more pioneer looking ones. The fancier ones were certainly sharper and of better quality. Had the couple become more successful and been able to afford better clothes and a better photographer?

Tanny looked more closely at the grainier photos. There weren't many of them. Two were of her great grandpa in front of the cabin. One was of a sour-faced young woman in a bridal gown. On the back it said, "Birgitta Inquist." *Birgitta?* Tanny remembered hearing that name too but was confused. Was her great grandma called Ingrida or Birgitta? The names were so similar. Perhaps the labeler had gotten mixed up about her name?

Tanny flipped over one of the images of the coon-skin capped ancestor, and the back said, "Samuel David Bender, 1875." *Samuel* sounded right. Tanny was sure that Samuel was the name of the original settler to that area in the Bender clan. Did he decide to be called David later, for some reason?

Tanny picked up another picture. It was Samuel and the sour-faced woman and, slightly off to the side, an indigenous woman. Tanny remembered hearing that Great Grandpa hired a local woman to help Great Grandma. But where was the sweet-faced Ingrida Inquist? And why was the sour-faced Birgitta pictured here instead?

In that same photo were three children, which Tanny assumed were Britt, David Jr. and Uncle Ivan, who died in the war. Though in this picture, two of them looked like girls.

Tanny picked up a studio picture of the sweet-faced "Ingrida" Inquist and her husband with their three children. David's ears stuck out. Ingrida's did not. Here was evidence that the ears were indeed Bender, not Inquist. Bender ears were the ears that the "godson" had. Tanny was certain now that the French godson was Britt's own child—Tanny's *cousin*—a Bender.

In the photo, there stood an obvious young Grandpa David, Great Aunt Britt, and one who must have been Great Uncle Ivan. Ivan had the fair colouring of the Inquists, while David and Britt had the brown-eyed, brown-haired look of the Benders. And look, David and Ivan had the sticking-out ears, though Britt had been spared.

Tanny looked again at the picture by the cabin with Great-Grandpa, the three children, the sour-faced woman and the indigenous woman. On the back was written, *Samuel, Birgitta, Nagamo,* and in front, *David, Serena, Mary* which must be referring to the children.

Now Tanny was very confused. She thought and thought. Was she conflating two generations of Benders? Was there a Samuel Bender married to a Birgitta Inquist, and then a son, David, who married an Ingrida Inquist? *How inbred were her ancestors?*

Tanny looked more closely at the Bender gentleman/gentlemen. Now it seemed obvious that she was looking at a father and son. They were strikingly similar looking, but not identical. That explained the difference between the pioneer-looking photos and the more settled looking photos. The original settler, Samuel, was in front of the cabin. The son, David, had the suit and could afford studio pictures.

Samuel's ears didn't *seem* to stick out (the pictures were grainy and he often wore a hat) while the son's did, as did his sisters' ears. So Tanny had two great ... uh.... Tanny counted on her fingers and finally had to grab a sheet of paper and write down the generations. Tanny's mother was Emily, whose father was David Jr., the brother of Britt. His father was David Sr. who married Ingrida (if Tanny was correct), the mother of David, Ivan, and Britt. And David *senior's* father was the original Bracebridge area settler, Samuel, who married Birgitta Inquist, and had David, Serena, and Mary. That made Serena and Mary (about whom she had *never* heard) her great-*great* aunts.

Tanny wondered what had ever happened to them. There were potentially many more "Bender" cousins through them (not that Tanny needed more cousins).

All of those three children had ears that stuck out. And strangely, they all had brown eyes and dark hair—at least as far as Tanny could tell from the grainy black and white photos. How strange that none of the children had any Inquist colouring.

Tanny looked at Birgitta's ears. Flat and ordinary. The only adult in the picture who had sticking out ears was the First Nations woman named "Nagamo."

Tanny stopped breathing. Was Nagamo the mother of all these children? Did Great-Great Grandfather Samuel have three children who were half indigenous and not Inquist at all? If that was so, what a scandal that would have been! No wonder Birgitta Inquist had such a sour face! (Though it did make David's marriage to an Inquist feel less like inbreeding).

Was this the picture Aunt Britt had wanted her to discover? Were the "Bender" ears not Bender at all but the lineage of this Indigenous ancestor? How did it happen that Great-Great Grandpa Samuel Bender had a wife, yet sired three mixed-race children with "the help"?

Tanny shook her head. Birgitta had (apparently willingly) passed these children off as her own, legitimizing them in a way that would never otherwise have happened in that day and age. Why? Surely, she could have cast the children and their mother off.

Samuel did have dark hair and eyes, just like the children. That gave believability to the children's colouring. David looked a lot like his father. It was the girls that had cheekbones and eyes that hinted at an indigenous bloodline.

Tanny was stunned. What a secret! Did her own mother know? Did any of the Benders know? This meant that every Bender since Samuel had some Indigenous blood. Until only very recently, that information would have been deeply shameful and to be hidden at all costs.

But Tanny felt no shame. In fact, she felt somehow a little more legitimate as a not purely European descendant living on all the indigenous land that had been stolen (whether she should or not). She also felt closer to Jeff, and very curious about Great-Great Grandmother "Nagamo's" story. Where did she come from? How did this arrangement happen? How had she felt about being the "help" and the mother of the children that she couldn't openly acknowledge were hers?

That is, of course, if she was indeed the children's mother, Tanny reflected. She realized that she was leaping to a lot of conclusions.

Tanny wanted to tell Jeff immediately, but Jeff was out doing a woodworking job for a Bracebridge resident. Tanny texted him, *I have something exciting to tell you when you get home.*

Jeff replied, *???*

Tanny reassured him, *No. I am not pregnant,* and added a laughing face.

And so Tanny called her mom. "Mom, do we have any native blood in our Bender ancestry? Where does all our dark colouring come from?"

"Oh, that old fairytale!" her mother laughed. "I never believed that rumour. You are descended from Inquists and Neufeldts, Benders and Raymonds—all good European families. There are plenty of brown-eyed Europeans from which you are descended. I don't know where any Indian blood would have come from anyway. Sorry, to disappoint you, honey."

Tanny felt irritated that her mother assumed she was disappointed. She wasn't. She was just curious about what was true. "So, okay...." Tanny continued, unconvinced by her mother's narrative, "Did both Great Grandpa and Great-Great Grandpa marry Inquists?"

"Where is this coming from?" replied Emily, sounding a bit suspicious. "Is someone feeding you scandalous tales about our family?"

Tanny was struck by her mother's defensive response. What was making her mother nervous that she should become defensive? "Oh, I just found some old pictures, and wondered about the family lines and what our Bender ancestors were like. That's all," reassured Tanny, trying to sound mostly uninterested. "I guess I didn't realize we had double Inquist ancestry."

"Well, you can't pick your ancestors. And if there *had* been a problem from cousins marrying, I'm sure it would have shown up by now in our family. I don't think you need to worry about anything at all." Emily paused and then added, "Your Uncle Paul is the one who cares about that stuff if you want to ask him your questions. He loves the history and the genealogy stuff. I never found it very interesting." Emily's tone implied that all reasonable people would find ancestry information dull.

"Okay mom. Thanks so much. Maybe I'll ask him," Tanny responded, her eyes following workmen wrestling a new window in the front door. The workmen had made a chute from the front bedroom window down to the lawn to send the broken plaster and wood down to the dumpster that way. But all new materials had to come in and up the stairs.

Tanny finished her call with her mother, asking about how the congregation was responding to Stephen's illness. Apparently, a few of the older members were feeling resentment that Stephen hadn't taken better care of himself. Tanny hung up feeling a little horrified at how self-centered some people could be. They didn't like being inconvenienced by Stephen nearly dying!?

Tanny had considered getting out for a walk, but a chilly rain had started to fall. Instead, she brewed herself some tea and tried calling her "uncle" Dr. Paul Bender. Dr Paul was in his seventies and had been a general practitioner in Kitchener until retiring very recently.

Uncle Paul was delighted to hear from Tanny, greeting her in his gentle gravelly voice.

As Tanny began to ask questions, Dr. Paul revealed detail upon ancestral detail, that would have made Emily's curly hair stand up straight.

Forty-Eight

April 13 to April 15

"Great-great grandfather Bender, the one named Samuel, *did* marry an Inquist, but they had no children because...?" Tanny was asking her Uncle Paul.

"I suspect she was what they used to call 'frigid.'," Dr Paul filled in for Tanny. "Today we might assume she had had severe sexual trauma or was simply asexual. But the stories that have trickled down all rumoured that she was happy to have Samuel go elsewhere for sex and was just as happy to raise the consequent children as if they were her own. When she claimed them as her own, people stopped wondering why there were no children from their marriage."

"Of course! What a practical solution." Tanny found herself saying. Now she felt sympathy for Birgitta. And she felt intensely curious about the woman called "Nagamo". "Was Nagamo treated well?" she asked.

"Apparently Birgitta was rather kind to Nagamo. Interestingly, Nagamo means, 'She is singing,'" continued Dr. Paul. "Perhaps that explains the musical talent that runs through the family. She seems to have come from the Deer Clan, but beyond that I haven't found any trace of her."

"Can't you just go by her last name?" asked Tanny.

"That's just it. The original tribal traditions never used the 'first-name, last-name' system that most Europeans use. Natives often had several single names, most given by friends to name a particular quality in them. "Nagamo" was possibly one of these names. She probably picked the name she liked best to offer to Samuel. But to track down a female indigenous from the 1800's using only a single name is no easy feat. And the farther we get away from her time, the less and less likely it will be that anyone might know who she was. We are several generations away already."

Tanny felt sad. If she had relatives in the first nations community, she wanted to know who they were. She really cared about family and kinship. Then she got an idea. "I know, Uncle Paul! What if I got a DNA test? Wouldn't that help me find out something about those roots?"

Uncle Paul chuckled. "It's not quite that easy, Tanny. But I love your enthusiasm. Let's both get tested. I am one-quarter indigenous, and you would be one-eighth—barring anything unusual on your father's side—and that would give us both male and female DNA in the family."

"Does that matter?" Tanny asked.

"It can," answered Paul. "There are a few ways to measure DNA; we can measure mitochondrial DNA—found in both men and women—and Y-DNA—which only the men carry. As you want to look especially through your mother's heritage, who was a Bender, your mitochondrial DNA will work fine. I want to look through my father's Bender DNA, which I can do with the Y-DNA test. If you wanted to look at your paternity, you'd have to get a brother to take the test. But for your Bender line, you can get the information you need from my DNA test."

"Pffff," Tanny snorted. "Another way women must be dependent on men. Yay," she said without enthusiasm. But she was mostly joking.

"I'm sorry," Uncle Paul said.

Tanny laughed. "Oh, don't worry about it. Let's get our tests and see what we find out."

"I have to warn you," said Dr. Paul. "Our DNA can only be matched to indigenous DNA if enough people from Nagamo's family have also gotten tested and given their consent to have their information available to searches."

"Oh." Tanny deflated. "So, we might not find anything."

"We might not. Not yet anyway. But perhaps in the future."

Tanny thought a while. Then she said, "So why don't all the Benders know this? Why did I have to guess and then ask someone besides my mom to find out? This seems pretty important." She had started pacing around the kitchen in Cedar Haven. Every time her eyes landed on the water-view, she felt an easing of her tension. She finally crossed the dining area and came to a stop in front of the big windows that looked out at the water.

Paul Bender said, "You must understand. The whites have traditionally considered the indigenous inferior. So, it would have been dreadfully shameful to believe that one was half or even one quarter indigenous not that long ago."

"Well, I know that Uncle Paul. But surely no one thinks that way anymore."

Paul made a noise of resignation. "Old habits of thinking die hard. I'm not ashamed of the idea at all. I think it is marvelously interesting. But my siblings and cousins would not hear a word of it. Only my first cousin, who left the church and so is completely ignored by most of the family, is keenly interested. She moved to Thunder Bay and made a good career for herself as a folk singer. Have you heard of

Serena Pelletier? She was big in the fifties and sixties. She fully embraced her herit-age and did everything she could to learn about her roots.”

“Wait, Serena Pelletier is a cousin!? Of course I have heard of her. Mom played some of her albums around the house when I was younger. She never mentioned we were related!”

“That is probably because Serena had the look of a first nations woman and spent a lot of time trying to seek status. She married a man with status. But your mom, among many others in the Bender family, are resistant to considering that there is any indigenous blood in the family. It doesn’t matter what evidence I have gathered. They militantly don’t want to know. So, I’ve learned to keep my discov-eries to myself. I have studied and researched our heritage for myself, discovering all sorts of remarkable things, that no one else in the family wants to know. I’m delighted to discover that you find this interesting!”

“I definitely do, Uncle Paul. Next time I’m in town I will try to get over and visit you to talk more about your findings.”

“You could also sign up on the genealogy website I use. Then I could share my research with you, and you could see all of the family tree I have built so far. I have over a thousand people logged, and I’m adding new faces all the time.”

Tanny agreed with enthusiasm. The two of them planned their DNA testing together and signed up. Dr. Paul offered to pay for Tanny’s test. “After all,” he said, “I am as interested in the results as you are.” Tanny got the information about the heritage tracking website and wrote down Uncle Paul’s login name so she could reach out once she had an account. She shivered with excitement.

“Did you know that Aunt Britt was a spy in World War Two?” Tanny asked her uncle. “Did you know she had a son in France that she had to leave behind?”

Tanny could practically hear Paul sit up.

“I suspected about the spy status, but all of that is still classified information. How could you know about it? And a child in France? I find that very hard to be-lieve. I will need to see your evidence of that. Please come visit soon with the docu-ments that lead you to these conclusions. If these things are true, what fantastic work you have done! I want to know your research methods.”

Research methods? Tanny thought. *Stumbling upon pictures and speculating?* She said, “Most of it—well, the child in France bit as well as being descended from Nagamo bit—is based on old photographs. Plus, I ran into a woman in Ben Kirk who knew Britt well during the war, and told me a whole bunch about her status as a spy and her falling in love with a Frenchman. His name was Lucien LaRoche, and he died before they could get married. She had a picture of Britt holding her baby which she gave to me—"

"Fantastic!" rumbled Dr. Paul. "Please come down soon. I must see these pictures."

After discussing the implications of these revelations, Tanny next asked Dr. Paul about Stephen's chances.

"He had a left anterior descending artery blockage, one of the worst kinds of attacks one can have. And Stephen was more overworked than anyone realized. He's lucky to have survived."

"But he is only, what? forty-two? Who has a heart attack at forty-two?"

Paul responded, "There is a history of heart disease in the Shantz family. And it's highly probable that his diet hasn't been top quality, as they would be struggling to raise their six kids on his salary. Liz will have to change the way she cooks for him going forward."

"So, Stephen's pay wasn't enough for them to eat well, so he gets a heart attack? That doesn't seem fair," Tanny complained.

"The ministers are paid fairly well in our denomination, but they are also expected to have lots of kids. I assume Steve and Liz wanted all their kids, but kids do eat into the budget. I also don't think the congregation realizes how hard he works. Pastors can be like mothers—expected to be available at all hours and have no needs themselves. Very few parishioners realize that most pastors work well beyond the standard forty hours a week. And we all know how Stephen loves his coffee. He was probably having all that caffeine to keep going. He's been known to have his "triple-triples," which are almost more cream and sugar than they are coffee. Those can't be good for you."

"Uncle Paul, tell me he's going to make it."

"All I can say is that each day that he survives increases his chances," answered Tanny's uncle. "The stent has done its job. It doesn't look like he will need open-heart surgery, which is a real blessing. Now we just hope his body will heal all the inflammation. That is the biggest barrier now. His body is not happy. All that overwork took much of his resilience away."

"Why didn't we know how hard he was working?"

"I've known for a while, but congregations are funny. They can feel entitled to ever-available, no-needs attention from the pastor. Imply that the pastor isn't available exactly when they need him, and they can get grumpy. They decide he is playing favourites—preferring to help certain parishioners over others. I've seen it happen. It does not go well."

Tanny thought about that. Had she ever felt like the pastor should be available the instant she needed him? She had to admit that she probably had. Maybe the pastor could have the occasional cold, but that was about it. And he still had to preach. Pastors couldn't take a Sunday off. Had she ever known a pastor be unable to preach due to illness? She couldn't think of a single time. So, they must have preached with fevers and nausea and who knows what else? What kind of system was that? She now felt very protective of all pastors' health. She said, "How dare the congregations be so self-centered! In this case, the workload could literally have killed their pastor!"

"You definitely have the Bender passion," chuckled Uncle Paul.

"Yay, the infamous Bender passion, otherwise known as mouthy and opinionated—not a popular quality in a woman," Tanny grumped.

"Don't you change one bit, Tanny," championed her Uncle Paul. "I don't think anything in this church would change if it wasn't for the mouthy, opinionated women pushing us to modernize. Women still wouldn't be allowed to vote or sit on the councils if it hadn't been for Britt's and others' insistence," he concluded.

Tanny felt remarkably seen and heartened. She felt a new wave of respect and love for this great uncle. She was really looking forward to further collaborations with him.

"Hey, Uncle Paul, do you know anything about a potential indigenous claim to Cedar Haven? I just found something in Britt's journals that mentioned something about that."

"You have Britt's journals!? Heaven's, girl, please may I see them? Might you loan them to me for a while? I'd love to read them."

"Of course, Uncle Paul! I'll set them with my suitcases, so I remember. It will be great to discuss them with you!"

"I have so many questions...."

"I will bring the letters between Britt and her friend from when they were both spies too."

"Child, you have made my day, my month, my *year*," enthused the senior doctor.

Tanny paced around the dining room table thinking about when she might return to Cliffside. Herman was having increasing problems. Both Jeff and the Bracebridge mechanic said she really should not try that trip in him anymore. So Tanny only used him to get around locally. She didn't feel great about taking Jeff's truck and making him have to use Herman while she was gone. She really needed a new car, but she didn't think she made enough consistent income to manage car payments.

Her wealthy client had booked her for many hours in the next several weeks, but after that she was having guests, and would not be using Tanny's service for almost two months. Tanny didn't like the idea of asking Jeff for help with the payments if her income wouldn't cover them consistently. But she might have to swallow her pride.

Huh. Was Stephen's health a matter of pride to him? Had he refused to ask for help until it was too late? She could relate to the unwillingness to ask for help.

Later that day Tanny told Jeff about the possible need for financial support if she got a replacement for Herman. Jeff encouraged her to look into a new car right away. He had been worried about her breaking down far from help. So together they went out hunting. They landed on a two-year-old Ford Fusion. She was royal blue, and Tanny loved her immediately.

"There's no way I'm going to lose Annie in a snowdrift," Tanny exclaimed with delight as they walked toward her new vehicle. "She is such a bright blue!"

"Annie?" asked Jeff, his arm around Tanny's waist.

"That's her name," declared Tanny.

"How do you know?"

"It just is," said the happy new owner.

Forty-Nine

April 16 to April 18

Jeff came home from his therapist determined to talk to Tanny about his triggers, and to reassure her he was aware and working on them.

Tanny greeted him at the door with Mack, both delighted to see him. Mack needed a walk and Tanny had lots of stories about her organizing gig that day. There was dinner and dishes, but eventually Jeff was able to get his lovely fiancée sitting quietly with him by the fire.

Jeff took Tanny's shapely hands in his and looked into her eyes. He was filled with dread, and everything in him wanted to do *anything but* discuss his defence mechanisms with Tanny.

He blew out his breath and lifted his head. "My therapist has been encouraging me to talk to you about my ... my triggers, and my tendency to withdraw into myself when I'm triggered."

Tanny's gaze remained steady and curious. Her hands were warm.

Jeff looked down at their joined hands. "You see, apparently, I have some abandonment issues, and my way to cope with feeling abandoned is to rely only on myself. The therapist called it an 'attachment disorder.'" Jeff looked into those warm hazel eyes again. Tanny looked tender. She was listening.

"I, uh.... So, this means that when I get triggered by reminders of abandonment, I withdraw into myself. I can come across as cold and short-tempered and ... like I need no one. I can push away those I love." Jeff's eyes begged Tanny to understand.

Tanny shrugged one shoulder and tipped her head. "But I've never seen these behaviours, Jeff. I'm not sure what you are telling me."

Jeff's heart started racing. *What if I lose her?* He took a fortifying breath. He was committed.

"Tanny, I love you more than anything in the world. The last thing I want to do is hurt you or drive you away. And ... and I'm not asking for a free pass on these behaviours if they show up. It's just that my therapist said it would deepen the understanding and trust between us if I'm honest with you."

Tanny looked puzzled and a little worried. "Are you saying you could hurt me? Are you saying you could resort to physical violence? I find that so hard to believe—"

"No," Jeff reassured her. "No. Not physical violence. I think it would come across as emotional abandonment. I wouldn't mean it to! It's just that when I'm triggered, I withdraw and feel like I can't trust anyone. I wall myself up and have all my defences on high alert against any potential threat. I defend *against intimacy,* because that feels safer." Jeff looked earnestly into Tanny's eyes, "But I don't mean to be that way. And the defensive feelings will pass. The person I want to be is *not* a fortress against the world. The person I want to be is your loving husband, and a participating and positive member of the community."

It was Tanny's turn to look down at their joined hands. She said, "So, if or when you get triggered, your behaviour could seem cold and defensive, but I need to trust that it's a trauma response, and that the Jeff I know will show back up when the trauma recedes. Did I get that right?"

Jeff was amazed at Tanny's fearlessness. "That's essentially what I need to warn you about: That you could feel rejected when what's really going on is from my childhood trauma. The last thing I want to do is push you away, even though it looks like I'm pushing you away." Jeff's voice cracked. "I'm sorry. I wish I wasn't so damaged."

"But Jeff, I'm damaged too! I have no doubt I have bad habits and defence mechanisms, and I don't even know what they are. Do *you* still love *me?*"

"Of course I do!"

"So please don't doubt my love for you." Tanny reached out and kissed his cheek. "I guess it will happen that we *do* doubt each other's love sometimes; I expect that that is part of the fabric of marriage. But as long as we're honest with each other and communicate, as long as we can apologize and make amends, and as long as we keep holding onto the foundation of our love, I think we can make it through anything."

Jeff embraced Tanny then, his heart beating out his love and wonder at this marvelous woman's courage. He felt he was the luckiest man alive.

Tanny felt very tender toward this precious man. She moved her hands slowly through his lengthening blond hair, gazing at his downcast eyes. She kissed his brow, then his stubbly cheek, then greeted his welcoming mouth with open warmth.

They moved their wordless communication upstairs and eventually fell asleep wrapped in each other's arms.

On Saturday evening, Jeff and Tanny learned that all the drains in the house and barn would be blocked for up to forty-eight hours starting Monday, while the new septic system installation was hooked up and tested. Jeff could stay at the Paramedic station or with Jacob and Eileen. But Tanny decided to head down to Cliffside for the duration, to visit her great-uncle Paul and to help Liz and Susan as much as possible. She moved her shift at Oliver's as well as her Tuesday organizing gig to later in the week to do so. Kate was happy to host her again, and Tanny would just have to figure out some way to explain to Emily why she didn't stay in her childhood home.

Before she left, Jeff took Tanny for a walk down by the water at the edge of Cedar Haven's property. It was a bit chilly, but not too bad for April in Brace-bridge. They watched the sun begin to set beyond the low hills on the western side of the lake. Jeff stopped Tanny and got on one knee, holding up a small box, opened to face her.

"Tanny, will you accept this ring as a sign of my promise to you?" he asked.

"Oh!" Tanny clasped her hands by her cheek and bent to look. Nestled in the velvety lining was a delicately woven ring. It had a deep blue stone in the middle with two smaller pink stones on either side. The band looked a bit like silvery white snakes or vines wrapping together, holding the three stones in their embrace.

Jeff rose to place the ring on Tanny's finger.

"The stones come from the earth around here. They are part of the Anishin-aabe traditional lands. The blue one is sodalite, which represents self-expression, truth, and communication – qualities that make me think of you." He slid the ring on Tanny's finger. "The pink stones are rose quartz. Rose quartz represents unconditional love, compassion, and healing – qualities which I hope to bring to our relationship." He held her hand so they could both look at the ring. "The metal is titanium, which is known for its strength and resistance to corrosion – it represents our relationship, holding what is best of us united."

Tanny had tears in her eyes. She had imagined an inexpensive little solitaire with a tiny diamond. She would have been happy with that. But Jeff had gone out and had this ring custom-made, carefully choosing each element for its meaning. She loved it instantly. It was one-of-a-kind, like their relationship.

Tanny threw her arms around Jeff's shoulders, saying, "I love it. I LOVE it! Thank you!"

After a big kiss, she dropped back down, gazing at the ring. Her heart was full. "Thank you, Jeff. I think my answer is still 'yes'." Tanny dimpled before she was folded into Jeff's embrace.

As Tanny drove south in snazzy new Annie she reflected on a conversation she had had with Bet Giddings when Bet hired her to help organize her attic.

In response to Tanny's complaints about the marriage-focused, singles-are-inconvenient attitudes in the church, Bet had said with affection, "You are definitely Britt's namesake. Britt loved that church with her whole heart; she too felt increasingly disillusioned with it through the years."

Bet shook her head and sighed. "Between you and me, I think Britt was being a bit controlling in her efforts to steer that congregation. She told me about her plan of puzzles and tasks. But I kept thinking, 'you can lead horses to water, but honestly, if they feel controlled or manipulated, they will refuse to drink.' Bet gazed at Tanny thoughtfully and shrugged. "I mean, horses may or may not drink for whatever reason. But *people* do not like being managed. I suggested she drop her plan to lead the Cliffside horses to drink, but she was determined."

"Huh," Tanny had said. "It never occurred to me that Aunt Britt was being controlling. I kind of thought her plan was brilliant; like, maybe *now* some of the people would wake up and start behaving better."

"But if *you* got a command from someone that implied you weren't good enough, and that you needed to shape up in some incomprehensible way to meet with their approval, wouldn't you balk?"

Tanny had been taken aback. That was much of her life with her mother. But she said, "But the tasks aren't incomprehensible. They are pretty simple."

"Yes, but, the whole thing implies a state of wrong-being, which could be insulting. Britt had an agenda about the congregation being different than it was. The very nature of her message was bound to set people's teeth on edge."

"But she was *right*!" exclaimed Tanny. "She was dead-on correct about the congregation being shallow and gossipy and judgmental! I was grateful she tried to do something about it."

"Because you agreed with her. What if you didn't? What if the person who created the puzzles and tasks thought the congregation should be more conservative? What if the tasks invited a more conservative outlook and a more insular mindset? How would you feel about following the instructions then?"

Tanny just felt grumpy.

"Oh, dear! I'm sorry I said anything, Tanny. Britt was an outstanding human being. I loved her with my whole heart. This is just my musings on her dynamic with that church. I don't know anything really."

Tanny was both mollified and humbled. Bet's observations had carried a lot more weight than she wanted to admit. It had not occurred to her that Britt might have been out of step in leaving such conditions in her will regarding the Cliffside congregation.

It was Tanny's own relationship with her mother that opened her eyes to how some congregation members might feel in response to Britt's complex conditions in the will. Britt was essentially holding the congregation ransom, forcing them to comply if they wanted to continue as a congregation in their home rather than lose nearly everything.

She drove in silence for many kilometres, chewing on these thoughts.

Aside from these thoughts, Tanny was looking forward to every aspect of this trip to Cliffside *except* for having to navigate her mother's expectations. She reflected that Cedar Haven was truly a haven for her, where she felt unconditionally loved and supported. As the pines and rocks flowed past her windows, she realized with a pinch in her stomach that her childhood home had never been a "haven." She had assumed it was because it had been the only reality that she had known. But as she reflected on it now, she noticed that she had often felt more comfortable, appreciated, and loved when she had hung out with Susan in Aunt Kate and Uncle Noah's house, or with Amy Hart and her sisters at their house. At home she had felt ... she had felt ... always under a critical eye.

These reflections made her wonder how many other children grew up in homes that felt anxious or critical and judgmental. She was realizing first-hand how hard that could be on one's sense of ease in the world. Tanny had lived in the constant sense that others were judging her, because it wasn't just in her home where she felt watched and judged. It had been at school and at church too. Many of the adults still lived in an appearance-based reality, where one's body size and shape were open for judgment as well as one's words, behaviours, and choices. It was a culture of perfection. Everyone was expected to be perfect already, not on a path of constant growth.

Tanny believed that Stephen Shantz had worked hard to replace the "look happy and perfect on the outside" culture with a "we're all on a path of growth and improvement" culture. The perfectionist outlook shamed and blamed mistakes (or swept them DEEP under the rug) while the "work in progress" outlook welcomed admitting mistakes, seeking health and growth as part of the work.

But so many of the older generation had been so steeped in the "admit no weakness or fault" culture that they seemed incapable of comprehending another way of viewing spiritual community. They continued to assume they were perfect. To maintain that illusion, they judged everyone else. There was no concept of walking companionably together towards spiritual growth in full self-understanding.

And so long as there was this large cohort of judging and controlling members, the church culture would have this toxic undercurrent that could be vicious in its gossip and passive-aggressive comments. She hated that she saw her home congregation this way! She hated that she viewed her mother this way. She loved her mother *but....*

Tanny had learned to be braced for criticism both overt and implied. She had become hyper-sensitive to hidden criticism thanks to her upbringing. Eventually Jenny had accused her of finding criticism where there was none, making Tanny more self-aware of the attitudes she was bringing to her relationships. *I tend to find criticism where there isn't necessarily any.* That insight had led Tanny to realize that she needed to disconnect completely from "what other people think."

Stephen Shantz had said to her once, "What other people think is none of our business." This idea was very confusing at first, because it seemed to Tanny that what other people thought was *everything*. But over time, as she learned what "codependence" was, she began to understand how important it is to know what *oneself* thinks *first*. She learned to disconnect somewhat from the gossip, judgment and criticism that could be rampant in the church community. She learned that *only some* church members operated by means of criticism and judgment and that those were not the people she wanted to pay attention to.

That's when Tanny began to notice all of the kind and loving church members. They had always been there, but they had not been yanking on her fear of criticism and her need to be liked. Once Tanny stopped listening to the judgmental members, she began to see the world in a kinder way. She began to be kinder to herself. She worked on treating herself the way she wanted to be treated. Tanny even began to realize how often the judgmental members were telegraphing their own fears and insecurities by being so gossipy. She both felt sorry for them and gave them a wide berth.

Tanny knew she covered up her childhood insecurity with bubbly, almost driven energy. She was passionately outraged whenever women were being demeaned or stereotyped. She loved the Phryne Fisher murder mystery books from Australia that portrayed an empowered, fierce, talented, and militantly independent woman. Phryne was also (conveniently) financially self-sufficient, which Tanny was not. Tanny would love to be a fierce protector of women's rights and to fight injustice too, to wear stylish clothes and never worry about expense. But that was not her reality. She wondered how many other financially strapped women couldn't be true to themselves or follow their dreams just because they had to work so hard simply to support themselves?

At least I have Jeff, and I have this incredibly fulfilling organizing work, even if it doesn't come close to a living wage yet.

Tanny sighed. She was fully aware that Jeff was not the only damaged one in the relationship. She resolved that as soon as she was making enough money, she would find herself a therapist too.

Meanwhile, she looked forward to learning a lot more about her Bender ancestors. Before she had left, Tanny had signed up for a free account on the genealogy website that Uncle Paul had recommended. She had linked to his account, and had been amazed to watch the people begin to populate her previously empty family tree. There was so much to look at! She had brought a whole packet of documents and photographs for her uncle to peruse. She was pretty sure that the conclusions she had drawn about her ancestors based on those documents would help them build even more facts into their joint database.

Fifty

April 18

Tanny pulled into Kate's driveway around one pm. She was expected for lunch at her mum's house, so she greeted Kate, lugged her bags into the guest room, and started the walk over to her parent's house. After the long drive, it felt good to stretch her legs.

Jenny and Will greeted her when Tanny arrived, Will echoing his mother's greeting.

After the niceties Jenny said, carrying Will toward the kitchen, "I just got the results of Will's assessment. He's got P.D.D.N.O.S."

"He's got P.D what?" Tanny asked, stopping in her tracks.

Jenny sighed and faced her sister. "Pervasive Developmental Disorder, Not Otherwise Specified."

Tanny said, "'Not otherwise specified'? "So ... what? "He's developmentally different but that's all we can say'?" Tanny reached her arms for Will who came to her easily. "That means you are smart and magical and adorable," she said to her red-headed nephew. Will rubbed Tanny's back as he loved to do. It seemed to be a pleasing tactile experience for him. His pacifier bobbed and his eyes looked off to the side.

"He actively avoids eye contact now," Jenny said. "The naturopath said to take him off all wheat and dairy." Jenny turned and walked into the kitchen.

Emily met them there having just gotten off the phone. "Hello sweetheart! Am I glad to see you! I'm hungry. I hope the trip went well."

Jenny grabbed Tanny's left hand having just noticed the ring. "Is this your engagement ring?" she asked with excitement.

"Yeah. It is!"

Both women gazed at it with delight.

"Jeff had it custom-made. Each element represents aspects of our relationship," Tanny explained.

Emily looked and said, "How ... unique!" She said, "Is that white gold? No diamonds?"

Tanny faced her mom. "It *is* unique. It is one-of-a-kind. It represents strength and durability, unconditional love, and communication, among other things."

"Represents?" asked Emily, looking with greater interest. "Did Jeff use correspondences to design your ring?" Emily was referring to a Swedenborgian teaching about the deep spiritual meanings of things.

Tanny felt despairing of her mom's need to make everything "Swedenborgian." Thinking quickly, Tanny decided that the world's ancient ideas that animals, rocks, and trees, have spiritual meanings *counted* as Swedenborgian correspondences, just to stop the awkward discussion.

"Yes mom. He used correspondences." *Who could say that the ancient beliefs weren't the same thing as "correspondences?"*

Over lunch they discussed Will being placed on a waiting list for a speech-language pathologist. They discussed Steve's survival and very slow progress.

"They are pulling someone out of retirement to come hold down the fort as Steve recovers. He arrives next week with his wife and will stay as long as needed," said Emily.

"Do you know who it is?" Tanny asked, wondering if it was someone she knew.

"Jeremiah Flint," replied Emily. Her voice sounded less than delighted.

"Oh no!" blurted Tanny before she could help herself.

"How do you know him?" Jenny asked Tanny. Jenny had never heard of the man.

"Mmm, I met his wife. I overheard her conversation with my client. Let's just say the Flints are waaaay over to the right of Steve and Jonathan."

"He's definitely old school," added Emily.

Jenny put her fork down. Will was down for his nap having eaten before Tanny arrived. "Wait, didn't Barbara's cousin marry a Flint?" she said.

Emily dabbed at her mouth with a napkin. "Yes. Dwight Millwood, Barbara's first cousin, married Jeremiah Flint's niece."

"We can always count on you to make the connections, mom," admired Tanny. "So, am I related to this Jeremiah Flint?"

"You do NOT call him 'Jeremiah'!" scolded Emily. "He is *Reverend* Flint to you."

"Yes, mom," said Tanny, feigning humility. She and Jenny shared a grin.

Emily was drawing with her hand in the air, thinking. "Let's see.... It's through the Starkeys. Your grandfather Smith was a Starkey, and Jeremiah's mother was a Starkey...." Emily twisted her mouth and squinted, still waving her hands, drawing. The common ancestor is ... Moses? Huh...." After some more stepping her fingers up and down in the air her face resolved.

"Yes. You are Reverend Flint's third cousin," Emily declared. "You are," Emily clarified, pointing at Tanny. "You are not. You're a Hill," she said to Jenny.

"But he's so old!" Tanny objected. "Are you sure he's not 'removed' a generation or two?"

"Nope," Emily assured her. "The generations can get offset through the years. If siblings are fifteen years apart and one of you is descended from the oldest and the other is descended from the youngest—"

"I'm going to have to get Uncle Paul to show me that on the genealogy program when I get there before I believe it." Tanny felt unhappy to be related to the man she had heard described in Ben Kirk. She hoped with all her might he wasn't as bad as he had sounded.

Dr. Paul lived across the street from Kate in the in-law suite at Brains' and Meghan's house. The house had been Paul's and his wife's. But Paul and Rachel swapped who was in the house and who in the apartment when Brains' family had grown beyond two children. When Rachel had died abruptly of a blood clot, it seemed to be good for everyone to have grandpa so close to his family as they grieved the loss of their mother, grandmother, and his wife. It had been over ten years since Rachel's loss. Dr. Paul seemed very content to have his son's family just the other side of a door.

Tanny was reflecting on all of this as she climbed the stairs up the bank to Paul's separate entrance. He let her into the cozy and messy living room.

"Hello, hello!" greeted the grizzled older man, backing away to let Tanny in.

Tanny hugged her "uncle" (he was some sort of cousin, some level of remove) greeting him in return. She shrugged off her jacket and handed him the packet she brought. "Here you go! Letters, photos, diaries—it's all there."

Paul's face lit up. He led Tanny over to a table where there was a large computer and lots of papers.

While he perused the many photos and letters, Tanny scrolled through his genealogy program. Tanny was excited to see that photos could be added to individuals' electronic files, and looked forward to adding an array of family faces along with the names.

As the afternoon passed, Tanny showed Dr. Paul the photos that had led her to conclude that Nagamo was the actual ancestor, and that the child in France was Britt's son, not just a godchild. Comparing the faces and looking particularly at the ears and brown eyes, Paul was inclined to agree with her. Then the letters between Grace and Britt during the war cemented the status of the young French child as Britt's son.

"Have you reached out to the family in France?" Paul asked.

"Well, no," Tanny responded. "I don't know if the child, whose name is Lucien Boucher, was ever told about his actual parentage. It doesn't feel right to just barge into his world announcing that his parents aren't his parents."

"I see your point," mused the bearded, kindly man. "But what if he *does* know, but assumes *we* don't want to be shocked by discovering this maiden aunt had been a mother?" He thought, tapping a pencil against the side of his hand. He said, "I bet there is a way to reach out to them without tipping our hand. I could open a friendly dialogue and test the waters...."

Tanny watched her relative with eager eyes. "I mean, that would be so amazing to be in touch with them. Maybe he'd like to come visit?"

"Remember that he is in his upper fifties by now. But maybe one of his children might like to come visit ... assuming they even want to know we are related."

"Oh yeah," Tanny acknowledged. "Who knows? But maybe someone is happy to acknowledge the relationship and would be as eager to meet us as we are to meet them? I guess we just wait and see."

Dr. Paul's eyes twinkled. "Well, I will reach out to them. And meanwhile I am looking forward to digging deeply into these journals and letters and getting copies of everything." He scratched his chin. "How long may I hold onto these things?"

Tanny said, "I would say 'forever' but I don't think it is up to me. You may keep them long enough to get copies of them all."

"Great. I promise to get on it right away," assured the sprightly older gentleman.

The two of them then arranged their DNA tests and were excited to anticipate their results. It would be many weeks before they found out anything, but Tanny was excited to have that process underway.

Tanny left Dr. Paul's place after a quick hello to Meghan, Brains, and kids on the other side of the door. They congratulated her on her engagement and Meghan described the ring as "really, really cool."

Tanny next had dinner with Susan and Jon, who ordered takeout, as they were both too tired to cook. Tanny picked it up for them and helped pay. She felt guilty at inviting herself over when they were so busy, but she also knew it was the only way to get to see them. Both Jon and Sue were looking careworn, but there was still a glossy shine of deep love polishing every aspect of their day-to-day.

Tanny thought the twins grew more each time she saw them. Though the adults couldn't discuss any of the scary and challenging things going on in the congregation in front of the girls, they managed some communication in code. The rest of the time they discussed Tanny's genealogical findings, the ongoing upgrades at Cedar Haven, and they shared joy over Tanny's engagement. The little family were all intrigued by Tanny's unusual ring. Both girls declared that they wanted rings just like hers when they got engaged, and Jon was impressed by Jeff's thoughtfulness and ingenuity.

Susan gave Tanny a huge hug and was incredibly happy that Tanny had found such a wonderful partner. "I really, really like Jeff!" Sue said. "He just *feels* right. I don't know how to explain it. I only hate the idea of losing you to Bracebridge. I will just have to get better at long phone calls."

"Facetime, baby!" Tanny agreed. "We'll find a way to stay in touch."

Tanny committed to cleaning house for Jon and Sue the next afternoon.

She would also be helping Liz in the morning, no matter what she needed. Tanny hoped she would get to go see Stephen in the hospital but knew that he might not be up to visitors. Also, Tanny visiting Stephen might not be the most helpful thing for Liz. She was expecting she would be cleaning or babysitting or doing laundry. Barb Millwood was going to be meeting her there, with Barb focusing on organizing the toys, the kids' rooms, the linen closet, and anything else that would simplify life for the Shantz family. Tanny secretly hoped she would get to work near or with Barb to keep learning organizing tips.

As Tanny was saying goodbye Susan said, "And tomorrow night is the big Pastor's council meeting when they were *supposed to* be discussing whether they kept separate worship services for the traditional group and the contemporary worshippers, or to combine the services into one, accommodating everyone and getting us worshipping together again."

"Oh yeah," Tanny remembered.

Jon said, "The council is still trying to decide if we go ahead with the discussion or table it, considering everything that has happened—the changes to the morale because of Britt's will as well as Stephen's heart attack. I mean, I have insisted on one service on Sundays anyway, because I'm not up to producing two services every Sunday. I am making the service a little of each style, and people can like it or lump it. It's just what has to be right now."

"Wow. I wish you all the best with that," empathized Tanny. "I guess I wish all the bickering and infighting would take a back seat because of the crises. But maybe not."

Jon replied, "The complaining has died down somewhat. The joint service seems to be moot now that there is no other choice. Of course, there are still a few members that won't come to church if I'm on the chancel."

"I can't believe that!" complained Tanny. "Imagine being that petty. I don't get it."

Right before Tanny left, Susan pulled her aside. Sue said, "I didn't want to say this in front of the twins, but we had our first ultrasound yesterday."

Tanny was suddenly on alert. "Is everything okay?"

Susan's sigh expressed resignation. "There is no doubt. We are having twins."

Tanny hopped from foot to foot, grinning broadly. "I predicted that, didn't I? The not-actually-Virgin-Birth, will be twins—a boy and a girl!?" She then calmed right down, composing her face. "I'm sorry. Is this terrible news for you? I will find a way to help you when they come."

Susan was smiling at Tanny's enthusiastic comment and then sudden sober question.

"That will be shortly after you are married, if the pregnancy goes full term." Observed Susan. "We will find a way to manage. I think Jon will be much more present and helpful than Duncan was able to be. Plus, the girls will be a great help, and my mom. Jon's mom might even come over for a few weeks to help and meet the babies. We aren't telling yet. We are hoping to wait until after the wedding, but if I keep growing at the rate I have been, people will figure it out anyway."

Tanny gave Susan a tight hug. "You can do this, Susan. And I *will* come down and help whenever I possibly can."

Fifty-One

April 19 to June 18

Tanny was heartened by her time cleaning for the Shantz's. Barb was always good company, and Tanny continued to absorb tips for helpful organizing – especially how to help the client find things in their new places if the organizer moved them. She left little notes: "If you are looking for your stash of random screws and nails, I have put them down with the rest of your hardware, sorted into categories." Tanny could not imagine the client missing a random pile of miscellaneous hardware from the back corner of the linen closet, but clients had their own internal logic, and one moved a client's items at one's peril.

Liz was at the hospital with Stephen. She was not around to answer questions, so Tanny and Barb used their best judgment and left notes of encouragement and information as they cleaned.

The word was that Stephen was improving at last. The spectre of death was receding with each passing day, and they were hoping he would be home by May first. He would still need a lot of rest and care, but Liz's hospital commute would be over, and the children would have their father in the home again.

"Imagine," said Barb, pulling a pile of jumbled sheets out of the linen closet to label and fold, "if they were in the States, they'd be facing frightening medical bills along with everything else. I certainly don't miss American health care."

"Not that it's that great here since the conservatives took charge of Ontario, but it is still so much better than what I hear about the U.S." Tanny agreed.

"Liz has been taking cooking classes at the hospital, learning how to change her cooking toward greater heart-health. She looks so tired all the time. I simply can't imagine how hard this has been on her and the kids. A bunch of us have lined up to bring heart-healthy meals after Steve comes home."

Tanny threw her arms around Barb's shoulders from behind and squeezed. "They are so lucky to have all this support. I *wish* I could do more myself."

Barb grinned and was careful not to drop the towels she had been moving. "It's a lot for all of us, but I'm impressed with how everyone is rallying to support the Shantz's and the Haley's."

Barb paused and said, in an aside, "Gosh, Jonathan Haley is a handsome devil. How does anyone stand it?"

Tanny laughed. She resumed wiping the baseboards. "I can honestly say I don't notice much anymore. The floor dropped out of reality for a while when he was first around. I could hardly breathe. But now he's just Susan's Jon. It helps that I have Jeff filling my whole heart and imagination. I can't imagine loving or wanting anyone more than I do him."

This time Barb threw her arms around Tanny. "I am so happy for you!"

The two cousins cleaned and chatted until lunch. It was Kate's turn to oversee lunchtime with the Shantz children, and she prepared enough to feed Barb and Tanny. After an active and lively lunch, Tanny gave her aunt and cousin big hugs and headed off to the Haley's to do some more cleaning.

Susan was having a good day. She wasn't suffering nausea, and her energy was better. She was able to clean with Tanny, and they had a great chat as they worked, solving all the world's problems and agreeing that they both knew best what the world needed.

They agreed that the church should just stick with the hybrid services and forgo any in-depth discussion about why and how to understand the other side's point of view. "As if Heinrich would ever do that work. I can't imagine him even trying to see the contemporary side's point of view," snorted Susan, scrubbing with extra ferocity at a stain on the carpet. "He's already called in sick for tonight, saying he adamantly votes for returning to the full conservative service."

Tanny groaned in frustration.

"Jon says—and you can't tell anyone he says this—'There's no problem a church couldn't solve with a few well-placed funerals.'"

Tanny burst into shocked laughter. "He doesn't!"

Sue grinned. "Apparently, it's a joke passed around in clergy circles. He doesn't actually mean it." Sue rinsed the stain and started stamping a folded towel into the carpet to absorb the water.

"It's delightful. Though conservative ministers probably say the very same thing with liberal members in mind," mused Tanny.

"No doubt."

Full of nurturing memories and refilled on time with her friends, Tanny was happy to return to Cedar Haven the next day. Jeff had told her the hook-up of the new septic system had gone without incident and the testing would be done by the time she arrived in the afternoon.

Tanny's heart began to sing as the rocks and pines appeared outside Annie's windows. She was excited to be making Muskoka her home, even with the chillier spring days and later arrival of summer warmth. It was just so beautiful. She felt her nervous system sink into greater rest as she heaved a big sigh.

She started singing, "I'm Coming Home," by Skylar Grey, swaying within the constraints of her seat belt and feeling happy.

April turned to May. Stephen did come home, still weak and on steroids to help his body combat the inflammation. Apparently, he looked appalling, swollen and sweating from the steroids. But he was home.

Rev. Flint and his wife had arrived, and Susan's descriptions of his first few sermons made Tanny's skin crawl. "There was the, 'Oh, you can't get out of bed to come to an hour of church, but you can watch hours of football on a Sunday?' guilt-trip sermon. And then there was the 'Swedenborg says angels don't laugh, so when you are laughing, you should ask yourself why,' guilt-trip sermon," described Susan. "Honestly. What is he thinking? Oh, and he picks the worst hymns! They are all about sin and shame and 'mortal weakness.' Jon has taken to playing funereal music at the interlude to accompany the overall feeling in the church since Rev. Flint arrived. It's his quiet rebellion and commentary on the change of tone. Flint seems oblivious to Jon's choices. Then sometimes, Jon will play something wildly optimistic, like Widor's Toccata, just because he has to counter all the doom and gloom. And I have had to do damage control with the girls on the way home from church just because Flint's children's message was so toxic. Finally, I started taking the girls out to Sunday school *before* the children's talk."

Tanny couldn't imagine how hard it must be on the more liberal members to have the church taken over by such a hard-nosed conservative. Maybe it would make them that much more grateful when Stephen was finally back? Steve himself must be suffering to know what sort of messaging was inundating his congregation in his absence.

"I bet Heinrich is happy," Tanny said.

"Oh, he is delighted. Jeremiah Flint is his new favourite person. They have the Flints over for cocktails and a meal nearly every Sunday after church. He must share with the Kaufmanns and Husseys though. They all want time with their new commander-in-chief. How can we be one congregation and be so divided in our attitudes?" Susan complained. "Jon preaches every fourth Sunday. The church was full on his Sunday except for the conservatives. Jon is sticking to half-contemporary and half-formal services. General Jeremiah insists on full old-school conservative services. So much for Stephen's effort to unite the congregation in choosing their worship style. The pastor's council opted not even to do the exercise, as it seemed pointless."

Tanny's calls with her mom saw her mother expressing more worry and control over Tanny's living in the same house as Jeff. It was because of General Flint's influence, she suspected. It made her feel sick to her stomach whenever her mother started again with religious worry. Emily had gone so far as to recruit Eileen and Jacob to her cause. Fortunately, Jeff's foster parents weren't interested in controlling the lovers anymore. They dutifully reported Emily's concerns but didn't add any pressure themselves. Tanny was deeply grateful for this. Tanny suspected that Jacob and Eileen didn't want to add any stress or conflict in their otherwise adult and respectful relationship with each other. Their lives were woven together through family and Cedar Haven stewardship. They saw each other often, and Tanny was pleased with the peaceful dynamic into which they had settled.

In mid-May Susan and Jon announced publicly that she was carrying twins again. Tanny again promised unwavering support, imagining herself coming for long visits to help when the twins came. Susan took Tanny's promises with the fistful of salt required. Tanny would be newly married and living three hours away. Sue said she was reconciled to the fact of having another set of twins.

The work at Cedar Haven progressed. Once all the new windows were in, the cost of heating improved. The demolition for stage two was done as well, so the construction dust was from cutting drywall and sanding plaster, rather than breaking down ancient, filthy walls. The new bathroom and laundry room were being framed in. Eventually a door would need to be knocked through to the existing bathroom at the top of the stairs for the use of the bedroom Tanny had been using. Jeff's room, Britt's former room, would have a new bathroom added between itself and the other south bedroom in the next stage of construction.

Meanwhile, the apartment neared completion, and the lovers moved out there. Tanny missed the generous spaces in Cedar Haven, but the weeks of construction had firmly convinced her that she no longer wanted to live in any house under construction. Once the current stage of construction was done, the next stage—renovating the south bedrooms and adding their bathrooms—would commence. Then finally, two bedrooms with dormers and a joint bathroom would be put in the attic. At least that gave Tanny lots of time to catalogue the possessions up there, curating and re-homing them in preparation for the renovation. They were looking at up to a year before the attic space was even started.

Spring advanced with every week, and Tanny had to adapt to black-fly season. Jeff wasn't bothered much by it, having lived his entire life in Muskoka. Tanny learned to hate the nasty insects, even buying herself a hat with netting so she could still take walks outside over those several weeks. She got many nasty bites about her head and neck before she purchased the hat. The screens in their barn apartment were new and solid, allowing them to welcome the fresh breezes despite the flying devils.

Tanny felt like a newlywed with Jeff in their barn apartment. It was gracious and quite charming. It took up about a third of the south end of the barn, with big windows letting in lots of light, especially into the basement portion of the barn. It had a lovely view of the woods and the water, sitting higher up the hill than the main house. The entrance, kitchen, dining, and laundry were on the walk-out basement level, with the charm of thick stone walls adding to the cozy feeling. The main level had a living area and bathroom, with the stairs to the loft bedroom tucked under the vaulted roof. It got plenty of sunlight and Tanny began to fill it with plants, too.

Tanny's DNA test arrived. She prepared it and put it in the mail to await the results. The instructions said it could be up to three months before the results were ready, which meant not until the end of July. Oh! How she wished the results would come sooner!

Jeff and Tanny were planning an autumn-themed wedding, set for October second. If her suspicions were correct about the Benders carrying some indigenous blood, Tanny especially wanted to show respect to what would be a part of both their heritages. They began researching modern wedding traditions being used in the Anishinabek community, not wanting so much to copy or mimic, but to incorporate some of the symbolism or traditions in a respectful way. Jeff had relatives with whom he could consult, and he had found a speaker of traditional

Anishinaabemowin who would be willing to say a blessing at the ceremony. Tanny was picturing using autumn leaves in her bouquet, and they would be married on the shores of Lake Muskoka, weather permitting.

Susan gently declined being the matron of honour; she would have her hands full having just passed seven months' gestation. She wanted to enjoy the day with Jon and the girls, with no added responsibility. And so Tanny asked Jenny, who was delighted to be included. Emily and Gilbert would keep tabs on William so Jenny could fully participate.

Tanny began planning her wedding even as Susan and Jon's "wedding celebration" approached. Stephen insisted that he would be able to do the ceremony by then, and it was looking like that would be true. Many of Jon's family members and a few friends were coming from South Africa, and the hunt was on for accommodations for them all. Susan and Jon now had a full bath and two bedrooms framed up in their basement, and they would be housing Jon's parents and one aunt, if they could get the work done in time.

Jon's two brothers were coming, but neither of their wives or children would be coming because of the cost and the school-year disruption for the kids. Jon would have loved to see his nieces and nephews, and for Susan to meet them, but that was not the reality.

The "wedding" was set for June nineteenth, which happened to be an important Swedenborgian holiday, called "New Church Day". Jon and Sue chose red and white for their wedding colours, because these were the colours connected with the holiday, and they found a way to have their wedding right after the church pageant which was about the Woman Clothed with the Sun.

They had considered casting Susan as the woman clothed with the sun with Jon being the angel Michael who rescues her, but they didn't want to confuse the children. "No, the angel Michael didn't actually marry the woman clothed with the sun...." It certainly made Susan notice how much the ancient tale in the Book of Revelation was like a fairy-tale, with a "princess" needing to be rescued from a dragon by a brave "knight", but in this case the woman also had a baby, and it was the *baby* being rescued... Susan pondered these things. As she herself was pregnant, the story felt even more poignant.

The reception would double as the usual June Nineteenth picnic. Weather permitting, they would be outside on the church lawn. Families could bring their food from home, but Jon and Sue would also be providing a spread for everyone, and there would be wedding cake and wine for toasts.

Tanny thought it was a brilliant idea. She and Jeff booked a hotel room because Kate was hosting Jon's brothers. The "wedding" and pageant were in the afternoon, which gave Tanny plenty of time to prepare with Susan. Susan was only just showing, which meant that she wouldn't be looking hugely pregnant in the wedding photos. Tanny was pleased about that. She wasn't sure why. She suspected that she felt protective of Susan, knowing most people's reactions to pregnant-bride pictures. She wished she didn't care. She wished the world wasn't so judgmental.

And just two and a half weeks after Jon and Sue's wedding celebration would come the meeting about the next puzzle and task. It was set for July eighth in the evening. July eighth, after which they would have thirty days to fulfill Britt's demands, or they lose the church, school, lands, and buildings.

Fifty-Two

June 17 to June 21

*B*efore the "wedding" Tanny got to spend a wonderful morning with Jenny, in which they got facials and mani-pedis, and talked in a way they hadn't in a long time. Jenny was taking Will to a speech language pathologist in Waterloo, paid for by the government. But it was also highly recommended that she hire a SLP to come to her home. As money was so very tight with the legal costs involved in the divorce, Jenny admitted that Gilbert and Emily would be helping her cover that cost. The man was said to be outstanding, but he was also very expensive.

"But Will is worth it!" Jenny insisted, almost tearful. "I will find a way!"

Tanny wished out loud that she could help with the cost. She then asked, "How soon will the divorce be final?"

Tanny knew about the nightmare Jenny had been going through in fending off Terry's attempts to contact her and reconcile. Jenny had had to get a restraining order against Terry, not just for herself but for their son. She had found a great lawyer who was helping her navigate the messy universe of divorce law. Tanny's heart ached for her sister. She knew it had been ugly with Jenny's husband. She knew how charming and manipulative he could be, and even how he had tried to recruit Jenny's mom to plead his case for him after Jenny got the restraining order. He was free and out in the world, living in a friend's basement. The only good thing about that was that he was still working, which meant spousal support was coming in.

Jenny admitted how ironic it was that much of that money was going to the divorce lawyer.

"It seems like poetic justice," Tanny championed.

"You always said there was something creepy about him," Jenny reflected soberly. "Why didn't I see it?" She looked pained and angry with herself.

"He was so charming and handsome and successful," Tanny replied. "He was Duncan's best friend. And he made a beeline for you. Of course you were dazzled!"

"No one had ever paid attention to me like that."

Tanny reached over and squeezed her sister's hand. "I think everyone was dazzled by him. They put him on the church board after only a year of coming around with Duncan. So please don't be hard on yourself."

After sitting for a while Jenny said, "And the divorce may not be final for another two years."

Tanny sat forward abruptly in her pedicure chair saying, "You are kidding me!" She startled the technician and had to apologize.

"It has been so exhausting just fighting to get him to stay away from me and Will, that we're only now starting on the separation agreement. It all must be done through the lawyers, because I refuse to be in the same room as Terry. So, it's taking a long time.

"But one thing I have discovered," Jenny continued, "is that he really values money. Whenever he starts trying to dispute petty things I remind him through my lawyer how much each dispute costs us in legal fees. He then realizes how much the lawyers are charging and stops dragging things out. It has sped up the process quite a bit. Selling the house was a nightmare until he gave up fighting. He honestly thought he would be coming back and living with us there! But to answer your question, it could be months before the *separation agreement* is done. Only then do we start the divorce proceedings." Jenny sighed, "I just want it all to go away!"

Tanny squeezed her sister's hand again in sympathy. They moved onto happier topics.

June nineteenth arrived with bright sun and slightly chilly temperatures. The community had been filling with guests from all over, and several were staying in the same hotel that Jeff and Tanny had selected.

Tanny and Jeff had met the rest of Jon's family in the days leading up to the wedding. Jon's parents were charming, and only a few years older than her own parents. They had a sun-kissed look and were both quite handsome and trim. His brothers were each incredibly good looking—one in a Chris Hemsworth kind of way, and one in a Zac Efron kind of way.

"Good grief! Tanny said to Conrad as they stood together at the rehearsal dinner. Gary was on Conrad's other side. "That family must have God-genes to produce such handsome men!"

Gary said, "Very pretty indeed," with appreciation.

Conrad said, "I was chatting with the one named Bradley. He started telling me how the black Africans were so much better off when the whites were in charge."

"He just got a lot less good-looking," Tanny responded.

"That was my thought," agreed Conrad. "Not that I was looking for a relationship." He hooked his arm through Gary's. "I've got the perfect man right here." He looked into Gary's eyes.

Tanny got the feeling that they would have kissed if it wasn't a public setting. The men just smiled at each other, then unhooked arms.

Jon had a cousin named Blake Pearson who arrived from Ben Kirk with his wife Harmony, and two small children. Harmony was Tanny's second cousin through the Neufeldts.

"The great family tree that is more like a braid," she murmured to Jeff after they had chatted with Blake and Harmony. "Who knew I was related to Jon from South Africa twice now, even if it is by marriage?"

"I feel like I have stepped into a giant web of relatives," Jeff replied.

"You kind-of have," agreed Tanny.

This was Jeff's first exposure to the music and pageantry at which Tanny's congregation excelled. The congregation sang in four parts, which was both beautiful and intimidating. He liked singing hymns, but he felt a bit strange singing the melody when most of the men around him were singing different musical lines than he was.

The school children and teachers did a delightful job portraying the main stories from the Book of Revelation, with a Chinese-style dragon wiggling and dancing around the grass, threatening the woman clothed with the sun. But the angel Michael chased the dragon away with the help of the school children, all brandishing foam swords. Together they saved the woman and newborn infant, and the sense of triumph and celebration was palpable. The joyful hymns celebrated the arrival of a promised new spirituality which would unite everyone and bring peace on earth.

"Oh! So, the Unitarian Universalists have it right?" whispered Gary, receiving a hard elbow in his ribs from Conrad. Tanny liked the way the skin crinkled around Gary's eyes when he grinned.

The wedding celebration happened immediately after the pageant, with Conrad and Tanny again walking down the grass aisle together before the wedding couple. Stephen was there, able to officiate, though he also sat a lot more than usual during the festivities and went home to lie down shortly after.

"You're not dead!!!" Tanny said when she saw him at last and gave him a big hug. "Good heavens you scared us!"

"I scared me too," Stephen admitted. "I am very clear now that I am not immortal." He had his humour back, but Tanny could tell he was still missing strength and endurance.

The ceremony proceeded just like a wedding, except there was no need to sign a license. It ended in a joyful recessional, with the girls skipping down the aisle in front of Jon and Sue. The couple beamed while walking back as flower petals floated over them, thrown by the nearest guests.

The ceremony held new meaning for Tanny. Instead of being involved in deep longing for her own love, she was full of rich anticipation and joy for her own approaching ceremony. And she was doubly happy for Jon and Sue. They were already married, yet this celebration somehow felt like a grounding—like their commitment was truly real. Tanny wondered why that was. Why did a big outward ceremony make a *spiritual* event feel *more real*?

She decided that there was some sort of power in ritual, just as that Lutheran minister had said. She was experiencing the truth of that.

The June nineteenth picnic commenced on one side of the lawn while the wedding party moved to another to have speeches and toasts. The wind had sprung up, so everyone had to gather close to hear the speeches. Bouquets, glass vases of flowers, and salt and pepper shakers were all put to use holding napkins down.

Alyssa insisted on offering a toast to God for bringing, "Mr. Peason Healy" to the church and to her mom. Susan waived her hand at the guests as if to say, "Just go with it," so everyone joined in toasting "Mr. Peason Healy," in the direction of Jon.

Tanny explained to Jeff, "Before Jon arrived, Sue's mom said a blessing asking for peace and healing for the church. Alyssa heard her say "Peason Healy." After Jon arrived, Steve introduced him after church as Mr. Jonathan Pearson Haley, and Alyssa decided that Jon was THE 'Mr. Peason Healy' that her grandma had prayed for…. She *still* thinks he was an answer to her grandma's prayer."

"Maybe he was," mused Jeff, looking thoughtful.

Jeff, for his part, was enchanted and intrigued by the whole thing. He could see the appeal in the close community feeling. The beautiful music and the artistry in the pageant were impressive. But the insider culture was also a bit off-putting. How hard was it for newcomers to find belonging in this this inter-related, culturally unique world?

He stood chatting with a fellow named Jackson, who was of Asian descent, and asked how he found it. Jackson had married a woman from the community. Jackson said that overall, he loved it. As an only child, he liked the feeling of having a big family. He did admit that he sometimes felt like a mascot. He had heard people mentioning his name as evidence that they were a diverse community. There was also a couple who had adopted children of African descent, and the members loved to list those children as proof of the congregation's diversity as well.

Jeff looked around at the overwhelmingly white-presenting group and wondered. Not that there was much diversity in Bracebridge either; there were a few brave folks, most from the Indian sub-continent, who had started businesses and restaurants there. But they were treated a bit like mascots too. Racism lived deep in the cultural sub-conscious. He worked constantly to stay aware himself and to treat each new person as an equal.

Jeff was also intrigued by some of the language used around the wedding celebration. Jackson had said that they often spoke of "marrying *into*" the church, as though marriage made you more of a member. Tanny had spoken to him about the way singles and widows (not widowers) were seen as incomplete and even threatening to the marriages in the church. Certainly LGBTQ+ people were 'threats' to the marriages somehow. It was a very heterosexual marriage-centric culture, much like a lot of conservative-leaning religions. Marriage was elevated to a holy and sacred status—perhaps not harmful in and of itself—but it meant that people got trapped in unhappy marriages they didn't feel free to leave. They were shunned if they got divorced unless "they could *prove* the other partner's genitals had been somewhere they shouldn't" as Tanny put it. Verbal and physical abuse didn't necessarily count as "just cause" for divorce in this church; neither did emotional or sexual abandonment. Tanny said that the marriage contract was held as *so sacred* that the church feared divorce more than spousal abuse. It was as if the marriage contract itself offered salvation, and so divorce meant ... hell? And was contagious?

The language in Jon and Sue's ceremony definitely spoke of marriage as most sacred. His pragmatic self liked the idealism but saw all the ways it could be problematic if elevated beyond real-world circumstances and realities.

Nevertheless, the beautiful weather, the happy people, the idyllic setting on an expansive green lawn beside a uniquely attractive stone church certainly implied heavenly happiness. He could see that it would be easy to fall for the fairy-tale. And the people were all so nice!

Jeff and Tanny talked a lot about his impressions after they were back in their hotel room. He expressed how remarkable the church culture had seemed and yet expressed his concerns as well. Tanny, having grown up in it said she would miss the artistry and friendships, but not the codependence or "weird vibes around singles." They decided they were not going to "marry *into*" the church. They would just get married.

After all the festivities, (having fielded only one set of obnoxiously prying questions about their living situation, from a woman named Margaret Inquist) Jeff and Tanny returned to their barn apartment at Cedar Haven. Tanny was falling in love with their new home. She especially loved the "peace and quiet" she experienced when she was far away from the church's expectations and gossip. She had only just named this sensation to herself. She knew she would miss the familiar faces and worship culture of her childhood. And she especially felt pangs during the hymns at the Bracebridge church. (Nobody did part-singing.) But she hadn't realized how heavily the spectre of "what others might think and say" had loomed over her life when she was in Cliffside. It returned whenever she went back there. But it was non-existent in Bracebridge. She didn't want to care what others might think and say about her. She wanted to be guided by her own conscience.

Grade eight graduation—something Tanny had attended every year when she had been able—happened in Cliffside after they returned to Cedar Haven. Tanny still knew the names of all the kids in Cliffside's little church school, and it was exciting to see another phalanx of young people launch into the public school system. She was a bit wistful that she would miss it. She was also aware that a bunch of Cliffside young people were graduating public high school, and she realized how many went out into the world rarely to return afterwards. A few married and brought their spouses to the community. Tanny supposed that those couples would be "married *into*" the church. But a great many more never joined as adults. She wondered if anyone was asking why.

Most of the young adults who went down to the college in Ben Kirk brought spouses back with them. It was always fun to get "new blood" into the Cliffside family braid. Many others stayed in the States with spouses they had met at school in Ben Kirk.

And babies were still being born who would go to the school. The school still seemed to be thriving, though the class numbers were dwindling. Tanny wanted the church and community to do well, despite the faults she found with it. She still loved her Cliffside roots despite everything. But she was deeply grateful that Jeff came from "outside" and had such a grounded, real-world perspective on her hometown. Sometimes his observations hurt a little. But he was never mean. And he was usually right. Tanny poured herself some tea in the stone-walled kitchen of their apartment and enjoyed the long, low rays of the sun out the window. It was near the summer solstice, and the sun wouldn't set until after nine pm. It wouldn't be fully dark until nearly ten. She took her tea up to join Jeff in the living room. They would sit and watch the sun set over the water. It was becoming a tradition.

Fifty-Three

June 21 to July 8

The renovators had moved into the south bedrooms in the main house. Tanny loved to peek into the newly finished northern rooms, each with their own dedicated bathrooms. There was still some finishing to do in them, but they were ninety percent completed.

Tanny was getting a mere trickle of organizing gigs, and so she was extra grateful for the shifts in the coffee shop. Most customers were decent tippers too, which helped as well.

The Cedar Haven board met regularly, mostly to stay up to date on the progress of the property renovations. The septic was working perfectly, and the new heating and cooling system would be operational by the last week in June. Tanny looked forward to when the central air would be working in their apartment. They had window units for now, but they were older and quite noisy. She found the constant noise wearing. The screen porch was progressing, but it was still mostly footings and sturdy posts. Jeff wanted to be sure that the porch supports could withstand many cycles of freezing and thawing given the wintry climate. He was also building in the capacity to add insulation in the future, in case they wanted to winterize it going forward.

Tanny rearranged her schedule for early July so that she could go down to Cliffside for the next puzzle and task assignment regarding Britt's will. She was expecting something much like the first set—a puzzle that might take weeks to solve, and a task that required the participation of many members in the congregation. She had been the one to crack the first puzzle with the help of little Will.

The dreadful Heinrich Knapp had been holding the congregation hostage with his refusal to complete his part of the first task until an act of fate? God? Random chance? Coffee? had removed the control from his grasp just in the nick of time.

Reflecting on Heinrich's attempt to dominate the church's future, Tanny had to agree with Bet Gidding's observations about Britt. Britt herself (posthumously) was holding the congregation hostage with this series of puzzles and tasks. Her intentions had been for good, but the consequences were wreaking havoc on the congregation members' nervous systems. Perhaps the situation had even contributed to nearly killing Stephen.

Tanny talked regularly to Susan, who was now cataloguing the awful sermons coming from Rev. Flint's pulpit. There was the "why aren't you giving more money to the church, you worldly, selfish people" sermon. There was the "since you are nothing but evil and selfishness, you can't trust your own thinking. So be led by your priests" sermon.

"When priests are just as evil and selfish as the rest of us, why should we trust them?" Susan asked, incredulous.

Tanny thought she had a point.

Being the treasurer for Cedar Haven had been fairly easy, as there were plenty of funds. Her job was to keep track of the money, pay bills as they came due, and report on everything to the board. The only questions that came up were when Tanny was looking back at Jacob's book-keeping and finding some sketchy transactions. Upon deep digging, the numbers came out even, so even if Jacob *had* been borrowing from the estate, he had ultimately put everything back. Nevertheless, that was embezzlement. It pained her to imagine that a man she had loved and trusted since she was a child had been embezzling from Britt and lying about it. She felt tainted somehow, as if Jacob's character defect might be contagious or even genetic.

As Tanny struggled to keep her own financial head above water, she had at least developed some empathy for Jacob, though she felt no temptation to steal Britt's wealth. Britt didn't owe her anything! Thanks to Britt's wealth she and Jeff had a place to live rent-free so long as Jeff remained property manager. That was more than enough.

With the renovations heading for the attic next, Jeff and Tanny had been gradually transferring the jumble of possessions from the attic down into the barn. The barn was built into a slope with ground level access to the main floor area. This is where the tractor and all-terrain vehicles were stored, and where Herman had sat while Jeff had been repairing it. It was also the level on which the extra furniture from the renovated rooms had gone, and where they put the attic possessions. Tanny had planned on sorting all the attic things during these months, but work and other activities kept bumping that task down the priority list.

Besides, Tanny had decided that she wanted to go through the items with family members and not by herself. She wanted more minds tending to these heirlooms. There were so many stories stored in those items, and she wanted to hear them all. Being on the genealogy website had particularly stimulated her interest in the stories about her ancestors' lives. Surely Jacob had some stories, and maybe Great Aunt Eliza Jane would know some things. Tanny's own grandma, Emily's mother, was in memory care. She had never been quite herself since grandpa had passed.

But Great Aunt Eliza Jane, Isaac's widow, was still lively and sharp-witted if frail. She had helped in the first "task" of feeding the hungry in her nineties. Perhaps she would have some stories to tell? Tanny resolved to interview her in the next few months. Who knew how much longer she would be around?

Meanwhile, Tanny started photographing various items from the attic and building a spreadsheet online for all the descendants to peruse. She would send out a link once she had a bunch of items with photographs and descriptions listed. Maybe some of her cousins might want an ancient pair of dress gloves, or an old photo? There was some wonderful furniture too, even if it was old fashioned. It was all made with real, solid wood!

Jeff and Tanny arrived in Kitchener in the early afternoon of July 8th. They opted for a hotel again, to keep things simple. Once they were settled, they headed over to Jon and Susan's. Susan was glowing. The nausea had settled down around the fourth month. Jon set about showing Jeff and Tanny the renovations he had started in the basement, planning to transform the large space into a large apartment. He showed where the kitchen was roughed-in as well as a nearly finished three-piece bathroom. A generous central area would be the living room, with space for three bedrooms along the far wall.

"It's almost going to be bigger than what you have upstairs! Tanny exclaimed.

"It seems like it," Jon said, "But it really isn't. We just have a weird layout upstairs. We have that large dining room in the middle and our 'third' bedroom is rather odd. We had hoped to rent the basement out to help with the mortgage, but with twins on the way, we may need those lower bedrooms sooner than we had planned."

Susan patted her belly and said, "We can try to keep the twins in the master bedroom for a while, but it's hard to imagine how we would make things work with just the main floor once they need their own bedroom."

"I want *this* bedroom!" announced Andrea, standing in an area that looked like it would be a master bedroom one day.

"I want *this* one!" claimed Alyssa, picking the next largest one. She had long ago accepted that Andrea was the dominant of the two of them and was used to making do with seconds.

"I think you two will share the big one," said Susan, "If you move down here at all," she added.

The church hall was overflowing when Jeff and Tanny arrived for the meeting about Britt's will. Many people came to say hi to them, congratulating them on their engagement and asking when the wedding would be. Tanny watched faces fall when she explained they would be having a smaller ceremony at Cedar Haven. She could tell that many wouldn't make the drive. She could even sense disappointment in one or two, as if they felt entitled to see her wed in her childhood church.

"But so many friends and family won't be able to come!" objected one moth-ball-scented woman.

Tanny reflected that Jeff deserved to have friends and family come just as much as she did. Most of his work buddies wouldn't be able to come down to Kitchener, so having the wedding in Cedar Haven meant that his crowd would be there for sure. The most important people for Tanny would make it up to Cedar Haven. That's what mattered to her, not being convenient for church members.

Many more people were delighted to hear about the wedding at Cedar Haven and asked to be able to see the pictures afterwards. That felt like love and support.

They found seats near Susan and Kate. They were surrounded by Bender relatives and cousins, as family tended to sit together.

Jon was up at the front with Stephen and the lawyers and Uncle Jacob. They had put them all up on the stage at a long table, to make room for more chairs on the floor.

The meeting started with prayers for a spirit of unity and God's guidance. Stephen read a quote from Swedenborg about trusting God's Providence, and then the meeting could begin.

The lawyers took turns reminding the audience of the terms of Britt's will and the consequences for fulfilling them (or not).

Tanny's stomach plunged at the reminder that the whole building and lands could pass from the possession of the congregation and be offered for sale, leaving the congregation homeless. It seemed decidedly unfair that Britt had set this situation up.

Jacob announced that the task would take place immediately, and once it was over, the puzzle would be handed out.

The group was then divided in half, with the second half moving to the sanctuary for their part. Tanny and Jeff moved to the sanctuary. Jeff was just an observer but was intrigued to see what was going to happen.

Once everyone was seated in the wood and stone space with the soaring ceiling, Stephen set up a flip chart with empty white paper on it. He drew two columns. One column was labeled "Them" and one was labeled, "Us".

He then wrote at the bottom, "two reds equal no points; two greens equal one point each; one red and one green equal one point to the side that chose red."

Tanny immediately did the math. She announced to the room, "So if we just keep picking red, if they ever pick green, we win. So, let's just keep picking red!"

Jeff looked thoughtful but said nothing. There was no other comment from the room, so they began. They picked red.

The message came that the other room had picked green. There was whooping and high fiving around the room. Tanny felt triumphant.

They picked red again. Word came that the other room had picked green. There was more whooping and rejoicing. So, they picked red again. The other room picked red. No points for anyone.

Tanny announced, "No matter what they pick, we have won, so long as we never pick green!"

The game went for several more rounds, with Tanny's group feeling increasingly baffled when the other room repeatedly chose green. It stopped even being fun, as their own points mounted, and the other group had no points.

Finally, the game was declared finished and Tanny's group returned to the hall. As they began mixing with the other group Tanny asked, "Why did you keep picking green?" She was genuinely baffled.

Susan, who had remained in the hall said, "Why did you keep picking red?" She was equally baffled.

"But we won that way," explained Tanny, sitting next to her cousin.

Jacob announced when everyone was quiet, "Something to know about this game; nobody said that *more points* made you the winner. The purpose of the game was for each side to get an equal amount of points; that would be true cooperation. Choosing red was a choice for power-over, where choosing green was a choice for cooperation."

Jeff murmured, "I wondered...."

Tanny wanted the floor to swallow her. *She* was the one that had set their team on the track to "defeat" the other team. It was all about winning for her when the real purpose was to practice mutual support. She buried her face in her hands, and crumpled over in her seat, making herself as small as she could. Jeff gently rubbed her back.

Jacob asked the team that had gone to the sanctuary how the exercise had felt. Conrad Knapp answered, "At first it felt great. We were on top and knew it. But after a while it was confusing. It stopped being fun. We didn't understand why the team here," he indicated the church hall, "kept picking green. It felt like we were missing something."

"Perhaps you were," offered Jacob. He then asked the crowd that had stayed in the hall how it had felt.

Dr. Paul Bender spoke up. "It was rather frustrating. We hoped the other team would choose green too, but they never did. They never did." He turned and faced the general crowd. "Why did you keep choosing red?"

Jacob said, "I think you were each operating on different assumptions. One group assumed that more points meant winning. The other group assumed that both teams getting points was how to win." Jacob looked over the room and read a document, "'The point was to experience the choices we make, to observe the feelings around the outcomes, and possibly to look at our assumptions about how to get ahead in life.' That is how Britt worded it. I will let you draw your own conclusions."

Tanny was still curled over in her seat. She was mortified. All this time she had been pointing at all the others who were ruining the church, when here she was, the one who had urged her team to "win". *She* was the problem in this case. She was the one who had urged her team to *beat* the other team, completely forgetting that the church was one group supposedly on the same side.

Jeff leaned down to her and whispered, "There is a way you were right. It was very clever of you to see how to get more points."

Tanny moaned. "But it wasn't about getting more points! It was about cooperating! I feel *terrible*!"

"Come here," said Jeff and pulled her up to sitting so he could set his arms around her.

"I feel so stupid!" Tanny groaned into his shoulder.

Jeff chuckled. "I love you so much, Tanny," was all he could say.

Tanny felt confused. Here, she had been a jerk so openly; she had led a whole group of people to act in a terrible way. And Jeff *loved* her? It felt like falling off a cliff. *How come he loved her when she was so terrible?* She clung to him and started crying. "You are astonishing. Please don't ever go away!"

"Oh. You are so doomed," he rumbled.

Tanny's tears turned to laughter.

Meanwhile, Jacob had asked for papers to be handed out to the crowd. Susan tapped Tanny's back with the stack.

Tanny straightened, wiped her tears with the back of her hand and passed the stack along.

The paper said,

Your answers lie in Hope.
Two quotes from the founding upholder of the law.
29 from Weber
14 from 2 Maples
30 from Frost
17 from Doering

And that was it.

"You have done your task."

"Didn't we fail?" murmured Tanny.

"You now have thirty days to find the answer to this puzzle."

"I guess not," murmured Jeff.

Questions burbled up from the floor. "Are these numbers of steps to or from something?"

Jacob answered, "I can neither confirm nor deny that."

Tanny sat up fully. "I think that means these *are* steps to or from something!" she whispered. She thought. The task was done, miraculously not ruined by her. If they solved this in a day or two, would they have to wait the full thirty day to find out? Or would they know right away that they were good for another six months?

Tanny called this question up to Uncle Jacob. Jacob conferred with the lawyers. He straightened up. The room fell silent.

"The lawyers say that you must be certain that you have the answer. If you call for a meeting to declare the answer and you are incorrect, you will have failed to solve the puzzle, no matter how many days are left of the thirty you were given. So be very sure of your answer before you ask to present it. It must be this way, or you could be calling us down here for every guess, over and over. You have only one chance to answer the puzzle, no matter when you choose to do so."

The room filled with murmuring.

Stephen rose to speak. "I don't know about you, but I need to go lie down. I turn this meeting over to Jon as my representative. You decide if you want to stay and work on the puzzle or go home at this time."

Stephen did look a little green, and Liz seemed happy to remove him from the meeting and get him home.

About half of the congregation was ready to go home as well. Another group, mostly younger members, chose to stay and try to figure out how to approach the puzzle. They were already talking about members' homes. The Frosts and the Doerings were members. But others were thinking it might be roads. Weber Street was a long road cutting through both Kitchener and Waterloo. But from where would they begin to count the steps? There was no road named Frost or Doering, but there was a #2 Maple Court....

Tanny felt exhausted and chose to leave. She and Jeff moved toward the entry-way with Tanny's parents. Susan was going home too, leaving Jon to oversee those staying behind.

Emily said, "I wonder if the 'Hope' reference has anything to do with Mount Hope cemetery?" The question hung in the air for a moment and then dropped.

Jeff and Tanny returned to their hotel. Before they fell asleep, Tanny made sure to show Jeff how much she loved him, no matter how tired she felt.

Fifty-Four

July 9

Tanny sat in the passenger seat as Jeff drove Annie toward the 401 to head back to Bracebridge. Tanny was looking at the puzzle set by Britt.

Your answers lie in Hope.
Two quotes from the founding upholder of the law.
29 from Weber
14 from 2 Maples
30 from Frost
17 from Doering

"I wonder if Britt *did* mean Mount Hope cemetery," mused Tanny. "And she says, 'answers' – plural – not 'answer.' That seems unusual. So does that mean there is more than one answer?"

Jeff shrugged. "Do you know where this cemetery is?"

Tanny looked up at the passing scenery. "Well, yes. It is in Kitchener, right near the border with Waterloo."

"Would it be well out of our way to take a look? I don't mind."

Tanny shifted and looked at her beloved. His hair was a good length now. In fact, it could use a trim soon. It was the same length all over, which meant it was a bit long around the ears. It was a honey-gold colour, like his eyes. She said, "I'd love that! Get off at the Wellington exit, and I'll guide you from there."

Eventually they were rolling along tree-lined Moore Street looking for an entrance to Mount Hope. It was already a warm day, so they drove a distance into the cemetery, finding a place to park in the shade. Soon they were standing on the grass looking around at the many headstones under the big trees.

"This cemetery goes back to the beginnings of the city here. Kitchener was called Berlin back then," Tanny said, walking slowly towards some of the closer headstones. A breeze ruffled her bangs.

They wandered some more. Jeff read, "Louis Kuntz." Then a little later he read, "Ubel, ... Krantz, ... Schmaltz.... All very German names."

"Yep." Tanny pulled out the paper with the riddle on it. "Two quotes from the founding upholder of the law," she read. "Founding upholder..." she mused. "'Founding' could be referring to a founding father of the city. So, someone from this general time period," she added, reading some of the dates around her on the stones.

"This Johann Schneider was born in seventeen ninety-seven," Jeff observed, eyebrows raised.

"Hey! If we're on the right track, we are looking for the last names of Doering and Frost, Weber and ... two Maples?" speculated Tanny, lifting her hair from her neck in the heat. She found a hair elastic and whipped her hair into a high ponytail.

Jeff loved watching her play with her hair. He loved the way her lifted arms changed the fit of her shirt. He focused on her words. Looking around at the trees he said, "A lot of these trees are maples. What if that clue is about *two trees*, not two people named Maple?"

"So, the headstone we are looking for would be '14' from two maple *trees*, not from 'Sarah and Isaac Maple?'" She grinned at him.

"That's what I was wondering," said Jeff, bending to read a headstone. "Dr. John Scott," he pronounced. A gust of wind pushed past him, and a shadow blocked the sun.

"No kidding," Tanny said in surprise, coming to stand beside him. "I think the Scotts were Swedenborgians. This must be an ancestor of the Scotts who live in Cliffside now. They are my cousins somehow."

"I'm starting to think you have a lot of cousins."

"Oh, believe me, I do!"

Jeff grinned to himself. As an only child, he liked the idea of having lots of cousins. He had a few relations on the Res, but he felt somehow separate from them. He had always felt separate.

The two of them wandered a bit farther and came across a large, squared pillar-style monument to the Weber family.

"Hey! Webers!" Tanny said. She looked at her copy of the riddle. "It says '29 from Weber'. Let's pretend that means twenty-nine steps." She looked around her. But which way?"

A breeze had kicked up, and some of the leaves were flipping their undersides to the wind.

Whichever way we try, we had better look quickly," Jeff recommended.

"I think there's a storm brewing."

Tanny looked up at the sky, and sure enough, the clouds now had a dark grey shadowing. The wind was gusting. "I pick ... that way!" announced Tanny, and she started marching sideways across the cemetery, counting. "Seventeen, eighteen .... Hey! This stone says 'Frost'." She looked around her, searching for other notable headstones. "What if the others are all larger headstones too? What is that one? She marched up to a tall narrow one – a squared pillar like the Weber's headstone. "'Davidson,'" she read. "That's not right. We are looking for Doerings...."

"And two," said Jeff, pointing to two tall maple trees standing fairly close together just a dozen or so steps away.

Tanny opened her eyes wide and gaped at him. "I think we are insanely close to the answer!" she squealed over the rising wind. Just then a small branch whipped by her, torn from a tree.

Jeff grabbed her elbow and turned her toward the car. "Unfortunately, it isn't safe to be outside right now. We need to get to shelter!"

Hand in hand the two lovers raced toward Annie. The rain started pelting down just before they got into the snug, dry automobile. They were wet but relieved to be out of the storm. The rain hammered on the car's metal hide as they looked out through the streaming windshield.

"Wow," Tanny remarked. "That came up so fast!"

"I think we might have been very close to finding the answer," Jeff added. "How frustrating that we had to run just as we nearly solved it." He started Annie and set the wipers to full speed. "Shall we go home?"

Tanny groaned. "I hate to give up when we're so close!" A decent sized branch fell onto the road about a car's length ahead of them. "But I think I'd like to get out from under these old trees even more just now."

Jeff had already started turning the car around to head to the exit. He sped onto Moore and then maneuvered them to a stretch of street that was not under such large trees. The few other cars they saw were driving slowly, lights on and wipers going like sixty.

The rain was driving in sheets now, and thunder rumbled.

Jeff looked at Tanny in apology. "I think we should just head home. I have a shift to get back for, and who knows how much this weather will slow down the drive."

Tanny sighed and agreed. They moved themselves toward the highway, not wanting to risk back routes and downed branches. As Jeff drove, Tanny texted her findings to Jenny, Conrad, and Susan.

"Be careful out there!" replied Susan. "There's a tornado watch in the area!"

Tanny looked out at the grey-green cast of the cloud cover and believed her.

"Gary and I will try to get over and continue the hunt after work," Conrad responded.

"Maybe William can help solve this one too!" responded Jenny, referring to how her son's interest in letters had given Tanny the hint she needed to solve the first puzzle.

Tanny felt excited, and wished she had a map of the cemetery so she could keep researching. She could find nothing online but a PDF of a tour that only showed a few of the many headstones.

The storm pelted down at times and seemed to ease at others as the couple made their way to the 401 and eventually to the 407-toll highway. They were more interested in getting home quickly at this point than saving some toll money. The storm seemed to follow them, twice making them pull over until the ferocity eased and they could drive again. They often passed other cars pulled over as well.

But as they turned and headed north, they seemed to head out of the storm front. The largely flat terrain of southern Ontario, especially as they moved into the farming belt north of Toronto, opened up to wide skies, where one could see quite a distance. They watched the towering, black-bottomed storm clouds recede in the rear-view mirror as they headed north toward Barrie. Tanny liked this stretch of the 400 highway, where there was little development and wide views.

At one point Jeff said, "My grandparents live down that way," and tipped his head to his right.

Tanny sat up. "What? Where? You never mentioned your grandparents. We should go visit them."

Jeff drove in silence a while. Then he said, "They disowned my father when he married my mother. They never wanted to see me. They didn't even come to my parents' funerals. They didn't want to raise me or have anything to do with me after my parents died."

"How terrible...." Tanny murmured.

"I know their names and their address. And I have never tried to meet them."

"But no wonder. They rejected and abandoned you. I'm not surprised at all. It must *ache* though."

Jeff reached over and held Tanny's hand a while. Then he said, "I can't stop wishing I could meet them—could *see* them. Would they look like my dad at all?"

Tanny said, "I support whatever you want to do. And if they treat you badly again, I will tell them what losers they are, and spray whipped cream in their faces."

Jeff laughed.

"Then I will throw maraschino cherries at them and tell them they are sundaes made of stupid." Tanny had a satisfied look on her face.

Jeff wanted to kiss her madly just then but needed to keep his eyes on the road. He squeezed her hand extra hard instead. The sky was continuing to look clear to the north, with bright sunshine. The storm clouds continued to recede in the rear-view mirror.

Tanny's phone dinged, and she looked down. "Susan says they are pretty sure a tornado touched down somewhere in the area, and are we okay?" Tanny quickly thumb-typed a reply.

She looked up and wondered about putting on some music or a podcast when Jeff spoke again.

"I was over in the Netherlands when Britt died. I was researching my Dutch roots. I found some cousins over there who welcomed me as family. They *looked* like family. They *felt* like family. I was considering moving over there where I had family who welcomed me, but my Dutch is terrible, and it is extremely hard to immigrate to the Netherlands, even with a family tie."

"Aww," Tanny commiserated. "For my part, I'm glad you didn't leave Canada."

Jeff squeezed Tanny's hand again. "Me too."

"Would you say something in Dutch for me?" asked Tanny.

Jeff thought a while and said, "Ik aanbid je, jij mooie vrouw."

Tanny looked flummoxed. "It sounded like you called me an icky, moo-cow."

"Nothing of the sort!" laughed Jeff. "Let's just say, I like you."

Tanny lifted a skeptical eyebrow his way. "Let's hope you said something better than calling me a cow."

Jeff lifted her hand to his lips. "Oh, I did."

"Wait!" Tanny said. "Spell what you just said for me." She lifted her phone up, pulling up Google translate. Reluctantly, Jeff spelled the Dutch phrase for her.

"Oh.... Oh, Jeff. You definitely said something nicer than calling me a cow," Tanny murmured once she discovered the translation. "Pull the car over right now."

So, Jeff did, and Tanny smothered her adored, wonderful man in many kisses.

It took an hour longer than usual to get home, thanks to delays from weather and other things, but at last they pulled into the long driveway at Cedar Haven.

There were a bunch of worker vehicles in the way, but at least Jeff and Tanny could find their way around them all to park near their apartment.

Tanny's heart was singing as she and Jeff unpacked their things in their new, smaller home. She had loved living in Cedar Haven proper but accepted that it was not theirs to live in, and that she had to be grateful for their charming barn apartment, which now had working central air! Oh! She would not miss the constant hum of the window units. Sometimes their sound had been soothing, but mostly it was tiresome, as everything had to be played or spoken louder just to hear over the constant hum.

Once they were unpacked, the couple toured the renovations and spoke to the workers. The southern bedrooms in Cedar Haven were having their new windows installed. One of them had an opening too small for the new window, and the workers were figuring out how and where to cut to accommodate the standard window and still have it look straight and balanced in the wall. Tanny was amazed by how many problems just like this one had come up during the renovations. No wonder renovations took twice as long as expected!

They found Aunt Eileen in one of the northern bedrooms, fluffing some pillows onto the newly fitted bed. The pine-branch-effect wallpaper was up, and the antique bookshelf was stocked with charming old hardcovers and some paperback vacation-reads. Eileen greeted them warmly, delighted that they were home.

"I must have missed seeing your car pull in," she said. "Which is a surprise, it being so bright blue."

Tanny, returning her aunt's hug said, "Are you giving me a hard time for liking bright blue? I think Annie is beautiful."

"She is hard to miss!" agreed Eileen, hugging Jeff. She looked with affection at Jeff and fluffed his hair. "You will be getting a trim before the wedding, I hope?"

Tanny watched, intrigued.

Jeff smiled at his foster mother. "I guess I'll have to, won't I?" he responded, winking at Tanny.

"He always looks a little mullet-y as his hair grows out," Eileen said to Tanny, making a face. "Once it's past a certain length it just looks like long hair, but there's always an awkward stage. I think it will be at prime mullet for the wedding." Eileen grimaced. "It's your choice, but I'd vote for a nice, traditional trim for the wedding." She rubbed her hands up and down Jeff's arms and then released him. "You do you. But please do consider a trim for the wedding. *Then* you can grow your hair out however you like."

"I will, indeed, be getting a trim, mom."

It was rare that Jeff called either of his foster parents 'mom' or 'dad', but it always touched Tanny. She was also feeling butterflies at the talk of their wedding. And what *would* Jeff look like in shaggy, longer hair? Her tummy flip-flopped at the imagining.

Jeff asked Eileen, "Mom, if my cousins from the Netherlands can afford to come, might they stay in one of these bedrooms? If the bathrooms are ready and the finished rooms deemed safe for use, might we have family stay in some of them?"

Eileen looked at her foster son thoughtfully. "You know, I think that's a marvelous idea. I will find a way to make Jacob think it was *his* idea, and then I'm sure he will support the idea too. We just need to make sure the rooms are truly ready for guests."

"I think we can do that!" said Tanny. "I love how this room has turned out. I can't wait to see how the others are going to look."

"We are calling this the 'Forest Room', I think," said Eileen. "What do you think?"

It was the room Tanny had stayed in when she first arrived. The new, generous windows really opened the view of the water and pines. The pine-motif wallpaper showed forest green branches against a golden-beige background, with these colours echoed in the bedding and furniture.

"I love it!" she said.

"Katrina Hawkins, the osteopath, apparently does some decorating on the side. She helped me find the bedding," explained Eileen.

"I never considered hiring a decorator," Tanny said. "I've never had the money. And there's something about managing by myself that is deep in my DNA."

"That might be your rugged American blood," Eileen teased. "It is nice to have a few extra pennies on this project to get professional help. It's really making a difference."

Tanny had to admit that Eileen was right. And if they wanted Cedar Haven to function as a guest house and retreat center, they'd need it to look top-notch and professional.

It was when Tanny and Jeff were sipping their tea and watching the sun set that she got a phone call from her sister Jenny, with Conrad and Gary in the background. "First of all," Jenny said, "A tornado really did touch down nearby today! It was in Ayr but just ripped up some trees in a field. There was no damage to any buildings. So, phew!" she said.

There was some conversation in the background and then Jenny groaned. "Gary just said it touched down in the Ayr-ea...."

Tanny moaned. "Punch him for me, would you please?" she asked her sister. She heard an "Ow!" followed by laughter in the background.

"But the biggest and best news of all," Jenny said, "is that we are pretty sure we solved the puzzle, thanks to your legwork!"

Fifty-Five

July 9, evening to July 10

"You solved it?" Tanny asked, jumping up and quickly switching the phone to speaker as Jeff came hurrying over.

"Yes. We are pretty certain. You were right about the two trees. We found the Doering's headstone, and using those four starting points, the Doerings, the Webers, the Frosts, and the trees, there was only one headstone in the centre of them all. A big, square pillar with the name of Davidson."

Tanny shivered. *Hadn't that been the pillar she and Jeff had been standing by when they ran from the storm?* Jeff's arm circled her waist, and he leaned closer.

"And you know how the puzzle said, 'two quotes from the founding upholder of the law'? Well, apparently, George Davidson was the first sheriff of Waterloo County. And there are two quotes from the Bible on the pillar, one for George and one for his wife."

Tanny's goose bumps got goose bumps.

"The puzzle says, 'Two quotes from the founding upholder of the law.'" Jenny's voice reported with great excitement. "They are lovely quotes." There was a pause. "Anyway, I'm sure this is the answer to the puzzle!"

"So, what happens next?" Tanny asked. "Do you have to call everyone back to another meeting?"

Apparently, Conrad had to take the phone as Will was getting fretful. "It turns out that your Uncle Jacob and his wife are staying over another night to visit with Kate, so they're still here. Jacob is checking with the lawyers, and the Bracebridge lawyer says that she will turn right around and come back for a meeting tomorrow night."

Tanny and Jeff's eyes met, and they knew they couldn't make the drive again so soon. Jeff had a shift coming up and Tanny was expected at the coffee shop the next morning.

"How I wish I could be there!" Tanny complained. "But I've got work, and so does Jeff."

"We all understand. We will keep you posted on the outcome of the meeting," reassured Conrad. "We will miss you! But we understand."

Tanny pictured the three of them gathered around Jenny's phone in what used to be her apartment. Gary and Conrad had seemed to be bonding with Jenny, which warmed Tanny's heart. She also felt a pinch of loss. That had been her place and her friends....

They still are your friends, dummy, her subconscious piped up.

Do I really wish I still lived in my parents' basement? she asked herself. The answer was a clear and strong, *NO*. Tanny reached over and kissed Jeff's cheek. She knew she was exactly where she belonged.

"Please do keep us posted," Tanny spoke into the phone. "And all good wishes that your answer is the right one. I mean, how can it not be?"

"We couldn't have done it without your leg work. It was a team effort."

Tanny didn't want to hang up. She was feeling a little nostalgic and homesick, despite her clear awareness that Bracebridge was home now.

"I love you, all of you," she said.

"Make that a double," Jeff said.

They finished their goodbyes and ended the call.

"Wow," Tanny sighed, stepping into Jeff's arms. "And so, they continue for six more months."

Jeff had leaned his head against hers. His slow, warm breath lifted the small hairs at her temple. Tanny hung in that space of anticipation as his nearness brought shimmering feelings in her belly. She kissed him then, in gratitude for his wonderful self, for his encircling arms, for everything he stood for, amazed that he seemed to feel the same way about her.

Jeff offered unconditional love, something that was new and marvellous. Jeff offered integrity and honesty, and she was HOME.

IN MEMORY OF

George Davidson
The first Sheriff of the
County of Waterloo
Born, Aberdeen, Scotland
May 14, 1814
Died, Berlin, Ontario
April 27th, 1881

....

*"Blessed are the pure in heart, for they shall
See God."* Matt. V.8

....

And of
His beloved wife
Margaret Garden
Born, Aberdeen Scotland
August 31, 1811
Died, Toronto, Ontario
Jan. 24th, 1894

....

*"Arise, shine, for thy light is come
and the glory of the Lord is risen
upon thee."* Isa. 60:1

....

THE END

See you all in 2026 when I begin
"God's Will,"
book three in the Cliffside Chapel series.

MUSICAL ACKNOWLEDGEMENTS

*Music has been a big part of my life and is a big part
of my characters' lives too.*

Kenny G: Jon and Sue walk up the aisle to "That Somebody Was You" featuring Toni Braxton as soloist with Kenny G on Saxophone. This song has significance to Jon and Sue, harking back to the New Years Eve dance 1998-1999. Produced by Walter Afanasieff, it is track 5 on Kenny G's album "The Moment."

The Windham Hill label: Many albums from the Windham Hill label have been soundtracks for my days. Most of it is acoustic and soothing – great listening for this ADD brain. Susan put on some Winham Hill music as Jon and Sue drove north to Bracebridge for their honeymoon. **Windham Hill Records** was an independent record label that specialized in instrumental acoustic music. They were bought out by BMG in the 1990s and are now a subsidiary of Sony Music Entertainment.

Karla Bonoff: In the 1990's it is not hard to imagine that Tanny had become a fan of the lesser-known Karla Bonoff. KB is a contemporary of James Taylor. Though known primarily for her songwriting for other artists, Karla has produced several albums, all of which I own and still play. When Tanny is walking to Jenny's she sings parts of "Way of the Heart", which is track six on the album named "New World." While in the shower at Cedar Haven, Tanny sings along to "Tell Me Why", "All My Life", and "Still Be Getting Over You", tracks three, four, and eight respectively from "New World."

"What a Wonderful World": is a song written by Bob Thiele (as "George Douglas") and George David Weiss. I came to know it through the recording by Art Garfunkel with James Taylor and Paul Simon (1978), which was a huge hit in the early 1980s, and performed by groups of amateurs (including myself) at many a wedding reception in those days. Tanny and Jeff sing along to it while they clean for Jon and Sue.

BIBLIOGRAPHY OR READING LIST

These books all influenced the writing of *To Rule Britannia*

Cameron, Julia. *The Artist's Way*. New York: G.P. Putnam's Sons, 1992. This book changed my life. This book unearthed my long abandoned and forgotten dream. This book opened the way and kept it open. Don't read it. Don't do the tasks. Don't finish it, or your life will change.

Clark, Bruce W.; Wallace, John K. *Geographie du Canada: Influences et Liaisons.* Montreal: McGraw Hill, 2000 (aka *Making Connections – Canada's Geography.* 1999) So. Much. Information.

Doran, Carol, and Thomas H. Troeger. *Trouble at the Table: Gathering the Tribes for Worship.* Nashville, TN: Abingdon Press, 1992. Immensely helpful work examining the growing schism over worship styles in many Christian centers.

Johnston, Basil. *Ojibway Heritage.* Toronto: McClelland and Stewart, 1976. Written by an Ojibway gentleman through an Ojibway lens.

Ross, Rupert. *Returning to the Teachings.* Toronto: Penguin Canada, 2006. Written through the lens of a white lawyer, this book offers an outstanding explanation of the differences between indigenous culture and "white" (Anglo-European) culture, and how poorly the white justice system serves the traditional indigenous peoples. It was eye-opening and life-changing for this reader.

Sault, Calvin. *A Traveler in Time.* Brantford: Self Published. Out of Print. Reflections on a life of healing and discovery.

ABOUT THE AUTHOR

Early Life and Community. Alison Longstaff Moore grew up in an intentional Christian community located in eastern Pennsylvania. Her upbringing was deeply rooted in the conservative Swedenborgian denomination, which shaped her identity and sense of belonging. This community was close-knit, with strong interconnections among its members, and Alison's family was an integral part of it. The teachings and traditions of the denomination played a central role in her life from childhood through her early forties.

Departure and Personal Transformation. In her early forties, Alison faced a series of betrayals and disillusionments within her faith community. These experiences led her to resign from the denomination that had defined her for so long. The decision to leave was profoundly difficult, as it meant losing her primary source of community, identity, and familial ties. In many ways, it felt as though she ceased to exist within the world she had always known.

After leaving, Alison was compelled to think independently and seek out new spiritual pathways. She pursued ordination with the liberal branch of the Swedenborgian church, which welcomed her warmly—contrasting sharply with the conservative branch that prohibited the ordination of women. The liberal Swedenborgians also respected Alison's autonomy, including her decision to end an unhappy marriage, without judgment or condemnation.

Remarkably, Alison and her first husband, Phil, continued to collaborate by providing marriage services for young couples, with Alison officiating and Phil playing the piano, even as they navigated their own divorce.

Evolution in Belief and Ministry. This book reflects Alison's journey as her beliefs evolved from traditional theological views toward a more dynamic and relevant theology. She integrates psychological insights to better understand contemporary social values, while always emphasizing Jesus' central teaching of loving one's neighbor.

Current Life and Ministry. Today, Alison resides once again in Kitchener, Ontario. She is married to her longtime friend and sweetheart from 1980, "Sam" Moore. Alison now serves as the pastor of the liberal Swedenborgian congregation at The Church of the Good Shepherd in Kitchener, continuing her ministry with a renewed and compassionate outlook.